Douglas Lindsay was born in Scotland in 1964. He currently lives in Belgrade, Serbia, with his wife and two children. This explains everything.

Also by Douglas Lindsay,
available from Long Midnight Publishing:

The Long Midnight of Barney Thomson

The Cutting Edge of Barney Thomson

A Prayer For Barney Thomson

Barney Thomson & The Face of Death

The King Was In His Counting House

Douglas Lindsay

This edition published in Great Britain in 2004 by
Long Midnight Publishing
Suite 433
24 Station Square
Inverness IV1 1LD
e-mail: info@barney-thomson.com

www.barney-thomson.com

A catalogue record for this book is available from the British Library

ISBN 0 9541 387 4 0

Printed and bound in Great Britain by
Mckays of Chatham plc, Chatham, Kent

Author's note

I'd like to thank the following hardy individuals who have contributed up to this point:

Bill Lindsay, for the wonders of Winona Wanderlip; Julie Logan, for all-purpose advice and pointing out the awful jokes, although clearly I've left most of them in; Lesley and Donald for copy editing and general ripping to shreds of the manuscript; Ewan MacFarlane and *Ross & Cromarty Enterprise* for support to Long Midnight Publishing in the beginning; Jane Urquhart, for maintaining the administrative end of the organisation during my incarceration in Serbia; and most of all to Kathryn for much of the above and everything else she's done along the way, and to Jessica and Hamish for driving me insane and contributing dutifully to my general descent into madness which so manifests itself in the Barney Thomson series.

For Kathryn

prologue

And the doughnut eaters shall inherit the girth

Melanie Honeyfoot's life was conducted to the tunes of children's rhymes and tv themes, which constantly played in her head. Pussycat, pussycat, where have you been; Bear In The Big Blue House; Tom & Jerry; To market, to market to buy a fat pig. Whatever seemed most appropriate at the time. She had found herself standing up in parliament arguing the finer points of a finance bill with her irritating opponent from the opposition, to the accompaniment of Winnie the Pooh. And every time she had to sit and listen to the First Minister, one of the old rhymes about kings came to her.

It wasn't that she had any children of her own. She had far too many things to achieve before she sacrificed her political ambitions at the altar of nine months of haemorrhoids, backache, alcohol deprivation, pâté and soft cheese deprivation, Prozac deprivation, chronic fatigue, heartburn, Carpal-tunnel syndrome, the inability to turn over in bed without the help of a crane, 24-hour vomiting and horrendous mental angst, concluding with God knows how many hours of screaming agony, to be swiftly followed by months of sleepless nights and tortured nipples, and years of no end of different types of stress and heartache.

The problem was that she had three brothers and four sisters, all of whom were festooned with children of various ages. All manner of the little buggers, whose company she was constantly forced to keep, and who were interested in her because they saw her on the tv every so often, which made her almost on a par with Bob The Builder and Pingu.

She awoke on an unusually warm and sunny Thursday morning in mid-September, having dreamt about Rolie Polie Ollie's Uncle Gizmo. Not unusual in itself, although the sexual nature of the dream had been a little disconcerting. She lay with her eyes closed, Rolie's theme tune playing in her head. Thinking of the day ahead. The mundane drudgery of the boxes in the office that were going to have to be dealt with; the appearance on Scotland Today, something that always had her ridiculously dry-mouthed and weak-kneed; the early meeting with the First Minister, Jesse Longfellow-Moses; the two-minute appearance in front of parliament, all because that spineless little SNP twat wanted to get his own ugly mug on the box.

The meeting with the First Minister was the only item on the list which gave her even the merest ghost of excitement. In the year and three months since his re-election the man had become encumbered by the most insufferable self-importance. Now that they had finally moved into the new parliament building at the bottom of the Royal Mile, and JLM at last had an office that he could truly call his own, his conceit had even started outstripping his criminality. The back benches were rumbling and the muck-raking in the press about JLM, which had been running ever since he'd been elected – infidelity, dodgy-dealing, cronyism – had begun to intensify. The fact that it had started spreading to the cabinet was the really interesting thing.

She was just entering the fifteenth rendition of Rolie's theme, when something made her open her eyes and turn to her left. A slight movement.

She was not alone.

The sudden sight of the shock of black hair was a bit of a kick up the backside of her poise, as she hadn't realised that she'd spent the night in anyone's company. Certainly the previous evening had been very relaxed and suitably alcohol-fuelled, but it wasn't as if she was in the habit of forgetting entire nights of her life.

'Hello,' she said, after the little breath of air had escaped from the back of her throat.

'Morning,' said her bedfellow.

'Did we, eh...?' asked Honeyfoot.

'Have relations?'

Very old fashioned. Honeyfoot nodded. This was absurd. The previous night had seen the usual crew down at Beanscene – ministers, deputy ministers and varying degrees of sycophant – drinking too many vodka mixers, talking interminably about the role of the Executive and JLM's presidential inclinations, and listening to one of those bollock-thumping acoustic acts that Beanscene uncovered in spades. And, as usual, at a little before eleven o'clock, she had left the bar alone. [Honeyfoot imagined that her romantic ambitions lay splattered against the rocks of a) your average man's mistrust of a female politician, and b) the world's obsession with scrawny women. For she was, as they say, no stranger to a doughnut.]

'Yes,' said Honeyfoot, 'relations.'

'No, no relations, although, to be honest, I wouldn't say no if you were to offer.'

Honeyfoot looked away, and glanced at the digital clock. 0639. The morning was bright and the pale summer curtains – the woman in the shop had described their colour as *supreme of August beige*, as if they might be something you had served to you with broccoli and sautéed potatoes – barely kept out the light.

'You've spent the night, though?' asked Honeyfoot.

Her guest laughed lightly.

'No, no, you're getting the situation wrong. I've just arrived. I see where you're coming from, though.'

Honeyfoot looked with a little consternation, and pulled the light summer duvet – featuring a design styled *pycnidium blue* – up closer to her neck. Then she noticed that her visitor was fully clothed.

'Why?' was all she said at first.

'JLM sent me,' came the reply.

'At twenty to seven?'

'Well, he kind of left the timing up to me, you know.'

Honeyfoot was unimpressed. Rolie Polie Ollie had been replaced, for some reason that her mind would not have been able to fathom had she had the time to try, by Hey Diddle-Diddle.

'You couldn't have, like, knocked?' she said. 'And come at least an hour later?'

Her early morning visitor smiled.

'Well, you know, these things are better done at peculiar hours.'

'What things?' said Honeyfoot quickly. She wondered what was coming. JLM bloody well wasn't going to sack her, was he? That would be so typical of the man. She'd supported him all the way and now he was about to do the old Thatcher trick. Keep a constant turnover of government ministers so that no one individual had the chance to get their feet under the table, unless they were completely incompetent and therefore no threat to the seat of power. How many more of the cabinet would be getting these early morning visits? And from the likes of this clown? Who the Hell did JLM think he was?

'The bastard better not be about to fire me,' said Honeyfoot. She felt a bit ridiculous, having this conversation lying naked in bed, the covers at her chin, still a little damp after her Uncle Gizmo-fuelled erotic dream.

'Fire? No, no, not fire. Much too vulgar. Much.'

'What are you saying?' asked Honeyfoot quickly, heart rate increasing, suddenly very concerned, suddenly thinking that this wasn't going to be so ridiculous after all.

'Well, all right, maybe fire isn't so bad a word.'

There was a swift swish of arm against *pycnidium blue* duvet and Honeyfoot was looking at a 7.62mm calibre handgun with silencer attachment. She attempted the word 'what', but there came nothing but a strange little ejaculation of air.

The last thing she saw was the smile of her killer. All transpired so quickly, she didn't have time to move. Or think. Or react in any way. Just die.

Doof.

A sterile thud, and man that was all she wrote for Melanie Honeyfoot.

The blood soaked into the sheets and into the duvet cover, so that it began to look less like *pycnidium blue* and a bit more like *hacienda maroon*. And, as Honeyfoot's killer blew purposelessly over the top of the silencer and rose smoothly from the bed, the clock clicked round to 0640 and Good Morning Scotland blurted on, with talk of a warm front, sunny blue skies and an Indian summer.

1

Then shall the dust return to the earth as it was: and the spirit shall return unto God who gave it

Sometimes when the sun hits you first thing in the morning, bursting in through open curtains and creeping slowly across the floor, the warmth on your face is glorious. A delicious sensation that conjures up myriad remembrances; of warm summer days lying in fields, the buzz of insects and white clouds lazily drifting behind trees; of ice cream in the garden and adults drinking tea; of sandy beaches and laughing children and cold seas trundling facetiously up the sand; of long cycles along country lanes, the crunch of tyres on gravel, the bike juddering in your hands; of lying on grass-covered hills, the burble of a nearby stream mingling with the distant din of a jet, inching across the blue sky.

And sometimes it just plain bites you on the arse.

Barney Thomson sat up quickly in bed, the sun harsh on his face. He looked around the room and did not recognise it. Nothing. Not the maroon carpet, nor the walls painted cream to pick out the simple floral design on the floor, nor the rich furnishings, nor the clothes folded neatly over the back of a chair.

He let his head fall back onto his pillow and pulled the light, summer duvet over his face. Lying covered up, with his head enshrouded, somehow seemed more natural and the ugly sensation with which he had woken began to fade. And in his shroud he tried to remember where he was, but nothing would come, his brain shooting in a hundred directions at once.

The knocking at the door came again, and he realised it was that which had brought him so sharply from his dreamless slumber and not the sun. He pulled the cover quickly from his face and stared at the door. Deep mahogany, solid and stern.

'Come in,' he said, and he barely recognised his own voice or even the words that came out.

The door opened and a young woman walked in, carrying a tray of breakfast materials. She smiled, her teeth were extraordinarily white, and she was dressed in dark blue. Neatly cut trousers and a top with a high, Chinese buttoned neckline. The outfit was edged with very fine red and gold, and had a beautiful presence of its own, of uniformity and of lavish, unnecessary expense.

'Nice to see you're awake, Mr Thomson,' she said, standing properly before him, after laying the tray on a large round table. 'We weren't sure what you would like to eat, so there's a selection.'

He didn't reply. She was partly blocking the sun so that it was hitting the back of her head and creating a halo effect around her bobbed blonde hair. She was beautiful. Pale. Almost celestial. And Barney Thomson suddenly wondered if he was dead.

'There's bacon,' she began again, feeling a little disconcerted by the silence, 'three types of sausage, scrambled eggs made the American way, toast, strawberry jam and marmalade, tea, coffee, milk and two breakfast cereals.' She paused, but still Barney stared at her, wondering. 'We can get you anything else should you require it, please don't hesitate to ask.'

He released his tight grip on the duvet and rested his hands on his chest. Suddenly he felt very hungry, the smell of the bacon crawling under his skin, much as it does.

'Bacon will be just fine,' he said. 'And toast.'

She smiled again and began to walk from the room, her movements balletic, her strides little hops from one foot to the next, until she stopped at the door.

'Mr Weirdlove will be along in about an hour, if you could be ready then,' she said.

Barney nodded, no doubt the look on his face belying his general immersion in confusion.

'Where am I?' he asked.

She smiled again.

'Mr Weirdlove will explain everything,' she said.

And she was gone.

Barney looked at the door for a while. Then the feeling of confusion was surpassed by the sweeps of hunger and he swung his legs over the edge of the bed and gingerly made his way to the breakfast table.

"✂

The next time there was a knock at the door, Barney was anew. He had eaten everything on the table, he'd had a long, glorious shower under stinging hot water, and he had dressed in the only clothes he could find in the room. An outfit not unlike that of the ambrosial creature who had delivered his breakfast.

He'd looked in the mirror, and wasn't entirely sure who was looking back. He was Barney Thomson, barber, that much was there. But the rest, what there must have been of his life, seemed distant and detached, as if the memories belonged to someone else. And so he had plunged into his breakfast, temporarily blanking his mind to the past.

He couldn't see much out of the window. A cobbled courtyard, renovated Victorian buildings across the way, walls of blue and roofs of red. He had wondered about the door and what might lie without, but something had stayed his hand so that he had not even bothered trying. The room was strange to him, but it was comfortable and reassuring and he didn't feel the urge to leave.

He'd turned on the television and watched BBC Breakfast for a while. Riots in Northern Ireland, murder in Jerusalem, the UN frantically withdrawing from another African hotspot as the machetes began to swing, economic meltdown, tension on the Kashmiri border, financial scandal and sexual excursions surrounding this quadriennium's US president. Nothing new there then.

'Come in,' he said, at the insistent knock, and the door opened. This time it was a man in his 30's, a small briefcase clutched under his arm. Blonde hair – bit of a Will Paton *No Way Out* – very sleek dark suit, plain tie. Parker Weirdlove.

'Good, you're ready,' he said quickly, standing at the door. 'Come on.'

Barney rose from the breakfast table, where he had been finishing off the cold remnants of the tray.

'You going to tell me what's going on?' he asked, unconsciously increasing the speed of his movements at the tone of his visitor's voice.

'I doubt it,' said Weirdlove. 'I tend not to get involved in minutiae. I'll get someone else to fill you in.'

'That's not really acceptable,' said Barney, as they walked out the door and began to stride quickly along a short hall of thick carpets and lavish artwork.

Weirdlove stopped under a painting of a distinguished looking man in his late 40's.

'Do you even have the slightest idea where you are?' he asked sharply.

'No,' said Barney, 'I don't.'

'Exactly,' said Weirdlove, 'so what are you going to do about it?' And he turned and walked on.

Barney raised an eyebrow. Well, being woken by a stunningly attractive woman carrying a stunningly attractive breakfast, featuring the main food groups of bacon, eggs, coffee and toast, wasn't exactly the same as having your toenails ripped off and your testicles cremated. So he made the only decision that was really open to him, and starting walking quickly along the corridor.

'Where are we going?' he asked.

'To see the First Minister,' said Weirdlove.

'Don't get it,' said Barney.

'Jesse Longfellow-Moses,' said Weirdlove.

They came to a short flight of stairs, down which Parker Weirdlove practically ran, then suddenly they were outside into the warmth of a glorious September morning. A quick walk through a small courtyard and then they were out onto the Canongate, the bottom end of Edinburgh's Royal Mile, and charging downhill.

'First Minister of what?' asked Barney.

'The Scottish Parliament,' said Weirdlove.

'Right,' said Barney. The concept of First Minister came back to him, but he had never heard of Jesse Longfellow-Moses. 'Should I know him?' he asked.

Weirdlove stopped suddenly, beside a small flight of steps. He fished something from his pocket and handed it to Barney. It was a pass to the Scottish Parliament buildings, already embellished with Barney's picture and signature.

'Don't lose it,' said Weirdlove. Then he turned, walked up the steps and swept into the foyer, Barney in his wake, at a gentle trot. Weirdlove showed his pass with a quick flick of his wrist, Barney followed suit, then they were through security and Weirdlove was walking up a flight of steps two at a time, up into the Assembly building, nodding at the occasional dark suited civil servant who passed them by in the opposite direction.

'You've been out the loop awhile,' he said, 'so you're excused. But there are a few do's and don'ts, so pay attention. You listening?'

'Aye,' said Barney, wondering which loop it was he'd been out of.

'You call him First Minister,' said Weirdlove, his voice crisp and neat like a butt naked skelp. 'Don't look him in the eye. Agree with everything he says. Do everything he asks. Speak when you're spoken to. Don't pick your nose, don't scratch your arse, don't adjust your genitals, don't pick food out your teeth, wax out your ear or gunge out your toenails. Don't breathe on him. Don't mention his wife. Don't mention policy. If he asks your opinion on something, give him his opinion, not yours. Don't talk about the weather. And never,' said Weirdlove, stopping abruptly under another portrait of Jesse Longfellow-Moses, so that Barney nearly walked into the back of him, 'never use the 'W' word.'

He stared with an unnerving intensity into Barney's eyes, daring him to ask what the 'W' word was. Barney nodded.

'Right,' he said.

Another look of conflagration from Weirdlove, then he turned quickly and pushed open a set of luxurious double doors, nearly taking out the Minister for Parliamentary Business as he did so.

'Morning, Nelly,' he barked at her, and she scowled and went on her way.

'Nelly Stratton,' said Weirdlove, turning up a set of carpeted stairs, under yet another beaming and very flattering portrait of Longfellow-Moses. 'Minister for Parliamentary Business. Nebby wee cow.'

Barney said nothing. Coming to terms with being in the seat of power, such as it was. And wondering about the man in all the portraits.

'You get all that, Mr Thomson?' asked Weirdlove.

'Aye,' said Barney. 'Nelly Stratton.'

'Not that, you idiot,' said Weirdlove. 'The instructions?'

'Aye,' said Barney, 'aye, I think so.'

'Good.'

At the top of this flight of stairs, Weirdlove stopped again, this time outside a door, at the end of another long corridor lined with more portraits of the esteemed leader. A security man sat at a desk, but he had already returned to reading his newspaper after catching sight of Weirdlove.

'We're here,' said Weirdlove. 'You ready?'

'Aye,' said Barney. 'Pumped.'

'Tone!' barked Weirdlove. 'Right, all the equipment you need is in there. The First Minister likes a Frank Sinatra '62. Get to work.'

'Sinatra,' Barney repeated.

'You familiar with it?'

'Absolutely.'

'You'd better be.'

And with that, Parker Weirdlove walked quickly away back downstairs, other fish to fry, other ministers to pop on the barbie.

Barney Thomson watched him go, then turned and looked at the door. It was a regulation affair; wood, plain, gold-coloured knob. And who knew what lay behind? Awash with confusion, head and body seemingly immersed in sludge, feeling like an antelope about to go to a lion party disguised as a wildebeest, he took a deep breath and opened the door.

2

The edge of jealousy

'You heard what he's done now?'

There were two of them in the room. Winona Wanderlip and Wally McLaven. She was the Minister for Enterprise, also burdened with the jobs of Minister for Science and Minister for Scottish Soup, or something or other. McLaven was Minister for Tourism, Culture & Sport.

Wanderlip was sitting at the desk, leaning back, her wrists resting on the edge of the wood, her fingers tapping. Loud staccato clicks from her long fingernails, except for the dull tap of the left hand ring finger, where she had bitten the nail down to the wire. McLaven was standing at the window, his back to her, staring blankly up Holyrood Road.

'Go on,' he said. Disinterested. He knew what she was like. Longfellow-Moses couldn't take a shit without her complaining about the toilet paper he used. Of course, the fact that JLM had his toilet paper delivered directly from Harrod's Water Closet Accessories Department, with every sheet individually stamped with his initials in gold leaf, and that he employed someone to actually do the wiping for him, meant that she had a point. Sometimes, though, he just couldn't be bothered listening to her. It was like having another wife.

'He's snubbed Graham again,' she said, crisply. 'He's coming up here next week to deliver the speech to the CBI, and JLM's not going. The man's an utter arse.'

'Look, Winnie, to be fair to the lad, Longfellow-Moses,' said McLaven, 'your man Graham'll deliver exactly the same speech he gave last year.'

'That's not the point,' she snapped. She hated being called Winnie. She had replaced her finger tapping with the incessant single tap of her right index finger. Her lips were thin and angry, she was breathing heavily through her nose. McLaven turned round, because he found her incredibly attractive when she was mad.

'Don't smile like that,' she said, at the cheeky look on his face.

'That Morse code you're tapping out there, Winnie?' he asked. 'Death to Longfellow, Death to Longfellow.'

She stopped tapping.

'It's not funny, Wally,' she said. 'Something's got to be done about him. He's just a guy, not some bloody God-king.'

'You should've stood against him,' said McLaven, shaking his head, speaking the line that he always gave her.

JLM had been elected party leader in the middle of the previous parliamentary term, after the resignation of his predecessor, who'd been caught engaging in sexual activity with a melon. Wanderlip had started a campaign against him, but had withdrawn from the leadership race due to a sharp dose of political expediency.

'That's old news,' she said, then she stood up quickly and waved a finger at him, as if she'd only just realised something. 'That's it, isn't it? Isn't it?'

McLaven shrugged.

'To be fair to you, Winnie, I don't know what you're talking about.'

She walked round from behind the desk, her arms bent, her hands cupping a pair of invisible grapefruit. Her blouse was tight, made tighter by the movement of her arms, and McLaven looked at her breasts.

'It's not old news, is it?' she said. 'It was thirty months ago. Thirty months. That's, like, not even three years.'

'God, Winnie, you *so* went to university.'

'It's nothing,' she continued, ignoring the sarcasm, 'but look what he's done. Just thirty months, and in that time he's turned himself into this thing, this dictator. It'd be bad enough if he'd been in power for years, decades, but this. We forget so quickly, Wally, don't you see? It seems like he's been there forever, we think he's got the popular support of the people, but he hasn't.'

He looked at her. He didn't say *he won an election last year*, because he didn't need to.

'Less than forty percent turn out,' she said in response to his thought. 'What the Hell is that? Did you know he's got his own private hairdresser starting work today? Excuse *me*? How many people has he got up there in that inner circle now? How many? All on the government payroll, all being paid for by the people of Scotland. What the Hell is that? He's got his nice new shiny building to play with, and he's building up his staff to go along with it. It's shocking!'

McLaven nodded.

'You know, Winnie,' he said, 'your breasts are just different class. Have you had, like, surgery or anything.'

She raised a finger at him, but didn't rise to the bait of the cheeky smile – the smile that had once fooled so many referees.

'It's serious, Wally,' she said. 'The guy's out of control. It's time we started doing something.'

'On you go, then,' he said, almost managing to look her in the eye. 'What's stopping you?'

'Christ, you know I can't,' she said. 'There's too much history. Everyone would think I was only doing it because I wanted his job.'

'You do want his job,' he said.

'It's bigger than that,' she said hurriedly. 'We've got to do this for the good of the country.'

'Aye,' said Wally. 'Aye.'

'But it can't be me,' she said, returning to the seat behind her desk. Wally watched her for a few seconds then turned away again – now that her breasts had calmed down – and looked back out at the early morning heat haze on top of the leaf-shaped windows that garnished the roof of the low central building of the parliament.

'We need it to come from someone who was part of his team. An insider.'

'I hope you're not about to ask me,' said McLaven without turning.

‘Don’t be ridiculous,’ she said, ‘someone serious. No, Melanie’s the one. Melanie.’

‘Speak to her then,’ said McLaven, disinterested.

‘I will,’ said Wanderlip. ‘She’s just not in yet today. Don’t know where she’s got to.’

‘Out shagging, I expect,’ said McLaven, although he didn’t believe it. He just had an in-built bloke’s need to say the word *shagging* every so often.

‘God,’ said Wanderlip, ‘it’s nine o’clock in the morning.’

McLaven grunted.

‘No, I’ll just have to wait until she gets in,’ said Wanderlip, stroking her chin. ‘In fact, it might be best for me to engineer a little disagreement between her and Jesse before I make my approach. Make her more susceptible to persuasion.’

McLaven glanced over her shoulder, but she was no longer talking to him. She was plotting aloud to no one but herself. He watched her for a few seconds, watched the wheels turning, then looked away again, out into the warmth of a bright late summer’s morning. The type of morning that reminded him of Italia ‘90, when he and the lads had been so close to soccer glory. Defeat to Costa Rica, and playing like a complete bunch of women against Brazil aside, of course.

3

The last king of holyrood

Barney stepped into the room, then stood with the door open, staring at the scene before him. Of the seven people already there, only one turned to look at him.

He wasn't sure what he'd been expecting of the First Minister's office. Sterility? Or perhaps overindulgent wallpaper and unnecessarily plush carpeting. The odd Van Gogh on the walls, a throwaway painting the bloke had knocked up one evening, in between the ear thing and quaffing endless bottles of petroleum-grade Bergerac. Probably a picture of the First Minister meeting Her Majesty, genuflecting just enough not to get his head removed. A photograph of the regulation wife and two children. Perhaps a Zulu shield he'd picked up on a trip to South Africa, when he'd been trying to pretend he was some sort of world statesman.

However....one wall was completely taken up with a mural, a magnificent painting of breadth and vision. A modern day sermon-on-the-mount, a throng at the foot of a hill, with Jesse Longfellow-Moses standing above them, his arms outstretched, beseeching them to follow his example, to live as he would have them live. A painting of breathtaking hubris, from the artist as well as the subject. JLM's face was warm and giving and magnificent, as if radiating God's light. And the faces of the crowd reflected that glory, as they gazed upwards in loving admiration.

The mural dominated the room, the rest of which almost conformed to the plan. Barney was still staring at it, awestruck, when the one person to notice him entering the room came and stood beside him.

'Close the door,' said the man, who was dressed with absurd cool. Sharp, dark suit, black tie, and £5000 shades, paid for by the taxpayer.

Barney dragged his eyes away from those of the painting of JLM, looked at the man, shook his head to get his mind back into the real world – if this was the real world – let the words finally sink in, said, 'Oh, aye, sure,' and closed the door.

'You're Barney Thomson, the barber,' said the man.

Barney nodded. As far as he could remember.

'The First Minister's waiting.'

Man In Dark Suit walked away from him and Barney's gaze followed his path to the huge, absurdly shaped windows which looked out over the white meringue of the Dynamic Earth building, with the sweeping hill of Arthur's Seat rising up behind. Standing at the window, his back to the room, was the First Minister himself, hands clasped behind him. Barney stared at the greying hair of the back of his head for a few seconds, then looked around the room at the rest of the entourage.

There were two women sitting at a desk, opposite the mural. They were both straight-backed, smartly dressed in a similar style to Barney, wore impossibly chic spectacles, and were punching away at laptops, engrossed enough not to have noticed Barney enter. Above the desk at which they sat was the regulation picture of JLM and Her Majesty, and only the best photographic technicians would have been able to tell that the picture had been digitally altered to show Her Majesty looking almost in awe of her new lieutenant.

Beside the desk, sitting in the corner on a comfy chair, was another woman, wearing a dog collar, reading the Bible. She was young, attractive, and Barney had trouble taking his eyes off her. When he did, he looked at the man who was standing before the mural, studying it intently. He might have been standing there for several hours, so intense was the look of concentration on his face. He too was a man of God.

The only other person in the room was standing at the window, mincing around a tailor's dummy. Arse out, knees together, lips pursed, hands fussing, nose in the air, he puttered around the dummy, tutting constantly. The mannequin was garbed in rich, blue silk and, rather than the usual crash-test face, its head wore a mask of JLM.

Barney shivered and walked forward. He had no idea from where he had awoken, but it felt like he'd now walked onto the set of some weird motion picture event. A government as depicted by Terry Gilliam.

JLM's desk was suitably grandiose, and an utter shambles of paper. Everything from Top Secret Foreign & Commonwealth Office files to brochures for Alaskan cruises and skiing holidays in the Italian Alps. It was a mess, as if every morning JLM opened up his mail, had a quick check through, then dumped it in a pile, waiting for a secretary who never came to clear it away. Under the pile were three phones, one of which was old fashioned and a virulent red colour, and Barney wondered to whom it might be a direct connection. The Kremlin? The UN? Pizza delivery? Swedish massage parlour? Westminster?

Ah, thought Barney. The 'W' word. Maybe his brain wasn't as dysfunctional as he'd thought.

Man In Dark Suit leant in towards the First Minister and whispered something in his ear. JLM turned immediately, he gazed upon Barney with curiosity for less time than it took him to assess a political opponent, then he broke into a huge smile and walked round the desk, warm hand of friendship extended.

'Mr Thomson, Mr Thomson,' he said, shaking Barney's hand vigorously. 'Can I call you Barney?'

I suspect, thought Barney, given the set-up here, you could call me anything you damn well please.

'Aye,' said Barney. 'First Minister,' he added.

'Wonderful, wonderful,' said JLM. 'Tremendous. Really marvellous.'

He finally released Barney's hand and stood staring at him, looking deep into the eyes, the smile never leaving his face.

'Lovely,' he said, after a while. 'How d'you feel? You've been through a lot,' he added, as if Barney was supposed to know exactly what that was.

'I'm all right,' said Barney. 'Not really sure what it is I've actually been through.'

JLM laughed, the big booming laugh he had first cultivated to draw attention to himself, but which now escaped from the barrel of his chest under almost any circumstance. When that had died down to manageable levels, he stepped forward and clasped Barney by the shoulder.

'Mr Weirdlove didn't fill you in on all the details, then?' he asked, smiling, then continued talking over Barney when he tried to reply. 'I'll get someone to take you through it later. Hope you remember how to cut hair, eh?' he asked. And the smile was still there, but this time Barney knew enough to know that there was a bit of an edge to the voice.

'No bother,' said Barney, not feeling anything like as confident as he was attempting to imply.

'Good, good, don't have to get one of the lads to give you a pair of concrete slippers and drop you off the Forth Bridge then,' said JLM, still laughing.

'Aye,' said Barney, because he had no idea what else to say.

JLM gave Barney's shoulders a squeeze, then looked around the room. Still the only one of the others to be paying them any attention was Man In Dark Suit.

'Right,' said JLM, 'let me introduce you to a few people. You've already met The Amazing Mr X?' he said, turning back to Man In Dark Suit.

Barney nodded and looked at Man In Dark Suit. He wanted to say, you're kidding me, right? He thought better of it, however. The Amazing Mr X might zap him with a destructor ray.

'Aye,' said Barney. 'Should that be *The* for short?'

'X,' grunted The Amazing Mr X, and JLM smiled.

'Security,' said JLM, 'got to have it these days. The Amazing Mr X is ex-SAS. Beautiful bloke, really lovely, really sensitive, but kill you as soon as look at you. Tremendous chap. Really lovely. A bit heavy-handed sometimes, but seriously, you need that these days when you're a world leader.'

Barney nodded. Perhaps he was on another planet.

'Come on,' said JLM, 'I'll introduce you to the rest of the team. One short at the moment, I'm afraid. Veronica Walters, my PA, blagged the big one in car crash last month, and I still haven't been able to replace her. It's all been a bit of a shambles since we moved in. Shocking surprise, as you can imagine. Terrible shame, she was a lovely girl. Really lovely. Very dear and sweet.'

Well, thought Barney, that explains the desk; but how could the First Minister not get a replacement? JLM led him towards the crash-test dummy. The dresser, who had been continually dancing around his latest creation, finally stopped at the approach of his master.

'Barney,' said JLM, 'I'd like you to meet Veron Veron, my dresser. Really super person, absolutely super. Smashing chap.'

Veron Veron held out a languid hand. Barney wasn't sure if he was supposed to shake it, kiss it or caress it, so he grabbed it roughly, gave it a quick shookle and took three steps back.

'Pleasure,' said Barney.

'I'm sure,' said Veron Veron, and he smiled ingratiatingly, waited to see if the boss intended to pronounce further and then buzzed back to his dressing.

'Lovely,' said JLM. 'Look, I'd better quickly run you through the others. I've got a ten-forty at the television studio, so you'll need to give me a bit of a tidy up before I go. My hair's been an absolute disaster since Phillipe's closed down.'

'Smashing,' said Barney, picking up the groove.

'Right,' said JLM, 'the two women at the desk are Dr Farrow, my physician, and Dr Blackadder, who's a bit of a psychiatrist. Between you and me,' he said, lowering his voice, 'I have the odd couch session myself, but really she's here to write psychological profiles on all those other wankers in the cabinet and on the benches.'

'Good,' said Barney. That, at least, made sense.

'Then there's my two spiritual advisors. The Reverend Blake, who's in the chair, and Father Michael. Bit of an odd one, to be frank,' said JLM, the voice lowering again, 'spends most of the day studying the mural. Very strange.'

'You're a religious man, then?' said Barney.

‘Christ, no!’ ejaculated JLM, ‘absolute load of pants. I mean, it’s ridiculous. Most of the voters never set foot in a church, most of them couldn’t give a bloody toss about religion, but you still have to be seen to be spiritual as a politician, or the press dump enormous amounts of faeces on you from the highest mountain. Bloody shambles. And, of course, you know what it’s like, can’t have one without the other, so I’ve got two of them here. And the study group’s recommending I draft in a Muslim, and I’ve just got to do it. Who knows where it’ll end?’

‘Aye,’ said Barney.

‘Right, smashing,’ said JLM, ‘that’s the team you’re going to be part of. Hope you like them.’

‘Lovely,’ said Barney.

‘Champion,’ said JLM.

‘Excellent,’ said Barney.

‘Smashing,’ said JLM. ‘Absolutely champion. Right, let’s get to it. I’ve got a seat set up in the bathroom. Saves getting the mess in here. You’re happy with a Sinatra ‘62?’

‘Should be,’ said Barney.

‘Think I’ll suit it?’ asked JLM, then walked off before Barney could answer.

Barney walked after JLM towards a door, which he could now see lay right in the middle of the mural. He looked down at his hands and held them before him, flexing the fingers. How long had it been since he’d cut anyone’s hair? He had no idea. He had no idea how long it was since he’d done anything.

As he followed JLM into the bathroom, The Amazing Mr X suddenly appeared between him and the First Minister and one of the two women at the desk finally looked up, glanced over her impossibly chic spectacles at Barney, studied him for a few seconds until the door was closed, then turned back to her psychological profile of Winona Wanderlip.

4

The parliament sits in the land

Melanie Honeyfoot's private secretary was sufficiently concerned about her boss's absence, to start trying to contact her as early as eight-thirty. She was generally never later than eight o'clock, and on a day when she was due in private with the First Minister at nine-thirty, it was usual that she would be in even earlier to prepare. So by 0821, Charlotte Williams had had enough of answering questions from people curious as to Honeyfoot's whereabouts, and had decided to go round to her apartment in Leith.

She walked briskly from the office, past curious glances, out of the building, grabbed a taxi that had just turned onto Canongate, then sat in traffic for twenty minutes, thinking that she was going to look very stupid if Honeyfoot had turned up at work two seconds after she'd left.

When she arrived she asked the taxi to wait, then stood outside the building for a minute, the glorious warm sun on her back, pressing the buzzer intermittently, reluctant to actually let herself in with the key that Honeyfoot had given her two years previously. It was one of the modern apartment blocks down by the docks, in between an area of dereliction and another exclusive housing development. Eventually she bit the bullet and her bottom lip and let herself in. Up the stairs, third floor, rang the bell and knocked a few times. Finally, feeling very nervous, she put the key in the lock, explanations of why Honeyfoot was not answering the door galloping through her head.

She could've spent the night at someone else's house. Worse, there could be someone else here, and they could still be at it. So carried away with the absurd concupiscence of lovemaking that they paid no attention to the phone or the door.

She pushed the door open, walked in and was immediately aware of the silence and the loud click that her shoes made on the parquet. She stopped, she listened, and at last her sixth sense kicked in, and she felt the hairs on the back of her neck press against the collar of her plain white blouse.

And now she knew. She walked straight for the bedroom, but slowly, vomit rising in her stomach. Didn't want to find what she was going to find. From doubt and concern that she was making a fool of herself, to the sure and certain knowledge that she was about to find Honeyfoot dead.

The bedroom door was closed. She hesitated, she stared at the handle. Suddenly she worried about fingerprints. Maybe hers would be the only other prints found on the premises. And she pulled the cuff of her blouse down over her fingers, gingerly turned the handle, and pushed the door open.

The extraordinary heat hit her first of all, from nothing more than the sun beating in through large south-east facing windows, on a balmy late summer's morning. She walked in and shivered, despite the heat. She felt cold; she felt death. She looked at the bed. She could almost sense the body of Melanie Honeyfoot lying there, dead through unnatural causes.

But the bed was empty. The duvet had been pulled neatly up to the pillows, and folded back. Almost as if it hadn't been slept in. She stood just inside the door and looked at the room. Trying to fathom the difference between what she could see and what she could sense.

Then the level-headed woman inside her, the person that saw rational explanation in everything, dismissed the strange intuition that had haunted her for a few seconds. The analytical triumphed over the deceit of imagination, and she walked quickly into the room to check for any sign of where Honeyfoot might have gone. And already she was thinking that the most likely explanation was that she'd been at someone else's house the night before and had been held up on the way to work. More than likely, thought Charlotte Williams, by the time she got back to the office,

Honeyfoot would already be there, and very displeased at Williams's absence.

And so, after a quick check of each room of the apartment – a check which revealed nothing that she did not already know about her employer – and a minute's reflection while looking into the dark waters of Leith docks, Charlotte Williams locked the door behind her and ran back downstairs to the waiting taxi.

✂

'You see,' said JLM, who was already in full flow, 'the people just don't understand what it's like to be me. The pressures, the tensions.'

Barney nodded. The bathroom was spacious and bright, with large windows looking out over Queensberry House and the buildings on up the Royal Mile, and more mirrors than your average Hollywood narcissist has in his/her entire mansion. He had been studying the First Minister's hair carefully for some five minutes and had yet to make a positive move. He felt a bit like a man sitting behind the wheel of a car after having been banned from driving for thirty years. He knew he used to do this, but wasn't exactly sure how to start.

'You all right back there,' asked JLM, 'you don't seem to be doing much?'

'Aye,' said Barney. 'I'm fine. A Sinatra '62?' you said.

'Yeah,' said JLM, 'I loved Sinatra. My kind of guy. Lovely. And deep. Very deep. Champion bloke. I see a lot of myself in the man. And he had great hair too, you can't argue that. Even when it wasn't his own, you know what I'm saying?' and he laughed.

Part of the problem, Barney was thinking, was that JLM pretty much already had a Sinatra '62. The line about it getting out of hand since Phillipe's had closed down was absurd; more than likely that Phillipe's had closed three days earlier. And so, as his mind worked its way out of the sludge in which it had been immersed since he had awoken that morning, the obvious fact dawned on Barney that he was cutting the hair of a man who was unnaturally obsessed with self-image. He was the First Minister, he would constantly be on television and in parliament, and making public appearances, visiting schools and hospitals. Of course he was going to notice every hair that was two-thirds of a millimetre too long. Especially when he was as dedicated to the promotion of his own image as JLM clearly was, what with portraits of himself ornamenting every wall.

And all at once, having understood the psychology of the man before him – something that all good barbers instinctively do – Barney knew where to start the cut, and what was required of him. He lifted the electric razor, he hooked on a no. 3 head, flicked the switch so that he felt the reassuring buzz of the razor in his hand, then moved smoothly onto JLM's neck.

'They say Sinatra had extraordinary nasal hair,' said Barney casually, getting back into the old barber routine, but not quite yet managing anything approaching insight. JLM chose to ignore him, as he studied himself in the mirror.

The door opened, and Barney noticed the flash of anger cross JLM's face that there had been no knock, an anger that died when Parker Weirdlove walked into the bathroom and closed the door behind him. The Amazing Mr X's hand flashed to the inside of his jacket, then relaxed.

'Good morning, sir,' said Weirdlove.

'Parker,' said JLM.

Weirdlove stood behind them, glanced at the folder he was carrying, then engaged JLM's eyes in the mirror.

'First up, you've got a 9:30 with Melanie Honeyfoot,' said Weirdlove, and JLM did a small thing with his lips to indicate disdain. 'She'll be pressing you for a further move on tax reform. Still looking to introduce a bill into this session. My sources tell me she has compiled some compelling evidence on the need for an introduction of a further levy on the Scottish taxpayer.'

He looked up and smiled wryly at JLM, who shook his head. Fortunately Barney was truly back at the helm, saw the movement coming, and made a smooth evasive manoeuvre.

'You're pencilled in for thirty minutes, but I'll get you out after five. Three if you really want. She's a no-show so far today, so I don't know what's going on there.'

‘A no-show?’ said JLM, and he did another thing with his mouth.

‘Television studio at 10:20 for the link up with This Morning, which’ll take place from 10:40 until approximately 10:45.’

‘Christ, five minutes?’ said JLM. ‘Bloody cheek. Who do they think they’re getting?’

‘They’re playing hardball. It was that or nothing. You’re on between Mel C talking about her new tattoo, and a woman discussing what went wrong with her vaginoplasty.’

Weirdlove looked up. JLM closed his eyes but remembered not to shake his head.

‘Tell me she’s going to ask us about what we’re doing for the arts and sciences and our plans for transport and the health service.’

‘You can try and swing it that way if you can, but it’s doubtful,’ said Weirdlove. ‘They’re looking to ask you about your affair and if you’re concealing any others. And they haven’t said anything, but it’s a fair bet she’ll bring up Hookergate.’

‘Oh, for crying out loud,’ said JLM. ‘Why am I doing this programme?’

Weirdlove ignored him. Because you’re desperate to get your face on television, regardless of the circumstances, he could’ve replied, but didn’t.

JLM engaged Barney’s eyes, and gave him a knowing look.

‘You’ll know all about Hookergate, I suppose?’ he asked.

‘Never heard of it,’ said Barney, who wanted to add, *I’d never even heard of you until this morning*, but thought better of it.

‘Bloody nonsense,’ said JLM. ‘My secretary who just pegged it, Veronica, Mrs Walters, was a lovely girl, really super. She rented out the apartment above my constituency offices in Perth. All above board, splendid business, no one was getting bitten on the bollocks. Now, she was a lovely girl, big rosy lips, bit of a looker, really, really champion lips, smashing lips. Red and full, you know the way lips can be. Liked to sleep around and what’s wrong with that? Anyway, there have been some ridiculous accusations floating around that she was a bit of a whore, and that she used the apartment for business purposes. Bloody nonsense.

And of course, I'm getting dragged into the whole bloody shambles. Bloody shambles, the lot of it.'

'You've to be back at Holyrood,' said Weirdlove, interjecting, 'for an 11:25 with the chairman of the subcommittee investigating changes to the Freedom of Information Bill.'

'More bollocks,' said JLM to Barney.

'You're doing lunch in the members restaurant with the leader of the Scottish Coastal Forum and the Deputy Minister for Rural Affairs.'

'Chap called Applecross,' said JLM to Barney, 'complete wanker. Scottish Coastal Forum for Christ's sake. Do we even have a coast anymore?' he added, obscurely.

'You have to be in parliament for questions at 2:30pm.'

'The usual bollocks?' asked JLM.

'Absolutely,' replied Weirdlove, 'although the leader of the opposition is scraping the bottom of a whole new barrel. He apparently wants to know if it's true that you don't let your children watch Disney videos.'

'Jesus Christ,' said JLM, 'do I have to go? Can't Benderhook take care of it?'

'You're penned in, I'm afraid,' said Weirdlove. 'You don't answer it this week, you'll have to do it next week.'

'Couldn't we fix Benderhook up to do First Minister's questions every week. Don't know why I even have to bloody bother with parliament. Everyone knows it just gets in my way. Got much better things to do.'

'You've got a 4pm with the leader of the committee on GM trials.'

'Good God, it gets worse,' said JLM.

'He's going to lobby for you to visit the trial on the Black Isle.'

Barney had almost finished the razor work and was now moving with assurance and confidence round the ears. It might be a day or two before he could cut with verve, panache, style and élan, but this would do for now.

'You mean like Jamaica or something?' said JLM.

'The Black Isle is just north of Inverness. It's not actually an island.'

'Christ,' said JLM, 'I'm not going away up there. For God's sake. That mob only ever vote SNP or LibDem, so it's not like it's worth my bloody time.'

'And you've got a 4:45 with Nancy Hackenbush.'

'God, you're going to have to help me out there,' said JLM.

'You want her to chair the Committee on Racial Equality.'

'God,' muttered JLM.

He caught Barney's eye in the mirror, and was about to utter something abject about the horrendous lot of a First Minister, when Weirdlove concluded.

'And you've two day's paperwork to catch up on, as well as what arrives today. You wanted to be up-to-date before your visit to Brussels tomorrow.'

'See,' said JLM, looking at Barney. 'See the life I lead. Everyone thinks it's wonderful, all this power. But it's hassle, you know, a bloody hassle. It's like this wonderful parliament building we've just moved into. It's a thing of beauty. It's like a naked woman smothered in white, Hawaiian honey. Lovely. Grows out the ground, that's what Miralles said. It was Dewar who sanctioned the whole thing, of course, but I couldn't have chosen better myself. But is anyone happy? Course not. They just bitch about how much it cost, and I get all the blame. Bloody nonsense. Don't know why I bother.'

'Why d'you do it then?' asked Barney, and Weirdlove gave him a look.

JLM examined Barney's face for any signs of acerbity or sarcasm, but decided that none had been intended.

'I was called,' said JLM grandly. 'I truly believe I was called.'

Barney nodded. Weirdlove shot JLM another little glance. The Amazing Mr X, as he had throughout proceedings, kept his eye on the door and said nothing.

5

Blessed are the storytellers...

Charlotte Williams arrived back in the office five minutes before Parker Weirdlove, Jesse Longfellow-Moses – who was sporting a quite delicious Frank Sinatra '62 – and The Amazing Mr X, trooped in, primed like coiled springs for their meeting with Melanie Honeyfoot.

And in those five minutes, Williams had made three calls, which were enough to ascertain that at the end of the previous evening, Honeyfoot had definitely returned to her apartment, on her own, and in a reasonably sober condition. There was no explanation as to why she had not slept in her own bed. In the claustrophobic world of Scottish politics, it would not be long before someone in the press got hold of the fact that Honeyfoot was unaccounted for and suddenly the story would blow up in their faces.

Weirdlove stood at Williams's desk, while JLM waited and looked around the other members of staff in the outer office, embracing them with the warmth of his munificence. The Amazing Mr X stood still, his hands clasped in front of him, a caged panther waiting to descend with awesome force and the opprobrium of high office upon anyone who might threaten his master.

'I take it Ms Honeyfoot has arrived safely?' said Weirdlove.

'She's not here,' said Williams, crisply, trying not to be daunted by Weirdlove.

'What d'you mean?' snapped Weirdlove.

'She hasn't, she's not,' said Williams, being daunted despite herself, 'she hasn't arrived this morning.'

'Where is she?'

'I don't know.'

'Do you think the First Minister's got nothing better to do with his time, Mrs Williams?'

'No,' she said, 'I mean, yes. I, eh, I've tried to contact Melanie.'

'How very wonderful of you,' said Weirdlove. 'The First Minister is leaving now. Should Ms Honeyfoot deign to show her face, please inform her that the meeting has been cancelled and, should she want another one, not to imagine that it will happen before the next session of parliament. Goodbye.'

Weirdlove turned quickly and walked from the office. JLM nodded at Williams, said 'Lovely, really lovely, thank you,' and followed Weirdlove. The Amazing Mr X made a quick scan of the office to see if anyone was regarding his employer with inappropriate levels of irreverence, then followed JLM a couple of paces behind.

✂

Williams immediately phoned building security and informed them of the peculiarity of Honeyfoot's absence. Building security made a few initial inquiries, decided that Honeyfoot's absence was indeed very peculiar, and by 10:00am had called the police. By 10:30 there was a team of fifteen officers in place, and by 11:00 the press had been informed, and within another quarter of an hour the media was filled with wild explanations of why Honeyfoot was absent from both her apartment and parliament.

And as she watched BBC24 in her boss's office, where one political 'expert', of whom she had never heard, expounded his theory that Honeyfoot had been kidnapped by Glasgow drug barons, she wondered if Honeyfoot was currently on her way into work and would be mad as Hell at her for starting this whole thing off.

✂

'What do you do all day?' asked Barney.

It was almost eleven-thirty. Barney had been sitting doing nothing for two hours. And now that he had cut the First Minister's hair for the month, he wasn't entirely sure what he'd be doing for the next few weeks.

The Rev Alison Blake, with whom he had fallen into conversation, laid down her Bible on a table and stared at the carpet.

'He more or less expects us to be here for him when he needs us,' she said. 'That's about it. You can fill your time as needs be.'

'So, are we stuck in this office?' asked Barney.

'Just about,' said Blake. 'This is our workplace.'

'But,' said Barney, 'I've cut the guy's hair. He's not going to need me for weeks.'

Blake laughed and smiled.

'You don't know him very well, do you? Take a look at that wall.'

Barney followed her gaze and took another look at the sermon on the mount; although Father Michael, who had not moved since Barney had first entered, partially obscured his view of the principal character.

'You think the man who had that painted on the wall of his office will not want his hair attended to several times a day?'

Barney shifted slightly so that he could get a better look at JLM's likeness. True enough, before he had gone off to the television studio, he'd had Barney give his hair a quick check over.

'It's madness,' said Barney. 'What do the rest of you do?'

'Madness ain't the half of it,' said Blake. 'Well, Veron fusses constantly over those damned outfits.' Barney turned to look at the dresser, hands on his hips, worrying over a tassel. 'JLM wears about one in twenty, they all look so ridiculous. In fact, Minnie ends up wearing more of them than he does. The two doctors sit at their laptops all day,' she continued, raising her voice to make sure they could hear, 'trawling the internet for sicko porn sites.' Blackadder smiled, Farrow flicked her the bird. 'Dr Farrow has to administer to the patient every time he has a sore throat and thinks he has a malignant cyst on his tongue. Dr Blackadder does psychological profiles of various people. She just makes stuff up, and throws in a few medical techno-terms to make it look good. He buys any old shit.'

Blackadder was still smiling and Barney felt a little out of place, as any newcomer would, not in on the in-jokes.

'They don't have to wear those glasses, by the way,' said Blake, 'he just thinks female doctors should look intelligent.'

'That's, em...' said Barney.

'The measure of the man,' said Blake. 'And the Father and I are here for spiritual guidance, which is a load of shit. Really, we're just here to advise on what reaction he's likely to get from the two churches when he does something moderately controversial.'

She stared at Father Michael and Barney followed her gaze. His head was inclined at the same angle, the hands were clasped in the same manner.

'Michael's a bit of a troubled soul, to tell the truth,' said Blake. 'Completely at odds with the whole priest thing, really.'

'Oh, aye?' said Barney.

'Yeah,' said Blake. 'Can't blame him. I'm always on at him to come over from the Dark Side, but then, I suppose if he did, he'd lose his job.'

'The Dark Side?' said Barney.

Blake laughed.

'You know what I'm saying. Probably shouldn't call it that.'

'You, eh,' said Barney, 'don't talk like your usual minister. The First Minister doesn't mind?'

Blake shrugged at first, then lowered herself slightly in the seat and her voice with it.

'Well, you know, I kinda balled him a while back, so I've pretty much got free-reign, what with him being scared I go public 'n all.'

Barney nodded. Balled. Right. Got you. That made sense. In as much as anything made sense to him.

'So,' he said, 'we don't get involved with anyone else in government.'

'God, no,' said Blake. 'We're JLM's people, and that's it.'

'Right,' said Barney.

And he stared at the floor and wondered about this preposterous set of circumstances into which he'd been thrown.

'So, how did you get here?' asked Blake. 'Everyone's got a story.'

Barney turned and looked into her eyes – deep, dark, impenetrable, and very, very attractive – and tried to think if he knew what that was.

'Not sure,' he said a while later, after he'd managed to draw his gaze away from hers, a look which had threatened to swallow him up. 'Been around a bit. Cut some hair. To be perfectly honest, I haven't a bloody clue. I'm kind of hoping someone's going to sort me out. Some of the past seems a bit dodgy, but I can't pin anything down.'

'Yeah?' said Blake. 'Sounds interesting.'

'Maybe,' said Barney. 'It's all a bit vague. Been a lot of murder in my life, I think.'

'Ooh, yummy,' she said, 'that sounds right up my street. Very biblical. Do tell?'

Barney determined not to look into her eyes again, as it disconcerted him to his core.

'Can't really remember. It's just a haze.'

'Yeah,' she said, enthusiasm drifting from her voice, 'I get like that sometimes as well. I'll see if I can find anything out for you.'

'Thanks,' said Barney.

They lurched into silence. Eventually Blake lifted her Bible and began to read once more the story of Jesus changing water into wine; but no matter how often she read it, no matter how she tried to view the story in her head, or what symbolism she felt she should be attaching to it, she couldn't help thinking that all it amounted to was the Big Fella helping out at a piss-up where they'd run out of booze. Barney looked up at the face of JLM, preaching to the converted, his eyes brighter and more radiant than in real life. Eyes that followed you around the room wherever you went.

✂

And across the city, across the old town and the new, over the traffic and the sweltering pedestrians, past the docks and out into the water, at the bottom of the Firth of Forth, a few hundred feet underwater, legs weighted with stones, stood the body of Melanie

Honeyfoot. To remain on the sea bed, to sway with currents, and to barely move an inch, for months and years and decades.

6

When my blue moon turns to fungus

The Slammer Bar was busy and smoky. Who'd have thought? In darkest Leith, at the corner of Coronation and Queen Charlotte Street, no one in the parliament even knew it existed. More to the point, political journalists would've licked a new born calf clean rather than have been seen dead in the place. So it was perfect for two people to meet in a quiet corner, surrounded by men and women who lived in the real world and gave nothing for their existence.

It was noisy in the bar, so that Winona Wanderlip had to lean across the table, her mouth no more than a few inches away from Parker Weirdlove's face. He could smell her skin and the lotion she had used to clean her face before coming out, he could see the tiny dimples in her nose, breathe in the white wine from her breath, so close that he could tell she was drinking an Australian chardonnay, crisp and full, delightful length in the finish, with hints of thyme, lavender and a double cheeseburger with regular fries and a large soft drink.

Wanderlip could smell nothing of Parker Weirdlove.

Wanderlip and Weirdlove went back a long way, long before Weirdlove's association with JLM. A distant past when bonds were forged and secrets created that each would take to the grave. More or less.

'He's cocking the whole thing up, Parker, you've got to see that,' she said to him, shortly after he had returned with her second glass of Australian white and his third mineral water.

'I know,' he said, defensively.

'And no one can challenge him. It's as if the entire party's completely impotent. It's frightening.'

'He's a charismatic man, Winona,' said Weirdlove. 'They all listen to him in parliament...'

'When he bothers to show up.'

'When they see him on the tv, I'll grant you, they hate him. He comes across as this patronising, condescending, ignorant clown.'

'Tell me something I don't know,' she muttered bitterly.

'As soon as they meet him in the flesh, they cave in. You've been there at cabinet. There's no end of times that one of them's turned up intending to take the guy to the cleaners and he just schmoozes his way through it. Half an hour later his intended assassin walks out of the meeting, wondering why it was he detested JLM in the first place. The man is smooth.'

'But it's bullshit!' she said forcefully.

'Who cares?' said Weirdlove. 'It's not about that. Politics isn't about substance and policies and forward thinking. It's about sharp suits, rhetoric, ball-busting confidence and knowing when to stab someone in the back. JLM has it to a tee.'

Wanderlip rested her back against the beleaguered wall cushion, let out a long sigh, and tapped her fingernails against her glass.

'And the economy goes to pot, the nation goes to pot, London laughs at us and the rest of Europe laughs at us. He looks bloody stupid, and we all look bloody stupid with him.'

Weirdlove smiled ruefully and also drummed his fingers on the table. He looked at the scratches and grooves that had been made over the years. He tried to let his face show his agreement with her, without uttering the words. For all their precautions, there might be someone listening after all.

'You heard what he's doing about the World Cup 2014 bid?' he said, looking up. He knew fine well that she hadn't, because the only person with whom JLM had discussed it was Weirdlove.

'Let me think,' she said, running her finger round the rim of the glass, 'he's going to commit to building ten new stadia in Scotland, and they're all going to be called The Jesse Longfellow-Moses Memorial Stadium?'

Weirdlove laughed. Winona Wanderlip was just about the only one who could make him laugh anymore.

'No' he said, smiling, 'but only because I haven't suggested it to him.'

'Don't,' she said, smiling.

'He's working out a deal with the Faroe Islands to do a joint bid,' said Weirdlove.

'The Faroes?' said Wanderlip. 'He's expecting a place with a population of sixteen to build two or three 30,000 seat stadia? What planet's he on?'

'He's not expecting them to do anything,' said Weirdlove. 'He knows by conjoining with them, we won't get selected. Even if we do, they'll fall flat on their end of the bargain, then we won't have to spend any money on it. Bingo. Everyone knows he doesn't give a shit about football, yet he looks like he's trying to do something noble and grand for the people. When it falls on its arse, it's not his fault.'

She shook her head and took another long drink.

'Why am I not surprised?' she said, voice a perfect New York take-off.

'I thought of it,' said Weirdlove, smugly. 'Rather clever.'

'Why am I not surprised?' she repeated in the same voice.

'Takes genius to get to the top,' he said, still smiling, and finishing off his drink.

'Not in Scotland it doesn't,' she retorted, then she leant forward again, pushing her drink to the side. 'Look, we have to get some momentum going. We have to start something, and you know it can't come from me. You know what the Hell Melanie's playing at?'

Weirdlove stared at the table again, where the initials KT had been rudely carved, then he placed his glass on top of the carving and lifted his eyes.

'No idea,' he said. 'Look, I'd better go. You sniff around the cabinet, see if there's enough unrest there to get anything going...'

'You're kidding me, right?' she said. 'To see if there's *enough*?'

‘I’ll sniff around the benches, gauge opinion, see if the time’s right. We good?’ he asked.

‘Yeah,’ said Wanderlip, settling back. ‘We’re good.’

Weirdlove rose from his chair and pushed it back. In doing so he bumped into a man with his pint of McEwan’s. A drop spilled, the man turned and gave Weirdlove the eye; but as usual, with people squaring up to the First Minister’s ADC, his opponent merely grunted and turned away again.

‘See you, Winnie,’ said Weirdlove, starting on his way. ‘Oh, and Winnie,’ he added, turning back, ‘I think he’s going to add a little something to your portfolio.’

Wanderlip’s jaw genuinely dropped. She already had more on her plate than anyone else in the cabinet.

‘I won’t let him,’ she said, indignantly.

Weirdlove shrugged, smiled and turned and walked quickly through the bar, leaving Winona Wanderlip and the rest of her Australian chardonnay alone at the table.

7

Someone else's toothbrush

Late at night, and Barney Thomson was sitting in a large comfy chair. He was back in his apartment, or prison cell, as he had begun to think of it, even though the door was not locked. He had watched television for a while, but nothing had grabbed him. Nothing seemed relevant, nobody on television seemed to exist in the world in which he existed. Now he sat with his hands on his knees, looking straight ahead, listening to Hoagy Carmichael, and waiting for tiredness to come over him so that he could go to bed.

He hadn't really spoken to anyone else, after his brief flirtation with the Reverend Blake. Father Michael had spent almost the entire day in awe of the mural; the doctors had buzzed away at their laptops; Veron had buzzed away at his dummy. JLM, Weirdlove and The Amazing Mr X had returned intermittently, and each time Barney had had to check JLM's hair. On the last occasion, before being dismissed, JLM had asked Barney if he could do a nice shave, and Barney had said he thought he could, although he couldn't really remember, and JLM had booked him in for a seven-thirty the following morning, and by the way, Barney would be travelling to Brussels with him. The First Minister needed good hair for his meetings with other influential diplomats.

Hoagy Carmichael was just singing about two sleepy people, and Barney was wishing that he could be one sleepy person, when there was a knock at the door. He checked the clock, quarter past midnight, but there was no skip in the heart, as there might have been at receiving a visitor at such a late hour. He felt like Mr Spock in *Star Trek III*. Like he was a thing, rather than a human being. Not, of course, that Spock was ever likely to feel like any more than half a human being, but you know what we're talking about here.

He got up, trudged the short distance over crisp carpet, and opened the door. One of the two doctors was standing outside, minus the spectacles, and dressed for the evening, a cool, pale blue blouse tucked into cool, pale blue jeans.

'Hi there,' she said, and Barney nodded. Couldn't remember which one of the two of them it was. Psychiatrist or physician?

'You've met a lot of people today,' she said, smiling, seeing the look on his face. 'I'm the shrink. Blackadder.'

'Aye, aye,' said Barney, trying to look cool, 'I know. It's late,' he added, because he thought he should say something, and it was the first thing that came into his head.

'Yeah,' she said, 'sorry. I just got off work, you know. I thought you might still be up. Parker wanted me to have a word.'

'Right,' said Barney. Then it clicked that he was supposed to invite her in, which is pretty much what any clear thinking man would've done already, with a woman who looked like Dr Rebecca Blackadder. Jesse Longfellow-Moses did not consider surrounding himself with people or things that were unattractive. 'You want to come in?' he said, attempting to cover for the fact that he'd just thought of it.

'That'd be nice,' she said, and she glided past him into the room, and he closed the door behind her.

'Most people call me Edmund,' she said, 'but it's getting a little tired. Rebecca's fine.'

'Rebecca,' he repeated, and looked at her, standing in the middle of the room, arms hovering at her sides. He felt awkward. 'Not sure if I've got anything to offer you,' he said, referring to a drink. His dinner had been brought to him by a different woman from the one who had delivered his breakfast. Same outfit, same hair, different gene pool. There had been a small menu card on the tray informing him that he was being served *an enchantment of chicken, with sun roasted potatoes, mango en papillote and caramelised comfit of whole-wheat pitta bread.* Very nice it'd been too. Accompanied by a half bottle of an outstandingly fruity

South African, which he'd polished off without appreciating a single drop.

'There's a drinks cabinet,' she said, pointing to the corner, 'but I'm cool.'

'Oh, right,' said Barney. 'Sit down,' he added, remembering some manners.

Rebecca Blackadder smiled and lowered herself into the single armchair opposite the one at which she knew Barney would have been sitting. Barney hesitated, then plumped himself down, subdued by the weight of resignation.

'Hoagy Carmichael,' she said.

'Aye,' replied Barney. 'I think I like it, but I'm not sure.'

'What's the last thing you can remember?' she asked, looking into his eyes. Would usually have a notebook at hand for this kind of thing, but sometimes it was better to be without.

Barney held her gaze for a second then lowered his eyes. He'd been thinking about this all day; and it had been a long, long day. He tried to think again, but it felt like such an effort and he just didn't have the will to do it. Maybe tomorrow, after a good night's sleep.

Outside they could hear the first heavy drops of rain, as the heat of the day which had lingered long into the night, had finally brewed up the storm which had threatened since late afternoon.

'It's just shadows,' said Barney, finally, although he did not look at her. 'I keep thinking about running across a moor, chasing someone, but I've no idea who or where or when. It's almost like it happened to someone else.'

'It did, in a manner of speaking,' said Blackadder, and Barney raised his eyes. 'You died just under two and a half years ago,' she said.

This, at last, had some effect on him, and a shiver worked its way down his back, as the rain began to gain momentum, so that there was now a loud tapping at the window. He still didn't look at her. So he was dead after all. It would certainly explain the bizarre world into which he'd been thrown.

'You were involved in chasing a murderer across open moorland in the Borders. No one knows if you fell or were pushed, but your body was found at the bottom of a cliff.'

Barney breathed out and nodded, but that information had done nothing to get him any nearer remembering the past. It was still an effort, it was still more than he wanted to think about. He looked up. His face was pale, his eyes weary.

'So, what is this? Heaven? Hell? Is this what Hell's like?'

'This is the real world, Barney,' said Blackadder. 'You were brought back, so to speak.'

Barney gazed at her. He had only vague memories of his past, he'd been dead, and now he wasn't anymore.

He just wanted to go to bed.

'I'm tired,' he said. And he was all of a sudden.

Blackadder nodded and stood up. The first roar of thunder exploded above them, although they had not noticed the preceding bolt of lightening.

'We can talk again tomorrow, if you prefer,' she said. 'It must have been a long day.'

'Aye,' said Barney, and he hauled himself to his feet to see her out. 'You're going to Brussels as well?' he asked.

'We all go everywhere with him,' she said simply, then walked to the door. She didn't agree with what had been done to Barney Thomson, and she pitied him. But there would be time to talk to him later, as long as it didn't all go dreadfully wrong.

'What kind of man is he?' said Barney, as Blackadder stood in the doorway.

She stopped, she engaged his tired eyes, she hesitated. The walls had ears, but then, she also knew that JLM would never get rid of her.

'He's just an ordinary man, several rungs higher up the ladder than he ought to be. They ran out of good men to run the Scottish parliament when Dewar died, and now we're all stuck with the likes of Jesse Longfellow-Moses. So, it's all gone to his head, and he can't get enough of it. Wants to leave his mark.'

'Should be a low-grade manager in the civil service,' said Barney. Which more or less hit the hammerhead on the nose.

She smiled and nodded.

'Absolutely. About the level that most politicians deserve to be.'

They exchanged one of those glances that Barney had never been able to fathom, then she dropped her eyes, turned and was gone. His eyes fell on the back of her jeans, the delicious movement of the hips. He closed the door quickly, then leant forward, his forehead resting against the cold wood.

So he'd been dead, and now he wasn't anymore. That made sense. It certainly explained the general feeling of being completely fucked up that was pervading every thought.

Barney turned slowly, then began walking round the room, switching off the small table lights. A quick detour to the bathroom, cleaned his teeth with what felt like someone else's toothbrush, then crawled into the cold luxury of the bed.

And in the background, as he drifted off to a nondescript sleep, he listened to Hoagy Carmichael, melancholy and slow.

8

The wisdom of the clowns

Though kings be clothed in armour,
wrought of gold and silver,
and cowed on bended knee,
the people come before them,
in awe of their munificence
so wise in their decree.
The kings of old look down from heav'n,
The blessed morn does rise,
Upon this new crowned king of earth...

'I'm stuck,' said JLM, pencil in his mouth.

Minnie Longfellow-Moses looked over the top of Blanche Wiesen-Cook's biography of Eleanor Roosevelt, eyebrow raised.

They were sitting up in bed, one in the morning, JLM with a cup of diet hot chocolate on his bedside table, Minnie with an Irish coffee. An Irish coffee of absolute in-your-face quality at that. JLM was wearing pink and white striped pj's, she was looking pretty hot in a silk, low cut Bravissimo thing.

'Speech to the European parliament?' she asked, to which JLM snorted; a sound which Minnie had ceased to find attractive a long time ago.

'You're kidding me? Don't give a shit what I say to that bunch of losers. I've left it to Parker. Even he'll probably farm it out to one of the press boys to muddle together for us. That lad at the BBC over there writes a good speech.'

She had turned back to her book within two seconds of him opening his mouth, but she continued the conversation with only a tenth of her mind on it; which was more or less what she usually gave to JLM.

'Don't you ever worry that he's going to rip the pish out of you one day?' she said. 'Get you to say something that you're not going to realise is really stupid or insulting.'

'What? You mean like referring to the Italians as wops?'

'I was thinking he might manage a little more subtlety than that,' she said dryly.

'I can spot subtlety you know,' he said, and she smiled. 'No, the guy knows who's boss when we show up.'

She nodded. Every day with Jesse Longfellow-Moses was a day waiting to blow up in his face, and she was amazed that he'd lasted almost three years without it happening more seriously than it had.

'So what are you stuck with?' she asked.

'My submission to the parliament arts exhibition,' he said.

She stopped reading and looked over the book at him again. She reached for the coffee and took a slow drink, getting the combination of whiskey, coffee and cream to perfection, then licked her top lip in a movement that would have had another man – one whose marriage hadn't staled many years previously – leaping athletically across the bed.

'The what?' she asked.

'Parliament arts exhibition,' he said. She noticed the forced air of nonchalance, and couldn't wait to hear what was coming next. 'There are a couple of rooms in Queensberry House that are still empty. Can't afford to install the sort of art they were intending to. So we're going to have a little exhibition thingy, with members of the parliament contributing. You know, poetry, paintings, sculptures, whatever. At the end of it, we'll sell some of the stuff off, keep some of the art in there. Lovely idea,' he added, 'really super.'

'And whose idea was it?' she asked.

He studied his notebook with intense concentration, pencil tapping against his teeth, as if he hadn't heard the question. Eventually he turned and looked at her, mouthed acknowledgement, and looked back at his work of art.

'Oh, mine,' he said. 'Really rather pleased with it.'

'So what are you contributing to this, then?'

‘Oh,’ he said casually, ‘I’ve got a few ideas. Doesn’t look like too many of the proles in the house will come up with anything, so I may end up with a separate section to myself. You know, First Minister, people are going to be more interested in what I’ve done than anyone else, anyway. Don’t you think?’

He turned to her, a very genuine look on his face. She nodded and smiled.

‘Yes, dear,’ she said. ‘So what are you working on at the moment?’ She took another slow sip of coffee, the glass over her face covering the amused smile. It wasn’t often that Minnie Longfellow-Moses had the chance to feel superior to her husband – only every time she spent more than two minutes with him. Which, fortunately, wasn’t very often.

‘Just a little poetical piece,’ he said. ‘It’s called *The Wisdom Of The Kings*. Lovely piece,’ he added. ‘Just looking for my final line.’

‘Go on,’ she said.

JLM studied his notebook again. Might not be too bad if Minnie came up with something. It wasn’t like she would expect joint credit.

‘The kings of old look down from heav’n, The blessed morn does rise, Upon the new crowned king of earth…’

‘With shit all down his thighs,’ said Minnie casually, turning back to Eleanor Roosevelt.

I’m not rising to that, thought JLM. For God’s sake, thought Minnie. The public, when they read that shite, will think it’s about Jesus. But I know who it’s about, the stupid arse.

‘Might just leave it ‘til the morning,’ he said. ‘Clear head.’

She reached for what was left of her coffee and ignored him. He poured his legs out of the bed, and headed for the en suite for final ablutions.

Melanie Honeyfoot’s killer was a little surprised upon hearing that the Minister for Finance had gone missing. The expected headlines in the Evening News, *Finance Minister Found With Brains Splatted Across Pillow* or *The Bitch Is Dead* or *Honeyfoot Blags The Big One* or *Honeyfoot: The Nation Celebrates*, had not materialised. Instead, it had become clear that someone had disposed of the body and tidied the place up. Bizarre. The killing had almost been a public service. Or so it had seemed, to one particular mind. Why not let the public in on the good news? Why tease them with the wonderful possibility of the witch being dead, but without letting them in on the truth?

Bizarre it may have been, but it did mean something. That rather than there being only one person in Edinburgh who knew who'd killed Melanie Honeyfoot, there were at least two. And so Honeyfoot's murderer knew that a deal more circumspection would be required when the next unfortunate victim hoved into view.

For there was little doubt that there would be more.

9

Bruxelles

'Winnie, Winnie, Winnie, Winnie, Winnie, Winnie, Winnie,' said JLM.

The hysterical screech with which she replied to his patronising tone was more than the second generation cell phone could cope with, and the words distorted so much that he couldn't actually understand what she said.

He held the phone away from his head so that the shrill shriek of the banshee was broadcast throughout the limousine. JLM looked at the other passengers, Parker Weirdlove, Barney Thomson, and crack bodyguard, The Amazing Mr X. He smiled wryly, a bonding typa thing with the other guys in the back – that could easily have been accompanied by the clink of beer bottles – feeling superior to women in general, and Winona Wanderlip in particular.

The last time JLM had added to Wanderlip's already absurdly overloaded portfolio, he'd done it face to face. In the ensuing few seconds he'd genuinely thought that she'd been going to rip his eyes clean out of their sockets with her fingernails. 'Next time,' he'd said to Weirdlove later that day, 'I'm doing it over the phone.' 'Very wise,' Weirdlove had replied.

So, JLM had just further shafted Wanderlip by adding finance, in the assumed temporary absence of Melanie Honeyfoot, to her list. And he'd done it over the phone, which was pusillanimous in the extreme but, as he'd said to Weirdlove, 'sometimes stupidity is the better part of valour', which hadn't really made sense, but he'd known what he'd meant.

'Winnie, it likely won't be for very long,' he said, after the cacophony of abuse had drifted off to a more low-key vilification.

'You know I'd give it to Eaglehawk, but I can't trust him. I do realise how you feel.'

'No you fucking don't, you wanker!' she screamed back at him. He looked with testosterone-fuelled superiority around the car, smiled wryly at the phone, shook his head, straightened his shoulders, and did his best 'who's king?' voice.

'Winnie, I shouldn't need to remind you who you're talking to,' he said.

'Damn right you don't!' she barked. 'I'm talking to a fucking idiot!'

'Look,' said JLM, very, very sternly, 'you're being very naughty. I'm too busy for this at the moment. Frankly I've got more important backsides to kick than yours. If you've got issues, you can bring them to me when I'm back tomorrow. I'll try and fit you in for five. If it's going to be a problem, perhaps you'd like to consider your position.'

The shrill cry of the Valkyrie began to rise, so he quickly clipped the phone shut and looked smugly around the car.

'Women,' he said.

The Amazing Mr X said nothing. The Amazing Mr X had his own issues to do with women, but they were mostly ones of respect, compassion and unfailing devotion. Especially towards naked women. Even more so, when there was more than one naked woman in a room at the same time. His bedroom in particular. That's enough about The Amazing Mr X and the women thing.

'She'll get over it,' said Weirdlove.

'And if she doesn't...' said JLM, and he dragged a finger across his neck, making the appropriate sound.

The car screeched dramatically to a halt at the Schuman roundabout, narrowly avoiding a limo-ful of Turkish diplomats, the passengers lurched forward, and at JLM's sign across the neck, Barney Thomson felt the strangest shiver surge through his body. The sign of death, and it seemed to bring back so much; yet, again, there was nothing on which he could put his finger, no picture of a scene from his past life that immediately came to mind.

'Barney,' barked JLM, 'what d'you think of women?'

'Not sure,' said Barney. 'They seem nice enough. Rebecca's a nice girl.'

JLM smiled knowingly and nodded at Weirdlove. Another little in-joke to which I'm not privy, thought Barney, but he hardly cared.

'She certainly is,' said JLM. 'Lovely girl, really lovely. You interested?'

That was something Barney hadn't even begun to think about, and he shrugged and stared at the floor. Didn't answer.

'What d'you think about the Euro?' said JLM suddenly. 'Barney?' he added, when Barney didn't raise his head, assuming the question had been directed at Weirdlove.

Barney looked up, a little of the 'about to get squished on the road' deer about him.

'Don't really know anything about it,' he said. 'Seems like a sensible enough idea,' he added quickly, assuming he was meant to say something. 'Ever contracting world, and all that.'

'Exactly!' said JLM. 'Exactly my thoughts.'

Weirdlove gave him a raised eyebrow. The Amazing Mr X was still thinking about women.

'So,' said JLM, 'I'm going to say as much to the European parliament. Would be damned good for Scotland.'

'We don't have that option on our own, though, do we?' said Barney.

'Ah,' said JLM knowingly. 'Not at the moment, we don't.'

And he and Weirdlove exchanged another knowing look, then JLM stared out of the window as the limo shot down Rue de Loi.

'Wonder what's happened to Honeyfoot,' mused JLM, out of the blue. 'Very odd.'

✂

Two minutes later and Winona Wanderlip was standing in James Eaglehawk's office. Big, bulging, bright red face, over-boiled like a lobster that's been in the pan for half an hour too long, extravagant hair, wild in every direction, chest heaving, a slight slaver at the mouth, incandescent with fury. In contrast, Eaglehawk looked like an FBI agent. Smooth, black-tied, groomed, pointy-chinned. Or what an FBI agent looks like in the movies, rather than in real life.

'You heard what he's doing?' she screamed at him.

Eaglehawk raised his hands to placate the stentorian outburst. He was sitting at the window, behind him the massive glass panels of the debating chamber, a September blue sky above. Of course he'd heard what JLM was doing. Wanderlip was always the last to find out. When JLM had added Enterprise to her brief, he'd told a group of visiting primary school children first.

'I know,' he said. 'It's cool.'

'You know already?' she screamed again, voice raised a pitch or two. 'It's cool? What the fuck is that? It's cool? When did he tell you?'

An easy one.

'Last night,' said Eaglehawk.

'So why didn't you tell me when I saw you this morning? We talked for about ten minutes.'

Eaglehawk held up his hand to indicate Wanderlip herself.

'Look at you, Winnie,' he said. 'You look as if you've got fifteen pounds of plutonium up your arse. Of course I didn't tell you.'

She emitted a low-pitch squeal.

'For crying out loud, Winnie,' said Eaglehawk, 'we all know what you're like. You're this exploding volcano. You've got this whole constantly pre-menstrual woman thing going on. I'm not going to go volunteering information like that.'

As he spoke, she crossed the point where, if she could literally have exploded she would have done, then started coming back down. Hands on hips – she frequently had her hands on her hips, even when she was in a good mood – heaving bosom gradually coming under control, lips on fire, nostrils doing all sorts of bizarre gymnastics, breaths short and sharp. Eaglehawk realised he'd ridden the worst of it, and made a note to thank McLaven for the advice: tell her to her face how bloody awful she is, and she'll respect you for it. As long as the home truth is coming from a man. And don't take it too far, or she'll rip your heart out.

‘You don’t think it’s odd,’ said Wanderlip, ‘that when the Minister for Finance goes missing, the First Minister doesn’t put the Deputy Minister for Finance in temporary charge? You don’t think that’s odd? Not even a little bit?’

Eaglehawk leant back, expelling a long breath. With a casual flick, he indicated the chair on the other side of the desk. Usually Wanderlip liked to stand over people, especially her ministerial inferiors, but she was coming down off the huge adrenaline rush of an out and out paddy, and needed the seat. So she slumped down, clasped her hands in her lap and crossed her legs. As if she was being interviewed by that aggressive idiot whom she always made mincemeat of on Newsnight Scotland.

‘Look, Winona,’ he began, ‘we’re not on tv here, we don’t have to bullshit anyone. Right?’

Wanderlip nodded. Slowly. Was this the preliminary step to him letting his guard down, and expecting her to do the same? Graham J Black, the Chancellor, had given her good advice when she’d first started. ‘Never let them see behind the veil. Never volunteer the truth. It doesn’t matter who you’re talking to. Never, ever, be honest.’

‘Right,’ she said.

‘Of all the ministers under JLM, you’re the only one who isn’t a no-hoper. The rest are all in it for the publicity or the free booze or the women. All right, there’s one or two who actually care, but you’re the only one with any real political talent. So, you’re the only one who’s any threat to JLM. He can fuck up all he likes, but if there’s no one else to replace him, then he’s there for the duration.’

She didn’t respond. He wasn’t saying anything new, nothing that she hadn’t thought before, nothing that the bloody Scotsman didn’t print every day. It was just new to hear it from one of her own.

‘He can’t be seen to fire you, but he wants you out. Right, how does he do it? By pissing you off so much, that you leave. Simple.’

'But aren't you pissed off?' she asked. 'Don't you think that you should've been given the finance job. What if Melanie never turns up?'

'You know something the rest of us don't?' he said, leaning forward.

'No,' she said quickly, 'why would I? You're avoiding the question.'

He rested his elbows on the desk. It was a pity, he was thinking, that Winnie had calmed down, because, as Wally was never slow to tell him, she was damned hot when she had a feist up.

'I've got my ambitions, Winnie,' he said, 'but they're long term. I've got plenty of other things going at the moment. For now, I just want to keep my nose clean, keep my job, and eventually my chance will come. That's all. Very, very equitable.'

Winnie. He'd reverted to Winnie. She stood up, feeling the anger beginning to rise again. Whatever colour he wanted to paint it, it was still yellow. Another bloody pathetic man too scared to stand up to Jesse Longfellow-Bloody-Moses.

She gave him a final withering stare, then turned and walked quickly from his office without looking back, without another word.

When she was gone, he waited another few seconds, could still hear the angry click of her shoes across the cheap flooring, then he lifted the phone and waited.

10

Political power grows out the barrel of a pun

'You're probably wondering why you're here?' said JLM.

In only a very short space of time, Barney had had enough. Every now and again JLM would throw some question or other at him, and Barney would skirt around the answer, because that's what Parker Weirdlove had told him to do. But who was it he was speaking to, after all? We are all one egg, as he remembered someone saying to him once. Obscure, and he wasn't sure why he remembered that and not a lot else. Maybe because it was so fundamental a principle. Anyway, after only a day and a bit in JLM's employ, he'd decided to be a little more honest.

'Not at all,' he replied. 'I'm here because you're obsessed with self-image, and can't stand the thought of getting your photo taken with so much as one hair out of place.'

A strange little noise escaped from the pit of Parker Weirdlove's throat. JLM looked sharply at Barney, as they sat in the small conference room in the bowels of the European parliament. Then he laughed lightly, the kind of laugh that Blofeld used to throw away before he pressed the red button and tipped someone into a tank of piranha fish. Casual, yet psychotic.

'That wasn't what I meant,' he said, voice cold, despite the laugh.

'Oh,' said Barney. Being forthright in entirely the wrong place. That reminded him of old.

'I'm in a very important position here, Mr Thomson,' said JLM. 'I don't doubt for one second that the First Minister of the country at the very heart of Europe's power infrastructure, needs to be impeccably turned out every minute of every day. I am a statesman, after all. The country looks up to me, and looks to me to play a vital role on the world stage.'

Barney nodded. It felt like it was time for some more honesty, but maybe not just yet.

'I meant, I expect you're wondering why you're here in this room, while the rest of the entourage is upstairs in the restaurant having lunch?'

All right, thought Barney, I picked up the wrong end of the stick there. Dr Blackadder, Veron, the Rev Blake, Father Michael and Dr Farrow were in a corner of the restaurant, tucking into frites and mayonnaise and steak au poivre etc. Barney was stuck down here, hanging out with The Amazing Mr X. The human equivalent of a flight on Easyjet.

'I hadn't actually,' said Barney, continuing his new honesty policy, 'but since you mentioned it?'

He had felt the slightest pang of regret at not having had the chance to travel with Blackadder, or to sit with her at lunch. Very odd; emotions within him that he didn't recognise.

'I like you,' said JLM, as if conferring some papal honour upon him. 'I like what you have to say about things. I like your opinions. You're a good sounding-board.' JLM hesitated. Barney hadn't really been aware that he'd said anything other than what he might have been expected to. Maybe that was it. 'You're sage,' JLM added. 'Very sage.'

'Thanks,' said Barney. Does it mean anything when an idiot tells you that you're sage?

'You know who you are?' said JLM.

Barney didn't answer, not being entirely sure how the question was intended.

'You're Peter Sellars.'

'Inspector Clouseau?' said Barney. That strange thing where he could barely remember the facts of his own life, but the minutiae of others' lives, the humdrum, the mundane, of television watched and purposeless gossip heard in barber shops, that was still there. That part of his brain had not been affected.

'Chance, the gardener in *Being There*,' said JLM.

‘Right,’ said Barney. Didn’t mean anything to him. Weirdlove cast a glance at JLM. Knew that his boss had never seen the film, had just heard about it and liked the sound of one of his staff being an advisor; didn’t realise that in any such analogy, it would be he himself who looked like an idiot.

‘Yes,’ said JLM, ‘a statesman can never surround himself with too many advisors. He himself just needs to be able to sort the cogent from the mundane. Lovely.’

‘Aye,’ said Barney, without much enthusiasm.

‘Anyway,’ said JLM, ‘Parker’s going to tell you why we’re all sitting in this dodgy little room in the arse of this miserable parliament.’

Barney looked at Weirdlove. A single eyebrow raised. Ready for more of it. This was bringing back life in the barber shop to him, no question. Men talking bullshit.

‘Listen up and listen good,’ said Weirdlove.

‘I love it when he talks like that,’ JLM butted in. ‘Champion.’

‘The First Minister has an agenda that few in the party know about,’ said Weirdlove, ignoring JLM, his speech having done the usual 0-120mph in half a second. ‘Correction, no one in the party knows about it. You learn this, you keep schtoom. The First Minister is trusting you with this, against my counsel. You got that?’

‘Just like government,’ said Barney. ‘Tell you a piece of information you don’t want to know in the first place, then threaten you so that you keep your mouth shut.’

JLM laughed. Weirdlove glowered. The Amazing Mr X didn’t even blink.

‘We’re about to receive a visitor from the German delegation. His name is Conrad Vogts. Only this group and about two people on the German side know this is happening. You understand what I’m saying,’ said Weirdlove, leaning forward.

‘I think so,’ said Barney, causticity creeping into his voice, which was new for him.

‘Tone!’ barked Weirdlove.

'Calm down,' JLM said to him, still amused by Barney in a paternal kind of a way, even though he was a couple of years younger than him.

'All right,' said Weirdlove, 'this is one of their top men. He's here to speak to myself and to the First Minister. You don't say a word. You listen, that's all. The First Minister wants you here, but that's where your involvement ends. You don't say anything. Not a word. Schtoom. Silence. You getting this?'

'Actually,' said Barney, 'you're beginning to confuse me a little.'

Another zinger of a look passed across Weirdlove's face. There was a knock at the door. The muscles relaxed around Weirdlove's mouth, JLM's shoulders straightened so that he became even more of a statesman than he'd been two seconds earlier, and as the door opened without invitation, The Amazing Mr X leapt to his feet, his hand reaching inside his jacket.

'Sit down, X,' said JLM, rising to greet the newcomer. The Amazing Mr X backed off. JLM schmoozed smoothly, as their visitor closed the door behind him and looked with interest around the four men already inside the small room. A room whose windows looked out onto a warm Brussels street, with cars and buses and no pedestrians.

'Herr Vogts,' said JLM, hand extended. 'Delighted you could make it.'

'I am tickled also,' said Vogts. A tall man, thick shock of greying hair, a warmth and ease about the thin face. Virtually no accent when he spoke English; if anything, a trace of American. And he spoke faster than Parker Weirdlove. 'I'll have a meeting with anyone who'll have me,' he continued. 'But then, most people won't have me. Especially women. Not that I'm interested in men, not in that way. Though at the same time I've got nothing against homosexuals. Some of my best friends are friends with people who know homosexuals, so that proves something, even if I don't know what.'

'Lovely,' said JLM, a little nonplussed. 'This is Parker Weirdlove, who you've talked to. And this is Barney Thomson, the government's principal advisor on fiscal matters.'

There would've been a time when Barney would've flinched. He nodded, rose from his chair, and shook Vogts by the hand.

'Hello,' said Barney, gruffly.

'I had you pegged as the barber,' said Vogts, 'but then, I never was much good with a peg. Especially when it came to hanging up the washing. That's why my wife divorced me. That and all those women. She just couldn't get enough of them.'

'Sit down, sit down,' said JLM, mostly to shut Herr Vogts up. Parker Weirdlove, having set up this meeting, which both he and JLM viewed as something of a fulcrum in their term of government, sat down and eyed Vogts with a great deal of suspicion. Barney Thomson didn't quite know what to make of him, but then that went for everyone he'd met in the past two days. The Amazing Mr X stared at the door, occasionally glanced at the windows, and thought of women.

'How can we help you?' asked Vogts, having nestled down into his seat.

'You will be aware of the delicate nature of this meeting?' said Weirdlove, before JLM could say anything.

'Oh, yes, delicate,' said Vogts. 'Like the fine hairs of a woman's pubes.'

'Yeah,' said The Amazing Mr X, in a low voice.

Weirdlove raised the sort of eyebrow that had many in the Scottish Executive reeling, but which meant nothing to the likes of Conrad Vogts.

'Yes,' said JLM, 'I rather like that. Lovely analogy. Really rather splendid.'

'No one in our parliament knows we're here with you, no one knows what we're going to talk about,' said Weirdlove, attempting added gravitas in the voice, to compensate for the fact that Vogts didn't appear to have any.

'Even I don't know what we're going to talk about,' said Vogts. 'Not that that's anything new.'

'We understand you're a bit of an expert on the Euro,' said JLM.

‘I am an expert on many things,’ said Vogts. ‘Hamburg, the 1983 European cup final, Monty Python’s Flying Circus, the comedies of the Marx Brothers. And women.’

‘Yeah,’ said The Amazing Mr X.

‘I am also considered an expert on the Euro,’ said Vogts, ‘although that’s probably because I speak very quickly on a subject that most people don’t know enough about.’

‘A tonic to hear such honesty in the political field,’ said JLM.

‘Ah, tonic,’ said Vogts, ‘I am also an expert on Indian tonic and its use as an alcoholic mixer.’

‘Lovely. Champion,’ said JLM. ‘Look, Mr Weirdlove is going to explain where we’re coming from.’

‘Indeed,’ said Vogts, and he turned to face him. ‘I’m all ears, although that’s only because the plastic surgeon misheard me. I was supposed to be all beer.’

‘The thing is,’ said Weirdlove, his voice shooting out even more quickly, as overcompensation for having a political interlocutor who he felt was kicking his backside, ‘it is clear to us that Britain’s policy of exclusion from the Euro-zone is a total disaster. It is affecting Scotland tremendously badly, and the Westminster government is moving far too slowly. We need to be decisive and audacious.’

‘So what are you saying?’ asked Vogts. ‘You want to take Scotland into the Euro zone separately? That’s not in your constitution.’

Weirdlove threw a quick sideways glance at JLM.

‘Not at the moment,’ said Weirdlove.

‘You’re going to have a referendum?’ asked Vogts. ‘I am much in favour of referendums. I think we should have referendums for everything. Governments should have referendums on where they’re going to buy their sausages.’

‘You’re a big advocate of referendums then?’ said Weirdlove, suspiciously.

‘They are the very essence of democracy,’ said Vogts. ‘The rock on which political freedom is based.’

‘We’re not going to have one,’ said JLM, loosely. ‘We’re going to push it through without telling anyone.’

'Lovely,' said Vogts, 'an even more fundamental political necessity. Don't tell the people anything if they're going to get in your way.'

'My thoughts exactly,' said JLM.

'I think we can do business,' said Vogts.

'Champion,' said JLM.

✂

Herr Vogts left the small room thirty minutes later, after reaching a broad agreement that someone would be seconded from Berlin, most likely Vogts himself, to help Weirdlove and JLM draw up plans to introduce the Euro to Scotland, completely bypassing Westminster in the process. The intention was to make the final statement with such grandeur and eloquence, and with some major European political alliances announced at the same time, that the public would be carried along in a wave of devolutionary excitement. In the meantime, JLM had to stoke the anti-English fires, which would be like peeling a banana, and investigate every legal loophole in the constitution that would help them subvert Westminster's control over Holyrood.

The financial plans would be drawn up with the help of the Deputy Finance Minister, James Eaglehawk, leaving the temporary Finance Minister, Winona Wanderlip, totally in the dark. When the fiscal coup d'état was announced, she would hear about it in the usual manner, from the press, her position would be untenable, in her own and in the public's eyes, and she would gracefully resign.

Following the Euro and further splits with Westminster, independence would be inevitable, backed by a rising swell of public opinion. JLM would be a hero and the father of the new sovereign Scotland.

A plan of the utmost cunning.

'What did you think?' said JLM, looking Barney in the eye. Waiting for words of wisdom from his latest sage.

Barney glanced at Weirdlove, who gave him one of his 'remember what I told you' looks. Barney turned back to JLM, having already determined to more or less ignore everything that

Weirdlove had said. He'd already been dead, for goodness sake. What else could they do to him?

'I think it's disgracefully dishonest,' said Barney. 'You've come to power on the back of parliamentary democracy, and in the past two days I've seen repeated evidence that you intend to ride roughshod all over it. It's prescriptive government at its most unhinged. You don't give a damn about the country or the people, you're only interested in the furtherance of your own political ambitions. You have total contempt for every institution and procedure that got you where you are, and if you think I'm going to exculpate you with some two second soundbite to make you feel good, as if you deserve plaudit for some sort of aesthetic spontaneity of thought, you're wrong.'

JLM nodded. Faint smirk of amusement at the corner of his mouth. The megalomaniac's ability to laugh at and easily dismiss home-truths

'I actually meant, what did you think of Herr Vogts?' he said.

Weirdlove steamed gently under his suit.

'Oh,' said Barney. 'Seemed like a decent enough bloke. Bit of a Mel Gibson Lethal Weapon **2** cut.'

'Lovely,' said JLM. 'Can we trust him?'

'Of course not,' said Barney. 'But then, he can't trust you.'

JLM laughed and rose from his chair. Like a flash, The Amazing Mr X was on his feet, checking the windows, watching the door, trigger finger twitching.

'Very good, Barney, very good,' said JLM. 'Come on, let's go.'

The Amazing Mr X pushed past Weirdlove, opened the door, checked the corridor, then indicated that it was safe for the party to leave the room. He walked out ahead and stood waiting. Rolling his eyes, Weirdlove breezed past him and strode purposefully up the corridor. JLM and Barney walked out together, The Amazing Mr X falling in behind.

'Barney,' said JLM, lightly taking his arm. 'Just a word. Don't ever speak to me like that again. It might just be that we send you back where you came from.'

'I don't even know where that is,' said Barney, not rising to the threat.

JLM gave him an ugly glance and upped his pace to walk quickly after Weirdlove.

'Oh, and Barney,' he said, turning under a large photograph of the Brandenberg Gate. 'Could you do me a Dean Martin '57 for my meeting with the Portuguese delegation? Apparently there's a woman as part of their team, bit of a looker, goes big for a man who can croon *That's Amore*.'

'Aye,' said Barney. 'No bother.'

'Champion,' said JLM, and then he strode on, came broadside with Parker Weirdlove, and immediately dropped into stern conversation.

11

Carry on up the revolution

The cabinet of the Scottish Executive was in full session. Almost full session. JLM wasn't in attendance, but then that was nothing new of late. In the three weeks since the resumption of parliament, he had not yet deigned to show his face at cabinet, having begun to think that there was little point in it. If any of his ministers said something he didn't like, he'd ignore them anyway. So what, he would voice to anyone who cared to listen, was the point of going in the first place? As First Minister, the man in control of the country's destiny, he had better things to do than listen to his government.

The difference from the norm was the absence of JLM's deputy, Fforbes Benderhook, an appallingly spineless Liberal Democrat. A man for whom political ambition went no further than sucking up to the First Minister's substantial butt, and who would attend cabinet on his behalf, reporting back diligently on any of the Labour members who raised even the slightest concern or dissension against any of JLM's policies.

He was the obvious one not to call to the meeting. The others, however, Winona Wanderlip suspected, were as fed up with JLM's grandstanding as was she. So the rest of the cabinet were there, with the obvious exception of Melanie Honeyfoot, who was dead, dead, dead.

They sat around the small table in Wanderlip's office. Winona, herself, at the head, and thereafter clockwise around the table; Peggy Filiben, Education, a nothing short of spectacularly attractive woman; the previously encountered Wally McLaven, Tourism, Culture & Sport, ex-Rangers, a man who thought culture was the ability to speak consecutive sentences without using the phrase 'to be fair', and who was sitting with his hand guzzling at Filiben's thigh; Malcolm Malcolm III of the Clan Malcolm, Health, ex-Westminster; Kathy Spiderman, Justice, a bizarre wee woman who would more normally have been found arguing the price of a toaster-of-uncertain-provenance down the Barrows on a Saturday morning, but who was a long-term ally of JLM's, turned bad; Trudger McIntyre, Environment and Rural Development, another futile Liberal Democrat, who had the whole Captain Mainwaring vibe to a tee; and finally, next to Wanderlip, Nelly Stratton, Parliamentary Business, a nebby wee cow.

'To be fair to the lad, JLM,' said McLaven, after Wanderlip had finished a long outburst on the trip to Brussels, which had succeeded a similar outburst on her being lumped with the Finance portfolio, 'just because we don't know what he's up to, doesn't mean it's dodgy.'

'If it's not dodgy,' said Wanderlip, 'then why not tell us what he's doing? Did you see it on News24? There were about five people turned up to listen to his speech to the European parliament. What was the point?'

'They bastards don't deserve him,' growled Kathy Spiderman, in that tone which suggested that she thought everyone in Brussels should be whipped with razor wire.

'The people of Scotland,' said Wanderlip, a group she regularly hijacked to support her views, regardless of whether or not they did, 'don't deserve for JLM to be buggering off around the world in search of fame, when he should be here addressing the issues affecting his own country.'

'Jesus Christ,' said Nelly Stratton, 'change the record.'

'What are *we* here for?' said Trudger McIntyre, softly, the first time he'd spoken, and they looked at him as one.

'What d'you mean?' asked Wanderlip.

'What do you do all day, Winona?' he asked. 'Plot? We're here to look after the problems affecting the Scottish people. While we're doing that, what's wrong with him promoting Scotland on the world stage?'

'Different class,' said Wally McLaven. 'To be fair to the lad McIntyre, he's got a point.'

Wanderlip looked at the two of them, then at the rest of the company, her mouth open in some amazement. She held Stratton's gaze for a second to see if she was going to get any support, but there was none forthcoming.

'Hello!' she said, with exaggeration, 'what has this man done in the past two and a half years? He's put so many restrictions on our individual powers that we can't do anything without him okaying it. For God's sake Wally, when was the last time you took a shit and didn't have to sign the toilet paper out of the stationery cupboard.'

'Jesus Christ,' said Nelly Stratton, 'every analogy wi' you has tae involve the stationery cupboard.'

Wanderlip slung some contempt her way.

'To be fair to the lad, Winnie,' said McLaven, whose judgement could be swayed by even the least persuasive argument, 'she does have a point. There's nothing happens in this building without JLM's name being on a piece of paper. I always thought it was good, solid, hands-on leadership. Really, though, there's the whole control-freak thing going on.'

'Thank you,' said Wanderlip, appalled that it had taken so long for McLaven to realise the obvious.

'Aye,' said Malcolm Malcolm III of the Clan Malcolm, 'but maybe it's because he's the most competent of the lot of us, and needs to be on top of everything.'

'Oh, for God's sake, Malcolm,' said Wanderlip, 'you can think like that if you want to, but I refuse. The man is out of control. He's got his own bloody barber now, did you hear that?'

'Aye, aye,' said McLaven, 'but to be fair to the lad, they say he does an excellent Dean Martin '57.'

'Stop it!' Wanderlip suddenly screamed, and McLaven ducked. 'Who cares? The point is, surely, that he is out of control. We have to do something about it. We have to think of something.'

'Go on, then,' said Peggy Filiben, from underneath McLaven's wandering hand. She too had, up until now, been silent. 'What's your plan?'

Wanderlip glanced to her left, checked out the look in Filiben's eyes. Then she gazed around the room. There had been voices raised in favour of JLM, but that was just from people who were afraid of him, and people too lacking in confidence to stand out from the crowd.

'We need someone to step forward. We need to act as a team, but we also need a leader to stand up to the man. Not just for our own good, but for the good of the people of Scotland.'

She looked sternly around the team. A hard look into every eye, thinking herself capable of reading the thoughts behind those eyes. Who would be brave enough, who would be spineless, and who, possibly, would be straight on the cell phone to JLM. Because, for all the discord in the ranks, she knew she'd taken a chance by inviting them all to the meeting. And part of her wanted JLM to know what she was up to, to hurry the thing up, bring their disagreement to a swift conclusion, because she felt she would ultimately triumph.

'Why don't *you* do it?' said Nelly Stratton. 'All mouth, nae trousers, as my mother used to say.'

'They'll see me coming a mile off,' said Wanderlip, not even looking at Stratton as she replied. Justifying herself to the others, not her accuser. 'We need someone to blindside them, someone they're not expecting.'

'I'll do it,' said the quiet, seductive voice. 'You're right. We need to stop him, before he bankrupts the whole country.'

Wanderlip looked to her left. She studied the eyes of Peggy Filiben, she saw the steel behind the outrageous good looks. It's always the women, she thought. Always. Men can talk a good game, they can act hard, but it's only ever the women who have the real balls to stand up to people.

As soon as Filiben had spoken, McLaven had withdrawn his hand. Something about a woman with real balls that makes you not want to grope her high up on the thigh.

'Good,' said Wanderlip. 'One day, the people of Scotland will thank you.'

'We'll see,' said Filiben, and the room dropped into a long silence.

✂

As Wanderlip had suspected might happen, within five minutes of the emergency and clandestine cabinet meeting breaking up, JLM's phone rang and he was given the news that the cabinet as a whole, and Peggy Filiben in particular, were to mount a challenge to his authority as First Minister. JLM thanked the caller, slipped the phone into his pocket, walked up the length of the private jet which was taking him and his entourage back to Edinburgh from Brussels at the end of a productive day, and settled into deep conversation with two or three of his closest circle.

12

Splat!

Peggy Filiben waved to the driver, smiled and stepped down from the bus, then started walking quickly along Grenville, where it splits off the Dunbar road. It was late in the evening, and the sun had given way to a humid night. The street was deserted, the closed doors and closed curtains of houses besieging the inhabitants in their private suburban melancholy. The bus driver watched Filiben for a couple of seconds, glanced in his rear view mirror, saw that the blue Hyundi which had been following him most of the way out of the city centre had parked a few car lengths behind, then he pulled out into the road and drove on, quickly crunching his way through the gears. As he turned the corner into Blythswood, another glance in his mirror and he noticed that the Hyundi had once again moved off, then it was out of sight and he had forgotten about it.

Filiben believed in using public transport. She didn't like the concept of private medicine or private financing of public projects. She was a good woman, a good socialist, honest, brave and forthright. And the media loved her, because she was gorgeous, and it allowed them to be fabulously patronising, which is one of the many things they enjoy. A Scottish tabloid had even offered her a couple of hundred thousand pounds to appear in their weekly magazine in her underwear. 'In immaculate taste, darlin',' the editor had said. Filiben had declined, and had marked them down for suitable retribution when she had the opportunity. Not that she was vindictive, but she hated it when people took politics lightly, and she herself had had to battle her good looks throughout her career.

And now she had just committed herself to the biggest gamble of that career. She didn't aspire to high office herself, having long held the conviction that more could be achieved from the cabinet minister positions than from the ceremonial post at the head. Indeed, if JLM had shown a little more respect for the Executive and the Parliament, she probably wouldn't have had any trouble with him jetting off around the world, playing the statesman.

She realised that Wanderlip was in it for herself, that she would use Filiben as the stalking horse, then should it get anywhere and JLM be ousted, she would move in and attempt to attain the leadership. But that was as it may be; she believed wholeheartedly that Wanderlip would be a vastly superior leader to JLM. A leader who would listen to her troops; who would trust others to do their given jobs; who would care more for her people than for her own career. She would be everything that JLM was not.

Peggy Filiben stopped at the side of the kerb. Looked left then right. The blue Hyundi was coming along the road behind her and she stayed at the edge of the kerb waiting for it to pass. As it approached, accelerating quickly, the smooth engine purring quietly through second and into third, she noticed the driver was wearing dark glasses and a woollen hat; a little odd for the hours of darkness on a sultry evening.

Her eyes flicked away, her head filled with random thoughts; of Winona Wanderlip and Jesse Longfellow-Moses, hair dye and anal implants and what to do on cold and wet Sundays in January.

She caught the movement towards her in the corner of her eye. Didn't even have time to turn. A flash of blue, the Hyundi careered off the road, bouncing on the kerb, so that when it struck her, the full force of it caught her at the top of her thighs. Approximately the same area that had felt the full warmth of Wally McLaven's massage.

The driver straightened the Hyundi on impact, Filiben was blatted aside like a balloon, and her head hit the ground travelling at 17.8mph. It was that which killed her.

The Hyundi sped on up the road, engine smooth and placid, the only sound having been the dull thud of impact, turned the corner in the opposite direction from the bus, and was on its way. And throughout it all, not a curtain twitched.

Peggy Filiben's body might have lain there undiscovered for some time. However, despite the killer's determination that this murder would go unseen, despite the precautions and due circumspection, there had still been someone there to bear witness. And as Filiben's body lay limp and spiritless on the pavement, another car approached along the road, and pulled up beside the corpse.

13

See those boats? I built them all. Do they call me Harry the boatbuilder? Nah. But you shag one sheep...

Barney Thomson, and the rest of the team, had been back in the country for a little more than three hours. He'd returned to his room, as he thought he should, but after another hour of staring at the walls and mundane methodology artworks, thin and crispy carpets and docudramas on the tv, he'd headed out onto the streets of Edinburgh, for the first time since his mother had taken him there at the age of seven. It had changed, as far as he could remember, in the previous forty-three years. Not that Barney knew he was fifty; or felt fifty; or looked fifty, for that matter.

Quickly found himself in the World's End at the corner of High Street and St. Mary's, with the tourists and the curious, ordered a bottle of American beer and a packet of peanuts, ensconced himself alone at a table in the corner, and watched the punters come and go, high tide low tide, the bar filling up, thinning out, and filling up again.

Strangely, after an hour or so, well into his third beer, he was quite happy. Enjoying the solitude and quiet of a noisy bar, watching the people of Scotland, as Winona Wanderlip called them, as well as the visitors of the world, savouring the cold taste of beer as it hit the back of his throat, and the haggis and chips which had just been delivered to his table. Still no nearer discovering the truth about his past and how he'd come to be in the employ of Jesse Longfellow-Moses, but it wasn't as if his life was horrendous. He was settling into it, going with the flow and not seeking the facts, in the belief that the facts would eventually find him.

He was feeling decidedly languid when the chair opposite him was pulled out from the table, and he smelled and recognised the expensive fragrance without immediately looking up from his plate.

'Edmund,' he said.

'Barney,' said Rebecca Blackadder, with a wry smile. She could ask people all she liked not to call her Edmund, but it never made any difference. It was the penalty she paid for having a cool name.

'Been looking for you,' she said.

'Been here all along,' he replied.

She took a sip from her gin and tonic and smiled again. Finally he looked at her, caught the movement of her lips across her teeth, the relaxation of the smile, the warmth and beauty in the eyes.

'How many bars have you been in?' he asked.

'Seventeen,' she said. 'Had a drink in every one.'

He nodded. Didn't say anything; didn't look at her. Smiled a little.

'Also looked in three pizza joints and four brothels.'

He gave her a quick glance.

'And did you eat pizza and shag some women?' he said.

'Some of the above,' she replied.

'Why are you here?' he asked quickly, looking at her this time, his voice losing the flippancy of two seconds earlier.

'Doctor's orders,' she said.

'Right,' he replied. 'And is the doctor going to tell me who I am?' And he shovelled some haggis into his mouth. It was delicious; spicy and crisp.

'You're supposed to work it out for yourself,' she said. 'I could tell you any old shit, and your brain would work its way round to creating memories to back that up.'

'If I died two and a half years ago,' he said sharply, 'how the Hell am I supposed to work out why I'm not dead anymore?'

She nodded, black hair moving across her forehead. Sometimes the untrained person could cut through the bullshit of the professional. In fact, she frequently had cause to reflect, it happened on a regular basis.

She leant back against the chair, looked at his plate. The smell of his meal nagged away at her stomach, but she'd already eaten. And Barney wasn't waiting for her to join him. But this wasn't Barney Thomson as the world had known him before. She didn't approve of him being here, of his very existence on the planet; but it wasn't his fault.

'Genetics,' she said.

'Ah,' said Barney. 'Go on.'

'You remember the Dolly the sheep thing?' she asked.

'Not really. Did they mix a human and a sheep?' he asked. 'They must've had difficulty finding the guy for that experiment. They put an advert in the paper. *Man Wanted To Shag Sheep. Previous Experience Preferred, But Training Will Be Given.* After a couple of days they only had thirty-three thousand applications.'

She was laughing. Barney Thomson made her laugh. And she was a woman. No one had ever been able to say that before.

'Not quite,' she said. 'Dolly the sheep was cloned from cells of a parent sheep. Advanced stuff, even now, but that was it, pure and simple.'

She hesitated. Barney ate his dinner.

'I'm listening,' he said.

'It's pretty controversial. But, you know how these things are. The stuff that was reported wasn't the half of it. There's another laboratory outside the city, doing all sorts of things the public knows nothing about. Even more cutting edge, even more frightening.'

She stopped again. Her voice had dropped lower and lower as she talked, and Barney imagined that she shouldn't be telling him any of this. For whatever reason, she was on his side. Although, then again, she'd admitted the night before that she was there at the behest of Weirdlove, and Barney had already come to realise that you couldn't trust Weirdlove any further than you could drive a Ferrari with liquid edible underwear in the petrol tank.

'So, where do I come into it?' he asked. 'Am I the result of a cross between a cow and a toilet seat, or something?'

'No,' she said, 'although there are some of them in the government.'

Again she stopped. Barney followed some unknown green vegetable around his plate, forked it with the last of his haggis, then took a long swallow of beer, draining his third and last bottle of the night, popped the last of his chips, and looked up at her.

'I'm going to go home now,' he said, 'or what passes for home. You want to tell me anything before I go?'

He didn't want to go home. He wanted to stay there all night, talking to her. But there was something in-built, making him back off.

'Your brain was kept in a jar for the past two and a half years,' she said, matter-of-factly.

William Matthews, 19, happened to be walking past their table at the time, and nearly dropped the five drinks he was carrying. In fact, he'd heard the words as 'your brain was kept in a bar', which sounded like a pretty cool place for your brain to be kept for that length of time.

'That explains a lot,' said Barney. 'Is it still in the jar?' he asked, which would explain even more.

'No,' she said, with a smile, 'I'm afraid it's definitely inside your head.'

'But it's been crossed with a sheep's brain? That would explain the woolly thinking.'

'Let me finish,' she said, suddenly extending her hand across the table and touching his. This had to be difficult for him, and he wouldn't be the first man to hide behind lousy jokes. Look at Jim Davidson. 'There's a laboratory near the coast, you know the type of thing. Looks harmless on the outside, bit of a run down farm. Don't even have any noticeable security, because they don't want to draw attention to it. They've been doing experiments in RCD since not long after the war.'

'RCD?' said Barney. 'That'll be what? Really Crap Doctors? Designer doctors, the government's answer to the GP shortage. You bring them out, they fuck up your health, then they get locked away in storage for the night. Coming soon, designer nurses, designer train drivers, designer ministers and designer advertising consultants. There's already five of them to every normal human being in the country, but they've persuaded the government that they need more.'

'Barney,' she said, softly, and this time she held a gentle finger up to his mouth; touched his lips. He shivered, he stopped talking. She held her finger against him longer than was necessary, held his gaze at the same time. Finally lowered her hand, and wrapped her fingers around his.

'This is pretty fucking weird, Barney, it's all right to be freaked.'

'Good,' he said, 'because I'm freaked.'

'Rapid Cell Development. They don't just clone the sheep or the mouse or the tsetse fly or whatever, they grow it to adulthood at an incredibly accelerated rate.'

'Why?' said Barney, interjecting where she had not intended to stop talking.

'Christ knows,' she said, shaking her head. 'Because they can? Because no one's done it before? Who knows what their reasons are? But there are always going to be people who'll pay for that kind of technology, so they're pushing it big. Have been for years.'

'So they took my brain...?' said Barney, and that very brain wasn't really computing any of this. It was as if they were talking about someone else.

'They took cells from it, and they grew you. This body you're in, they grew in less than two years.'

He stared, he gazed, he gaped, he wondered, he marvelled, he doubted, he mistrusted. His mouth was slightly open. He reached for the bottle, put it to his lips, forgetting it was empty.

'I'll get you another,' she said.

'No, go on,' he said quickly.

‘The one thing they can’t do yet, is develop the brain at the pace of the body. So, when your body had reached the adult state they were looking for, they removed the brain, and transplanted your original brain.’

‘Which had been kept in a jar,’ he said.

‘Yeah,’ she said.

‘I’m sceptical here,’ he said. ‘I mean, I realise I’m messed up, ‘n all, but what you’re saying, that has got to be bullshit.’

‘You’d like to think so,’ she said. ‘But if it was, you wouldn’t be here.’

He leant forward, then he sat back. He glanced round at the other customers, he tapped his fork on his empty plate. Scraped it around, dug up the few morsels that were left.

‘Bollocks,’ he said, finally. ‘I mean, why me? Why not do it with George Harrison or Jimmy Stewart or some scientist or other. Why me? Why Barney Thomson? What did I ever do?’

‘Availability,’ she said. ‘First law of construction, whether it’s buildings or people. You can only work with the materials available to you. They have a guy on the inside at St Andrews University, that’s where your brain was being stored.’

‘In a jar,’ said Barney, with melancholy.

‘Yeah,’ she said. ‘Really, you don’t have to keep going on about the jar. There’s not that much difference between a jar and anyone’s head. You were a trial, not a lot more than that. Then Jesse found out about you, knew that you were this renown barber guy, and fancied having you as his personal hairdresser. Parker did the rest. They kind of switched you on a couple of days ago.’

Barney spun the beer bottle around so that it toppled and rolled along the table. He grabbed it just before it fell, then repeated it. Switched him on.

‘I’m losing credulity here,’ he said. ‘I’m not sure, but I have memories of being this murderer kind of guy.’

‘That’s what everyone thought,’ said Blackadder. ‘But after you died, a government inquiry was established to examine your life. More or less exonerated you of everything you’d been accused of in the past. Two minutes after that, you weren’t news anymore.

The press forget in seconds, and the public trundle along in their wake. So, now you're just like this new guy. A new life, a new body, new everything.'

'Still miserable as fuck,' he said with contemplation, reading the label on the bottle, trying to grasp at normality.

She squeezed his fingers, her hand never having left his.

'We'll see what we can do about that,' she said.

Barney engaged her eyes and automatically lifted the empty bottle to his lips to cover his vague discomfort with the close attentions of a woman.

Did it sound plausible? Of course it didn't. But then, just because you don't comprehend something, doesn't mean that it can't happen. It wasn't like he understood the physics behind nuclear fission, wind, the evolution of planets or why women have more orgasms, but it didn't mean they weren't all true.

He took the bottle away from his face because he realised he looked like an idiot. Tore his eyes away from hers, looked at the floor of the bar and contemplated that it would, at least, explain why his very existence seemed to be such an anachronism.

14

Nuthin' much

A similar scene to the one that had unfolded with the strange disappearance of Melanie Honeyfoot, re-enacted itself in the Scottish Executive the following day when Peggy Filiben failed to materialise for work. She'd had a six-thirty with a journalist from the Mail on Sunday – she'd always enjoyed giving the press total access, but doing it spectacularly early in the morning, especially on a Saturday – so when Mike Holgrum was present at her office, and she wasn't, the alarm had been raised. Peggy Filiben never missed an opportunity to talk to the press.

So the media had it even before building security or the police, and Holgrum jumped with both feet at the coincidence of two cabinet ministers going missing in the same week. Before alerting anyone to his suspicions, he had established the last person to see Filiben at the parliament and how she'd travelled home from work, he'd spoken to the bus driver who'd dropped her off, and he had visited the scene and discovered blood on the pavement, not that far from the bus stop. He'd stopped short of breaking into her house, then he'd finally informed the police of his enquiries, two minutes before he'd informed everyone else.

The day flew by in a torrent of media speculation and frantic police investigation. And at the end of it, the authorities had nothing more than the sighting of Peggy Filiben alighting from a bus, never to be seen again. They had confirmation that the blood on the pavement was indeed hers, and that was just about that. The members of the cabinet had been forced to reveal that they'd been in session, what with that being the last time that any of them had seen her alive. None of them, however, gave voice to the possibility that there might have been a connection between the meeting and Filiben's disappearance. That would just have been too implausible and frightening to think about.

The bus driver had vaguely remembered the blue car, but that was about as far as it went. 'All look the same, don't they?' he'd said.

And it just so happened that the driver of the Hyundi was as surprised as everyone else that Peggy Filiben had disappeared. The plan had been for her body to be found, squished to a pulp, on the pavement. So, there was something suspicious going on. Above and beyond the fact that members of the cabinet were getting murdered.

And so the fifteen officers that had been put onto the task of locating Melanie Honeyfoot were multiplied five-fold, the press screamed murder, there were cries of serial killer to be heard in the corridors of the parliament, and there were more than a few people in Holyrood looking over their shoulders and wondering who was going to be next.

15

Shagtastic!

Monday morning, the weekend having slipped quietly by. The Sunday papers had questioned the disappearance of the two Cabinet ministers right enough, but it hadn't managed to get quite as many column inches as the beginning of the latest *Pop Idol* series. Already there were complaints of bias about the lack of Scots selected for the televised stages; and the uproar had pushed the mystery of the disappearing cabinet women definitively onto the inside pages.

Politicians had to learn their place in this personality driven age; the trouble being that most of them still thought that they dined at the top table of public interest. And if the press weren't all that concerned about the spectacularly attractive Filiben, they were unlikely to be too bothered if any of the rest of them disappeared. (Apart from those cabinet ministers who'd played football for Rangers and Scotland, and who were a little bit cheeky.)

Wally McLuven had been allowed to cherry pick his deputy minister at the office of Tourism, Culture & Sport. Patsy Morningirl was a lovely girl, with a bit of a gorgeous-but-thick-as-mince look about her. Whenever there was any comment in the press to be made about Tourism, Culture or Sport, Wally himself would be there, cheeky and cheery as ever, with a ready smile, quip, and saucy hand up the skirt of the nearest female journalist. The male journos loved him because he'd played football, the female journos loved him because there was always the chance they'd get to shag the man who'd scored three goals for Scotland in World Cup Finals. So, the fact that his deputy was a complete and utter eejit meant little, as her existence in the Executive was almost totally nugatory. Even the press weren't that interested in her Amsterdam-hooker looks, because they had Peggy Filiben to gawp at.

To cut more quickly to the point, Patsy Morningirl was there because Wally McLaven had banged her a few times, she'd threatened to tell his wife, and he'd got her the position. Although he had also attached the caveat that if he was going to have her around on a regular basis, then he would be allowed to continue banging her. Patsy had agreed.

So, when Winona Wanderlip strode past McLaven's secretary – who attempted to stop Wanderlip charging in uninvited, but thought, who cares and gave up – and marched into his office, it was to find Morningirl flat out on top of Wally's desk, pants to the wind, skirt at her waist, and Wally with his breeks at his ankles, pumping away like a ferret.

'Oh, for God's sake,' said Wanderlip, 'can you two just try not doing that for like two minutes?'

They looked at her. They kept at it. Wally was in fine form, and Patsy was almost enjoying herself.

'Hi, Winnie,' said Patsy, 'he's all yours in a few seconds.'

'Won't be long,' said Wally.

'Should I wait outside?' said Wanderlip.

'No, no, no, no, no, no, no, no, no, noooooooo!' said McLaven. Then he collapsed in a temporary heap on top of Morningirl.

He lay there, panting heavily. She lay under him, moderately content with her lot and looked to the side. Half-smiled at Wanderlip, in a 'we're all women together' kind of a way.

'Terrible about Peggy,' said Morningirl.

'Yes,' said Wanderlip.

'Lovely girl, too.'

'Yes,' said Wanderlip, wondering how long Wally would need to recover. The first time she had interrupted them having sex, she'd been embarrassed. But now, on what was possibly the twentieth occasion, it had dropped to zero on the Mortification Scale.

Morningirl sighed heavily.

'Still,' she said, perking up, 'if Peggy's dead it'll make me the best looking bird in the government. I might get a bit more coverage.'

'Very forward thinking of you, Patsy,' said Wanderlip.

'And I'm telling you,' said Morningirl, 'if anyone offers me money to pose in my Adam Ants, I'll drop the old skirt in seconds.'

'Lovely,' said Wanderlip. 'Wally, have your dylithium crystals been recharged enough for you to have a conversation at all?'

Wally exhaled a long breath, turned and gave her a cheeky wee grin.

'I know you're desperate to see, 'n all, Winnie, but could you turn your back a minute?' he said.

Wanderlip tutted loudly, turned and looked at the photographs on the wall of McLaven's office. There were approximately fifteen photos of Wally's footballing heroics, mostly scoring goals for Scotland. There was a good one, however, of a spectacular dive he'd made in the last minute to get a penalty against Celtic. (There wasn't a photo of him blootering the penalty three miles over the bar, however.)

There was a scurry of little feet across the floor and Morningirl appeared beside Wanderlip, the tops of her legs clamped together.

'See you later, Winnie,' she said.

'Aye,' said Wanderlip, dryly, 'we could go the ballet together or something.'

Morningirl vented what passed for a laugh, something akin to the noise a hyena would make when, well, it'd just been shagged by Wally McLaven. And she was gone.

Wanderlip turned round. McLaven was sitting demurely behind his desk, tie straight, jacket on, ready for business.

'Can't the two of you go to a hotel or something?' said Wanderlip.

'It's more daring this way,' he said cheekily.

'What d'you mean daring?' she protested, sitting down across from him. 'You don't give a shit if you're caught. JLM's caught you at it before and all he did was congratulate you and take Patsy's phone number.'

McLaven laughed.

'I'm just a brazen hussy, darlin',' he said, being Elvis.

'Bloody marvellous,' she said, then dropped the condemnation and leant forward. Serious face.

'You been thinking what I've been thinking?' she asked.

McLaven considered this for a few seconds then shook his head.

'You know, Winnie,' he said, 'I seriously doubt that.'

'Peggy volunteered to step forward on Friday, and now she's gone. Blood on the pavement.'

'Yeah, nightmare,' said McLaven. 'She was gorgeous too.'

'That's not really the point,' said Wanderlip.

'Oh, it is,' said McLaven. 'It means all we're left with is you, Kathy and Nelly, for god's sake. You'll admit yourself, you're no oil painting, and Nelly, well Jesus-suffering-fuck, there are no end of issues with that face of hers. And Kathy? You know how if you give a dog a bone and then two minutes later try and take it away again. She looks like the bone.'

'Christ, Wally!' she said, becoming agitated by his immature cheeky cheeriness, 'it's not a beauty contest.'

'Sure it is, Winnie,' said McLaven. 'It's all about presentation. There's nothing under the surface that matters anything like as much as how it's put forward, and who's putting it forward. It's not what you say, it's whether the public want to shag the person who's saying it.'

She groaned, Wally smiled at himself.

'Hey, that's pretty good,' he said. 'If I say that in the right place it might end up in one of those books of quotations. What d'you think?'

'Wally,' said Wanderlip, 'Peggy could be dead.'

'I know,' he said.

'She very possibly could have been murdered.'

'I know,' he said.

'And,' said Wanderlip, going on a bit, 'murdered because she was intending to challenge JLM's authority.'

McLaven shook his head, held both hands up in a restraining gesture.

'Settle down, Winnie,' he said. 'You don't know anything of the sort. She could've been killed in a regular hit and run.'

'Where's the body?' she said, voice a little higher-pitched than previously. 'Definition of a hit and run, is that you hit someone, then you clear off. You run!'

'Well, I don't know,' he said, defensively, 'maybe it was a hit, clear up your mess and run. That might be the latest thing with these people.'

'What people?' she demanded.

He sighed big, he leant back, he placed his elbows on the arms of the chair and put his face into his hands.

'I don't know, Winnie,' he said. 'I just don't think you should go picking up the wrong end of the stick and beating about the bush with it, that's all.'

She exhaled a long, resigned breath. Maybe she should look into it more herself, make her own enquiries, before shooting off at the mouth. First things first; if Peggy was killed because of what was said at the cabinet meeting, who was the grass?

She stood up. Maybe she was talking to the grass right now. So what if he was cheeky, cheery and smiley? It was the same persona he'd had on the football field, and it had allowed him to get away with no end of dirty fouls and dodgy dives in the penalty box; made the fans more forgiving when he missed sitters from two feet.

'I'll speak to you tomorrow,' she said.

McLaven put his hands on the desk and tapped out the beat of *Hello Goodbye*.

'Aye,' he said. 'Don't worry about any of it, Winnie.'

She brushed off the remark with a swish of her dark hair and was gone. Wally looked at the closed door for a few seconds, then lifted the phone. Thought better of it, hung up, then stretched his legs out under the desk and pulled up his underwear and trousers.

16

Unnatural selection

'Seriously, Barn,' said JLM, 'the plebs just don't understand the pressures. It's hard to know what they're thinking some days. Listen to this.'

Barney was kind of half-listening. He'd had a slow weekend where, had his personality been a little more developed, he would've been lonely. He'd trudged the streets of the capital, he'd found bars and restaurants, he'd spent the money that was mysteriously placed on his tray every morning with his breakfast.

Then, back to work for Monday, and he had spent another day in the company of the team, travelling around Scotland in JLM's wake. A whirlwind tour of the west coast, glad-handing voters in Ayr and Kilmarnock, Girvan and Largs. Not for a minute did JLM's face show anything other than a complete contempt for his public, and an obvious desire to be at some important conference in Rio or Kuala Lumpur. He had travelled the area in the new First Minister's Train, which had been decked out at a cost of three and a half million pounds, and which caused immeasurable inconvenience to the rail network every time it was used. (The public had yet to be informed of its existence, and were generally told about leaves on the line, or of an idiot driving the train. When JLM arrived at the station, there was always the limo there to pick him up.)

Whilst making his enforced visits to schools and factories and old folks' homes etc. etc. the entourage had stayed on the train, reading the Bible, fussing over expensive tailoring, checking medical records, doing whatever it was that they did every day. Barney had sat in a corner of the train, variously viewing his colleagues with suspicion or ill-ease. Wondering what they thought of him. They probably all knew about him, where he had come from. All knew that he was this freak of science, an abhorrent blip in humanity, an unnatural selection, and no one could be at all sure what would become of him, how the unnatural selection would develop. Weird growths on his skin, new limbs, another head, a bizarre enjoyment of Saturday night television. He could be the subject of a horror movie in ten years time. *The Elephant Barber*, or *The Barber Who Was Scientifically Reborn And Who Turned Into A Glutinous Amorphous Mass, Slimed Over Everybody, Drowned Whole Communities With Exploding Suppurating Sores And Didn't Have Much Luck With Women.*

They'd probably need a snappier title than that last one.

To further plunge his melancholic, confused mind into the mire of turmoil, muddle, chaos and disarray, he'd had another chat with the Reverend Blake. It'd been late on in the day, while JLM had been undertaking his final engagement of his whirlwind tour – to Nardini's in Largs, where he partook of some strawberry ice cream, and acted like he holidayed in Largs and Millport and Rothsey all the time. In fact, he'd been jetting off to the Indian Ocean for longer than he'd had the ambitions which now so clouded his judgement.

'You're looking a bit down,' the Rev Blake had said to him.

Barney had turned away from the carriage window and the meagre view of grey cloudy skies above the buildings.

'Aye,' he'd replied. 'Been a long day doing nothing. Sitting here making sure that that arsehole's hair looks all right every five minutes. Bloody waste of time.'

'Well,' she'd said, 'we all felt the same when we first got here, but you'll get used to it.'

'Why?' he'd said. 'Why should I get used to it? Why should I spend another minute here?'

Alison Blake had given a little shrug of the eyebrows. Her right hand had fiddled with her dog collar. Her eyes had flitted to Father Michael, who had spent the day studying 13th century art, depictions of the birth and of the death of Christ, then back to Barney.

'I suppose you owe them, to an extent,' she'd said.

'What d'you mean? Because I'm this freak of weird science, and they've brought me out into the world for people to gawp at me?'

'Weird science?' Blake had said, curious, and then her face had relaxed, the eyes had widened and she'd nodded. Sagely.

'What?'

'You've been talking to Edmund?' Blake had said, lowering her voice. 'Always a mistake.'

Barney had breathed deeply, closed his eyes, tried to totally empty his head of all thought, failed, opened his eyes again.

'Go on,' he'd said.

'She's prone to the odd flight of fancy,' Blake had said. 'A bit loopy. Expect she told you some story about rapid cell growth and brain transplants and the like.'

Barney had looked at Blake, although his eyes and his mind were off someplace else.

'Aye,' he'd replied.

Blake had sighed, cast a sideways glance at Dr Blackadder, a pitying look, and had turned back to Barney.

'Barney, really, someone should've said,' she'd said. 'Rebecca's a bit, I don't know, not all there. I'm not saying she doesn't know her stuff, because she does. She makes up these psychological profiles for JLM, and she's on the bloody nose, every time. It's just, she's way off beam herself. Christ knows what a psychological profile of her would look like.'

'Are you allowed to use the name of Christ like that?' asked Barney.

'Yeah,' she'd replied, dismissively. 'Look, I'll come round to your room tonight. I'm just along the corridor. We'll have a wee chat. I've been speaking to Parker and he's told me the truth about your being here. Asked me to have a word. What d'you say?'

Barney hadn't known what to say, hadn't known what to think, hadn't known what to do. So he'd said yes, and now he was back in Edinburgh, and once more seeing to the hair of JLM, before he attended an evening engagement at the Chambers of Commerce.

For this evening he wanted to look like George Clooney, which was going to be a bit of a stretch.

'I don't know that I want to,' said Barney, in response to JLM's instruction to listen to his annihilation of the proles.

'Don't care,' said JLM. 'I'm wandering round a supermarket or something, I don't know. What was it X?'

'A fish canning factory,' said The Amazing Mr X.

'Whatever,' said JLM, as Barney studied the back of his head for the seventh time that day. 'This ignorant, plebeian little scrote, pops up from under her white overalls and stupid little hat, and asks me what I'm going to do about bullying in schools. I mean, who do they think I am? You think bloody Churchill bothered about bullying in schools? "I don't care if the Germans are in Kent, wee Johnny got his head splatted against a gatepost by Big Wullie." Pants! Utter pants. I mean, I'm the First Bloody Minister for Christ's sake. I don't have time to bother my arse with the day to day stuff. I'm out there, taking care of the big issues. The world stuff, not namby-pamby ten year-olds who can't look after themselves in the playground. Bloody nonsense.'

The door to the bathroom opened without a knock. In a split second The Amazing Mr X had a grenade launcher armed and primed on his shoulder, only to be forced to stand down when Parker Weirdlove walked in, clipboard at the ready.

'Are you nearly done, sir?' he asked.

JLM caught Barney's eye in the mirror.

'Barn?' he said.

'It depends,' said Barney. 'If you want your hair to look all right, well, by Christ, after fifteen haircuts today, believe it or not it looks fine. If you want to look like George Clooney, that'll take a little longer. Say, a few years for the bone restructuring, another couple for plastic surgery, then another ten while you learn to brainwash everyone you're talking to so that they can't see that you look nothing like the fucking guy.'

JLM smiled in that patronising manner.

'You know, Barn,' he said, 'I've sponsored your presence here, I don't think that's overstating the mark. Do you, Parker?'

'Not at all, sir,' said Weirdlove.

‘No, not at all. Indeed. Lovely. And I have to be honest, Barn, I’m getting a little tired of your downright rudeness. You may masquerade it as honesty all you like, but you are taking advantage of my good nature. So, well, I think we probably understand each other.’

Barney nodded and fussed around the corners of JLM’s hair with a comb and a pair of scissors that weren’t going anywhere near his head. (If he’d removed some hair every time he’d attended to the lad JLM’s napper, the man would’ve been bald by the previous evening.) Well, it seemed he had to consider his position. His past life was coming back to him like lumpy porridge. Vague, meaningless chunks in amongst the general morass; the old shop in Partick, his insane mother, something about a monastery, the details were drifting back in ambiguously connected clumps, the exact meaning of which he had still to put together. However, no matter how much of that came back to him, it wasn’t going to tell him what had happened after he had died, if he had indeed been dead. It didn’t tell him what had brought him here, into this ridiculous menagerie. It was all very well biting the hand that was feeding him, but perhaps he should wait until he had his life sorted out before he went making mincemeat of the man. It was ridiculous, absurd madness, but sometimes you just have to bite the antelope on the arse.

‘Certainly, sir,’ he said to JLM. ‘Would that be a George Clooney *From Dusk ‘Til Dawn*, or a George Clooney *ER*?’

‘Actually,’ said JLM, settling back, relaxed and vaguely smug that he had established his superiority over another of the lower classes, ‘I rather fancy a George Clooney *Batman & Robin*, that would suit me, don’t you think?’

‘Most definitely,’ said Barney, just about managing to keep the tone from his voice.

He studied JLM’s hair, laid down the scissors, and started, well, farting about with a comb and some mousse. He’d never seen *Batman & Robin*, for crying out loud. Who had? He’d never watched *ER*, he’d never seen *From Dusk ‘Til Dawn*. In a few glorious months, at some previous stage of his hirsutological career, he had crammed thousands of pieces of pointless information into his head, so that he could talk to almost any customer on almost any subject. The films of George Clooney; the complete works of Kierkegaard; the geography of the female sexual organs; all thirty-seven French expressions for cut-and-blow-dry; two thousand and one reasons why the moon landing never happened; the history of Christianity and how the real Jesus was in fact the deputy manager of Burger King in Casablanca; fourteen different ways of saying *There is a man molesting women on the promenade* in Italian. And, of course, while his life and the story of who he was, was only coming back to him in sepia tinted sound bites, he could remember every single piece of pointless information and what passed for wisdom in the barber's shop.

To cut a long story off before it becomes gargantuan, he had no idea what a George Clooney *Batman & Robin* looked like. But not that it really mattered, as there were just plain not that many things he could with JLM's hair in any case.

'So,' said JLM, catching Weirdlove's eye in the mirror, 'the speech is done?'

'Yes, sir, it is,' said Weirdlove, 'and I think William's done a good job. Kept it short, as you requested, and a few jokes in at the start at the expense of the Tories. Lovely one about Westminster which might have the Prime Minister twitching in his pants…'

'Champion.'

'There are going to be a few journos there, so you'll have some questions to answer.'

'You got a prep folder?' asked JLM.

'Yes, sir. I've kept it brief. They're mostly likely to ask about Honeyfoot and Filiben. If you think they've been murdered...'

'How the dazzling fuck should I know?'

'Exactly, sir,' said Weirdlove. 'What you're going to do about replacing Filiben, until we know exactly what's happened to her.'

JLM looked troubled at having to give some thought to an executive matter.

'Who's her deputy?' he asked.

'MacPherson,' said Weirdlove.

'Don't know him,' said JLM. 'I think we should probably transfer the responsibility to the Minister for Enterprise, don't you? Enterprise, Education, makes sense to loop them together.'

Weirdlove nodded, making a note on his clipboard. His lips twitched. Barney fluttered away around the fringes of JLM's hair, making it marginally more bouffant. The Amazing Mr X stared at the door and waited.

'Do you want me to patch the call through to Ms Wanderlip for you, sir?' asked Weirdlove.

JLM looked troubled, made a show of studying his watch and thinking. Shook his head; Barney saw it coming, and diverted the mousse massage just in time.

'Just not enough minutes in the day,' he said. 'I'll call her later. If we have to announce it to the press before she knows about it, I'm sure she'll understand.'

'Absolutely, sir,' said Weirdlove.

'Lovely,' said JLM. 'Anything else?'

Weirdlove drew a deep breath, studied his notes.

'Just one other thing, sir,' he said. 'The Herald's picked up on a story about a suspected Rwandan war criminal living in Glasgow. Looks like they're going to try and make something of it. Might get a little sticky.'

'What did he do?' asked JLM.

Weirdlove studied his notes. His face contorted slightly as he reread the details.

'He's accused of helping to take injured Tutsis to a hospital, to the point where it was horrendously overcrowded. About three thousand people in a hospital for a few hundred.'

'And that's a crime?'

'Then he set fire to the hospital and burned them alive. His men macheted to death anyone who tried to escape.'

There was a pause. Barney swallowed and glanced at Weirdlove. JLM lowered his eyes, while the picture of what had happened unavoidably came to mind. Even The Amazing Mr X looked up.

'Jesus,' said JLM. Then he shook his head. 'Where is Rwanda anyway?' he asked, regaining normal transmission.

'Central Africa, sir,' said Weirdlove. 'East of the Congo.'

'Africa?' said JLM. 'God, you live and learn, don't you? All this time I'd been hearing about Rwandan war crimes, I thought it was one of the Baltic states or something. So it didn't happen in the Second World War?'

'No,' said Weirdlove, slowly. '1994.'

'Christ,' said JLM, 'nobody's going to give a shit then. Just leave me to it, I'll say all the right things. We done?'

Weirdlove looked back at his notes. Reread over the story of the Rwandan war criminal. Wanted to say something else, but knew the tone in JLM's voice. He could leave it for another day.

'Yes, sir,' he said.

'Excellent,' said JLM, 'lovely. Barn? You done?'

JLM admired his new hair, which was barely different, in the mirror. Barney, who wanted to stick the scissors into the back of his head, nodded and laid down his tools.

'Clear,' he said.

'Champion,' said JLM, standing up. 'Absolutely lovely. Come on, team.'

And, as he marched to the door, The Amazing Mr X leapt up to dive out the door in front of him, checking the outer office for terrorists, spies, hoodlums and journalists.

17

Uh-oh...

The Rev Blake was dressed in civvies; fuck-me boots, blue jeans and a thin, maroon crushed velvet top. She wasn't wearing any underwear, either, but Barney Thomson had yet to notice. She had her glass of white wine, Barney had a bottle of Miller. (Barney Thomson never used to drink American beers at home. Now here he was; he'd be at the Coors Lite next.) She was on the sofa, he was sat opposite on a large comfy chair. Another woman back at his place, a minister at that, and it seemed no more or no less surreal to him than the rest of the previous few days.

'You just have to watch what she's saying, that's all,' said Alison Blake, forcing a discussion about Rebecca Blackadder, that Barney didn't want to have. 'She's a bit of a loose canon.'

'Aye, whatever,' he said. 'Don't really want to talk about her.'

'I understand,' said Blake. 'I realise it must be difficult for you. You've been unconscious a long time.'

Barney eyed her suspiciously, took a swallow of beer, set the bottle down on the small table at the side of his chair.

'Unconscious, eh?' he said. 'What story are you going to tell me, then?'

Blake leant forward, and the shifting position of the v-neck and the movement of the top against her chest, gave Barney the first inclination of the no-underwear thing. Tried not to think about it.

'The truth,' she said earnestly. 'You can trust me.' Was on the point of invoking God, but thought the better of it. He would either believe her or not; God wouldn't come into it.

'All right,' said Barney. 'Tell me what you know.'

She rested her forearms on her knees. Held her glass in both hands between her legs.

'You were chasing a man called Leyman Blizzard across a moorland in the Borders,' she said, crisply. Tell it quickly and convincingly. Be honest about the face. The same rules applied as when teaching the word of God to sceptics.

Barney nodded. Leyman Blizzard. The name did more than ring a bell. Blizzard, the old bugger. Had murdered Katie Dillinger in the church.

'Go on,' he said.

'You fell off a ledge, smacked your head on a rock. You were found the following morning, having been out on a cold, wet night. Comatose. Another half hour and you would've been dead.'

'All right,' said Barney, 'sounds plausible so far.'

'You were in hospital for over two years. It was a big thing at first, because of your past. Barney Thomson caught and in a coma, all that kind of stuff. Headlines in the newspapers for a while. Strathclyde Police launched an inquiry, then at some stage Blizzard handed himself over and told his story. There was, to be frank, a bit of revisionism done on your life, and you were more or less exonerated for your past crimes.'

'That's what Rebecca said.'

'At least she got something right,' said Blake, caustically. 'Big news one day, might as well be dead in a ditch the next. Having handed himself in, Leyman Blizzard obviously changed his mind, and he managed to escape. So, he was that month's celebrity psychopath. Centrefold in Playloony. The whole nine yards.'

Barney nodded. Long term unconsciousness was a bit more credible as an explanation.

'How did I get to be here, though?' he asked.

More credible perhaps, but he doubted whether anyone in this situation would be able to convince him of the veracity of any explanation.

'You were just languishing in a hospital. The serial barber that time forgot. Happens to everyone that's famous for five minutes. Your wife divorced you...'

'My wife?' he said, and another large part of his life came moseying back in on a lame horse.

'There was an obscure question to parliament about you one day, from some obscure MSP. Disagreement about whether or not to turn off the life support. Jesse got interested. He may look like this absurdly egotistical narcissist, but there's a decent man in there somewhere. Got interested in your story, got you moved to a private medical facility. The Father and I, well, we've been saying our prayers for you. I know what I look and sound like sometimes, but I do have faith. The effectual fervent prayer of a righteous man availeth much.'

That'll be the Bible then, thought Barney.

'It can make a difference,' she continued, talking through his thoughts, 'and with you, well it did. Last week you started showing signs of improvement. Sudden indications of brain activity. And, well, JLM decided to have you moved to our apartments. We were waiting for you to wake up. Here you are.'

Barney stared at the floor, the thin carpet, cold and clinical. Another day, another story. Only difference being that this time it wasn't in the realms of scientific fantasy.

He sat back in his chair, stretched out, pressed his hands against his face. Left them there. Just wanted everyone to leave him alone. Had been interested the night before when Blackadder had told her story, but now he didn't want anyone's concern, didn't want to hear any more stories. Left alone in a dark room for several days, and he'd probably come up with the answer himself.

He jumped at her touch; her soft fingers against the back of his hand. Felt the gentle whisper of her breath and then her lips against his forehead. A delicate kiss, lingered over only briefly and then she knelt down on the floor.

'You don't believe me,' she said.

Barney took his hands away from his face, opened his eyes, but didn't look at her. Stared at the ceiling. Swallowed.

'Don't know what to believe,' he said.

She ran her fingers down the side of his face, a tender touch, let her hand linger beside his lips. After a few seconds, he found himself kissing her fingers.

'You can put your faith in me, Barney,' she said. 'Put your faith in the Lord. He will show you the way, I promise. The people that walked in darkness have seen a great light: they that dwell in the land of the shadow of death, upon them hath the light shined.'

He turned and looked down at her, her pale face a few inches away in the dim light of the evening room. He felt like crying, he felt like breaking down into a billion separate molecules, or melting into a hundred gallons of water, so that he could just wash away.

Her hand was still against his face; she lifted her eyes, her mouth, she lifted her head close to his, he could smell the scented soap with which she'd washed half an hour earlier. Her lips met his, soft and gentle, and he gave into them and melted into a hundred gallons of water so that he was washed away.

Well, for God's sake, let's not get carried away. They snogged and then she led him off to the bedroom, where the lad Barney gave as good as he got.

18

The first bite is the deepest

Two o'clock in the morning, JLM was lying in bed reading one of his press scrapbooks. He'd been keeping them since he'd made his first speech to the Scottish Labour Party Conference in Perth as a teenager, thirty years previously. His favourite ones were from just before he became First Minister, when the press were in the business of talking him up; which contrasted markedly with their attitude since he'd become First Minister, when they'd done everything to drag him down.

So that was what he was reading now, as he lay alone in bed with his nightly cup of diet hot chocolate. An article entitled *Cometh The Hour, Cometh The Man To Save Scotland*. There were several on the same theme, as all the Scottish broadsheets had rallied to his cause, following the ignominious departure of his predecessor.

It made comforting late night reading after a stressful day. Bloody Ayrshire, he'd thought, as he generally couldn't be bothered heading any further west than Livingston. No end of mindless questions from the buggering minions during the day, a good speech wasted on the suits of the Chambers of Commerce, and then a grilling from some bloody awful Herald journalist – a man who he'd ensure would never again darken the press room door when JLM was in attendance – about the Rwandan thing, a subject he just wouldn't let go. So reading his own press from a while ago was the equivalent of the warm cup of chocolate at his bedside. Solace at the end of a lousy day.

Tomorrow, however, he hoped for better things. There was a G8 conference coming up in Toronto, and he was determined to be there. As far as he could tell, he had as much right as the bloody PM, and just because the PM had rebuffed the suggestion when he had run it by him, did not mean that there wouldn't be other ways to try and force the issue. So he would be having a meeting with a representative from the Canadian government. That, and Herr Vogts would be arriving from Germany for some serious work on how to bypass Westminster on the introduction of the Euro.

He was just rereading the paragraph about his unusual breadth of vision, when he heard a bit of a stramash downstairs. Raised voices, thumping footsteps, and he looked at the clock. Minnie was away for a few days, attending a conference on women's issues in The Hague. Piece of bloody nonsense, JLM had thought, but it got her out of his hair for a while, and allowed her to feel that she was making a contribution to the world. Besides, it didn't do him any harm to be seen to have an effective wife.

He was still contemplating why she would be back this early, when the door to his bedroom was thrown open and Winona Wanderlip careered into the room. She looked wild and exciting, her hair tossed to the skies, much of it defying the fundamental laws of physics. Her beige summer jacket was pulled to one side, as if someone had made an ineffectual grab at her arm and she had been in too much haste to sort it out. Mouth wide and pouting, heart pumping like a piston, adrenaline coursing through her body at a rate of a hundred and seventy-three pints a minute, she stood in the centre of the bedroom.

Behind her, a bit beleaguered and looking a wee bitty embarrassed, came The Amazing Mr X, who came and stood next to her, although not so close that she could've had a swing at his nuts or anything.

'Sorry, boss,' he said to JLM. 'She scared me.'

'That's all right, X,' said JLM. 'You can wait downstairs. Ms Wanderlip won't be staying long.'

At those words she fizzled some more, a strange noise escaping from her body, like the sound of rain on electricity pylons. The Amazing Mr X looked at her with a mixture of fear and contempt, then turned and walked from the room.

JLM waited until the door closed, then closed the scrapbook over and straightened his shoulders.

'Winona,' he said. 'You've got one minute and then I'm calling the police.'

'What the Hell are you playing at?' she said.

'I'm only trying to run the country the best I can,' he said, disarmingly.

'I know what you're up to. You put every single job in the government onto my plate, and when eventually cock-ups start getting made, you can blame me and kick me out. Either that or I choose to jump ship. I'm not bloody stupid.'

'Winona, you credit me with too much guile,' he said.

'Do I bollocks, you bollocking idiot,' she barked. 'Anyway, it's not guile, it's arrogance and superciliousness and disdain and narcissistic up-your-own-arse-ness. Well, I'm here to tell you you're not getting away with it. I've had enough.'

'Oh, well, have you now?' said JLM slyly. 'What are you going to do, Winnie? Throw your teddy in the corner? Withdraw your £1.50 a week from the tea club? Write a letter to *Woman's Weekly* maybe? Lovely. Or perhaps to the agony aunt in the Daily Record? Dear, whatever the Hell her name is, my boss is giving me too much responsibility. I'm only a woman, how am I supposed to cope?'

She didn't pounce immediately. She was no unfettered wolf leaping at the injured deer; no savage lion, all muscle and teeth, jumping on the exhausted wildebeest; no vicious anteater, sticking its snout into the hill and gobbling up all the workers, who'd been happily building a swimming pool for the little 'uns. She waited. She stood over the bed, trying to control her anger. She'd had therapy, that was no secret. Rage control. Hadn't had the choice after the judge had ordered it, following the incident over the last parking space at Murrayfield. All the exercises they'd taught her to go through, they all pushed from different directions in her mind. Think one thing, think another, concentrate, concentrate, don't lose control.

'You're time's up, number seven,' said JLM. Voice as dismissive as he could make it. Loved nothing better than winding up Winona Wanderlip.

She lost control. And when she moved, it was with a surprising speed, agility and a nimbleness that belied her slightly clumsy bearing. JLM, who had been assuming the usual steam out the ears, throw the odd handbag, scream a bit, and then leave, banging the door behind her routine, was caught totally unawares.

She stepped forward, threw back the covers and, like Johnny Weismeuller or Mark Spitz, dived forward on top of JLM. Pitched it perfectly, so that her face landed smack beside his crotch, then with her mouth wide so as to encapsulate the full breadth of his tackle, she bit down hard. Kept her teeth closed for a second, shoogled her head from side to side a bit, then stood up.

Just for a wee moment or two, JLM was silent. His face turned white. His mouth was open, wider than Wanderlip's had been two seconds earlier. There were tears in his eyes.

'Is that all you've got to say?' said Wanderlip, having stood back up and regained her composure.

A weird hissing sound escaped from JLM's throat. He was clutching his testicles. His whole body was numb, apart from the screaming pain at its centre.

'Here's what you're going to do,' she said, firmly. 'You rearrange the distribution of work within cabinet by close of play, or I go to the press about the amount of money you're spending on that bloody entourage of yours. And the train. And everything else. You got that?'

He didn't reply. He was still in no position to talk, as he began to curl up into the foetal position.

Wanderlip turned and walked slowly from the room. Stopped at the door, faced him, tried not to smile.

'I would've thought I might've had to open my mouth a bit wider than that, Jesse,' she said.

And with that last put-down she was gone.

Jesse Longfellow-Moses curled up into a ball and began the rest of his long night, which was sure to be a painful one.

19

International barber of mystery

Tuesday morning. Barney Thomson stared at the remains of his breakfast, which he'd demolished with some vigour in a little under twenty minutes. The usual full works, and he'd already decided to give himself just another couple of mornings of it, before laying off and settling for cereal and grapefruit, before his heart clogged up and he was dispatched back to wherever it was he'd come from.

The news was on in the background, mostly talk of the chaos surrounding the Executive, what with its missing ministers and workload generally being amalgamated into one department. It was the first time he'd really focused on it, what with his head generally being all over the place. But sure enough, here he was, back in the saddle, cutting hair, and there was quite possibly a multiple murderer on the loose in the city. This thought having occurred to him, and having brought back no end of memories from his previous existence, he stopped thinking about it and decided to wallow in the events of the night before instead.

To put it bluntly, for the first time in so long he couldn't remember, he'd had biblical relations with a woman. And it'd been brilliant. He may have been dead or unconscious for two and a half years, but there was plenty of life in the old pistons, no mistake.

So, and you can't take this away from the big fella, there was a smile on his face. Alison Blake may have been called by Christ, but it hadn't stopped her shagging like a horse. She had left at some time after three, a final kiss on his warm lips, and a promise of more to come.

There was a knock at the door. Barney glanced at the clock. He was due with JLM in fifteen minutes to get his hair prepped for an appearance on Radio Scotland. This would be someone come to collect him. Or it might possibly just be Alison Blake come back for some nefarious sexual purpose. (A whole new world had suddenly opened up.)

He approached the door. It crossed his mind to take the chance that it would indeed be the Rev Blake, and to do it naked, with his manhood upstanding before him. Good sense prevailed, however, and he opened the door fully clothed, and rather tentative. Which was just as well, because Detective Chief Inspector Solomon wasn't used to seeing naked men at this time in the morning.

'Aye?' said Barney. Still had a little marmalade on the edge of his mouth. Some sixth sense told him it was there, and he licked it off as Solomon produced his badge.

'DCI Solomon,' he said, 'and yes, before you ask, I'm wise as fuck. This is Sergeant Kent. You Thomson?'

'Aye,' said Barney. 'Suppose I am. And you're right, you do look wise.'

'None of your sarcasm,' snapped Solomon, albeit with a certain good-humour. 'You got a minute, because we're coming in?'

'Since you put it like that,' said Barney, stepping back and allowing them entry. 'I'm due with the First Minister in fifteen minutes.'

Solomon grunted.

'Appearing in another carpet commercial, is he?'

'Radio Scotland,' said Barney.

Solomon smiled ruefully, as Barney closed the door.

'Wouldn't want to be seen on the radio with bad hair,' said the DCI.

'Exactly,' said Barney, smiling.

Having gained access, and the confidence of the interrogatee with a little banter, Solomon stood in the middle of the room and looked around. Had wondered how it was that the First Minister had been keeping his employees. Had a good eye for a quality sound system and DVD/digital tv set up. This was the best.

Several thousand pounds worth of the taxpayers' money in those alone.

Barney watched them, wondering what they were up to. Here to arrest him for sleeping with an agent of the Lord? Perhaps it was in that morning's newspapers. *High Ranking Barber Shags Vicar, Sentenced To Death.* Or, *Thomson In New Outrage Against Society.* Or maybe they had put two and two together, arrived at sixty-four, and were here to arrest him for the murder of the disappearing cabinet ministers. *Reprieved Barber Can't Kick Killer Habit. Born Again Hirsutologist Cuts Swathe Through Cabinet; Citizens Erect Monument In His Honour.* Could be anything.

'So,' said Barney. 'They're going to be expecting me soon. You going to arrest me before then?'

Solomon grunted, shook his head.

'Nah,' he said. 'Why'd you think we'd do that?'

Barney shrugged. No reason, he thought. He looked at Sergeant Kent, a quiet man, who was staring solemnly out of the window at the morning sun. Wishing he was somewhere else, thought Barney.

'Why're you here then?' asked Barney.

'Thought it was about time we checked in,' said Solomon.

He eyed Barney for a few seconds, then decided to go for it. When he started talking, his voice raced along like Parker Weirdlove or Herr Vogts. Maybe, Barney thought, a few seconds in, there's trouble with the tape speed inside my head.

'Expect there's been a couple of people told you some things about why you're here, where you came from and that kind of thing. Yeah?' he asked, then zipped on to the next sentence without pausing for Barney to answer. 'Well, whatever you've heard, forget it. I don't know what kinda shit these goons here'll have been trying to get you to believe, but you can't trust any of 'em. And I mean, any of 'em, even the religious ones. Hell, they might be the worst.'

'So why am I here?' said Barney, with some resignation.

‘You’re part of an undercover police programme,’ said Sgt Kent, suddenly from out the blue. Barney raised an eyebrow. Even Solomon gave Kent a swift look.

‘That’s novel,’ said Barney. ‘Do elaborate.’

Solomon jumped in before Kent could say anything else.

‘There’s a fella at St. Andrew’s University been doing some research into the criminal mind,’ he said quickly. ‘Between you and me, the guy’s an absolute fucking fruitcake. And he stinks to high heaven, never fucking washes, spends so long in that lab of his. Anyhow, he’s been doing experiments reactivating the brains of dead criminals.’

‘Ah,’ said Barney, butting in. ‘That sounds plausible.’

‘Cutting edge work,’ said Sgt Kent, nodding. ‘The man’s a leader in his field.’

‘Yeah,’ said Solomon, giving Kent another destructor-ray glance. ‘Whatever, to cut out most of the crap, on our behalf he will fit the brain of a dead criminal into a fresh corpse. Do all sorts of reactivating shit, then bingo, you’ve got a new person.’

‘The trick is,’ said Kent, ‘that the doctor has isolated the gene that leads to criminality, and he removes it. It’s really pretty clever.’

‘What Dr Fucking Einstein here is trying to say,’ said Solomon, ‘is that we end up with a person with rare insight into the criminal mind, but who has lost the will to commit criminal acts. Bingo.’

‘Brilliant,’ said Barney. ‘Don’t believe a word of it.’

Solomon laughed again. It was a nice laugh, and he knew not to use it around real criminals because it was totally inappropriate.

‘Yeah,’ said Solomon, ‘I can see why. It’s pretty fucking weird, there’s no denying that. But, my man, it’s true.’

‘Then,’ said Barney, ‘whose body is this? It looks exactly like me?’

‘Good point,’ said Kent.

‘Yeah,’ said Solomon. ‘The doctor does this thing where he implants the memory of your new body, so that’s how you remember yourself looking.’

‘You’re making this up,’ said Barney.

'There's weirder fucking things than that in life, Mr Thomson,' said Solomon, 'and they're true.'

Barney laughed.

'You've persuaded me,' he said, smiling.

'Thought I might,' said Solomon.

'The strangest thing is,' said Kent, and Solomon started silently mimicking his speech, 'that the doctor couldn't find the criminal gene in your brain.'

'Ah,' said Barney. That would tie in with what he was beginning to remember about his past life. 'You must be disappointed.'

'Why?' said Solomon and Kent together, and they scowled at each other.

'Pht! goes your insight,' said Barney, doing an accompanying little hand manoeuvre.

'Well,' said Kent, 'we don't think so.'

'Yeah,' said Solomon, '*I* don't think so, I can't vouch for anyone else. You've been around a fair amount of shit in your life, so we're confident. You're our man on the inside of the Executive, and we're pretty sure you can come through.'

'Marvellous,' said Barney, and finally he sat down on the settee opposite where the two police officers were standing. He settled back, he looked at them expectantly. Something like this had been inevitable. Later in the day it seemed reasonable for him to anticipate visits from the Flying Squad, the FBI, MI5, MI6, the CIA, NASA, Blue Peter, the Royal Society for the Protection of Birds, and Thirty-Seven Year Old Puerto Ricans For A Safer Eurotunnel. 'What exactly is it you'd like me to do?'

'Well,' said Solomon, 'your remit has kind of changed in the last few days.'

'Dramatically,' said Kent.

'Would you shut up?' said Solomon. 'Whose show is this?'

'You're taking an age to get there,' said Kent, sullenly.

Solomon hesitated on the brink of a 'can it, Sergeant' type of remark, pointed a finger, didn't say anything, then turned back to Barney.

'There's been murmurings about Longfellow-Moses and the death of his secretary. Bit of a weird business. So, we decided to try and get someone on the inside. A plant. Get a closer look, gather some evidence, you know the score.'

'Be a snitch?' said Barney.

'Mole,' said Solomon. 'When the First Minister decided he wanted his own hairdresser, we got the doctor to activate you and planted you in the middle of the forest.'

'So what makes you think that removing the criminal gene is going to turn anyone into a mole personality type?' asked Barney.

Solomon shrugged slowly, while giving Kent a quick 'don't even start talking' glance.

'There are certain rewards in it for you,' he said. 'But we can talk about that later.' Solomon checked his watch. 'Look, you'll have to be going soon. To cut the bullshit, we now need you to poke your nose into the cabinet's business, if you can. Find out who's behind these two disappearances. You think you can do that?'

Barney smiled. It was like he was being made a deputy. How utterly bizarre; if it was true. Couldn't believe anything, of course.

'You mean, can I be discreet, perceptive, incisive, trenchant and shrewd?' he asked. 'I seriously doubt it.'

Solomon smiled. Kent regarded Barney with a little suspicion.

'I'll speak to you again in a couple of days,' said Solomon.

And with that he walked past Barney, Kent in his wake. Barney smiled at them, then shook his head and stared at the carpet. Just how many more explanations about his presence here was he going to receive?

The door opened and closed again, and Barney let out a long sigh and drummed his fingers on the arms of the chair. Maybe it was time to just walk out. Get out of this prison of a hotel room, out of Edinburgh, because this city wasn't his city, get on the road and see where he ended up. He could go and live overseas for the first time in his life. He could be Barney Thomson, International Barber of Mystery. He laughed at the thought.

There was a cough behind him.

He rose quickly and looked at the door.

Parker Weirdlove was standing inside, arms folded across his clipboard and chest. Must've crept in silently, as the police officers departed.

'Who the fuck were they?' he asked.

Barney Thomson did not answer immediately.

20

Make it so

Longfellow-Moses looked as though he was studying the work Barney was doing on his hair – today he'd requested a Gregory Peck *Mocking Bird* – but his mind was elsewhere, grappling with big thoughts, whilst trying to ignore the continuing throb in his loins. Weirdlove was standing in the corner, checking his clipboard. The Amazing Mr X was standing silent, mean and tall, by the door.

'Can you get some figures for me?' said JLM, from the depths of his reverie.

Weirdlove looked up from the bullet points he had noted down to help JLM negotiate his way through the radio appearance; they consisted mostly of differing ways to shift the conversation away from his sexual affairs, Hookergate, his other dodgy business affairs, his denial of Disney videos to his children, and the Rwandan war criminal thing.

'No problem, sir,' he said. 'What kind of figures would you like?'

'Space,' said JLM, and he pursed his lips in a Churchillian kind of a way. Looked sombre and serious and statesmanesque.

Barney raised an eyebrow. The Amazing Mr X stood poised with his surface-to-surface missiles primed and ready to rock.

'How d'you mean that?' asked Weirdlove. As he said it, he glanced suspiciously at Barney, as he had been doing for the past half hour. He did not believe that the two men who had been leaving Barney's room as he arrived, had been Jehovah's Witnesses.

'It's just so vast,' said JLM. 'I mean, seriously, it's like this lovely, huge, enormous blancmange.'

'D'you actually know what a blancmange is, sir?' said Weirdlove.

'Whatever,' said JLM. 'There was some show, used to be on tv, where they said that space was the final frontier. Can't remember what it was called. Lovely stuff. Anyway, you know, they were right. Space is like this, well, thing.'

'What kind of figures were you looking for, sir?' asked Weirdlove, recognising one of his boss's flights of fancy, wanting to get to the crux of it, so that he could shoot it down in flames and then move on to something worthwhile.

'Have you any idea,' JLM began, 'of the size of NASA's annual budget?'

'Is this a test, or are you wanting me to find out?' said Weirdlove dryly.

'God, Parker,' said JLM, 'I don't have that kind of info at my fingertips. Find out, man.'

'$13.6billion,' said Barney. 'That's about £7billion, give or take.'

JLM smiled, gave Weirdlove a wry 'you'd better keep up' look. JLM had been impressed so far by Barney's general silence and good behaviour since they'd had their little chat.

'Lovely,' said JLM. 'Thanks, Barn. What's our annual budget?'

'About £24billion,' said Weirdlove quickly, annoyed at himself that he was actually bothered that he answered before Barney. 'That's about $40billion,' he added.

'Yes, thank you' said JLM, 'I can do the math.'

Weirdlove shot an imaginary dagger into the back of JLM's head. JLM looked statesmanesque and pondered his position.

'All that money more or less accounted for?' he asked. 'Our 24 billion, I mean. It's rather a lot, isn't it? You'd think there'd be a few spare pennies.'

'Is it all accounted for?' said Weirdlove, wearily. 'Every last penny, sir. And we've still got three hundred year old hospitals, the central belt road system is hopelessly inadequate, our tourism policy is shambolic, the rail network is wretched, the councils are impotent and bankrupt, our social services are in chronic decline, our fisheries policy in disarray, police numbers are plummeting, there's an increase in reported crime across the board, the prisons are overcrowded yet arrest rates are down, anyone of any talent, be it in sport, business, science or the arts must go to England or abroad to meet their potential, the west is riven by bigotry and sectarianism, education is desperately short of money, the exam system is in chaos, the young feel let down and ignored, the old feel betrayed, your care for the elderly package is a prescriptive hash job, and the rest of us in the middle can only find the strength to carry on because our applications to emigrate to Australia have been denied. All that, and our football's shite and BBC Scotland comedy output is pathetic. There are,' he said, voice slowing at last, 'no spare pennies.'

'Be that as it may,' said JLM, waving a dismissive hand, 'how d'you feel about instigating a space programme of some description.'

Weirdlove breathed deeply. Barney continued to study the back of the royal head, and wondered if Gregory Peck's hair ever actually varied from film to film. Like his facial expression.

'We could probably push it through parliament without too much trouble,' said JLM, continuing unabashed. 'I could give them one of my vision speeches, you know the ones. Space is just such a lovely thing, don't you think? How much d'you think it would cost to have a space programme of some sort, Parker?'

Weirdlove mentally tapped his brain on the clipboard. Count to ten. Count to ten. Don't lose your temper.

'It depends what you were looking.....'

'You see,' said JLM, cutting him off, and raising his temperature a little further, 'I was reading this article in the Herald Tribune. Did you know that NASA are still using the same rocket technology as they were in the 60's? Did you know that not only have they not made advances in manned space flight, they've actually regressed to the point where it would take longer now to get a man to the moon, than thirty years ago. It's madness! Complete madness! There's a big universe out there. It's beautiful and lovely and delicious. And we're stuck down here. It's time someone did something about it.'

‘Well,’ said Weirdlove, starting again, ‘it depends what you’re looking for, sir. If you want to buy a box of fireworks out of Woolies, let them off and get someone to make a note of their trajectory, that’ll probably only cost you about a tenner. If you want to push the boundaries of rocket science and send men into deep space, that would probably take up most of our 24 billion. Course, we’d have to shut down the schools, the hospitals, the prisons, the police forces, the fire service...’

‘We could call it,’ said JLM, oblivious, ‘the Jesse Longfellow-Moses Space Research Centre. Lovely ring to it, don’t you think?’ he said. ‘I’m sure I could push that through parliament. What d’you say, Barn?’

‘It would certainly be something for the country to rally around, sir,’ said Barney, sounding like Jeeves. Then he gave Weirdlove a defensive look which said, ‘that was what you told me to say’.

‘Indeed,’ said JLM. ‘Get me some figures, Parker, will you?’

‘Have you a specific objective in mind?’ asked Weirdlove, barely masking the acerbity.

JLM looked at the ceiling, as if pondering the stars. Barney stood back, having finished the cut. Hands off, and the man looked more or less the same as he did whether he was supposed to be George Clooney, Frank Sinatra, Gregory Peck or Ella Fitzgerald.

‘Men on Mars by the year 2010,’ he said grandly.

‘Right,’ said Weirdlove, making a note, ‘and do you want to bring any of them back alive at all?’

JLM hesitated. Would the public think the mission a failure if the men never got back? Probably bloody would, the ignorant bastards. They never cared about the boundaries getting pushed; always had to pee their pants every time somebody pegged it in the furtherance of human knowledge.

‘Don’t care myself,’ said JLM, ‘as long as they send pictures. But, I suppose we’d better or the press’ll get on their bloody high horse.’

‘Very good, sir,’ said Weirdlove.

JLM finally noticed that Barney had finished. He examined the hairstyle for signs of Gregory Peck-idity, found them, stood up and walked round the chair.

'Champion,' he said to Barney, slapping him on the arm. 'Smashing job. Right men, let's go and kick the BBC's arse for them.'

The Amazing Mr X leapt to open the door, jumped out ahead of JLM, checked the vicinity for spies and terrorists, then cleared the First Minister for egress.

21

The lad wally takes his final dive

'Different class,' said Wally McLaven, rubbing his hands together. 'That's what I mean by quality. Absolutely brilliant. That's the kind of thing that makes all the difference in life. Real quality, to be fair. Different class. Now, can you show us your other breast?'

McLaven was recruiting a new secretary. Just because some people had moved on in the world, and thought that it was horribly sexist, disgusting and primitive to ask a teenage girl to show you her breasts before you considered offering her a job, didn't mean Wally couldn't still exist in the Dark Ages. Amanda Cartwright was his fourth interviewee; two of the previous three had downright refused to take their clothes off and had been asked to leave; the other had reluctantly given Wally a look at her breasts, but had stopped short of offering a feel, despite Wally's claims that he was making sure she was lump-free.

Amanda Cartwright, however, was altogether more accommodating. She popped the second of her boobs out into the open, and Wally leant across his desk for a closer look.

'Lovely,' he said, 'really wonderful. Have you had any work done, anything like that?'

'Oh, aye,' she said. 'I got implants when I was sixteen. What d'you think?'

'Beautiful, babe,' he said. 'They're top quality breasts. And how have the implants affected the feel of the breast. Are they still as supple as before the operation?'

'Oh, aye,' said Cartwright. And she stood up, leant towards him so that her breasts were almost in his face, and said, 'Why don't you try them out for size? And I've also had my labia minora clipped, if you want to check 'em out.'

There was a loud rapping at the door. Wally woke up.

He sat up quickly, having been slouched massively in his office chair, enjoying a midmorning doze. He was due in committee at some point, but he couldn't entirely remember when. They were to have some ridiculous discussion about Scottish opera; as if anyone gave even the slightest shite about it.

'Come in,' he said, straightening his tie and running a hurried hand through his hair. Quick run of the tongue over the teeth to make sure there was no obvious food remaining from the leftover curry that he'd had for breakfast.

The door opened. It was his secretary, the spectacularly unattractive Miss Rutledge. He had spent most of his year incumbent in the post being horribly rude to her in the hope that she would resign, thereby allowing him to get a younger, better looking model installed.

'What?' he said, sharply. 'I'm busy here.'

'You've got a message from the First Minister's office,' said Karina Rutledge. 'Wants you to meet him in Conference Room 6F.'

'6F?' said McLaven. 'That's like, what? Is that even in the building? Are you sure you took it down right?'

She bit her tongue, once again. The four hundredth time this year. The ignorant little bastard was going to get his comeuppance one day. One day soon.

'6F,' she said again, sharply. 'It's on the ground floor. It's where they have regular meetings of the Culture Council, but there's no reason why you're going to know anything about that, is there?'

'Enough of that tone, Miss Rutledge,' barked McLaven. 'When's the meeting?'

'Now,' she said. She swivelled, closed the door and was gone.

And, seeing as her back was turned when McLaven left the office a couple of minutes later, it was the last time she ever saw him. Alive, at any rate.

✂

The First Minister was squirming through his radio interview, and not just because his knob ached when he sat in certain positions. For once he was extremely pleased that he wasn't on television. Despite his great hair. He didn't have too much influence on the BBC, but he was working at it, and when he'd established a bit more of a salient into the organisation, the first thing he was going to do was get Bertie Shaw shagged out of his position as midmorning talk show bastard. Lovely chap though he'd thought him up until now.

'You cannot deny the right of the Scottish people to know whether there are any more skeletons in your closet, First Minister?' said Shaw, who was having a great time. Getting to rip the pish out of the First Minister, in full knowledge that the public would be enjoying every second.

'Really,' said JLM, 'this is intolerable. I've answered the question a hundred times now. The details of my previous mistake have been given a full and proper public airing, and Minnie and I now consider the matter closed.'

'But you haven't answered the question,' said Shaw, exasperated.

'What question?' exclaimed JLM, exasperated.

'Did you have any other affairs?'

'I answered that at the press conference four months ago,' JLM snapped.

'I think that's debatable,' said Shaw, as much as a wee aside to his audience, 'but why not answer it again here and now?'

'Can I ask you a question?' said JLM, with command, attempting to gain control of proceedings.

Parker Weirdlove was standing behind him, shaking his head. The whole thing was inevitable, and if JLM hadn't been so keen to get his face on every newspaper front page, every magazine cover, every tv show, even every radio broadcast, a thinking idiot's Victoria Beckham, then he wouldn't constantly walk into these giant cow pats.

'Well,' retorted Shaw, 'you can, after you've answered mine. Are the Scottish people going to find out that you've had more than one affair, First Minister?'

'My question,' announced JLM, with solemnity and spunk, 'is why are you so concerned with tittle-tattle and gossip? I think you might find your listeners would much rather hear about our policies for the Health Service and the modernisation of the rail network.'

'Indeed, First Minister,' said Shaw, and from beneath the desktop he produced a barrage of that day's newspapers. Weirdlove groaned. JLM bristled. The Amazing Mr X just wanted to grab a microphone and start singing. 'That's very interesting, because yesterday your Health Minister, Malcolm Malcolm III of the Clan Malcolm, issued new government guidelines for the financing of the NHS in Scotland, and not one of today's papers picked up the story. Instead we've got *First Minister Hides From Rwandan Question*; *True Cost of JLM's Euro-Jolly*; *JLM Blunders Again*; *Hookergate Refuses To Die Despite JLM's Machinations; Good Hair, Shame About The Policies*; *Wanderlip Bites JLM On The Cock*, and *Longfellow-Moses Parted My Red Sea And Walked Right In, Claims £200/Day Whore.*'

JLM hurrumphed.

'Your ministers can issue all the guidelines they like, First Minister, but if the people don't trust the taste of the ice cream, they're not going to be interested in the cone. Are there any more affairs from your past or present, that the public have not so far been told about? Yes or no?'

JLM breathed deeply. Looked up to catch Weirdlove's eye, but he was standing out of sight. Enough of a hesitation, couldn't be seen to linger over it.

'What I think your listeners will be more concerned with is the fact that there is this clear mistrust of the First Minister. I was elected by the people...'

'Less than forty percent of them,' barked Shaw.

'Let me finish. Last May, I was duly elected by a majority of the voters in this country. I have a mandate, directly traceable to the people of Scotland, and I think those people will be getting extremely fed up with your line of questioning.'

‘Perhaps,’ said Shaw. ‘But all you have to do is answer the one simple question, First Minister, and we’ll move on. Have you betrayed your wife with more than one woman? Yes or no?’

‘There you go again,’ said JLM, laughing in a pompous manner, thinking that he had the moral high ground…

And on and on they went, fifteen minutes with the interviewer never moving on to a second question, and JLM never answering the first. JLM thought he performed very well; imagined that the listeners were outraged on his behalf; he’d taken the superior position, treating Shaw with just the right mixture of contempt, acerbity, sarcasm, brio, panache and élan. He’d ground Shaw into the dust, and Shaw had ended up looking ridiculous. A masterful performance.

Then there was the other point of view. Of one thousand, three hundred and forty-one e-mails sent to the BBC, only one criticised Shaw. The Scotsman the following day led with *JLM ‘Admits’ Affairs Through Equivocal Denial.* The Sun went further: *JLM Shagged Loadsa Birds.* The Press & Journal went off on a slightly different tack: *North-East Man Finds Stone In Peach.*

So, while JLM left the studio, head up and feeling good about himself, Parker Weirdlove knew that he’d just witnessed another PR catastrophe. Or then again, he wondered, as he walked in the wake of a slightly limping JLM and The Amazing Mr X, perhaps he’d known what he’d been doing all along. By extending the discussion on his extramarital affairs, when he himself might be sure there were none to be uncovered, he had allowed Shaw to squander the opportunity to ask him about the Rwandan issue, the Cabinet murders, the cock-up over health care for the elderly, Hookergate, the absurd joint bid with the Faroes for World Cup 2014 and the rumour that Winona Wanderlip had bitten him on the old meat and two veg.

Maybe he wasn’t as stupid as he looked.

Wally McLaven humphed his way down the stairs. It’d only been a couple of years since his playing days had drawn to an injury-hit climax down at Ayr, but already the fitness was gone, and the weight had piled on around his middle. And as he humphed, he mumbled disparaging words against JLM and all who sailed in him. Dragging a man away from a sensational dream. Bloody idiot..

He searched along corridors and down paths. Committee rooms were always a mystery to him. He was actually on three of the parliament's committees, but had only ever attended one of them; a fact which wasn't going to change just because they were now in new premises.

Eventually stumbled across Conference Room 6F by accident, knocked, waited, no answer, and so he pushed open the door and entered.

He stopped. Felt the strangeness in the room. The blinds were drawn against the morning sun, and the room was in half-light. Occasional shafts of sunlight swept through the air, illuminating the dust. McLaven knew that JLM wasn't going to be here, and in that instant he realised that as he'd walked down he'd heard a radio playing, with JLM being interviewed live. Funny how some things don't compute, when your mind is elsewhere.

'Close the door,' said a voice. A woman.

Soft and low and, well, delicious. Wally McLaven smiled and nodded to himself. So that was it. These things always fell into place faster than you imagined they would. He'd been summoned down here to perform.

He recognised the voice, couldn't quite place it. Couldn't see who'd spoken, but he closed the door behind him and walked into the room. Heard the footsteps, turned to his left. She was walking towards him, having been standing in a dark corner. Not dressed in the least provocatively, but that didn't necessarily mean anything. There wasn't a bit of clothing on the planet that Wally McLaven couldn't have disengaged in under three seconds.

'Oh,' he said, which wasn't much of a greeting, but if he'd had a vote, he wouldn't have cast it for the woman who was walking towards him. Not that she was unattractive, but there was something about her. Still, he was here now, he hadn't had sex so far that day, and Patsy was in Inverness doing some ridiculous tourist thing. Any old magazine in the dentist's waiting room. 'Hi, babe,' he said, imagining a good recovery.

'Glad you could come,' she said, the voice oozing sex.

'Give us a few minutes, Hen,' said McLaven, laughing. 'Different class.'

'You up for it?' she asked.

'Oh, aye,' said McLaven. 'You must've heard all about me, eh?'

'I certainly have,' she said, as she came up beside him.

She smiled, glossed red lips a little parted. White teeth, a mouth that you could spend years on. Wally started to schmooze in a faintly ridiculous manner; being a man who believed all his own press.

'You've come to the right man, darlin',' he said, accompanying the words with his usual cheeky grin.

She put her hands on his neck, a gloriously gentle touch, soft fingers caressing his skin down either side, sending goose bumps all the way down his back and arms. He shivered. He closed his eyes. He felt her warmth and her cool sophistication at the same time. This was going to be wonderful. He waited.

She head-butted him with immaculate precision, busting his nose open. He groaned, stumbled back. He opened his eyes in time to see the swift movement of the knife taken from somewhere at her back, two-handed, up over her head and then brought swiftly down into his forehead. Buried it.

Wally stared up at her, his body hovered in suspended disbelief at the evil which had just been inflicted upon it, then he fell forwards. His killer jumped smoothly to one side, and the corpse of Wally McLaven plunged down onto the carpet and crumpled into an uncomfortable heap.

She stood over him for a few seconds, walked to the door, opened it a cautious inch to check the way was clear, and then stepped out into the light of the corridor on a late summer's midmorning.

✂

She hovered a while in the vicinity, still feeling the thrill of the kill. Waiting to see if anyone would come along to clear up the mess. Ten minutes, before an uncertain pusillanimity got the better of her and she left the area and placed an anonymous phone call to building security to get them to check out Conference Room 6F. It took her quarter of an hour persuading them that such a conference room actually existed, and by the time they got there, a further thirty minutes later, the body of Wally McLaven had already been moved on, leaving nothing but a few blood stains on the carpet.

To be fair to Wally's killer, as Wally himself might've said, she was a little confused when she heard.

22

A predestination of seven cheeses

The word spread quickly through the parliament. Wally McLaven had been added to the list of Honeyfoot and Filiben. Missing, leaving but a meagre trail of blood. The cabinet of ten was now down to a cabinet of seven. Winona Wanderlip heard the news while she was sitting as part of the Further Education Committee, which was debating an increase in student grants, even though there was absolutely zero public funding to sustain such an increase.

Wanderlip broke down in tears, in the moment of Wally's death finally realising that she'd loved him. Or maybe had just loved the idea of him; so different had he been to the man who had left her at the alter.

She'd recovered her composure quickly, had not left the committee room, had blown her nose, wiped away the tears, had started to programme her mind to forget all about Wally McLaven, had begun to nibble again at the non-existent nail on her left ring finger, and had directed the committee back the way of business.

However, no matter how much they talked of other matters, her mind kept returning to the fact that another of her supporters was gone, there would be another space for JLM to plug with his own man. And strangely, despite what had gone before, it never occurred to her for a second that she was about to have Tourism, Sport & Culture dumped in her lap, so confident was she that JLM would give in to her threat of the previous night. And you know, such was the constant reminder of the lingering pain in his knob, she was right.

✂

JLM heard the news in his car, travelling back for an annoying appearance before the Cultural Affairs Committee. Another bloody waste of time. His thoughts were far more focused on the imminent arrival that afternoon of Herr Vogts, who was due to spend three days, mostly with Weirdlove, establishing a base position for Scotland's entry into Europe, a position that would be impenetrable. This was to be followed by his meeting with an official from the Canadian government, to discuss an invite for JLM to the next G8.

He had to be reminded of who Wally McLaven had actually been, as he'd only met him a few times in the past year. Was surprised to find that he was a Labour member, as he'd generally considered his pointless good natured bonhomie to be in complete alignment with the Liberal Democrats. 'At least it gets me out of having to appear before that bloody committee,' he'd muttered.

He had returned to his office, where he was now standing at the window, vaguely wondering why it was that members of his cabinet were slowly disappearing, one by one. Still half expected McLaven to show up, after having been pumping some idiot secretary in an obscure part of the building. Honeyfoot was a loose cannon, of whom he'd had a very low opinion, and he would not have been at all surprised to discover she'd buggered off to the Caribbean on a whim, with some muscled half-wit she'd met in a bar. But Peggy Filiben. She was too honest and too committed.

'I need spiritual guidance,' he said suddenly, turning round to face his entourage.

Veron Veron froze dramatically, mid-sequin; the lady doctors looked up from their laptops; Barney Thomson rolled his eyes, shook the paper, and went back to reading about the panic that was being wrought throughout the parliament by the latest proposed boundary changes; Parker Weirdlove raised a bit of an eyebrow; The Amazing Mr X loaded up his Kalashnikov. Which left the two people in question.

The Rev Blake looked over the top of Jude; Father Michael was once again engrossed in the Sermon on the Mount.

'Reverend, Father,' said JLM, 'the inner room.'

On the other side of his office from the en suite, there was a smaller office which had so far been little used, because he was spending so much time in the bathroom having his hair attended to.

'You really ought to release a statement to the press, sir,' said Weirdlove. 'They're baying.'

'I thought you were writing that?' said JLM tetchily.

'I've done it,' said Weirdlove, with equal tetchiness, 'but I do think they might be looking for a personal appearance of some description.'

'Bloody shag,' muttered JLM, as Blake and Michael waited in divine expectation.

'And you should call an emergency cabinet meeting,' said Weirdlove.

'Oh, for crying out loud,' said JLM.

And with that he marched into his inner office, followed by his two religious advisors, while Parker Weirdlove lifted the phone and went about organising the emergency cabinet meeting and press conference which he felt the First Minister should attend.

JLM appeared at the door.

'How are you getting on with the, you know, space thing?' he said.

A small vein throbbed high on Weirdlove's temple.

'Getting there, sir,' he said.

'Champion,' said JLM, and he closed the door and disappeared to hear the comforting words of his agents of the Lord.

✂

'So,' said Rebecca Blackadder, some time later, sitting down opposite Barney in the restaurant. 'You got shagged by Alison, then?'

Barney stared at his *supreme of Devonshire turkey in a salmon nage with crystallised bananas and a redcurrant coulis in a comfit of profiteroles, with chips*. Why was he not surprised?

'Aye,' he said. 'On the radio, was it?'

He looked up. His voice sounded hangdog, but there was a light in the eyes that Blackadder wouldn't have recognised had she known him before. He was no longer a man who was most comfortable feeling sorry for himself.

'Could tell by the way she ignored you all morning,' she said.

'Ah,' said Barney. He'd obviously noticed that Blake was ignoring him, but was cool enough about the whole thing not to feel like a piteous rejected teenager. 'That what she usually does?'

'Yeah,' said Blackadder. 'She's pretty much had every one of us in that room. Apart from Father Michael, of course. Did her best, but you have to admire the man's commitment to the cause.'

'Haven't spoken to him,' said Barney.

'Not many of us have,' said Blackadder, and she tucked into her *parfait of cauliflower in a predestination of seven cheeses, with an explosion of thyme and an epidemic of rosemary*.

'Funny woman, all the same,' said Barney.

'You could say that,' said Blackadder. 'Pious when it suits her, that's our Alison.'

Barney nodded, forked another piece of banana, munched it and then washed it down with a wee sip of a fruity Californian chardonnay, robustly bodied, exquisitely finished, with hints of Kate Winslet, summer fruits and the Oxford Dictionary of Literary Quotations.

He looked around the canteen, sparsely occupied. It was elegantly decorated, fine pictures on the wall – apart from the ones of JLM – rich carpet, an atmosphere of stilled refinement, which quite went against most of the politicians who dined there. However, as they also had to pay for their meals, and it was expensive, it was not much used. Another waste of money. JLM's entourage had their meals paid for, and so ate there every day.

What did the police seriously think he could do, thought Barney, mind rambling. He was a barber or, more appropriately, a stylist, which was what he'd become. He wasn't anybody's man on the inside of the cabinet. He was in no position to investigate the disappearance and possible murder of three members of the

Executive. Was he supposed to ask the waiter if he had any ideas?

'So,' he said to Blackadder, deciding he might as well get on with it and dive clumsily into the murky waters of investigation, 'what d'you make of all these disappearances?'

Rebecca Blackadder toyed with a piece of Swedish-cheddar enrobed cauliflower and licked an imaginary particle of sauce from the corner of her mouth.

'You interested for any particular reason?' she said.

Barney shrugged. Where previously he would've looked like a giraffe in pink pyjamas with an inflated condom on his head when trying to look inconspicuous, he had now learned the ability to blend.

'Nah,' he said casually, and she bought it. They were in the government buildings, the cabinet were dropping like flies; it'd be odd if they didn't talk about it.

And that's when he had his first incisive thought on the subject. There were all these people in JLM's office, hanging out endlessly all day, doing nothing. It wasn't as if they never spoke to each other. Yet none of them ever talked about the cabinet. And neither did JLM, apart from when Weirdlove forced him into it. Barney himself wasn't acting suspiciously by raising the subject, the rest of them were suspicious by not raising it.

'Just seems kind of weird,' he said.

'Well,' said Blackadder, taking an expensive napkin to her chops, 'it's one of three things.'

Barney raised an eyebrow, continuing to fill his face with food.

'Oh, aye?' he said.

'One,' she said, and she began to count them off on her fingers. It's the age of the visual aid after all. 'There's a bit of cosmic payback going on. God, they're all politicians. You think the people are the slightest bit concerned? Hell, no, they're cheering. Look, before today there's been two of them gone AWOL, and it's not even been the headlines in the papers. The public are more interested in joke tv like Pop Idol and Big Brother, or the latest freak millionaire, or how many minutes Robert Downey has lasted out of rehab this week. If they give a shit about any politician, it's JLM and who he's shagged or who he's ripped off or who he's going to shag or rip off. With the exception of Wally, public recognition of the cabinet is absolute zero. The cabinet are nothing, masquerading as marginally more than nothing. I know the reasons JLM ignores them are completely wrong, but the essence of it is right. They are individually and collectively a complete waste of space.'

By the time she'd finished her wee speech, Barney was almost done with his meal. She had a nice voice, all the same, and he was quite happy to sit and listen to it all day.

'Aye,' he said, 'but who's actually doing it?'

'Don't know,' she said with a shrug. 'A disaffected public, maybe.'

'All right,' he said, 'what about two and three?'

'Two,' she said, 'JLM is getting them all bumped off one by one, until he's the only one left in the government.'

'Don't think so,' said Barney. 'The way he operates at the moment, he might as well already be the only one in the government. Why bother to authorise murder? He might be able to worm his way out of the corruption and sex scandals, but even he'd have a job getting away with a pile of corpses.'

'Fair point,' she said. 'So, here's my third idea. They're not actually dead, any of the three of them, despite the blood that's been found at the scenes of two of the crimes. They're all going off somewhere secret to plan a coup d'état, and they're going to march triumphantly into Edinburgh at some point in the next few weeks, to regain control of the country.'

'That'd be fun,' said Barney.

'It certainly would,' she said.

'Does JLM have the Army on his side?' he asked.

'You know,' she said, 'I don't think JLM has anyone on his side. Apart from that idiot X.'

'What about Weirdlove?' said Barney.

Blackadder gave a very slight shrug of the shoulders with accompanying face.

'Good question, Barn,' she said. 'Good question.'

And that was all Barney was going to get from Dr Rebecca Blackadder, who soon after signalled a change of conversational direction by discussing a spangly tassel top that Veron Veron had designed for JLM to wear to a rumba night at the Scottish Labour Party Conference.

23

To cabinet, to cabinet, to buy a fat pig

JLM looked around the table at his cabinet colleagues. There had been chatter amongst them before he walked in, but they'd all bowed to his greatness and quietened down upon his arrival. Now they were waiting for him to pronounce. He had yet to decide what he was going to do with the Tourism, Culture and Sport brief, assuming that Wally's return was not imminent. The only clear thing was that he couldn't possibly give it to airhead chick, Patsy Morningirl.

JLM himself was still feeling battered from a bruising and rumbustious press briefing. He had been asked twenty-three questions in all, split more or less down the following lines: who did he think was murdering his cabinet colleagues? (3 questions); was it true he'd had sex with three prostitutes in one night? (4 questions); had he murdered his secretary? (3 questions); what was he going to do about all the Rwandan war criminals living in Scotland? (2 questions); was he ready to admit that he had defrauded the taxpayer of more than £2m? (3 questions); just how hard had Winona Wanderlip bitten his cock? (6 questions); was he prepared to admit that his policy on care for the elderly was in total disarray? (1 question); and what did he call that hairstyle he was sporting? (1 question). The last one was the only one which he'd answered directly.

Furthermore, the bastarding BBC had broadcast the whole bloody thing live. When he found out who was responsible, that was another pair of bollocks which were going to get a good sharp rap.

He pretended to look through the papers which Weirdlove had given to him for the meeting, gave the appearance of making a few final mental notes, and looked up at the quickly diminishing throng of the cabinet, now reduced to Wanderlip, Malcolm Malcolm III of the Clan Malcolm, Nelly Stratton, Fforbes Benderhook, Trudger McIntyre and Kathy Spiderman.

'Well,' said JLM, with a half-hearted smile, 'seems like there are only seven of us now. They'll be calling us the Magnificent Seven. That'll be lovely, don't you think?'

He looked around the pond of disinterested faces. As his eyes drifted past hers, Wanderlip made a small gnashing movement with her teeth, sending deep psychological discomfort straight to his groin.

'Can I be frank?' said Nelly Stratton.

'Oh yes, please,' said JLM.

'It'll more likely be the Invisible Six and the Up His Own Arse One,' she said, looking at the others for confirmation. Only Wanderlip nodded.

JLM tried to laugh it off, but he almost choked on it.

'Very good, Nelly,' he said.

'Or,' she continued, 'the Doomed Six and the Narcissistic One.'

'Yes,' he said, nodding.

Behind him a small smile came to the lips of Parker Weirdlove. The Amazing Mr X looked out of the window, checking for snipers.

'Or how about,' said Stratton, running with the joke, as all the best comediennes do, 'the Discombobulated Six and the Vainglorious One?'

'All right, Nelly,' said JLM in fluent schoolteacher, 'I think we know where you're coming from.'

'The Neglected Six and The Unbelievably Conceited One,' she said quickly.

'Enough!' ejaculated JLM. 'Can we get down to business?'

There were a few nods around the table, albeit only from the men.

'That'll be a first,' said Nelly, and Wanderlip nodded this time. 'You usually storm in here, issue a few decrees, then walk out.'

'And what makes you think I'm not going to do that this time?' said JLM quickly.

And he stared sharply at them all, attempting to quieten any further dissension in the ranks.

'Right,' he began, 'Wally's gone off, don't know where. At first I suspect we all thought he was just banging some pointless little bit of skirt, but if that'd been the case he'd probably have been back in under five minutes. No, it would appear that he has gone the same way as Melanie and Peggy, wherever that may be. I doubt any of us has any idea, although I'm sure that won't stop the police from making their usual unnecessarily brutal enquiries.'

He looked around the table. Here we go, each and every one of them thought, already started to prattle on without actually saying anything, admiring the sound of his own voice, and not in the least interested in what anyone else has to say.

'So,' he continued, 'we have to consider what we're going to do with his portfolio, such as it is.'

'Whilst also considering the redistribution of Peggy and Melanie's portfolios at the same time,' chimed in Wanderlip. And she ground her teeth together for effect as she said it.

JLM stared across the table, and he suddenly had a thought. A wonderful, delicious, magnificent thought. The bloody woman had clearly left his house the previous night and phoned up every newspaper on the planet to tell them of her knob-biting proclivities; off the record, no doubt. So, since it was already out there and he did not consider he could be any further embarrassed by the revelation, why not make the most of it? Why not, and this would really give her a good solid thump in the nads, get the police to charge her with assault. And bloody grievous assault at that.

An arrest, a charge, a court hearing, he could get Dr Farrow to take the teeth imprints from his penis, and bingo, Wanderlip would have a criminal record. At some stage along the way, hopefully fairly early on, she would be out on her ear. And, if he wanted to rub salt into the gaping wound, he could bring a civil action once she'd been found guilty of the assault charge. Say,

£4m, that'd be a good round number. Embarrassment, loss of fertility, stress, throbbing loins, there was no end to the things that he was suffering because of her unprovoked attack.

'Absolutely, Winnie,' he said. 'Quite right. Lovely. We must do something about that.'

And suddenly the day did not seem so bleak. He had the perfect route to getting rid of Wanderlip, Herr Vogts would be arriving in less than half an hour to begin formulation of the Euro plan, he was confident he could brush off most of the other difficulties that the press kept banging on about, he was about to instigate an invite to the next G8 and, if he was really fortunate, whoever it was who was one by one removing his cabinet for him would continue to do so, and he would have to pay them even less attention than he currently did.

He glanced out of the window behind Wanderlip's head. The sun was indeed shining.

'Champion,' he said. 'I'll get the Finance and Education portfolios back where they belong, and promote MacPherson and Eaglehawk appropriately. Parker, get me some recommendations for two new deputies in those departments. And we'll need to find a new Minister for Tourism and the rest of that portfolio. Leave Patsy where she is as no.2. I'm open to any suggestions from the table, otherwise Parker if you can come up with a couple of names.'

He looked around the room once more. This time his shoulders were straighter, his voice was more confident, he filled the end of the room with his presence.

'Lovely,' he said, when there were no immediate calls from the floor. Of course they weren't going to suggest any names. There was so little talent in the parliament, they would struggle to come up with a single nominee to be in charge of the tea fund. 'Right, we need to get back out there and present a united, solid face. Until we know for sure what's happened to Melanie, Peggy and Wally, we have to carry on as if nothing's happened. We fill the gaps, we carry on, we kick arse. We stand together, and united we stand, united in the stand against everything that our enemies stand for. We're in it together to the bitter end, through the rough and the smooth. We each stand or fall by the collective actions of the collective. We are one, and the one is all of us. We eat as one, we breathe as one, we shit as one. We eat, breathe and shit kinship in the face of adversity. This will be our finest hour! Are you with me?'

Of the six people around the table, all the men had stopped listening to him at around the time that he'd started sounding like Winnie the Pooh. Wanderlip had heard it all and gave JLM a suitable look of contempt.

'Sounds like you're going to pish all over us again,' said Stratton.

JLM nodded and smiled disarmingly. At least you're switched on, you nebby wee cow, he thought.

'Right people,' said JLM, shuffling his papers like he was a newsreader, 'we're through. Let's get out there and kick some backsides.'

'Excuse me,' said Wanderlip, as the men in the room began evacuation procedures. Each of them slumped back into their seats with a resigned sigh. What was the stupid arse going to say now?

'Yes?' asked JLM. One word, a very, very patronising tone.

'Is there the slightest possibility that we could discuss policy, now that we're all in the same room?' said Wanderlip. 'I've got some major issues here, you know. There's a rumour that MotoCell are thinking of closing their communications factory in Bathgate.'

'Why's that a problem?' said JLM. Weirdlove regarded him with a raised eyebrow.

'Several thousand jobs!' said Wanderlip, in a duh-huh tone. 'You know how many millions we, the Executive, have plunged into the bloody thing? We have given them massive government support to keep the factory going, and now it looks like they're just going to pull out, moving the entire operation to Azerbaijan.'

JLM nodded soberly. The loss of thousands of jobs never looked good. Of course, none of the decisions around MotoCell had ever had anything to do with him. It was all the work of his predecessor, Wanderlip and the chancellor in Westminster. So, it could all work out well for him.

'You know, Winnie,' he said, 'I don't even know where Azerbaijan is. Anyone else got any points?'

The men were all keen to get going, and had nothing to say. Nelly Stratton could've talked all day, but just didn't see the point. Wanderlip was too apoplectic to speak. The words would eventually come, but not before JLM had said 'Champion!' and walked out the room, Weirdlove in his wake, The Amazing Mr X ahead of him, armed with rocket launched CS gas canisters.

✂

Twenty minutes later Nelly Stratton was standing at the window of a small ancillary room on the top floor of the Assembly Building, with nothing but towels, brooms, cleaning fluids and large packets of rough-around-the-edges toilet roll for company. Looking out at the sun on Arthur's Seat, the tourists still pounding their way to the top, to be buffeted by the winds that always blow up there.

She was waiting for someone. Another of her little clandestine meetings, of which she generally had one or two a day. This was a little different however, as she wasn't looking to undermine the idiotic leader of the Executive. She had had enough of his total elimination of parliament in the decision making process. As Minister for Parliamentary Business, she was offended by his complete disregard for the seat of government, and she had not been at all fooled by his stupid Three Musketeers speech at the cabinet meeting. However, she had other concerns for the moment.

She was here to find out more about the disappearance of her cabinet colleagues. Not that she was sure the person coming to visit her would be able to help her out, but she had a feeling. With Honeyfoot, she had been unconcerned. Filiben had been a little more troubling, because there was a possible connection with her intended challenge to JLM's authority. But Wally, this was the one which had hit Stratton the hardest. Wally was harmless, the political equivalent of a mild dose of feminine itching. If someone wanted him out, then they might possibly want them all out. It could even be that Stratton's was the next neck on the chopping block.

The door opened, Stratton turned away from the window and the warmth of the sun on her face. The man glanced again along the corridor behind him, stepped into the ancillary room and closed the door.

'Mrs Stratton,' he said. 'A pleasure to be called to another of your little conflabs.'

'Cut the shite, Parker,' she said, 'and tell us what's going on with all these folk going missing.'

24

Eaglehawk rolls up his trouser legs and joins the fellowship

'Herr Vogts!' said JLM, broad smile on his face, 'delighted to see you. Come in, come in!'

JLM was in his inner sanctum, where he could sit, like Jean-Luc Picard, and dispense management wisdom to the lucky few who got to enter. Barney was sitting by the window of the expensive and warmly decorated little room, having spent the previous ten minutes agreeing with everything that JLM had been saying.

Vogts was shown in by The Amazing Mr X, who closed the door behind them, and took up position where he could view all avenues of entry and egress, thermonuclear handgun at the ready.

'The sun is shining,' said Vogts, smiling. 'I thought I was in continental Europe.'

JLM laughed. He was about to quip, that's what my government has done for this country, when Vogts added, 'At least until I saw the rubbish on the streets and all the young girls pushing prams, eh?'

'Yes,' said JLM, with a little less enthusiasm. 'X, any idea what's happened to Mr Weirdlove?'

The Amazing Mr X turned sharply, at hearing his letter.

'Weirdlove?' he said. As JLM's personal bodyguard he took no interest in anyone other than the First Minister. He glanced quickly around the room, making sure Weirdlove wasn't in attendance, then had a quick but pointless swatch at Holyrood Road three floors below. 'Don't know,' he said.

'Sit down, sit down,' said JLM to Herr Vogts. 'Everything to your satisfaction so far on your visit?'

'More or less,' said Vogts, 'although can I just say that there's not been enough women, alcohol or loud pointless singing. This is a bizarre way to run a government.'

'Can I organise a coffee or something for you? said JLM, attempting to hold up his end of the conversation.

'*Or something* sounds good,' said Vogts. 'Can I get a beer? A German beer, not the coloured water that you drink in this country.'

'X,' said JLM, 'can you locate Herr Vogts a German beer, please?'

The Amazing Mr X looked concerned.

'I'm not actually allowed to leave your side, sir,' he said, as if he was barking orders on a parade ground.

'Do you come with me when I take a shit?' asked JLM carefully. 'Or when I go to bed with my wife? I don't think so. X, you are authorised to do things other than stand at my shoulder holding onto my wiener. Now, go find a beer.'

Reluctantly, The Amazing Mr X left his post.

'You'll remember Barn Thomson?' said JLM, indicating Barney.

'Oh yes,' said Vogts, 'the barber.'

'Financial wunderkind,' said JLM.

'I didn't get that impression,' said Vogts

'Lovely, lovely,' said JLM. 'Now, you'll be spending most of the next few days with Mr Weirdlove, my principal political advisor. And there's one other I'd like to be involved in the consultations. I trust you've had useful discussion with your people in Berlin as to how we can solve our little problem.'

'I have had several very constructive meetings,' said Vogts

'Good, good,' said JLM.

'On one occasion,' said Vogts, 'we constructed a ten foot tower out of beer mats, until that idiot Voeller nudged it accidentally. Hasn't been able to hold his beer since the botched vasectomy.'

'Yes,' said JLM, 'that wasn't quite what I meant.'

Barney sat looking from one to the other with vague amusement. His mind, however, was strangely on the cabinet murders, if that's what they were. How he could glean information to help solve them, and how he could possibly extricate himself from this ridiculous position.

The door burst open and in strode Parker Weirdlove, looking a little dishevelled around the chops, having run along the corridor. Didn't like to be late for anything, even if it was only JLM.

'Gentlemen!' he barked, as he marched in. 'Just had a few things to which to attend.'

'Such as?' said JLM.

'Herr Vogts,' said Weirdlove, nodding at the guest.

Vogts returned the greeting with a casual wave of the hand.

'Mr Weirdlove,' he chimed, 'you look as if you've been making big love!'

Weirdlove smiled uncomfortably, nodding at JLM and Barney. Looked embarrassed. Having been in such a rush, he hadn't had time to mentally prep himself for Vogts.

'Well,' he said, 'I don't think so, Herr Vogts.'

'Don't be embarrassed,' said Vogts, 'we have a saying in Germany. In government, there is more than one way to fuck the country. Clever, no?'

JLM laughed that big booming laugh of his. Weirdlove smiled and wondered how he was going to get out of the next few days. Barney hadn't been listening.

The door opened without a knock, and in walked James Eaglehawk, the new Minister for Finance. The initial idea of bringing him in on the Euro plan to undermine Wanderlip had now been overtaken, but his was still the kind of devious, duplicitous and positively venal mind that was required for the project. Sharp suited and sharp chinned, he stood before the throng.

'First Minister, sir,' he said.

'Lovely,' said JLM, 'glad you could make it, James. Herr Vogts, this is James Eaglehawk, our new Finance Minister.'

'A pleasure,' said Vogts, taking Eaglehawk's outstretched hand. 'You have a name of many birds.'

'Yes,' said Eaglehawk, with supreme cool.

'I once knew an English girl called Greattits, but I think that was more a statement on her physical attributes than her actual name.'

'The same could be said about my name,' said Eaglehawk, with effortless panache. 'I swoop like the eagle on unsuspecting prey, I hover above the ground and know every inch of my territory like the hawk. I am a hunter, and the hunted are my prey.'

'Splendid,' said JLM, in an effort to cut him off.

'The beasts of the forest are my victims,' said Eaglehawk, continuing despite JLM's best intentions.

'It's the breasts and the forest that are my victims,' said Vogts, 'and I think we know what kind of forests we're talking about.'

'Enough!' said JLM. 'Gentlemen, I have other business. I'll leave you here to begin the formulation of the plan. Remember these three things: complete discretion, precise execution, and no bollocks. Got that? Champion.'

JLM rose from his chair, regarded the room with a generous smile and clasped his hands together in a roguish manner, as if he was about to go out and give a wench a good slap on the arse.

Barney watched him with the same bemusement with which he was currently watching everything. Would not be surprised if he was about to be left alone in a room with Weirdlove, Vogts and Eaglehawk to discus Scottish fiscal matters. Might as well have the future of the country's economy in the hands of someone who had no idea where to even begin.

'Barney!' said JLM, 'come on, I've got a very important meeting with a mademoiselle from the Canadian government, and I'm looking for a Christopher Lambert *Highlander III*.'

'Hah!' said Vogts, as Barney rose. 'I knew you were the barber.'

'Of course I'm the effing barber,' said Barney dryly, as he walked past.

'Need to speak to you later about a little law suit, Parker,' said JLM quickly, having just been caught in the middle of another lie. Then he marched out, leading Barney from the room. Just as The Amazing Mr X galumphed in, carrying a Stella Artois...

✂

'You see,' said JLM a few minutes later, once more at the whim of Barney's can of mousse and dashing blow drier, 'you can trust some of your people some of the time, but not all of them all of the time, you know what I'm saying? That's why I've got the three of them in there formulating policy. Over the next couple of days I'll take each of them to the side and have a wee chat, make them think they have my ear, that they're my man on the inside. Play them off against each other, find out who's really on my side.'

'Is that what you do with the cabinet?' said Barney, with cool.

JLM snorted.

'Well, I suppose I used to, but they're just so pointless now it's not worth my time. I'm the government, not them.'

'Someone thinks them important enough to murder,' said Barney. Very smooth and entirely natural introduction, he thought. Maybe this detective business wasn't so difficult.

JLM shook his head.

'You're right,' he said. 'Can't understand it myself. Why kill something that's so insignificant that it hardly matters that it even exists? I do think it's more likely, however, that they're not dead and that they're collecting somewhere, intent on pulling some stunt, marching back to Edinburgh to take over the parliament. If they're not dead, I've got a good mind to arrest the three of them. What d'you think?'

'At the very least,' said Barney. 'In fact, if you reinstated the death penalty for treason, assuming they're not already dead, you could have them killed.'

'Very good, Barn,' said JLM, catching his eye in the mirror and nodding. 'What d'you think X?'

The Amazing Mr X, who was standing at the back of the bathroom, one eye on the window, one on the door, had been thinking about women again. However, he didn't want to be seen not to be listening to everything the boss said.

'Delicious,' he said.

'Yes,' said JLM. 'Delicious. A very good way to describe it.'

There was a knock at the door. The Amazing Mr X went through several body contortions in an effort to get himself into position to receive an attack.

'Come in,' said JLM, who didn't always share his bodyguard's flair for the dramatic.

The door opened, and Rebecca Blackadder stuck her head into the First Minister's boudoir.

'Edmund!' said JLM, looking at her in the mirror. 'What a treat. Is there anything I can do for you?'

'Building security are here, sir, I think you'd better come out.'

'Goodness me, Ed, I've got an important meeting in half an hour, and I need the right hair. What is it?'

'Nelly Stratton, First Minister,' said Blackadder.

'Christ,' he muttered under his breath. 'What does the nebby wee cow want now?'

Blackadder looked at The Amazing Mr X, exchanged a glance with Barney, stepped into the room and closed the door behind her.

'She's been reported missing, sir. Same set-up as McLaven. No sign of a body, but blood on the carpet.'

JLM let out a long sigh and turned round. The Amazing Mr X looked a little concerned. Barney raised an eyebrow; there goes another one, he thought, and he wasn't progressing very far with his investigation. Maybe it wasn't so easy to be a detective after all.

'Jesus,' said JLM. 'For crying out loud. You sure she's not just gone for a pint, or something?'

'Blood on the carpet,' Blackadder repeated.

'Maybe she was shaving,' quipped JLM.

'Your hair looks lovely, sir,' said Blackadder. 'I think you should come out.'

'You're right,' said JLM, glancing around at the mirror. 'My hair does look lovely. Thanks, Barn.'

And finally JLM rose and walked to the door, out to face another little crisis in his government.

As what counted for panic once again embraced the parliament building, the killer of the nebby wee cow sat back and relaxed with a hot cup of joe. At first she'd thought she might hang around and wait for building security after she'd made the call; ensure that they found the body before whoever it was who was cleaning up after her. And then she'd thought, sod it. I'm the killer, I should be in charge, I'll do it my way. I'll start toying with the idiot.

And so, after she had stabbed Stratton in the neck with one delightfully fluent ping of the knife, she'd removed the right shoe of the Minister for Parliamentary Business, then carefully cut off her big toe and placed it in a small polythene bag and into her coat pocket. Then she had bound the foot and put it back into the shoe. Then she'd left the scene of the crime, a small ancillary room on the top floor of the Assembly Building, returned to her office and placed the call to building security. More than likely, she thought, the body would be gone by the time they got there. Highly unlikely, however, that the ad hoc undertaker would notice that Mrs Stratton was not complete.

She sipped her coffee, munched on a fig roll, and pondered the variety of naughty things that one could do with a severed toe.

25

The comedians

Finally the media had something decent into which to get their teeth. Rather than the vague disappearance of a couple of cabinet ministers, they now had two more vanishing in the parliament building itself, leaving blood on the carpet at that. *The Executive Cull Picks Up Pace*, boomed BBC Scotland at six-thirty. *Arch Diver & Nebby Wee Cow the latest to go missing,* said Scotland Today. *Government in Crisis*, thundered Newsnight Scotland, with the appropriate graphic displaying the exponential curve of the presumed slaughter of the cabinet. *Disney to sue First Minister at refusal to let his children watch Jungle Book*, said Channel 5. *Britney's underwear in new love triangle*, said Sky News.

For a few hours only, the media were more interested in the death of the very minor celebrities of the cabinet, than they were in JLM and Hookergate or Disneygate or World Cup 2014gate. By the following morning, the disappearance of McLaven and Stratton would not be front page in many of the newspapers, but they dominated the television for a few hours.

Barney was back in the very comfortable cell of his room, watching the television reaction to the latest news, when there was a knock at the door. Much as there was every night. It seemed to Barney like he was the new thing in town. *What are you doing tonight? I'm going to see the freak, Barney Thomson.* He didn't immediately leap up, only vaguely interested in who it might be. Some other messenger of his past, more than likely, with another explanation as to who he was and where he'd come from. *Actually son, you came up the Clyde on a banana boat. As a matter of fact, you're a holographic image. It's a wonder what the people at Lego are doing these days. Apparently they made you out of bits of body that other people didn't need. You're a low-cal, decaffeinated zombie, fully back to life but with none of the slime.*

He wearily walked to the door, sort of hoping that it would be Alison Blake returned to quash the rumours of her indifference. It would give him something to do, if nothing else.

Solomon and Kent were waiting outside, hanging around like a couple of blokes who didn't know what to do with themselves, looking up and down the corridor.

'Solomon and Kent,' said Solomon.

'I remember,' said Barney. 'I only saw you this morning. I thought you were going to give me a few days?'

'That was before the roof caved in,' said Solomon.

Barney nodded. True enough. There'd been a one hundred percent increase in the death rate. If it continued at this pace they'd all be gone by the day after tomorrow. And where would the country be then? Well, actually...

He stood back and ushered them in, nodding at Sergeant Kent as they passed.

'By the way,' said Solomon, 'who did you tell people we were? They're looking at us like we're cowboys.'

'Jehovahs,' said Barney, closing the door.

'Jesus Christ,' said Solomon. 'Couldn't you have said we were serial killers?'

Barney walked over to the drinks cabinet. Cracked open a Bud, turned to the others.

'Get you anything?'

Kent shook his head.

'You got any unblended malt in that thing,' said Solomon, expecting the answer no.

'Seven different types,' said Barney.

Of course there are, stupid, thought Solomon. This is where the taxpayer's money is going to, after all.

'I'll take a Glen Ord if you've got it,' he said.

Barney checked, nodded, cracked open the small bottle of Glen Ord, poured it and passed over the glass.

'What's the big secret with you guy's being police?' asked Barney. 'Four cabinet ministers have disappeared. The place is swarming with you lot.'

'Not us,' said Kent.

'Did I say you could speak?' said Solomon, going straight into his Bill & Ben routine with Kent. 'Look, this whole thing with you, nobody on the force actually knows about. We're investigating the murder of Veronica Walters. That's our thing. The boss just thought that since you were on the inside, you might be able to make a few enquiries. So, we're kind of a liaison. We're not technically involved in the cabinet murder investigation. We have access to what they know through the boss; we'll pass on to him anything that you can come up with.'

'The left hand doesn't know what the right is doing?' said Barney, settling back in his comfy chair.

'Yeah, but the dick knows everything,' said Solomon, 'and that's what matters.'

Barney smiled.

'Never let it be said that a man's brains aren't in his dick,' said Kent.

'Shurrup,' said Solomon.

'All right,' said Barney, 'what d'you want me to do? Seriously. I'm just a guy. I'm not a detective, I can't manipulate people, I'm not particularly adept at the deductive process. With the exception of Longfellow-Moses I don't know anyone in the cabinet. I may be on the inside, but I'm probably on the inside of the wrong box.'

Kent started to say something, but was silenced by a raised hand from his superior, so he slumped down onto the sofa that Barney's women usually sat in, plonked his feet on the coffee table and shoved his hands in his pockets. Puffed his cheeks out so that he looked like a baboon and let out a long whistle of air.

Solomon watched the display with contempt, took a swift wee shot of Glen Ord, then turned to Barney.

'We're at a loose end here. There's four of these comedians gone missing and we've no idea. Now security's been stepped up in the last day, pretty tight in the parliament buildings. I'm not saying that no one could get in, but whatever was done to McLaven and Stratton was more than likely committed by someone who works in the building. Which begins to narrow it down, because the two we had before today went missing outside the building. So, you following me?'

'Like a dog,' said Barney.

'Good,' said Solomon. 'We've got one thousand, three hundred and twenty-three people working in the complex who aren't dead yet. We have to work on the assumption, until something better comes along, that it's one of them who's committing the murders. Right, where do we go from there? Why would anyone want all the members of the cabinet dead?'

'Apart from the obvious,' chipped in Kent.

'Ignore the monkey,' said Solomon, 'because even the obvious doesn't apply. The First Minister has totally removed power from his ministers. They've maybe still got one Hell of a lot of paper to push around, but when it comes to real responsibility and power in the decision making process, zip! Why should anyone have a grudge against any of them, when none of them have made a decision in the past year?'

'Very good,' said Barney. 'So what, you've also eliminated everybody in the building from your investigation?'

'What would Sherlock Homes say now?' wisecracked Kent.

'Ignoring the sideshow,' said Solomon, 'the logical conclusion is that it's someone, or a group, who have direct dealings with the cabinet. The people in each of the government departments don't really have too much business with the cabinet, except through their minister. So, to cut the crap, we're looking at a member of the cabinet itself, someone from the First Minister's office who has regular dealings with the cabinet, or one of the civil servants who has to deal with the cabinet. Sound good?'

'Sure,' said Barney. 'Have to start somewhere.'

'Exactamundo,' said Solomon. 'So, we realise you don't have access to all those groups. But what we're asking you to do is to integrate into the group you're already in. The First Minister's men and women.'

'I've already shagged one of them,' said Barney. Boys will be boys.

'Hey,' said Kent. 'Excellent.'

'Yeah,' said Solomon, 'very good. Find out as much as you can, find out what they know, if any of them have dealings with any of the other two groups. Most of all, find out about Weirdlove, 'cause if ever there was a sinister motherfuck on this planet, that guy is it.'

'Aye,' said Barney. 'You must've seen him this morning as you left.'

Solomon shook his head. Kent gave Barney one of those suspicious little looks that he threw his way every now and again.

'Nope,' said Solomon. 'Why'd you say that?'

Barney shook his head. Because I was presuming he came in as you two left, he thought, but didn't say. Perhaps Weirdlove had ghosted in through the closed door. Perhaps he'd been in the room all along.

'Doesn't matter,' said Barney. 'Look, I'll see what I can find out. What d'you want me to do? How should I contact you?'

Solomon reached inside his coat pocket and produced a small red flag on a small brown pole. Kent rolled his eyes and hurrumphed.

'When you think you've got something for us, doesn't matter how insignificant it seems, stick this in the window of your room. We'll get in touch.'

'You're kidding me?' said Barney.

'He likes to pretend,' said Kent, getting to his feet, 'that his life is a movie. All undercover trickery and car chases.'

'Can it, Kent,' barked Solomon. 'You got anything to tell us, Barn, you put this in your window. You got that?'

'Whatever you say,' said Barney, and he saluted.

'Right,' said Solomon. 'We're out of here. Come on, Superman.'

Kent made a face at Solomon's back and followed his leader to the door. As he passed Barney he put his hand on his shoulder, squeezed, and said, 'Well done on shagging the vicar, mate. Excellent.'

And they left.

When the door was closed, Barney turned round quickly, wondering if Parker Weirdlove was going to be standing inside again, as he had been before. Not this time, and Barney slumped back down into his seat.

'How did they know I slept with the vicar?' he muttered to the room.

26

Give it up for the rubettes!

It was half-time at the 70's retro show at the Royal Concert Hall in Glasgow and the appropriate generation had packed out the auditorium, to watch the usual remnants of one of the century's darker decades of musical output. Of the eleven acts on the bill, there were at least two versions of the Bay City Rollers, an octogenarian line-up for Mud, featuring none of the original band members, Alvin Stardust and his 300lb codpiece, and a varied selection of has-beens, never-weres and be-glittered psychopaths whose egos had remained trapped on Top of The Pops for close on thirty years. It was, to be fair to the lads Fat Bastards, an appalling show. And the audience was fifty-three per cent larger than for the previous night's performance from Scottish Opera.

In the middle of the back row, as inconspicuous as a person who was on Reporting Scotland every other night could be, was Winona Wanderlip, decked out in an enormous Rubettes hat, which she'd possessed since she was ten and had grooved along to *Juke Box Jive*. Along with an absurdly enormous pair of dark glasses, of the variety sported by Peters out of Peters and Lee, it made her blend in with the seventies crowd, so that no heads were turned in her direction.

The man sitting next to her was dressed in a suit and tie, much as he always was. He stood out a mile, but still no one paid him any attention. Something about him made people not want to be caught looking at him.

'It's got to be one of the cabinet,' said Wanderlip. 'Seriously, who else is interested? I don't even see JLM having anything to do with it. He just ignores us all anyway, so why bother killing us off?'

'Quash the rebellion,' said Parker Weirdlove. 'It's good dictator skills. The slightest hint of trouble, and you ditch the ringleaders. Melanie was getting arsey; you said yourself that Peggy came out of your illicit cabinet meeting prepped to make a challenge; Nelly was, well, Nelly.'

'And Wally?' said Wanderlip, giving him a sideways glance.

'Exception to prove the rule,' said Weirdlove. 'I don't know.'

'You know something you're not telling me?' asked Wanderlip.

'Not at all,' he said. 'If JLM wanted rid of people he could just sack them. You're a bit of an exception, because you're this thing in the press. But the others; Jesus, you can tell what it's like. There're four of them dead or missing, and apparently there's only one paper leading with it tomorrow. No one cares.'

'So who then?' asked Wanderlip.

'It's impossible, Winnie,' said Weirdlove. 'Impossible to say. Maybe Eaglehawk. Took out Honeyfoot to get promoted, then he takes out a few others just to make it look like there's a serial killer after you all. Who knows? I'd just watch your back, given what's happened to your colleagues.'

'Thanks,' she said. 'I needed those comforting words.'

'I'm just saying, that's all,' he said, raising a defensive hand.

Wanderlip looked around the crowd, bathed in interval light. Was the killer here, in amongst the crowd? Had she been followed from Edinburgh, and at some stage of the second half, while the audience danced to Middle of the Road, would a silent bullet come whizzing her way?

She stared at a man who looked uncomfortable in his tartan flares and tartan denim jacket and wondered if he could be the hit-man sent to blend in and get her. Or then again, maybe he was just a poor sap who'd been feeling like a complete idiot since his wife had made him get dressed in his retro-gear.

You could just never tell. It could be anyone. It could be Parker Weirdlove.

Winona Wanderlip shivered and turned to listen to Weirdlove, as he started to tell the story of the future of Scotland in space.

✂

Late in the evening, Alison Blake lay back, her head resting on her right hand, her right hand resting on her pillow. She had just extinguished her post-sex cigarette, exhaled the last lungful of smoke through circled lips. She had the warm, luxuriously relaxed and contented feeling about her body that comes with post-sex cigarettes and occasionally even comes with sex.

Today had been the usual dismal run with JLM, getting to spiritually advise him for three minutes, knowing that every word she spoke was either going straight over his head, or not even reaching his head in the first place.

She ran a contemplative hand through the hair of the man lying flat out next to her; the only man who she could call regular in her wide ranging pantheon of sleeping partners.

'That was heavenly,' she said, although it hadn't been. It'd been *all right really*, or *could do better*, or *one day you might get the hang of it, but I'm not holding me breath*.

The man stirred but said nothing. His hand moved under the covers and touched the bare skin of her stomach, gave her a wee affectionate squeeze, and was then withdrawn back to the safety of his side of the bed.

'No problem, baby,' he said eventually. 'Like strawberry blancmange.'

✂

Conrad Vogts also had an interesting evening. Sitting up until quarter to midnight, playing cards with James Eaglehawk and wiping him out for several hundred Euros, whilst having a long and involved chat about the possibility of Scotland's entry into the Eurozone, without the barbed interjections of Parker Weirdlove. (Vogts had also wanted to have a long and involved chat about Scotland's entry to the Eurovision Song Contest, but Eaglehawk hadn't been so concerned about that.) Vogts recognised JLM for what he was; all show, all PR, all political ambition. Eaglehawk was shrewd however, an operator prepared to bide his time, a man who would not be seen to make mistakes. There were few in the voting public who would buy a used car off him, but then only because there are a million people selling used cars. If you needed a used car, and there was only one person selling them, you wouldn't really have any option.

So, after several hours of gin rummy, a few beers and a couple of fish suppers, Conrad Vogts and James Eaglehawk had reached something of an understanding about the future of the Scottish Executive, and about the future of Scotland itself.

They had also reached an understanding on the future of Jesse Longfellow-Moses, and about the number of his days.

27

Preparing for war and the illumination of the masses

The unnatural heat wave continued into the following morning, Edinburgh and the rest of Scotland, waking to the seventh balmy day in a row. The newspapers were full of pictures of kids with ice cream all over their faces, near naked shots of gorgeous bits of tottie prepared to peddle their dignity for a few moments in the sun, and the usual talk of global warming and water shortages. The odd unscrupulous editor pulled library photos or articles that they'd used the last time there was hot weather for more than a day and a half.

So interested were the papers in the weather, that it had become something else to keep the cabinet murders off the front pages. Not that they didn't make the most of it on the insides: *Two More Gone, As Nation Rejoices*, The Scotsman; *Four Down, Six Of The Bastards To Go*, The Herald; *McLaven Falls Faster Than He Used To In The Box*, The Celtic View; *The Nebby Wee Cow Didn't Deserve To Die But Who Cares?*, The Daily Record; *Wanderlip & Spiderman The Only Two Left With Breasts (Or Balls) In The Cabinet*, The Sun; *North East Man Grows Potatoes*, The Aberdeen Press & Journal. The story *German Flies In On Secret Mission To Align Independent Scots To Euro*, was buried on page 56 of the Financial Times. No one noticed.

For this seventh day of hot weather, JLM finally decided he would like something a little seasonal to be going on with, so had asked for a Paul Newman *Long Hot Summer*. For the first time in ten different hair styles, it was actually going to involve Barney in removing some hair.

Which was what he was doing, as he went through the normal morning rigmarole of Parker Weirdlove outlining to his boss the day ahead, JLM cussing and muttering about what a waste of time it all was, and of The Amazing Mr X, standing very still, listening for the slightest sound that might herald an assassination attempt and warrant the use of the self-loading, hand-held bazooka which he had started carrying around with him.

'Look,' said JLM, suddenly, butting into Weirdlove's outline, bringing a well-practised death-ray look from his sidekick, 'I'm really not interested in all the press stuff and this bloody annoying appearance in parliament. I mean, really, the cabinet don't bloody do anything, it hardly makes any difference that they keep dying. Government in crisis, my arse. The fewer of them there are, the better we'll all get on. Can't argue with that, can you, Barn?'

Barney nodded.

'Absolutely, sir,' he said, drawing another scorcher from Weirdlove.

'No, we need big stuff,' said JLM. 'You manage to rearrange that thing with the Canadians we had to cancel because of Stratton and that absurd business with her blood?'

'Had to put it off until next Monday, I'm afraid,' said Weirdlove, to the accompanying groan. 'We'll fit it in between your appearance on *Celebrity Who Wants To be A Millionaire* and your appearance before the Parliamentary Committee on Misappropriation of Public Funds.'

'Christ!' said JLM, turning round, catching Barney unaware this time, and getting a good old slice of the hair on the back of his head removed. 'I'm appearing on *Who Wants To Be A Millionaire*?'

'Well,' said Weirdlove, 'it's only the Scottish version. It's hosted by Craig Brown, and they're dubbing it *Who Wants To Be An Underachiever*?'

'Still,' said JLM, 'tv is tv. Mustn't forget that. What was that other thing you mentioned?'

'Not important,' said Weirdlove. 'And I've got some initial costings for you on the whole space thing.'

JLM nodded, as Barney went about repairing his shattered work of the last few days. The Paul Newman *Long Hot Summer* was about to turn into a Bruce Willis *Any Movie In Which He's Got A Baldy Napper*.

'Yes,' said JLM, 'space. I've been thinking about that, and you know, perhaps it might be a little extravagant. What d'you think?'

'Indeed, sir,' said Weirdlove, 'I believe the voting public might prefer it if you concentrated on the health service and transport for a while.'

'God, Parker, bugger them!' he said. 'We have to think big picture here. Big Picture! I was just thinking, that once we go UDI, the bloody English might pop their heads above the parapet and think about sending troops or something. What d'you think? So I thought maybe we should have some bollocking good defences established, and a few tricks up our sleeve, if you know what I'm saying. Lots of troops, heavy fighting equipment, a bit of a navy and an air force, then bollocks to the bloody English. We'd be in the whole Taiwan situation. Maybe they'd be able to beat us, but it would take them so long and they'd get such a bloody nose out of it, they'd know better than to try. Once we've got our independence, well, we can start to be a bit of a player on the world stage. Send our boys on peacekeeping missions to Africa and the like. That'd be champion, eh?'

Weirdlove couldn't think of an immediate reply. Sometimes, despite everything, JLM still left him speechless.

'And, well, with all that kind of thing, that kind of input to the world stage, all the pomp and all that, we might be able to supplant the bastarding English on the permanent council at the UN. What d'you think? We in with a shout?'

Weirdlove still did not reply.

'Barn?' said JLM, looking for a response from someone.

'Lovely idea,' said Barney. 'You yourself might even manage to become the first head of government to become UN Secretary General whilst still in power.'

Weirdlove rolled his eyes.

'Jesus, Barn!' said JLM, 'that's bloody brilliant. Does the UN constitution allow that? Whatever, anyway, champion. Parker, here's what I want you to do. I need proposals for creating our own armed forces. When we split away from the bastards down south, we'll get a percentage of the existing military, but we need a good solid infrastructure before then. I need figures, and I want a judicious balance between land, sea and air. We need to think about options to get us the finance. I'm talking, just off the top of my head here, privatising the entire health service and introducing health insurance, handing roads over to industry and letting them put tolls on every motorway, A and B road. I'm talking privatising education, letting the people pay for their children's schooling right from the off. I genuinely think they might like that, more of an input and everything, you know?'

He paused while he wondered if there was any other way in which he could help the people of Scotland by absolutely shagging them.

'There must be no end of different ways we could hand control of the country back to the people, don't you think? I'm sure we could persuade them of the need for this, particularly if we invoke the threat of an invasion from the English.'

'For example,' said Weirdlove, 'I expect you could persuade the civil service to pay the government for the privilege of working for us.'

'You know, Parker,' said JLM, 'I think that might well be the case.'

JLM lapsed into silence, while he considered the glory of his plans. Yet to notice that Barney was giving him a slightly downgraded haircut on the one he'd asked for. Weirdlove looked through his notes to see if there was anything else he could tell the boss which was liable to scupper the smooth running of the day. But given that he was able to bluster his way through any question about murder, Hookergate, fraud, or any other business, it didn't seem to matter.

'And I was thinking,' said JLM, as Weirdlove folded the clipboard under his arm, and waited with a patient smile, 'I was reading Linklater in Scotland on Sunday at the weekend. A good article about the Second Enlightenment. I think we should aim for that, don't you? Scotland should be this place where big ideas are born, we should be enlightened and erudite as a nation. I was thinking of founding a kind of Longfellow-Moses trust, you know, establishing a series of centres around the country, where the intellectuals of the day could meet and debate the ideas that I was handing down from above for the advancement of society. The Jesse Longfellow-Moses Enlightenment Forum, I thought we could call it. How's that sound?'

Weirdlove didn't answer.

'Barn?' said JLM.

'Champion,' said Barney.

The Amazing Mr X stared out of the window and thought about *Tom & Jerry*.

JLM finally noticed his hair, looking quizzically in the mirror.

'Is that what Paul Newman looked like in *Long Hot Summer*?' he asked.

Barney stood back and observed the symmetrical beauty of JLM's US Marine haircut.

'Near as dammit,' he replied. 'Near as dammit.'

28

God is not a man, that he should lie

Once JLM had marched from his office with his brief for the day and a spanking new and very short haircut – 'I love it! I love it!' Veron Veron had cried – Barney returned to the midst of the others. The two doctors worrying away at their laptops; Veron busying himself at his dummy, this time creating an elegant, but unnecessarily elaborate thing for JLM's meeting with a Thai prince that had been pencilled in for three weeks hence, (but which was destined never to happen); Father Michael absorbed in whatever hidden messages he was divining from the sermon on the mount; and Alison Blake buried in her Bible, and now avoiding Barney like he was, well, a religious freak or something.

Barney had two pieces of mail, which was unexpected. One internal, one external. He made himself a cup of tea, sat down in the large comfy seat next to Blake, said 'Morning,' with a smile, and got a nodded grunt of a reply, and opened the first of the two letters.

It was from a woman in Aberdeen, who had given him her home phone number, her cell phone number, her business phone number, her e-mail address, her business e-mail, business fax, business cell phone, home and business addresses, car registration number, date of birth, chest measurement and what size of big pants she wore. It read:

> Dear Mr Thomson,
> I've noticed in the last couple of days how wonderful the First Minister is looking. What with his new hair, I suddenly realise that he's been telling the truth all this time and that his

policies are brilliant and the right thing for Scotland.

You are a God. Will you marry me? I'm not a great catch, but I make a lovely pie and my personal hygiene is mostly impeccable.

Please contact me. And please don't think I'm desperate, but I'd really like to start a family, and my husband's not interested.

Yours, hopefully,
Lillian K McEwan

Barney read it a couple of times, wondered if he should give it to security or something, then slipped it into his pocket and thought he might show it to Blackadder later to get a psychiatric profile of the woman.

The second letter had come through internal post, and was only marked up with his name, which had been typed in Garamond. He opened it, unfolded the letter. It read:

> You've had contact with the police. Meet me at 10am in conference room 3c, Queensberry House.

Barney read it again, four times. He looked at the clock. A little after nine. He glanced around the room to see if anyone was staring at him. Was it one of these comedians? Unlikely. But who had heard that he'd had dealings with the police? Was it an open secret? Did everybody know details of every single visitor he had in his room? *Oh aye, Barney had the police round last night, and he knobbed the vicar the night before, he's also had Blackadder round there, but he didn't sleep with her, and the invisible man's been in there as well for a haircut, but of course, no one saw him...*

He folded the paper into his pocket, looked up again quickly to see if he could catch anyone staring at him, didn't, then sat back and sipped on a contemplative cup of tea. Wasn't due to administer to JLM's hair until almost eleven, although there was now absolutely nothing that could be done with it. It was just too plain short for mousse. In fact, Reporting Scotland would lead at lunchtime with *The Latest Disappearance From the Cabinet: JLM's Hair*.

Barney closed his eyes, relaxed and gave up thinking about who it was he was going to meet and how they knew he was the Fed's man on the inside.

✂

Barney left JLM's office at 9:45. Didn't make any excuses, on the basis that that was only more likely to draw attention to himself. Managed to not even glance over his shoulder as he went.

Took about ten minutes to find 3c, wondering all sorts of things as he went. Was he about to get murdered? Or was it a joke that they played on all the new boys, and he was about to walk into the middle of a meeting of some select committee and make a total idiot of himself?

The cupboard was bare when he arrived. A tiny little room, a small table with a few chairs. A whiteboard on one wall, so that all the consultants who came in could write their drivel, and three windows looking out at the sky, which today was a warm and hazy pale blue.

Barney stood at the window looking down at the Canongate, and across the city at the grand architecture and columns and buildings, old and new. Edinburgh kicked Glasgow's arse, and there was just nothing Glasgow could do about it. But he had Glasgow in him, and whatever had happened to him two and a half years ago, whichever of the three stories were true, it was still there.

So lost was he in his contemplation of the city, that he hadn't even noticed that it was almost quarter past ten by the time the door opened. He turned, hands in pockets, sucked from his reverie.

Father Michael closed the door, stood still, nervous, edgy. It was the first time that Barney had looked into his eyes, and he could tell all manner of things were going on in there. And strangely it relaxed him, made him realise that he was the confident one in the room. He was in charge. All things are relative, all self-confidence measured against those with whom one is dealing. Barney's self-confidence was so much greater than before in any case, and this was not someone to instil doubt within him.

'Father,' said Barney.

'Mr Thomson,' said the priest, and his voice was small and thin, and Barney wondered how he ever managed to project himself from a pulpit.

'What can I do for you?' said Barney.

'You've been speaking to the police,' said Michael, words very quick, very quiet, almost as if he didn't want Barney to know he'd spoken them.

'I've been speaking to a lot of people,' said Barney. Obvious, already, that he was spending a lot of time around politicians.

Michael stared at Barney, deep into the eyes, trying to work him out. There was nothing there for him to latch on to, however. But then, it had always been one of Michael's problems. He couldn't read people, he couldn't get inside their hearts or their minds.

'I've got my suspicions,' said Michael. Still tentative.

'Oh, aye,' said Barney. 'What are you suspicious about, exactly?'

'These murders,' said Michael quickly. 'The Cabinet.'

Barney folded his arms across his chest.

'Go on,' he said.

'No proof,' he said. 'You'll really have to find that yourself. Or maybe the police,' he added. 'Maybe the police could try and find the proof, if you tell them what I'm thinking.'

'Why don't you tell them?' said Barney.

Michael swallowed. Glanced nervously over his shoulder at the closed door, six inches behind him.

'I'm too unsure,' he said. 'You're their man on the inside. I thought perhaps you could do a bit of prying, investigating. Try and discover something more concrete before speaking to them. I don't know,' he concluded, to reaffirm the complete lack of confidence he had in what he was saying.

Barney studied Michael's face, his eyes, the lines at the corners of his mouth. Was he always lacking in confidence or was it because he had no conviction about the lies he was spouting?

‘I’m listening,’ said Barney sternly, making no effort to put the man at ease.

‘Dr Blackadder,’ said the priest quickly, again almost as if he didn’t want Barney to have understood what he said.

‘What about her?’ retorted Barney.

Another messenger of God was about to dump on the only person he had felt able to trust since he’d got here.

‘I know how she seems,’ said Michael. ‘I know how she comes across. Very caring, very concerned and involved. But I’ve been watching her for months now, I’ve been waiting for something to happen.’

‘Why didn’t you tell someone?’ said Barney.

‘You mean the First Minister?’ said Michael, quickly.

‘Or Weirdlove,’ replied Barney.

‘No,’ said Michael, shaking his head. ‘No. You can’t trust Weirdlove. Don’t ever trust him.’

He looked earnestly at Barney, pondering his next words.

‘And the First Minister,’ he said, uncertainly. ‘You can’t talk to him about her. I don’t know what it is, but she’s got something on him. Something in their past. He’ll never get rid of her. He can’t.’

‘And?’ said Barney, not giving him any space, not letting up. ‘What has that got to do with the Cabinet?’

‘Whatever it is, this thing, this thing in their past,’ said Michael, the words clumsy and forced, ‘she’s doing something. Acting on his behalf, maybe. I don’t know.’

‘She herself has killed the four of them, is that what you’re saying?’ said Barney.

‘No!’ said Michael, horrified at being pinned down, ‘no. I don’t think so. She’s got a lot of friends in different places. Maybe she is doing something, I don’t know. Maybe she’s got nothing to do with it, I just know what she’s like, I know there’s this thing between them.’

The words finished tumbling from his mouth. Barney leant back against the window ledge, felt the warmth of the sun on his back.

‘So, he said, ‘there’s a thing between them. Something that has possibly led to something else, involving something or other, all tied up with something from some time in their past. You're losing the credulity of your audience here.'

Michael closed his eyes, breathed deeply. No wonder he had made a lousy parish priest; no wonder he could never persuade anyone of the veracity of God's word. He looked at Barney.

'I know how it sounds,' he said.

'Then you'll know why I'm sceptical,' said Barney.

Michael swallowed and rubbed his hand across his chin. Hadn't shaved that morning and he felt the sharp edge of his bristles. Barney watched his hands, the nervous movement of his fingers. Was he doubting him because he didn't want to believe him? The same way he had doubted the Rev Blake. He liked Blackadder. It felt good being around her, he enjoyed her company, he wanted to see her after hours. The thing with Blake, well that had just been what it was and nothing more. He had something with Blackadder, a connection that nothing from his slowly returning memory suggested he had ever had in the past.

So, was he doomed to doubt every word he heard spoken against her? And would he go on doubting it right up until the point where he was added to her victims?

'I'd better go,' said Michael, suddenly, the words a rush.

And before Barney could question him any further, he had opened the door, checked the corridor, and was gone.

The door closed over with a click, and Barney was left alone with the heat of the sun, in a small musty conference room. The blank whiteboard stared down at him from the wall. He turned and looked out at the day, could smell the warmth from outside. Closed his eyes and was transported to the Campsie Fells above Glasgow, where on days like this his father would've taken him and his brother. Back when he was young, very, very young. His family came back to him, his first thoughts of them, apart from his mother's killer instincts, since he had awoken.

He felt the weight of loss upon his chest, brought on by the smell of a warm morning in September. He turned away from Edinburgh, walked round the small table, out of the conference room and back into the troubled times of the Scottish parliament.

29

Plank

The parliament was in full session. Jesse Longfellow-Moses was open for emergency questions.

The parliament only sat on two days, Wednesday and Thursday, with First Minister's questions on the Thursday afternoon. However, with the unexpected events surrounding the government, the opposition had managed to bring forward questions by a day, hoping to catch him off guard. And, knowing that they were actually unlikely to catch him with his pants down over the cabinet murders, they had decided to throw a few other unexpected fast balls his way. They didn't have to be big issues, their badly advised thinking had been, they just had to catch him unawares to make him look stupid.

They were going out live on the BBC, and so the place had jerked into what passed for life, as it usually did once a week. Open house on the First Minister, the chance to get their muzzles on the gogglebox, and every member was in place at their little stations, Sunday best and a quick brush with whitening toothpaste before appearing.

'And furthermore,' said the leader of the opposition, a spineless little plank who was leading his party into the kind of oblivion that the Conservatives had successfully aspired to in Scotland, 'findings from a study at the University of Dundee have revealed that up to five species of insect and spider, indigenous only to Scotland, are becoming extinct every year. In the light of these shocking findings, can the First Minister put our minds at ease about the Executive's commitment to green issues, the environment, the greater Scottish ecosystem and the ecology of the planet?'

There were one or two mutterings in agreement from around the chamber. A few silent groans of disgust. Winona Wanderlip slumped deeper into her seat, fingers tapping dully on the desk in front of her.

Fucking Hell, she thought. If only I was leader of the opposition. There are a queue of things with which to absolutely rip the pish out of the man, any one of which would have most politicians slavering over their breakfast, and this idiot asks what he's doing to protect bugs. In one question she could belittle Longfellow-Moses in front of the country. She could be Ed Murrow; she could be Denis Healy sending Geoffrey Howe packing. She could be the one to make the man crumble before the nation. But she was stuck in the Labour Party, and even the slightest hint of rebellion would get too many backs up. No one likes unrest. No one likes a troublemaker.

JLM rose to his feet, looking smugly through the set of dry answers that the civil service had prepared for him. None of them related to the bug question, because no one on the planet had expected a bug question. But then, that was because no politician worth his salt on the planet would be so stupid as to ask a question about bugs.

'Perhaps my learned friend,' JLM began, a cheeky smile on his face, the one he'd borrowed from Wally McLaven and would now no longer have to return, 'thinks there are not enough insects in Scotland in the summer.'

There was a ripple of laughter around the auditorium. The leader of the opposition shook his head and tried to appear aloof.

'Is it,' continued JLM, 'that he would like a large percentage increase in the amount of bites on the arse that the average holidaymaker gets in the Highlands in August?'

There were guffaws, as well as a few frowns at the use of language.

'I agree,' said JLM, after casting a superior smile around the audience, 'totally. We could pass it on to Visit Scotland. Here's a wee catchphrase. *Want To Be Pustulant, Suppurating and Vile? Come To Scotland and Visit Argyll.*'

Uproar. Parliaments are generally fairly soft audiences for the comedian; like churches and doctors' surgeries, people aren't really expecting a laugh, so even the slightest thing gets them going. When the experienced politician decides to go for it, the crowd are putty in his hands.

'We could do scratch 'n sniff weekends,' he said, in that mock serious manner beloved by the politician who fancies himself as Billy Connolly. 'Spend an hour naked in a field on Skye in July, then spend the remainder of your holiday feverishly clawing at your body, until you've surgically removed all the bites, but also have no skin left.'

Not so many laughs this time, and the experienced house speaker in him knew that he had passed his peak. Time to finish off the stupid little eejit.

He waited for the noise to abate, he looked around the sea of expectant faces. The sun smiled vigorously on him through the huge windows which dominated the upper walls of the debating chamber. He lifted the papers so that they would be the stick with which he would beat his opponent. They all knew what was coming; some of them held their breath. The leader of the opposition thought, here we go, but cursed the advisor who had persuaded him to ask the question. 'Show that he's not in touch with the bread and butter issues of life in Scotland,' that had been the thinking. Genius.

'This is a great nation,' said JLM, sombrely. 'We have been great in the past, and we will be so again. The Second Enlightenment is coming, sponsored by this government, this Executive. My colleague, Malcolm Malcolm III of the Clan Malcolm, issued a precise and far-reaching paper outlining the future of the Health Service in Scotland only two days ago. The integrated transport policy is coming together.'

He took a statesmanlike pause. Jesus, thought Wanderlip, you're not all going to let him away with this, are you? Someone have the balls to say something! The paper on the Health Service was nothing more than rehashed ideas. No new money, no new thinking. A disaster! There was no integrated transport policy, unless you called collectively ignoring all the problems at the same time, integrated. How could they all just sit here?

'No one is saying that the environment is unimportant,' he continued. 'This government is fully committed to that end. Recycling bins up 5% in the last two years. Legislation forcing industry to explain why they're dumping toxic waste...'

'But it doesn't actually stop them dumping it!' cried a brave little soul from the back. Good for you, thought Wanderlip, at the young woman's voice. At least two of us have testicles in this place.

JLM laughed in the slightly arrogant way that he somehow managed to get away with.

'There will always be arguments from the small-minded about technicalities,' he said, throwing the line away, along with the comment. 'As First Minister it is my position to see the bigger picture, it is my place, my curse, my bane, my affliction, to stand at the window of Scotland's predestination, looking out over the landscape of our heritage and how it leads us onto the promise of our destiny.'

'What the fuck...' muttered Wanderlip, and one or two others, as JLM got carried away.

'Four of my cabinet have likely been murdered in the past few days,' said JLM, 'these are dark times. But yes, I will rise above them, I will lead Scotland onto new glories, a new place on the world stage. We must concentrate for the moment on filling these cabinet positions from within the wonderful ranks of MSP's I see sitting here before me today. '

Another pause while he let the compliment sink in.

'This nation can be great again, and will be great again. This government has grand ideals, a grand vision, and we will realise that vision. This will be the legacy of my administration, this will be the empire on which the purport of our inheritance will be weighed.'

Oh, for crying out loud, thought Wanderlip. Any bloody excuse and he's off on a screaming tangent.

'We will rise and conquer!' exclaimed JLM, coming to the conclusion of his *tour de ridicule*. 'Scotland! Scotland! We will be kings!'

Some idiot couldn't stop himself applauding, and then the next thing anyone knew, there was a tumult of cheering at their great leader's grand vision.

'Fuck's sake,' muttered the leader of the opposition beneath the noise, 'I only asked him a fucking question about beetles.'

✂

Kathy Spiderman left First Minister's questions early. Not because she thought it was the most ridiculous, over-the-top, absurdist nonsense that she'd heard JLM come out with in some months – although it was – but because she had been summoned by the same type of note that had earlier summoned Barney Thomson. And, in a strange coincidence, it had also summoned her to the same little conference room on the top floor of Queensberry House, with large windows and a lovely view out over the sun roasted bottom end of the Royal Mile.

She opened the door to be greeted by the sight of someone leaning on the window ledge, one of the two windows opened wide, allowing in a gorgeous zephyr to douse the humidity.

'Awright?' said Spiderman. 'What's this?

The person at the window glanced round; although Spiderman had already recognised her from the rear view.

'Just catching the breeze.'

Spiderman stood by the door and looked out the window. What were any of them doing inside on a day like this? What was the point in any job when you couldn't just blow it off and make the most of the few glorious days that God gave you? It was one of the reasons why, despite the general appeal of power and the ability to control others' lives, Kathy Spiderman had already made the decision to stand down at the next parliament. Already kicking herself that she'd stood for re-election a year earlier, and hadn't opted out like the twenty-one others; the ones who'd realised that they were wasting their time.

She walked forward, took her place at the window, leant on the ledge and looked down. She could smell the warmth, and it took her to summer holidays when she was young, playing in the streets all day until her mum shouted for her when the sun was still low in the sky. Hopscotch and football and hide and seek and whatever was the big event at the time, whatever that summer demanded they imitate.

'It's beautiful,' she said, still curious as to why she'd been called up here, but this was better than having to listen to Jesse Longfellow-Moses give the parliament details of his latest vision.

'Yeah.'

She turned and looked at the person who had called her; faced flushed with the sun, as if she had been here a while, elbows on the ledge, holding a cup of water in both hands.

'You want a drink?' she asked.

Spiderman looked at the clean, clear liquid, imagined diving into it, submerging, becoming enrobed in still water, the cold touching her skin, removing the discomfort of the day.

'Aye,' she said, and the drink was put into her hands.

She didn't hesitate. Cup straight to her mouth, didn't see it coming. The poison was so fast-acting that she did not even have time to pass the drink back before it took effect. The cup slipped from her hands, she turned and stared, mouth open, gasping for clean air.

'Wh....,' was forced from the back of her mouth, and then she slumped forward, so that her midriff was resting on the window ledge. Her weight nearly took her over, but after a wobble or two, she came to rest, arms dangling over the side, feet still on the floor.

The location of the axis made it easy for her feet to be lifted up. Spiderman's killer hesitated, enjoying the first moments of her death. A few seconds and she would splatter onto the Canongate. Let the Undertaker clear that one up.

The killer put her hand on Spiderman's belt. Then she heard a sudden swish of movement behind her. Started to turn, her hair catching the sunlight, like some shampoo ad überchick. Whomp! and she collapsed in a heap at the feet of Kathy Spiderman, bludgeoned crudely over the head with a heavy duty stapler. The weight of her, sliding down the inert legs, caused Spiderman's corpse to fall back into the room, tumbling over her killer's body, where it came to rest, their heads beside one another, so that it seemed that they were almost in intimate conversation.

Like Smith and Jones.

30

A little light lunch music

Barney Thomson took a late lunch in the parliament restaurant, having given JLM's napper a final brush up and polish just before he'd departed for questions. So it was, that as JLM graced the chamber with his magnanimity and courage, Barney was beckoned from his solitary lunch of *piquant of asparagus on a mutton of beef, with peaches en croute and the chef's delight of liquorice crème anglaise*, blended delightfully with a spicy Argentinean red, mellow on the throat, but unnecessarily vulgar on the stomach and downright vicious on the bottom, with hints of citrusy fruits and non-biological warfare, to share lunch with the Three Musketeers, boldly going where no one had gone before to solve all of Scotland's fiscal difficulties.

It was Herr Vogts's doing, as he had really wanted to ask Barney a few questions about men's hairstyling. Weirdlove hadn't been too impressed, Eaglehawk only mildly curious.

Barney walked over in response to the beckoning finger, plate in one hand, savage glass of wine in the other, and took his place at the fourth seat. The others were sharing a bottle of a rumbustious German white, for use as an accompaniment to meat dishes, as a drink on its own, for mixing cement, or for a hundred other practical uses around the building site; and they were eating a variety of things off the chef's menu, which involved compotes and nages and God knows what else.

'You can be our D'Artagnan,' said Vogts, smiling.

Barney laughed.

Weirdlove thought the analogy stupid.

I want to be D'Artagnan, thought Eaglehawk.

‘Well, I think I’m older than the three of you, but if that’s how you want to think of me,’ said Barney.

‘You’re only as old as the woman you feel, eh?’ said Vogts laughing.

‘Old ones are the best,’ said Barney.

‘Jokes are only as old as the woman who laughs at them,’ said Eaglehawk, who would try and compete with Vogts’s Groucho routine every now and again, but always ended up sounding like Zeppo. The poor bastard. No one laughed.

‘You can take an idiot to water, but you can’t make it think,’ said Weirdlove caustically, and the other three gave him a quick glance and wondered at which of them the jibe had been aimed.

Weirdlove had known from the start of the day that there was something going on between Eaglehawk and Vogts. He had left them alone the night before, expecting that they would go their separate ways soon after, but it was immediately apparent to him that that had not been the case. He had consequently been suspicious all day.

‘What did you do to Jesse’s hair today, Barn?’ said Eaglehawk, jokingly, deciding to ignore Weirdlove. ‘He looked like a criminal.’

Barney shrugged. ‘Inevitable,’ he said. ‘If the man’s going to get his hair seen to eight times a day, and he’s going to bob around like a ferret while he’s in the chair, accidents are bound to happen.’

‘And you can’t say that the criminal look does not suit him,’ said Vogts.

‘I wouldn’t speak those words too loudly, Herr Vogts,’ said Weirdlove, lowering his voice.

Herr Vogts gave his new chum Eaglehawk a knowing smile and stuck a ravaged and toffee-ised carrot into his mouth.

‘So,’ said Barney, coming to the end of his meal, while just about coming to terms with the feral monstrosity of the wine, ‘what can I help you with? Looking for some layman’s input into your duplicitous shenanigans over the Euro, presuming you’re all experts here.’

'Actually, I just wanted to ask you if you could give me a Gerd Müller, '74,' said Vogts.

For some reason that he could not explain, Barney knew exactly what a Gerd Müller '74 was going to look like. About to agree to it, when Weirdlove launched in.

'Yes, Mr Thomson,' he said, 'perhaps you could give us a layman's view of Scotland joining the Euro independent of Westminster. It'd be very interesting.'

'Well,' said Barney, after draining his glass, and giving it the required two seconds' thought, 'let me see...'

He looked round the table. No JLM here to offend. Didn't think it bothered him if he rubbed any of these men up the wrong way.

'Financially, it'll probably do you good. I say that from a position of complete ignorance, but trading wise, I can't see that it's a bad thing. From the public's point of view, you've got to get the press on your side, the tabloids as well as the business papers. Don't get the tabloids, then you're just going to get ridiculed. Having said all that, ethically and politically the way you're doing it is outrageous. A terrible affront to the voting public. Jesse is a mile up his own arse, not content with being principal politician in a pointless little country on the outskirts of Europe. But you three? I don't know what the story is with any of you.'

Vogts smiled ruefully. We've certainly all got our own reasons, he thought. Eaglehawk regarded Barney with suspicion, reading into his words the implication that he, he himself, James T Eaglehawk, was also up his own arse. Weirdlove gave Barney the sort of look he'd given him when he'd spoken to JLM in the same manner, destructo-rays pinging out across the table.

'Ah,' said a sweet voice behind Barney, 'a lovely little conspiracy of four, all men together.'

Barney turned, recognising the voice, smiled at her. Rebecca Blackadder, dressed in black, still wearing the unnecessarily cool spectacles that JLM demanded of her. Vogts smiled also, what with her being a beautiful woman 'n all. Eaglehawk regarded her with the contempt in which he held most women that he wasn't having sex with. Weirdlove breathed deeply. Didn't entirely trust

Rebecca Blackadder, even if he sometimes manipulated her into doing his bidding.

'Sorting the world out,' said Vogts.

'I bet you are,' she replied. 'Well, you won't need Barney for that, will you?' And she looked expectantly round the others.

'True enough,' said Weirdlove, without tone, without humour, 'he's said quite enough. We should be getting on. Come on, gentlemen.'

He rose, turned and left without so much as another glance at the doctor. Eaglehawk nodded at Blackadder and Barney and followed Weirdlove from the restaurant.

'I'm only here to make sure Mr Weirdlove does not disappear up his own rectal passage,' said Vogts smiling, then with a nod and a wink, he too was gone.

'Don't mind if I sit down?' said Blackadder, after watching them leave the room.

'Sure,' said Barney. An absolute pleasure.

'What was that all about?' she asked, stirring her coffee.

'Nothing much,' said Barney. 'Just great men, doing great things.'

'In historical events,' said Blackadder, 'great men – so called – are but labels serving to give a name to the event, and like labels they have the least possible connexion with the event itself.'

'Very good,' said Barney. 'Tolstoy?'

'Totally,' she said, taking a surreptitious sip of coffee.

'Very nice. You must.....'

There was a noise at the door, and they looked up to see three police officers standing in the entrance. Barney looked at Blackadder, caught the merest hint of worry before it was removed quickly from her face.

'Ladies and gentlemen,' said the plain clothes officer of the three, to the few who remained in the restaurant by this time, 'can I ask you all to please remain in your seats. There's been a reported incident in the building, and we need everyone to stay where they are for the time being. Someone will be along to speak to you soon. Thank you for your co-operation.'

A be-suited civil servant with a pole up his bottom rose from his seat to toddle off and protest about how busy he was, and couldn't he be an exception? Barney looked back at Blackadder, raised the merest hint of an eyebrow.

'Another minister, do we think?'

She nodded.

'Yeah,' she said, 'I was going to say. I heard someone mention it before I came in. Apparently Kathy Spiderman's been reported missing, although no one knows what's happened to her.'

'Oh,' said Barney. And he fiddled with his cutlery, scraping the last remnants of food from his plate. And you didn't think that another one of these clowns going missing was worthy of a mention? He looked up at her, to see what was going on inside the head, but the face was as inscrutable as ever. 'She was Justice, was she?'

'Yeah,' she said. 'Whatever that was supposed to mean.'

Barney nodded. How many left? How many more would die before he had actually discovered anything worthwhile for Solomon and Kent? But then, it wasn't his business. Why should he feel this weight of expectation?

'How many of them are left now?' he asked. 'Cabinet ministers.'

Blackadder stared at the ceiling, as if she had to think about it.

'Five,' she said, lowering her eyes, 'including JLM, of course. And assuming that Spiderman's really gone, and she's not just sitting in some cubicle somewhere crying because someone's hurt her feelings.'

'Right,' said Barney, trying to sound casual. Assuming that undercover detectives usually sound casual as they go about their business. 'Who're the other four?'

Blackadder gave a little knowing nod – Barney assumed, again, that it was the nod of someone who knew the person she was speaking to was in the employ of Federal agents – and started counting them off on her fingers.

The two uniformed police officers had taken up position at the door; the plain clothes character had gone off somewhere to beat someone up.

That's just an unfair generalisation.

'Benderhook,' she began, 'JLM's deputy. An all right kind of a guy if you want, say, a punchbag in your living room, or someone to rest your feet on while you're watching tele, but otherwise he's a complete woose.'

'A perfect politician.'

'Exactly. There's Trudger McIntyre, Environment & Rural Development. Just the most inept of men you could imagine. No idea about politics whatsoever. Only got the job because JLM shagged his wife once, McIntyre knows about it, and blackmailed himself into the post.'

'Fine behaviour,' said Barney.

'Totally. Malcolm Malcolm III of the Clan Malcolm, Health. Bit of an idiot, but heart in the right place, all that stuff. Very interesting family history of mental problems, which he shows signs of inheriting, but I haven't spilled the beans on that one just yet.'

'Except to me.'

'I can trust you,' she said, and you know, thought Barney, there might just have been a wee bit of an edge to the voice. 'Which leaves Wanderlip, who's as much of a bane to JLM as anyone is going to be. Minister for everything else. Bit of a nippy sweetie.'

Barney nodded. Didn't know any of them, but then, why would he?

'Of course, there's the two who've just been promoted in because of the first two deaths, and then there'll be three more promoted in,' she said. 'And so it goes on.'

'Who'll be next?' said Barney suddenly. That was what really mattered now. That was what always mattered; whose neck was next in line?

'Could be any one of them,' said Blackadder, the shrug in the tone as much as her shoulders.

'You, 'em,' said Barney, unsure if he was getting into very obvious routine questioning territory, 'must have done profiles on all the victims for JLM.'

'Yeah,' she replied.

'Anything there to connect them?' he asked.

'What?' she replied, 'the Cabinet thing isn't enough? The fact that every few days they all used to sit down in the same room together isn't, like, a connection?'

'Well,' said Barney, a little on the defensive, 'you know, sometimes you draw obvious conclusions, and sometimes those obvious conclusions are wrong. That's all.'

Blackadder nodded, gave him an appreciative look.

'You're right,' she said. Then she paused, toyed with her spoon, ran her finger along the edge of her coffee cup, said, 'You seem interested. In these murders.'

Barney did the casual thing, which he almost had to a tee.

'Isn't everyone?' he said. 'The cabinet's getting murdered one by one. Jesus, it's huge!'

'And yet,' said Blackadder, 'no one in the country gives a shit.'

And that was about the size of it. Barney held her gaze for a minute, then looked away. Drifted lazily around the few groups who were now marooned in the restaurant. One or two in hushed conversation; a group of three men who were talking about the Rangers-Feyenoord game that night; a couple discussing whether Scotland were ever going to beat England at Twickenham again; four women debating the merits of vibrators with revolving peas inside them, you know the type. These were people who worked in the parliament and even they didn't care that another member of the senior-most committee in government had gone AWOL.

It seemed to make sense, suddenly. Whoever was carrying out these crimes wasn't doing it for political motive. Why bother? Why do something this bad, for this little effect? So, if it wasn't political, it was personal. A grudge. Maybe against the cabinet as a whole, or perhaps for every death, there was a different reason.

'Come to dinner with me tonight,' said Blackadder suddenly, breaking into his rare insight. 'I know a place, outside the city.'

Barney looked deep into the dark eyes. Go out of the city. That was a strange thought. Despite all the murder and chaos so close by, he felt strangely safe and protected in the city. But then, she was a psychologist. Maybe she knew; maybe that was why she wanted him to go with her for the evening.

'All right,' he said. Heart beating just a little bit faster at the thought of a night out with her alone. The added imperilment of uncertainty. 'That'll be nice.'

'Yeah,' she said, smiling wickedly, 'it will.'

31

And after all, what is a lie? 'Tis but the truth in masquerade

JLM was staring intently into the mirror, regarding his hair with grave uncertainty. He was back in his office en suite; Weirdlove was not in attendance, still cosseted with Vogts and Eaglehawk; The Amazing Mr X was at his station by the window, B-52 at the ready; Barney was poised behind JLM, waiting with an almost total lack of enthusiasm for his boss's pronouncement.

'It's too short!' JLM ejaculated eventually. 'Too damn short, Barn!'

'That's 'cause you jumped about like a jack-in-the-box while I was cutting your hair this morning,' said Barney. 'If you're going to live by the sword,' he added, 'you're going to get a shite haircut.'

JLM hurrumphed. He was going to have to speak to the press, again, and for all the cabinet ministers that were dropping like flies, frankly he just knew they were going to ask him about his hair.

He looked at his watch, pursed his lips, shook his head. Another fifteen minutes and he was going to be out there, on the lawn at the side of the parliament, shirt sleeve weather, sun on his nearly bald head, overlooking Holyrood Palace, prepared with all manner of concerned statements about the quickly diminishing cabinet, and they were going to ask him what he was doing with his napper.

'Could you do me hair extensions or something?' he said, cocking his head to one side.

'You need hair to attach the extensions to,' said Barney glibly.

'Yeah, yeah, I suppose,' said JLM. 'What about implants then, you know like Elton John and all that mob?'

You'd look like a fucking idiot!!!! thought Barney.

'That'd be great,' said Barney. 'But we'd have to pluck hairs from your pubes to implant into your head, and it's not like you don't have hairs in your head. You just need to let them grow.'

'Pubes?' said JLM, frankly shocked.

'Yeah,' said Barney. 'That's why Elton John didn't mind. I mean, those kinds of guys pluck their pubes anyway, don't they?'

'Do they?' said JLM. He looked troubled, believing everything his barber told him, and looked away.

'Any other options?' he asked, after shivering through the thought of his pubic hairs being physically extracted.

Barney took a pace back and studied the hair again. Here we go, he thought, back in the old routine. Give the customer a bit of bullshit, spin the usual crap, get them to feel good about themselves.

'What about purple dye, or something,' said JLM.

'Look,' said Barney quickly, before JLM suggested a wig, spray paint or crayon, 'you hair's fine. It suits you. It's the whole Michael Stipe thing going on. The voters'll love it, the press'll think you're cool'

'You reckon?' said JLM, already buying into his new superstardom.

'Absolutely,' said Barney. 'You know, I wouldn't be surprised if you got asked to model some new suit or other on the Milan catwalks. You could be the face of Scottish Euro-chic with this haircut, you know what I'm saying? You'll be the toast of, I don't know,' hesitated Barney, momentarily running out of bullshit, 'Monte Carlo and all that mob. St Moritz.'

JLM looked critically at Barney in the mirror. Bloody rubbish, he thought, but when your ego is hungry, it'll pretty much eat any old gruel thrown its way.

'Sounds good,' said JLM suddenly. 'You know, you might be right. I like it.'

And he looked at his shit hair through new eyes.

'Really,' said Barney, 'the press are going to be more interested in the disappearance of Kathy Spiderman. This is the perfect time for you to be statesmanlike. Proud, dignified, not cowed in the face of all this murder and mayhem. Defiant in adversity, resplendent and magnificent against the odds, prepared to look the terrorists of the world, or whoever it is that's perpetrating these crimes, squarely in the eye, and to declare that Scotland will not be defeated, democracy will be not be vanquished, and that you, Jesse Longfellow-Moses, will not be shaken in your determination to make Scotland great once again.'

Even The Amazing Mr X gave Barney a bit of a sideways glance.

JLM turned round, rising from his chair.

'Brilliant, Barn!' he said, 'bloody brilliant! Can you write all of that down quickly? You think you can do that? Do you?'

'If you're desperate,' said Barney.

'Brilliant,' said JLM. 'Right, I love that stuff. Maybe you can start writing speeches for me. Champion. Let's go and kick some arse.'

For the first time in their acquaintance, Barney and The Amazing Mr X exchanged a knowing glance, and then they were charging from the bathroom, on their way to prepare JLM for the biggest press briefing of his tenure.

JLM gave a long speech, before taking any questions. He outlined his government's and his own personal stance on the murders; the way ahead; the full force of the law was looking for the perpetrators of the crimes; Scotland would not be broken; blah, blah, blah, blah. Spoke for a full fifteen minutes – with passion, fluency and heartfelt courage – before the first question. Which was:

'First Minister, Russell Hargreaves, Scottish Daily Mail. What's with the new haircut? You look like a wank.'

Barney returned to his room a little after six. Due to be picked up by Rebecca Blackadder at seven. Just under an hour to relax, listen to some Hoagy, catch a bit of the news on the tv – Scotland

Today were to lead with the claims of *fix!* surrounding the ejection at the latter stages of the Scottish entrant on Big Brother, followed by a feature on JLM's hair, followed by talk of Celtic asking Pele to come out of retirement for £125/week, and finally, squeezed in before the weather and a story about a little girl who'd spilled her ice cream, the account of Kathy Spiderman's unexpected disappearance – have a shower and get garbed up in as plain an outfit as he could find in his wardrobe.

Of course, when life seems simple and laid out before you on a plate, it generally goes tits up. There was a woman waiting for him, as he let himself in. Sitting facing the door, jacket off, gin and tonic in her cool paws. Legs crossed, outrageously chic spectacles removed, so that her piercing blue eyes became even more striking. Not that she was especially attractive, although there was a certain vicious beauty about her mouth.

Dr Louise Farrow was the latest JLM babe to pitch up at Barney's place.

'Hi,' said Barney, closing the door behind him, not in the least surprised to see her. It pretty much only left Veron Veron to show his face and give him advice. And X, of course, although he was fairly confident X wouldn't have anything to say. 'You took your time.'

She smiled.

'Thought I'd let some of the shit get flushed away before I made an appearance.'

'Very thoughtful,' said Barney, and he went to the fridge, cracked open a beer, and slumped down into the seat opposite her.

She had left the office about twenty minutes earlier than Barney, although he had barely noticed. Of all of them, she was the one who came and went the most. But then, of all of them, she probably had the least to do. JLM hadn't actually been ill, even slightly, since he'd ascended to power.

'So?' said Barney, and left it at that. Did not feel beholden to any of these folk when they turned up.

'What have they told you?' she said. Sharp voice, a chameleon zinging its tongue out to snaffle a bug.

'Who?' said Barney, although he knew the answer.

'About why you're here,' she said.

Barney took a long drink. Immediately, no bullshit, no crap, no attraction, just an acute tongue, powerful eyes and he trusted her totally. You make instant judgements in life. Whatever he was beginning to feel for Rebecca Blackadder, he wasn't going to feel for this woman; whatever had passed through him in his feelings for Alison Blake, he wasn't going to feel for her either. But he was sure of her.

'In a coma,' he said, voice matter of fact. 'The other two have had me dead and my brain kept in a jar. In one, transplanted into someone else's body, in the other a whole new body grown genetically using my DNA.'

The ice in her glass clinked as she tipped it into her mouth; a lovely sound for a warm late afternoon of an Indian summer. Barney took some beer, wondered what was coming. *Actually you're from space. As a matter of fact, you're an insect. It's hard to believe, but we're actually in another dimension; it's all related to Membrane Theory*

'And you believed any of that crap?' she said.

'Not really,' he said, having already given them a fair degree of thought. 'The coma one had a bit of a ring of authenticity to it, but at the same time, I don't know. Didn't sound quite right.'

'Good,' said Farrow, 'because it's bullshit. Ping, you wake up one morning in a strange bed, fully functional after two and a half years in a coma. Bullshit. And the other two you can just forget. You know how many synapses they'd have to attach to do a brain transplant? Jesus, it's fictional stuff. Total bullshit.'

'Aye,' said Barney, 'that makes sense. I suppose you're about to tell me the truth.'

She lifted her eyebrow at his acerbic tone, took another swish of g&t to accompanying music, laid down the glass, lifted her briefcase, which Barney had not noticed sitting beside the chair, took out a hardback book in glossy dustcover, and tossed it over to him.

Barney held her gaze for a few seconds, and then looked at the book. *Barney Thomson: Urban Legend*. On the cover was a rather severe photograph of Barney, and the man in the picture resembled not in the least the man Barney saw when he looked in the mirror. He looked inside, checked the date of publication, the previous year, and leafed quickly through the pages, looking at some of the photographs. Closed it over, felt a strange sensation gripping his inside, the hand on his guts slowly tightening. Not a feeling he'd had when listening to any of the other contrived explanations.

'You're not Barney Thomson,' she said, coldly. 'Although, I suppose, it depends on what you say makes the man. Life is full of that kind of bullshit question.'

'Explain,' said Barney.

'Barney Thomson died two and a half years ago. Chasing a guy called Leyman Blizzard across a moorland in the Borders. Fell off a rock, broken neck, and that's all she wrote. Big news at the time, some fella researched this book, looked into all the shit you were supposed to have committed in your time. Big surprise, discovered you'd done very little of it. Hence the title of the book. Barney Thomson is this urban legend, nothing more. And an urban legend from which society is very quickly moving on.'

Barney was listening, his beer attached to his lips. Drinking slowly, paying attention. Already it had a ring of truth to it that the others didn't.

'Who am I, then?' he said, and he suddenly found he had trouble getting the words out of his mouth. Did he really want to know?

Farrow shrugged.

'No one knows,' she said. 'You're just a guy. You were found late last year wandering about the docks at Leith. In a daze, no one had any idea where you'd come from. You were suffering from amnesia. Doctors did a few tests, decided that you'd likely never recover. There was talk about giving you a new life, inventing a life for you.'

She paused, Barney could feel the scrutiny of her eyes as Farrow searched for signs of belief or doubt. He said nothing.

'A couple of months ago, JLM finished reading the book you've got there. Fascinated by it, the myths that grow up around people.

Knew about Leith docks man, decided he'd create his own Barney Thomson. You were kept in hospital, kept hypnotised for weeks, and they implanted the life of Thomson into your head. That's why it'll feel so hazy, because it's all bullshit. It's also all been taken from that book; you read it, see if you can remember anything that's not actually printed there. You'll struggle.'

Barney nodded, held the book in his hand. And this time, unlike the others, his brain didn't seem to be in fugue when hearing the story. It all sounded possible; men lost their memories, men were hypnotised, people could be brainwashed to think anything. It felt right.

'Why you?' he said suddenly.

'Everyone's got their motives,' she said. 'You either trust people or you don't. My motives are just letting you sort out the truth from the crap, nothing else. Altruistic, if you like. No reason why you should believe me and not the others, but that's up to you. I suppose I don't really give a shit whether you believe me or not, I just thought you should know what you're dealing with. Any other stories you'll have heard will just be JLM and Weirdlove messing with your mind. You're their toy. It's like they're picking the legs offa spiders.'

Barney looked at the cover of the book, felt no connection with the face of the man displayed there, then laid it down on the floor at the side of his chair.

'Rebecca?' he said.

Farrow drained her glass, felt the chill of the ice cubes falling against her top lip, laid the glass back down on the table.

'Maybe you should just work it out for yourself,' she said. 'She works for JLM.'

'We all work for JLM.'

'She goes round to the official residence every night after work, did you know that?'

'So what are you saying?' said Barney, quickly.

Farrow hesitated, as if pondering whether to give him any more. She could tell Barney no end of stories about Dr Blackadder.

'You're the new kid on the block. A bit out of sorts, a bit weirded out by it all. A nice guy, honest face, easy to trust.

You're their man on the inside. You'll get to know people, those people will trust you with confidences, you'll pass them on to Blackadder.'

'I don't know anything,' he said defensively.

'Don't you?' she asked, and he thought of Solomon and Kent. 'And even if you don't know anything yet, they're thinking long term. You'll learn plenty over the next few weeks and months. JLM's a big picture guy, you must've figured that.'

'Oh, aye.'

'So, you're just part of the picture. He gets a cool barber to cut his hair, and he also gets an agent on the inside of all kinds of places to dig up information for him. An agent operated by Blackadder. Look, what's the best way to torture someone, to get information out of them?'

Barney thought about it, shrugged his shoulders, said, 'Roast their testicles. Stick matches under their fingernails. Drill their teeth.'

'Take them to dinner and buy them a beer,' said Farrow. 'You torture someone, you create resentment and bitterness. They might tell you what you want to know, but then they're more likely to not tell you anything or to lie. If you want the truth and a lot of it, you have to make someone trust you and like you, you have to make them want to take you into their confidence. Rebecca's a psychiatrist. Not only does she know all that shit, she's good at it too. She's a pro. She's this thing, lovely manner, nice eyes, nice mouth, men want to sleep with her, God, most women want to sleep with her. She's delicious. Something about her. People tell her stuff, and she tells all of it to JLM, and so, JLM's power within the Executive grows.'

Barney tipped his head back, tipped the last of the bottle into his mouth. Swallowed, slowly lowered his head and rested the bottle on his knee. Dr Louise Farrow lifted her briefcase and rose from the chair.

'Think about what I've said. There's no reason for you to believe me over any of the others, it's entirely your shout.'

'Where do the murders come into it all?' said Barney, stopping her in her tracks as she walked past him.

She didn't look him in the eye; stared straight ahead, thought about it, finally looked down at him.

'For all the bluster and the over-the-top bullshit, Jesse Longfellow-Moses is an incredibly sinister and dubious man. The team he is supposed to work with, a team for whom he has obviously no respect whatsoever, are getting murdered one at a time. Coincidence? Might be. But if it's not, you also have to look at Rebecca, because she's the one closest to him.'

She hesitated. She was standing right beside him, close enough to reach out and touch his face. A tender gesture, but she knew it would mean nothing to him.

'Just be careful around her,' she said. She let her eyes linger upon him for another few seconds and then she walked slowly away.

The door closed behind her, Barney leant down and lifted the book. Studied the picture without opening the cover for a full five minutes, then let the book drop onto the floor. Stood up, walked to the window. A night out with Rebecca Blackadder, and the evidence, such as it was, was building up against her.

Was it time to put the flag in the window for Solomon and Kent? But then, who the Hell were Solomon and Kent? If he was prepared to believe the story that Farrow had just told him, then what did that do to the credibility of Solomon?

'Jesus,' he muttered, turning away from the bright late afternoon sun towards the fridge. 'It's Miller time.'

32

One in the head for the Trudgemeister

The Cabinet Murderer, or Kabinet Killer, as the Sun had dubbed her when they bothered mentioning it, had been pissed off about being whapped over the napper, just as she had been about to proactively announce the death of Kathy Spiderman.

She kept changing her mind. She had Nelly Stratton's toe, which she intended using to toy with the Undertaker. It would turn up in the post, or on someone's plate of chips, tests would be done, and then the world would know that Stratton wasn't hanging out at Disneyland Paris. But suddenly, with Spiderman, she'd thought how wonderful it would be to tip her over the edge, to let her be spread across the Royal Mile; but again her plans had been thwarted. She'd only been unconscious for a few minutes, but it'd been time enough for her stalker to clear up after another one of her murders; so Spiderman was only missing presumed dead/on holiday/plotting, instead of being meat paste on the Canongate.

Strangely, the Kabinet Killer wasn't all that concerned about who her stalker might be, she was just getting extremely annoyed about it. The fact that someone was doing it at all was the issue, their identity was secondary. She would find out soon enough. For the moment, she was more concerned with working her way through the cabinet until they were all dead. Or at least, until all but two of them were dead.

✂

Trudger McIntyre, the Minister for Rural Affairs and the Environment, had been assigned two police officers as protection. He called them Bill and Ben, despite the fact that it didn't seem very sensible to mock the people who'd been assigned to take the bullet for him. Still, Trudger was an artless man, who could think of no reason why anyone would want to kill him, regardless of whether or not they were one by one murdering the rest of his cabinet colleagues.

The thing is, though, that if you're not a psychotic murderer yourself, and you're not trained in the right field, you're not going to know how a psychotic murderer thinks. So, some sleight that you've pulled at someone else's expense, while seeming trivial to you, might seem like a damned good reason to commit murder to your everyday loony. Which, as just so happens to be the case, was about to befall Trudger. Or, the Trudgemeister, as he'd tried to become known in the parliament, to no avail.

So, there he was sitting in the Tolbooth, enjoying a pint of Thatcher's Dry. Very, very tasty. Washing down some alarmingly tasty pub food, involving divans and home made elements and the like. Had dispatched his bodyguards to a nearby table as he wanted to eat alone and in peace. Finished his meal, took the last slurp of Thatcher's, and stood up to go to the toilet. As he rose, he found Ben at his side.

He looked at Ben, he looked at Bill who had also risen and was standing at the ready.

'Look, Ben, I'm just going for a slash,' said Trudger. 'You feel you have to come and hold my cock?'

Ben took a step back, hurrumphed a bit, and puffed out his chest.

'Don't worry,' said Trudger, 'I'm not going to escape through the bloody window.'

He walked to the toilet, Bill and Ben returned to their seats and started talking about sports. They had already eyed up everyone who had been to the men's and knew it to be empty. They'd counted them all out, and they'd counted them all back again. However, they just hadn't thought laterally. The outer door to the ladies and gents was shared; they hadn't thought about the ladies, hadn't noticed the woman with the dark glasses and black, black wig who had disappeared in there half an hour earlier and who had yet to emerge.

Trudger stood at the urinal. Had the toilet to himself, which you might think was fortuitous for his killer, but actually it was fortuitous for the others who'd decided not to use the toilet at that time, as his killer would've taken out any sundry volunteers to the slaughter. Trudger took his pish, let's not go into too much detail here. Gave the whole thing a shake, was about to tuck everything back inside his big purple pants, when the Ride of the Valkyries descended from on high. Having suspended herself between cobwebbed pipes and the corners of the ceiling, she released her hold, transferred the knife from her teeth to her hand, and buried it to the hilt into the top of Trudger's head, as she free fell on top of him.

The two of them collapsed in a big heap on the floor, a tangle of arms and legs, Trudger's body twitching. The killer pulled the knife, raised herself up and then buried it back into his body, through his ribs, into his heart. Hesitated, contemplated cutting the heart from the chest, but wisely decided that she should not push her luck.

She stood up, did not even bother to look back at the sixth member of the cabinet to die, cracked the bones in her fingers, checked herself in the mirror, straightened the wig, and walked quickly, but unhurriedly, back out into the bar, past Pinky and Perky, or whatever it was that Trudger called them, and on out the door.

And, as she went, smiling at the thought of Trudger's body being imminently discovered by the next poor sap being summoned to the urinal of necessitation, a ghostly figure appeared as if from nowhere in the men's toilet. He stood over McIntyre's body watching the blood run onto the tiles, and heard the outer door of the toilets swing closed, as the killer walked back into the pub.

Then he locked the main door into the men's and set to work.

By the time Bill and Ben decided that Trudger was taking an inordinately long period of time, even for a man who might've decided to take a dump, he was just nowhere to be found. There was blood right enough on the toilet floor, but there was no sign of the big fella anywhere.

Bill and Ben had struck out.

33

Ooh-be-dooh

Jesse Longfellow-Moses stood in his office, taking in the scene outside, the window open slightly to let in the evening. The sun was on its way down, and although it was still warm, he could sense a change in the air. Tomorrow would be cooler, the day after would be a return to the usual drab awfulness of a regular Scottish early autumn.

Most of the team were long gone; only Veron had lingered this evening, finishing off a sequinned orange lamé creation, which he considered ideal for JLM's speech to Glasgow City Council, but even he had been away nearly an hour.

And all that time, JLM had stood alone looking out over Dynamic Earth and the rise of Arthur's Seat. Imagined himself up there, if he could ever be bothered his arse to walk up it, looking out over the city, back up the Forth towards the bridges, and in the other direction, away out to sea. Grand plans and visions fighting for attention in his head, along with the rampant insecurities which he fought so hard to quash, and which constantly told him he wasn't good enough to be where he was; that his visions were foolish, his plans for the country, folly.

At least this country suited him, no doubt; what kind of world was it where people were more interested in instant fame and celebrity, the brief lives of others to be discussed over breakfast and then tossed out with the empty packet of Cheerios? What kind of country was it whose people would vote insatiably for *Pop Idol* and *Big Brother*, but wouldn't bother their backsides voting for political representatives who could shape their lives?

Or was that another folly that the entire parliament, that parliamentary democracies everywhere, made? They didn't shape anything. It's the media who wielded real power, it's the media who shaped lives, it's the media who decided what we talked about over breakfast. *Big Brother* was real democracy, much more so than voting for one pointless politician unsuited to the job of running a council or a government or a European parliament over another. Who was more powerful, Murdoch or Bush? And even if you were to answer the latter, who would be more powerful in a years' time, or at the utmost, five years' time.

And so, to add to the insecurities, the doubts would return about what ends he could finally achieve, and the realisation that to achieve greatness, to really affect people's lives, politics was not a tenth of the career route that was the media. Perhaps politics should serve as nothing more than his entry pass into the media. He was already taking up every offer to appear on television and radio that came his way.

He was watching the path of a small single-engined plane as it headed north, when the door opened behind him. It closed again, whoever it was remained silent, waiting for JLM to turn around. He breathed deeply, his hour of solitude and reflection over.

'There's been another one,' said Parker Weirdlove.

JLM finally turned. Weirdlove was just inside the door, clasping his clipboard as ever to his chest. JLM said nothing, asked the question with his eyebrows.

'McIntyre.'

'Thought he had a couple of bodyguards?' said JLM.

'He was taking a piss. Just vanished into thin air, leaving a little blood behind.'

'Course he has. Any clues?'

Weirdlove shook his head.

'So who's left?' said JLM. 'Me, Winnie, Benderhook and Malcolm? Anyone else? I forget, I see them so little.'

'No,' said Weirdlove, 'that's it. You should be careful. Where's X?'

'Sent him off to get some dinner, told him not to come back until nine. I'm safe enough here.'

Weirdlove took a couple of paces forward.

'What makes you think that?' he said, quietly.

JLM looked at him suspiciously.

‘Why d’you say that?’ he said.

‘Stratton, McLaven, Spiderman, they all disappeared in the building,’ said Weirdlove. ‘You shouldn’t think that you’re invincible, especially when X isn’t about. We’ve no idea who’s doing this.’

‘No,’ said JLM, ‘we don’t. What d’you think the police are doing?’

‘They don’t have a clue,’ said Weirdlove. ‘Have you spoken to the Chief Constable?’

‘Yes,’ said JLM. ‘Decent enough chap, but he was more interested in my views on Disney videos, and why I wouldn’t let my children watch them. At least it’s all affirming my sentiments on the cabinet.’

‘No one gives a shit about them?’

‘Exactly.’

‘On the matter of the Disney thing,’ said Weirdlove, looking at his clipboard, ‘the Walt Disney Corporation has issued a claim against you, stating that by not allowing your children to watch their product, you’re damaging the image of their company, etc, etc...’

‘How much?’ said JLM.

Weirdlove searched through the document for the figure, raised and eyebrow when he found it.

‘£360m,’ he said.

JLM laughed.

‘Well, it’s good publicity at least, eh?’ he said.

‘Cracking,’ said Weirdlove. ‘You’ll be shagged if you lose, however.’

‘Well,’ said JLM, sitting down at his desk, and looking to sort out a final few things before The Amazing Mr X arrived and escorted him home for the night, ‘I’m not going to lose, am I? I take it, just like whoever started the story in the first place, they’ve yet to realise that I don’t actually have any children.’

‘Well,’ said Weirdlove, ‘you’d think that might be an issue, but they appear to know that already.’

‘Go on,’ said JLM wearily. Neither of them realising that they had already spent longer talking about this than they had about the disappearance of Trudger McIntyre. A man might be dead, an actual human being and everything, but it was nothing against the power and interest of a giant entertainment concern. In his own actions, he justified his thoughts of earlier. Media, media, media.

'They accept that you don't have any children,' said Weirdlove.

'This should be interesting,' said JLM.

'But they contend that when you were first asked the question you dealt with it with a wry smile.'

'They've actually used the expression 'wry smile' in their statement?' asked JLM, with, well, a wry smile.

'Yes, sir,' said Weirdlove, 'they have. They accept that you thought it amusing to be asked a question about your children when you don't have any, but they contend that by not quashing the rumour you allowed it to grow into this urban legend typa thing, so that most people now not only believe that you do have children, but that you don't let them watch Disney product.'

'And they think they've lost £360m worth of business in Scotland?' said JLM. 'Jesus, they don't do that much, do they?'

Weirdlove hesitated, but thought he might as well tell the truth and watch the smile come to the boss's face.

'They're citing you as a major player within Europe, and as a consequence, your words have had an impact across the continent.'

JLM did indeed smile. A major player in Europe? Cool. These guys were American, most of them probably thought that Scotland was a town in England. Yet, they were aware enough to think that he, Jesse Longfellow-Moses, was a major player in Europe. Jesus. How unbelievably smooth was that? Would Blair or Chirac or Schröder be sued for that much? Probably not.

'Champion,' said JLM. 'D'you think I should stop my children eating at McDonald's and Burger King?'

'Definitely,' said Weirdlove, smiling.

34

A nice spot of dinner, put your foot in it, go home alone

Barney had had a nice bit of beef for his dinner. Actually it'd been called a *monastery of prime Szechwan chateaubriand, enveloped in a parfait of blackcurrant roulade, with a fondant of kohlrabi and a splodge of Somalian potatoes*, and at first it had kind of reminded him of *The Thing* with Kurt Russell, but he preferred to think of it as a nice bit of beef. Rebecca Blackadder had had fish and chips. Together they'd shared a stunning bottle of Norwegian claret; firm bodied and well-liposuctioned, enormously lengthed, capaciously flavoured and well fruity, with overtones of jammy dodgers and Jock Stein.

They were onto dessert, although a bit behind the curve. It was one of those dining experiences in someone's front room; limited menu, stunning food, place small enough that you could hear every clink of every glass, every throwaway comment, every slurp of coffee, from every table. The other diners had already munched their way through a selection of after dinner mints. Due to Blackadder's late arrival at Barney's room at the beginning of the evening, they were still champing their way through a plethora of mild cheeses on sesame biscuits.

They had talked of many things; flippant conversation about the world and music and television, and the more they talked and followed different paths of conversation, the more Barney remembered, the more aspects of life he discovered lurking in his memory. And all the time, as he became more and more sucked in by Blackadder's deliciously soft voice, he had the words of Louise Farrow guzzling at the back of his mind. The voice, the atmosphere, the wine, the food, the casual conversation, occasionally straying off into real meaning, it was all part of the *torture*.

As dessert crunched to a conclusion and the coffee arrived, Barney became aware that they were holding hands across the table. Wasn't sure how they'd got there.

'I just loved what you did with his hair today,' she said, after a lull in the conversation, during which they had gazed at the candle, flirted with each other's eyes. 'He looked pretty stupid.'

Barney smiled.

'Yeah,' he said. 'Didn't really intend that, but he was jumping up and down in his seat like a one year-old. Swiped off a big bit of hair I didn't mean to.'

'And you had to even it up?'

'Exactly,' said Barney. 'I think he looks all right. The no hair/short hair brigade'll vote for him. I think I managed to persuade him of that.'

Blackadder shook her head, smiled at the thought of the man. All part of the plan, imagined the Farrow-brainwashed Barney, but he was switched on enough to know not to trust anyone. Treat everyone with suspicion until you are absolutely dyed-in-the-bollocks certain of them, that was his motto.

'He's just bizarre,' she said, and it was at least the fifth time in the evening that she'd started talking about him. But then, wasn't it natural? Doesn't everyone with an absurd superior, spend their life bitching about him to their colleagues and anyone else they can get their hands on. 'Full of these great visions, but doesn't realise that the people don't give a shit about politicians anymore. None of them. Look, the country doesn't even care that the cabinet are all dead.'

'Aye,' said Barney.

'It's like when he decided he wanted *Highland Cathedral* to be the national anthem.'

Barney shook his head.

'Don't know it,' he said.

'It's this glorious tune, beautiful words, it's what Scotland's been looking for. If hearing *Flower of Scotland* sung by a large crowd makes the hairs stand on the back of your neck, this'll make you dissolve into a pile of mush. It's gorgeous. Give it time, let people get to know it properly, make it a thing, it'd be the people's choice. But Jesse leaps in, tells everyone that it's his decision, so of course they say, you're a politician, you can stick it up your arse. The press rise up in arms, there's uproar for a coupla weeks, then Jesse has to back down. Bloody stupid. Now, if the Sun or the Record had decided that *Highland Cathedral* was going to be the national anthem, bing! you've got it. Groundswell of opinion, people trust what their papers tell them, and it's shootie-in. But Jesse's only a politician, that's what he doesn't realise. He has no say.'

Barney nodded in agreement. That was certainly the truth. Just a wee coincidence that JLM was coming to the same conclusion at approximately the same time.

'What d'you think of Dr Farrow,' Barney suddenly found himself asking, to fill a moment's silence. Closed his eyes briefly as the words left his mouth, as he'd been telling himself all evening not to mention it. Wanted to believe in Blackadder, wanted to believe Farrow was the fraud. But while his heart spoke loudly, his head nagged with greater insistence that Blackadder was the pretender.

She looked at him closely, watched the brief closing of the eyes. Hand was retracted under the cover of putting sugar into coffee.

'What d'you mean?' she said. 'Has she been to see you?'

Be cool, Barn, he thought. Be cool.

'You've all been to see me,' he said casually. 'Except Veron of course. Don't know what's the matter with him.'

'What was Louise saying?' asked Blackadder, bit of an edge to the voice, thought Barney, or was he just looking for there to be an edge to the voice? Could go round in circles all evening. Maybe he should just be honest with her. That's what friends do.

'Usual stuff, you know. You've all taken it in turns to turn up on my doorstep and tell me my, what'd you call it, provenance. Like I was some sort of antique. My favourite was Weirdlove telling me I was a vampire. One of his family.'

'No, seriously,' said Blackadder, not letting him away with cheap jokes, 'what did Lou say? I know we look like a bit of a team 'n all, but then it also means I know her better than most. You've got to watch her. She's not one to trust. What did she say?'

Well, he thought, doesn't do any harm to give her a bit of the truth, doesn't mean I have to mention the part about her and JLM being bosom buds.

The waitress arrived at the table, sensed the change in atmosphere, as surely as JLM had sensed the change in the weather, so did not make any light remarks, as she had been doing throughout the evening. Cleared away the cheese board, piled plate on plate, asked if they wanted more coffee, which was a bit daft seeing as neither of them had touched what they already had, and made a swift exit. *Having a fight at no.3*, she said, when she returned to the kitchen.

'She said that I wasn't Barney Thomson. Not my body, not my brain.'

'Who are you then?' asked Blackadder suspiciously.

'Just some unknown guy with amnesia. I've been brainwashed to think I'm Barney Thomson, so I do. I might as well be him, if no one else is.'

Blackadder toyed with the salt cellar. Tapped a finger on top of it.

'If that's the case,' she said, and her words drifted off. Had carelessly begun the sentence without knowing where it was going. Whether or not it was true, and how was Barney supposed to know, it had a ring of truth. The story she'd told him had been given to her by Parker Weirdlove. How far would she trust *him*?

'What?' said Barney, but she had no reply. She toyed with her spoon, finally lifted her coffee now that it was cool enough to drink without slurping.

He shrugged it off, and eventually the conversation moved on from Dr Louise Farrow, but the tide had turned, the feel of the evening had changed, with words barely spoken. And so, at the end of the night, each was vaguely suspicious of the other, and they parted with a kiss on the cheek and, at least on Barney's part, no little regret.

✂

Late in the evening, the cooling north wind having risen, Winona Wanderlip arrived at the town centre apartment of Parker Weirdlove. He greeted her on his doorstep without enthusiasm, ushered her in quickly, stood in the hallway in his t-shirt and boxer short pyjamas that he'd been wearing in bed. She had stepped out in a white blouse and thin skirt, unprepared for the cooler weather. Goose bumps on her arms, flush around the cheeks, fabulously erect nipples.

'You know you shouldn't come here,' said Weirdlove, quoting a line from two out of every three 9pm movies on Channel 5.

'Did you hear about Trudger?' she said, and Weirdlove could feel the shiver in the voice. Not being caused solely by the cold outside. Knew she was afraid.

'Where are your bodyguards?' he said.

'Gave them the slip,' she said, and she shrugged her shoulders at the look he gave her. 'I couldn't let them know I was coming here.'

'Well, you shouldn't have come here,' he said, sternly. 'Look at you, Winnie, you're scared.'

'I'm not bloody scared!' she cried. 'But there's only me, Benderhook and Malcolm left from the original cabinet.'

'Duh huh!' said Weirdlove, smacking the palm of his hand off his forehead, 'well why are you out without your bodyguards then?'

'I needed to talk to you,' she said. 'And I can take care of myself,' she protested.

'That'll be why you're terrified, then,' he said.

'Stop saying that! I'm not terrified, just because I'm a woman.'

'Look at you! You're shivering, you've got goose bumps all over your body, and your nipples are like big lumps of play-doh.'

She swallowed, looked down at her chest, shook her head in embarrassment, turned, walked a few further feet down the hall, turned back to face him.

'Christ!' she said, exasperated, 'all right, I'm scared. I'm fucking terrified! Are you happy, Parker? Six of my colleagues are gone, probably murdered, there are only three of us left, four including Jesse, and I could be next. They're going for us one by one, and the police know dick! We're sitting ducks. So what if I shook off the bodyguards, did they do Trudger any bloody good?'

'Only 'cause he let them out his sight,' said Weirdlove coolly.

'I'm not letting someone watch me wipe my arse, Parker!' she yelled. 'We're supposed to be living in a civilised society. Look, I'm here now, whether you like it or not. Are you going to offer me a drink?'

Weirdlove breathed deeply, considering his position. It wasn't entirely unheard of for JLM to show up at his place, although it was rare and he would be unlikely to instigate a search of the premises. Even so, it would be unfortunate if Wanderlip were to be discovered at his flat under these, or any other, circumstances.

'Personally, Winnie,' he said, a little more casually than he was aiming for, 'I don't think you've anything to worry about. Not at this stage.'

'What does that mean?'

'I just,' he began, 'look, I think you'll be fine. Whoever this is, maybe they're not aiming at the cabinet, you never know.'

'You're kidding me, right?' she said. 'You're saying that someone is just haphazardly murdering people in Edinburgh, and bugger me, but if it isn't just the case that, entirely at random, the victims have all be part of the cabinet. Fuck me, who would've thought? Odds have to got to be, say, at least fifty to one. Maybe even double that!'

'Winnie,' he said, 'calm down.'

And, to her surprise, he opened the door again.

'I'd give you a coat,' he said, 'but if JLM saw you he might recognise it as mine.'

The objections to the stupidity of that came to the tip of her tongue, but the fact that he was throwing her out was the far, far greater slight.

'Don't do this, Parker,' she said.

'I'll speak to you, tomorrow,' he said coldly. 'If we get the chance, although we're going to be pretty busy.' Last day with Vogts and Eaglehawk. Maybe it was time to cultivate friends to shore up his position. But then, only the right kind of friends. 'Tomorrow,' he repeated firmly, when she didn't move.

Wanderlip hesitated, felt the old familiar rage well up inside her. Count to a million, don't completely cut yourself off from him, she thought, even though he deserves it. You never know, you never know.

And so, stabbing her fingernails into the palms of her hands, she walked quickly past him and on down the stairs which led to the front door.

Parker Weirdlove watched her for a few seconds, but closed the door before seeing her vicious glance over the shoulder. He held his hand against the door for a while, as if considering his position, and then walked slowly back down the hall and into the bedroom.

'Well,' said the man who was sitting up in his bed, reading House & Garden. 'Nipples like big lumps of play-doh, eh? I wish I'd seen that.'

Weirdlove scowled, shook his head, pulled back the sheets and climbed into bed.

Once more unto the breach, dear friends, once more; or close the wall up with our English dead!

35

In the wee small hours of the morning...

Minnie Longfellow-Moses returned from The Hague curiously late. Jesse was sleeping soundly, the sleep of the self-righteous, empty cup of diet hot chocolate on his bedside table, along with some musings that he was jotting down, intent on formulating them into a book of some description for publication in the next year or so. It would be his *Mein Kampf*, his *Das Kapital*, the broad statement that laid down the founding principles of Mosesism. She lifted his notebook, cast an uncritical eye over the misty ramblings on the future of the welfare state, and how the best way to promote a good health service is to have a healthier population, and the best way to ensure that people are healthier is to hit them in their pockets if they're not. *You'll see*, he'd jotted down, *how quickly people cut down the fags and fish suppers, start jogging to work and cramming in the apples and pears, as soon as you make them have to pay for their trips to hospital.* It would be a guiding principle. The state would help those who helped themselves. And it was a sure-fire way to get away from the modern culture of lack of self-responsibility. Everyone would be in charge of their own destiny.

The perfect society, that was the conclusion he'd reached. And he'd written those words at the top of the page as a good title for the work. It won't be a long book, his final thought had been as he'd drifted off to sleep, but it's not about length, it's about history.

Minnie Longfellow-Moses placed the notebook back on JLM's bedside table, couldn't even summon the interest to smile wryly.

‘That’ll get you far, Jesse,’ she said softly, and she turned and walked into the bathroom.

Winona Wanderlip took a long time to get off to sleep, a thousand political intrigues and connivances scrambling about, part of a giant muddle, in her head. The cabinet murders, the deaths of so many ineffectual people, it was so utterly pointless. It had to be someone close to them, someone with a vested interest in the cabinet’s handling of the country. Perhaps it was that old spy thing; where they’d cause a plane crash to cover up the fact that they were assassinating one person. It might be the same here; they were really only after one member of the cabinet, but they were killing them all to make it look like a more general vendetta.

That, and so many other conspiracies, feasted on her imagination as she lay listening to the sound of traffic on the South Bridge. What use had the police been? They had interviewed everyone in the parliament building about ten times, and they hadn’t a clue. They must’ve spoken to someone who knew what was going on, or someone who was responsible, and they’d been unable to notice. And what use were the two officers, one sitting outside her bedroom door, the other in the sitting room? What were they going to do when a killer silently broke in through her window in the middle of the night and struck her down?

The police were no use, the case of Trudger had shown that the bodyguards were no use. It was going to take a spark of inspiration to solve the mystery, and by Scooby Doo, if she wasn’t just the woman to do it. And if, in the course of her investigations, she was to discover that Jesse Longfellow-Moses was in any way implicated in proceedings, then it might turn out nicely after all.

What to do about Parker Weirdlove, and what had become of their special relationship, was another question which vexed her greatly. So much so, that she had turned the picture of him which sat beside her bed, face down on the table. Tonight she did not want him watching over her while she slept.

✂

As for JLM's team:

Parker Weirdlove slept very easily. No trouble visiting the old land of nod, when you have justice and honesty as your passport. All it takes is a little self-belief.

Veron Veron slept equally well.

The Reverend Blake began the long night alone, but did not continue as such all the way through.

Dr Louise Farrow sat up late into the evening, surfing, checking everything from FBI files to a variety of medical histories, until there came a knocking at her door.

Dr Rebecca Blackadder got back to her room, sent a few e-mails, wrote a few notes, considered a few things. Went back out again after midnight, had a couple of drinks, and was not unaccompanied when she returned to her room at a little after two.

The Amazing Mr X stayed awake all night, worrying over whether he should have taken the night off, leaving the job of guarding JLM to the two untried police officers. The Amazing Mr X never slept.

Barney Thomson, be he either composed of the old Barney's brain, body or memories, or a combination thereof, lay awake for several hours, bedroom curtains open, staring at the ceiling. Neither restless nor unhappy, brain a gentle buzz, thinking about Blackadder, wondering if there was a real connection between them, and wondering if he had just done the right thing. For on returning to his room, he had bitten the bullet and placed the flag in the window for Solomon and Kent. Solomon had arrived an hour and a half later, minus his Robin, had listened to Barney's reservations about Dr Blackadder, had cracked a few gags, and had gone on his way. Barney had thought to raise the matter of Solomon's tale of his past, but had decided to leave it for another day, and a clearer head.

And Father Michael had a very interesting evening, which involved sex, murder and rock 'n roll, which would've gone down very badly with his superiors had they known about it. The Catholic Church hates rock 'n roll.

James Eaglehawk and Conrad Vogts had another long evening, which stretched into the wee small hours of the morning. A mixture of business and pleasure; on the one hand plotting Eaglehawk's ascension to power in the Scottish Executive, with German and European backing, on the other, reminiscing about long nights in the Bavarian Alps, filled with beer, women and tall tales of beer and women.

James Eaglehawk and Conrad Vogts were becoming firm friends. Jim and Bertie, as they now knew each other.

Poor old Jim Eaglehawk. A simple man who, despite being very careful, despite spending years in politics watching his back and avoiding uncertain alliances, was blinded by his own duplicity into not seeing the duplicity of others. And so, he did not see Conrad Vogts coming, not in the least.

Which does not leave many people to be considered.

The vast population of Edinburgh slept soundly, or not, in their usual manner, quite unconcerned about the bloodletting that was taking place in the Executive. Earlier that evening there had been rival radio phone-in shows; Radio Scotland against Radio Forth. Radio Scotland had been discussing the massacre of the cabinet; Radio Forth had been discussing whether there should be strip bars in the centre of Edinburgh. Radio Scotland had fifteen calls, twelve of which had asked them to talk about something more interesting. Radio Forth had three hundred and twenty-seven calls.

So, that just leaves the last two members of the cabinet, who have more or less been absent from the narrative up until now. Malcom Malcolm III of the Clan Malcolm, Minister for Health, and Fforbes Benderhook, Deputy First Minister. You might be thinking, well they're shadowy figures, they might well have something to do with the general slaughter of all their compadres. Or you might be thinking that they're nothing more than the red uniformed guys who used to beam down to the alien planet with the big spunkmeister himself, Cpt James T.

Well, as the night slowly lingered its way around to an early morning, the sun rising behind banks of grey cloud, and the Indian summer came crashing to its knees, both Benderhook and Malcolm were dead. One with a bullet in the brain, much in the same manner as the late Honeyfoot; the other, the unfortunate Malcolm, his head rather brutally panned to a pulp with a beautiful bedside lamp he'd picked up in a Christmas market in the southern Belgian town of Dinant.

They had both been guarded by the requisite two policemen, men who were obviously ineffectual in either case. Benderhook's guards were completely oblivious to their charge's murder, or disappearance, as it appeared, until he didn't materialise for breakfast the following morning. Malcolm's guards, much to his murderer's discomfort and guilt, had had to be surgically removed before the head pulping sesh had begun.

In the case of Benderhook, his killer had dispatched the Deputy First Minister with precision and panache, and had then turned and legged it for Malcolm's house. That the body of Benderhook would then be removed, so that it looked like the man might've just nipped out for a McDonald's breakfast, would be of no surprise to her.

However, with the bloody bludgeoning to death of Malcolm, and the completion of her night's work – indeed the completion of her task as a whole – the killer had decided that perhaps it was time to discover the identity of The Undertaker. And so, she'd faked her departure from the scene, on the assumption that she was being watched, and then had crept back to hide in the shrubbery and await The Undertaker's arrival. And her marginal sneakiness would be rewarded, for at last, after eight Cabinet murders, the identity of the person cleaning up after her heinous crimes, would finally be revealed to her; and it would make no sense whatsoever…

✂

The slaughter of the innocents of the Scottish Executive Cabinet had come to a conclusion. Eight of the originals down, only Winona Wanderlip and Jesse Longfellow-Moses remained. And although it was of virtually no interest whatsoever to the people of Scotland, Wanderlip would at least feature in one newspaper story the following day:

> **WINNIE IN NIPPLEGATE SHOCKER**
>
> Phworr! As Labour stunna, Winnie Wanderlip, stepped out into the cold last night, on her way to a select Edinburgh nightspot, passers-by drooled at her breasts, as her corking nipples walked down the road at least four inches in front of the rest of her. 'They were like pine cones,' gasped stunned pedestrian, Wullie McGinest, 18.
>
> Several people called the emergency services, as chaos threatened to engulf the city centre.
>
> 'We've just never seen nipples like them,' claimed shopkeeper, Alvin McAndrew, 36. 'Traffic ground to a halt, and I saw several people almost killed by drivers distracted by her enormous protrusions.'
>
> Wanton Winnie was last night unavailable for comment, but a close friend told us, 'Winnie is really proud of her nipples, and loves to show them off. She's a big tart really.'
>
> Last month, Wanderlip issued a statement denying having had collagen injections in her nipples, and several other parts of her body. She is 38.

Lovely stuff.

36

One Vision

Barney watched the Scottish news the following morning. They actually led with the murders of Malcolm and Benderhook, although they treated it more as a comic cuts type of thing, the presenter ending the report with the words *'who'd be a cabinet minister, eh?'* and a wry smile. Barney wondered if Solomon had immediately put a tail on Blackadder, and whether she would now be exonerated. Or would he have moved at the pace that the rest of the police force had moved? The Chief Constable had been on that morning, and had excused his Force's poor performance in the investigation up to that point with the statement; 'Obviously we're putting all available manpower into the investigation. However, with the visits of Michael Douglas and Catherine Zeta-Jones to play golf in recent days, and the award of an honorary doctorate in 'Cool' to Sir Sean Connery at Heriot Watt University, we have had to prioritise. Once the Daniel O'Donnell and S Club 7 concerts are over, we'll be able to place more manpower onto the protection of what is left of the Executive, but I think at this stage that most people will understand that it would be extremely bad for the city of Edinburgh, and Scotland as a whole, if anything was to happen to a celebrity.'

Can't argue with that, Barney had thought, as he'd tucked into his bacon, eggs, black pudding and sausage. (His honourable intention of moving onto healthier breakfasts after a few days, had dropped by the wayside, to accompany his vague feeling that he really not ought to be here at all.)

The day ahead read like most other. It was Thursday, so JLM should have been in parliament for questions, but with that having been brought forward a day, he was taking the opportunity to get back out amongst his people, which he loathed doing, but felt was probably necessary. He would get his face in newspapers and on television, and he could spread the word of his grand vision, not only for the country, but for the entire world. So, given that he was visiting a shopping centre in Perth, (where he would stand on a box and preach), Stirling Castle, and a cheeky wee tea shop in Drymen, he was going to have to have good hair. Barney was on call, due for his first session in a little under twenty minutes.

He was just watching a football report on Rangers' new signing – a West African who, it had transpired, had never played football in his life, which made it embarrassing that Rangers had just given him a £2m signing on fee. 'The main thing,' claimed McLeish, 'is that he's not Scottish' – when there was a small scraping sound from behind, he swivelled round, and saw a small piece of paper on the floor, having just been pushed under the door.

He rose, dashed to the door, swung it open, leaving the paper on the floor, and looked along the corridor for the unexpected mailman. Whoever it was, however, had gone, and Barney was of no mind to go chasing after them.

He lifted the paper, closed the door. Returned to his table, took a slurp of tea and another piece of toast, then unfolded the message. It was typed on a piece of A5 stationery from JLM's office, as follows:

The end to this is in sight. Come to conference
room 12, Assembly Building, at eight o'clock
this evening. Tell no one.

Not surprisingly it was unsigned. That would've given the game away a bit.

The end to this is in sight. Barney bit into another contemplative piece of toast and let the paper fold itself back over. The end to the murders he presumed, but then, it was nothing to do with him. He'd been partially drawn into it because of the interference of Solomon and Kent, but he still didn't feel part of it. Why drag him off to a conference room? Unless, of course, he was to be the next victim.

He dabbed his lips with a napkin, eyed the last piece of toast like a velociraptor eyeing up Sam Neill, then pounced on it like an unfettered tyrannosaur swooping on the baby lamb that was a lumbering diplodocus, armed with butter and strawberry jam.

✂

There was a bit of an uncomfortable atmosphere in the room. Winona Wanderlip had come to see JLM, hoping to get him on his own, but they were together in his inner office with Parker Weirdlove, and the inevitable Amazing Mr X.

'There are only two of us left,' said Wanderlip, stating the blindingly obvious.

JLM, however, displayed the fact that he had been thinking about his grand vision for the world, by answering, 'Two of whom?'

'The cabinet!' she barked, turning round from the window, where she had been looking out, chewing endlessly on what was left of the nail on her left-hand ring finger.

JLM and Weirdlove exchanged a glance between boys, of the 'here goes the premenstrual woman again.'

'There's Eaglehawk and McPherson,' he said. 'And we'll sort out the other appointments over the weekend, won't we Parker? Either promote the deputies, or find someone else if the deputy is only window dressing, like Patsy whatshername. Don't worry, Winnie, I won't land it all on your plate.'

'Exactly, sir,' said Weirdlove.

'Jesus,' said Wanderlip, 'is it just of no concern to you that all these good people are gone, probably murdered? The Executive is in complete disarray. Christ, there's this monumental shambles.'

'Winnie, Winnie, Winnie,' said JLM, and she could've swung for him, 'there's only a shambles in government when people perceive there to be a shambles. Let's face it, there are only two ministers in the Executive that anybody in the public could pick out of a line-up. You and me. We're both still here, aren't we? I mean, really, politicians don't actually do any work, do they? It's the Civil Service that does the work. How many Civil Servants have been killed, Parker?'

'None,' said Weirdlove, as they moved easily into their Sir Humphrey routine. Wanderlip seethed.

'So has the work of the Executive been affected at all?' said JLM, smoothly.

'Not at all, sir,' said Weirdlove. 'Of course, that might be because the Executive doesn't actually do anything.'

'Whatever,' said JLM, engaging Wanderlip in the eye, and being so condescending he was kicking condescension on the arse, 'all politicians are here for are to make decisions and appear on television. The fact is, and I think I can say this because we're among friends here, none of that lot ever got to make any decisions because I wouldn't let them, and any time the networks want someone to appear on the tv, it's either me or you and your premenstrual routine.'

'Jesus,' she muttered.

JLM let the smirk drift casually from his face, let the look of superiority slide from Weirdlove's oozy visage, which took a little longer, let the near explosion of rage from Wanderlip die down.

'There's about to be a new dawn in Scotland, Winnie,' he said, and Weirdlove raised an eye at him.

'What d'you mean?' she asked.

'You can either be with us, or bow out of government, it'll be up to you,' said JLM.

'What are you talking about?' she asked with greater insistence. 'A new dawn?'

JLM did something fiddley with his hand, as if he was Gandalf or something.

'All things will be revealed in good time,' he said mystically. 'I do think, however, that the slaughter is over.'

The words fell softly from his lips. Wanderlip felt the hairs rise suddenly on the back of her neck and press against the collar of her maroon blouse. She glanced at The Amazing Mr X, but the big fella was staring out the window, away off in one of his dream worlds. She looked at Weirdlove, and the look he returned was as impenetrable as ever; and for some reason, the phrase 'the eyes of a killer' popped into her head. She shivered, turned back to JLM, who was half-smiling at her in that vacuous way of his.

She played his words back in her head. Were they just the empty hopes of a politician, hollow words meant to put her at ease. Or was there something more sinister? Was Longfellow-Moses armed with some prior knowledge? That was what she had felt, but even then, ten, fifteen seconds later, the moment was gone and the statement seemed innocent once more.

'You know something?' she asked.

JLM laughed that big, booming laugh of his. Of course, thought Wanderlip, nothing to make you laugh like all your political colleagues getting murdered.

'I'm a political animal!' he said, the voice loud on the tail of the laugh. 'You have to admit, Winnie, I'm this thing. I'm Jesse Longfellow-Moses. I'm not just the First Minister of the Scottish Executive, I'm a major player on the European stage. Schröder, Berlusconi, Blair, they've begun to look to me for wisdom and leadership.'

JLM had looked away from Wanderlip and was staring at some indistinct point on the ceiling as he spoke, and God knows what he was seeing there. Wanderlip and Weirdlove exchanged a look, but JLM's ADC remained inscrutable.

'Jesus,' he continued, 'I even had Lord bloody Robertson on the phone to me yesterday.' It had actually been Lord Roberston's private secretary, telling JLM that George was getting his hair done for the foreseeable future. 'Next week I'm off to Italy and Switzerland, and I'll be popping into Berlin on the way back. That's the position we're at, Winnie. I can just pop in to see these people. I'm a player, Winnie, a player. I'm at the top table, no question. Even Bush wants to meet me, but I'm putting him off, you know. No rush, eh? And the Pope, he's another one, but I'll tread lightly there, you know. Don't want to piss off one half of Glasgow at this stage. Leave it a while. I said to the lad, Pope, 'sorry mate, but you'll just have to wait.''

He was meandering spectacularly, as he was prone to do when he became carried away with his own august majesty. He suddenly snapped out of it, as he came down from his cloud. Looked at Winnie, and she could see that the flicker of madness was still there.

'What was I saying?' he said.

'You lost me,' she said, caustically.

'Yes, yes, champion,' he said. 'I'm a political animal, I know things, feel them in my gut. It's why I'm here and why you're just the Minister for Enterprise. Christ, Winnie, people don't even know what you mean by that. Anyway, I know you're not of my calibre, but I hope I can make you understand. I'm a political predator. I feel things, I know what's happening, even if I don't know all the facts. Do I know who's been off killing the cabinet? No, absolutely not,' he said, and she noticed the slight unconscious movement of the eyes as he said it, 'but do I genuinely believe deep down in my bollocks that these killings are over, yes I do. You have my word,' he added with finality and a certain triumph, his eyes once more firmly engaging hers.

Wanderlip studied his face for a few seconds, as he stared at her intently. She looked at Weirdlove, she nodded her head. The hairs on the back of her neck had long since calmed down, during JLM's coronation speech, but the feeling of disquiet was still there, the room still stank of the atmosphere of unease which had pervaded since his seemingly glib statement about knowing that it was all over.

Head still nodding, like a plastic dog in the back of a car, lips pursed, she walked slowly past them, opened the door and passed through into the outer office, closing the door behind her.

She let out a great sigh, then engaged the eyes of the single member of JLM's team who happened to be sitting in the office at that point.

'You the barber?' she asked.

Barney Thomson nodded.

'Suppose so,' he said, 'but if you wanted to tell me different, I'd probably be prepared to believe you.'

She closed her eyes briefly at another man speaking in riddles, then walked slowly from the office, not looking at the mural as she went.

37

Thrown to the sharks

'What about Wanderlip?'

James Eaglehawk looked up at the shark which was swimming overhead. He shivered. How thick was this glass, he wondered? How many million gallons of water were behind it? The pressures must be enormous. Day after day, week after week, months drifting into years. How often did they check these things? His mind rambled on. These places were always making cutbacks, weren't they? There's not an institution on the planet not making cutbacks. Did they put the proper manpower in place to check for cracks in the infrastructure of the tank? A systematic regime of inspections? Wasn't it inevitable that at some stage the glass would crack, the tunnel underneath the tank would fill up with water, and the people who happened to be under the aquarium at the time would either be drowned, or be eaten by the bloody great sharks that were swimming overhead. He could tell they were looking at him; one shark in particular. It cast a brazen glance at him every time it passed by. It was circling, just waiting for the first fissure to appear in the infrastructure of the glass, the first chink in the armour. Then, fucking voom! it'd be down like a shot, eating Eaglehawk for breakfast.

He shivered again, could almost hear the sound of his bones crunching as the shark bit massively into his midriff, could imagine the shark enjoying the *meringue of braised guinea fowl* which he'd eaten the previous night, could see the look in the shark's eye as it champed his testicles. Human testicles were probably a delicacy for these things.

'What you having today, Sharky?' one would say to another. Eaglehawk thought of sharks as speaking with Australian accents.

'Me, mate? I got lucky, cobber, I've got some human 'nads for my supper.'

'Fabulous, mate. You got any to spare?'

'Come on, mate, there's only two of them and they're pretty fuckin' tiny.'

'What?' he said, dragging his eyes away from the shark who was going to kill him, back to Conrad Vogts.

Vogts smiled.

'You're imagining the shark eating your testicles?' he said.

No one, and especially not a politician, likes to know that someone can read their innermost fears. Even the slightest hint that the façade has been breached, and you're in trouble. Good thing, then, that Vogts was an ally…

'No, no,' Eaglehawk said, completely turning his back on the shark, although he could still feel its eyes burrowing into him. 'I was just imagining swimming with them in the Caribbean or somewhere. That must be so cool.'

'Indeed,' said Vogts, seeing through the lie. And Eaglehawk knew he could see the lie, just as Vogts knew that Eaglehawk knew. Eaglehawk didn't know, however, that Vogts knew that he knew, so we can bring this thing to an end.

'What about Wanderlip?' Vogts repeated. 'Where do you see her fitting into all of this?'

A figure of authority approached them, in an all-in-one. Short, bobbed blonde hair, fairly attractive.

'Gentlemen,' she said, 'could you step back onto the conveyor, please?'

Eaglehawk shot her a glance, nearly gave her a 'do you know who I am' speech. Or, more to the point, 'do you know who I'm about to be?'

'Certainly, certainly,' said Vogts, 'we only got off so that you would come and speak to us. You are very beautiful.'

'I can tell you're not Scottish,' she said, as the two men followed her instruction.

'I'm from Koblenz,' said Vogts, as he started to move away from her. 'A beautiful city on the Rhein. You must come and see it one day. We could take a cruise together. Drink wine by moonlight, watch the clouds through castle parapets, make love all night beneath the stars.'

She ostentatiously glanced down at his lunchbox and smiled.

'All night, eh? What drugs are you taking?'

'Just the opiate of your beauty,' said Vogts with a smile.

'Aye, I'm never done travelling to continental Europe,' she said, turning away as the conveyor belt began to take Vogts and Eaglehawk around a corner. But she had a wee smile on her face, no question. And the young lad coming along the belt who had heard the exchange, saw her smile and thought that he might have a go himself, if she was that easy.

'Hey, Hen,' he said, as he passed her by, and she turned to him, still smiling. 'I'm fi' Glasgow. Fancy coming doon the Clyde wi' me for a shag?'

The smile died on her face, just as the retort died on her lips when she saw the two children with their parents coming behind the lad who'd had a go. She turned away, the delight of the flirtatious moment gone, and went about her business.

Vogts turned back to Eaglehawk, still smiling. Eaglehawk had ignored the exchange, and was keeping a close eye on the shark, which he was sure was following him now that he was on the move. Was there some way the shark could get out of the tank? Maybe there wasn't a lid on it, because they assumed that the sharks couldn't climb over the sides. This bastard could, though.

'Talking of beautiful women,' said Vogts, 'what about Wanderlip?'

Eaglehawk attempted to return to the present. Shook off the presence of the shark, tried to think about Winona Wanderlip.

'She'll have to go,' said Eaglehawk, in a low voice, casting glances around at the other visitors. There was no one within a few yards, however, and in any case everyone else was there to look at the fish, rather than for reasons of political intrigue. Vogts was also there to look at the fish, which was why he'd dragged Eaglehawk out to North Queensferry.

'Of all the cabinet ministers that could have been murdered, Melanie aside,' continued Eaglehawk, 'she's the one we needed taken out first. This psychopath is doing us a favour, no question, but we could’ve done with the loony bastard getting rid of Winnie first of all.’

‘Unless,’ said Vogts, and his tone made Eaglehawk forget the sharks just for a few seconds, ‘she is behind it all.’

‘Why?’ said Eaglehawk, even though he was not at all disposed to support her in any way. ‘The only person between her and the position of First Minister is Jesse. Why get rid of people who might’ve supported her?’

Vogts raised his eyebrows.

‘Go figure, as our American friends might say,’ he said. ‘Women are strange creatures, and let us not pretend to ever know their thoughts. Politics is the social equivalent of a woman; no one ever knows what their political opponent, or even their political ally, is thinking. And so, a woman in politics, my God, is the most explosive of combinations. If ever there was an eruption waiting to happen, it is such a woman, and your colleague, Winnie, most certainly fits the bill.’

Eaglehawk nodded.

‘Too right,’ he said.

‘So,’ said Vogts, ‘what are you going to do with her?’

Eaglehawk turned away from Vogts. Immediately found himself staring at the shark. Shuddered big, turned back to Vogts, the fear still crawling over his body.

‘Throw her to the bloody sharks,’ said Eaglehawk, and he held Vogts’s gaze for a second, then dropped his eyes. ‘Let’s get out of here,’ he said, ‘this place gives me the creeps.’

And off he charged, in search of the great outdoors.

38

Doubt that the stars are fire

The First Minister and his entourage were in a barber's emporium in the shopping mall in Perth. JLM had done the rounds, given his soapbox speech to an enthusiastic crowd of Japanese and American tourists, who'd thought he was an actor doing a Winston Churchill impersonation for their benefit, gladhanded a few bemused passers-by, who'd thought that maybe he was someone off *River City* or *Chewin' The Fat*, and finally had hit upon the idea of visiting a barber's shop, commandeering one of the chairs and getting Barney to publicly perform on his hair.

Barney had no problem with this, except for the obvious point, that there was very, very little he could actually do to JLM's hair.

There were four chairs set up, a busy little establishment, three barbers working away as JLM held court, the junior barber turfed aside to sit and read the paper while Barney applied a blunt razor to the back of JLM's scalp.

'You can't underestimate the importance of a quality men's hairstylist,' said JLM, approximately his fifteenth platitude since arriving in the shop.

As with the fourteen previous examples of banality, the other three barbers completely ignored him. There was the usual strained atmosphere that pervades any establishment during the visit of an unwanted dignitary. The commonplace conversational topics, from St Johnstone's footballing travails, to whether Rangers and Celtic should head off and join the English Premiership or a more appropriate league like the Small-Minded Sectarian Self-Possessed Filled With Mediocre Foreign Talent And Shite At Football Conference, and from the Fatty Arbuckle theory on why it takes four men to insert a light bulb up someone's arse, to lengthy discussions on naturalistic fallacy and the error of defining good in empirical terms, were cast aside, to be replaced by discomfort and reticence.

One of the barbers had asked Barney what the Hell he intended to do to JLM's hair, given the shortness of it, and Barney had replied absolutely bugger all, it's all about fooling the customer and making them think they're having good done to them. After which the barbers had viewed Barney with a little less animosity, realising that he was being dragged around in JLM's absurd wake, rather than being a driving force behind the man's delusions.

So, the shop went about its business, as JLM pronounced on a variety of vacuous points; the perfect politician.

'They say that getting your hair cut by another man is only one step up from chimps picking fleas out of each other's hair,' said JLM. 'But they're wrong!'

One of the customers almost asked who 'they' were, because he'd never heard anyone say that before, but decided that silence was the better part of curiosity. He was in the middle of having a rather dubious *Russell Crowe, Gladiator* visited upon him. The other two customers currently being attended to were being given respectively an *Oliver Reed, Gladiator*, and a *Third Tiger From The Left, Gladiator*. (The shop was doing a special *Gladiator* weekend. To tie in with the whole thing, Barney had decided he was giving JLM an *Unnamed Baldy Man In The Coliseum Crowd, Gladiator*.)

The Amazing Mr X stood at the door, looking up and down the shopping mall, the people once more decked out for cold weather, the young ladies, who two days before had been baring substantial amounts of flesh, now totally covered up in polyunsaturated clothes of various descriptions. X was disappointed.

'Gillete, Wilkinson Sword, oh yes,' said JLM. 'Makers of fine razors, the pair of them. Absolutely.'

And so JLM went on, as Barney took a strangely long time to not cut his hair. He was rather enjoying the comfort and safety of the barber's shop, which he hadn't expected. But here he was, back where he had spent most of his working life – possibly – and feeling very much at home. The smell, the stillness, the relaxed atmosphere, albeit a relaxed atmosphere compromised by the presence of the First Minister. He felt at home. Back in the saddle. He was an F-15 pilot, having spent years in double wing exhibition jobs at air shows, back at the controls of a fighter. He was Good King Richard, back from the crusades, ready to kick Prince John's arse. He was East Berlin after the Wall had fallen. He was Clint Eastwood in *Space Cowboys*. He was Bill Clinton after he put the Monica thing behind him. Well, let's not get carried away.

However, he couldn't drag it out for ever, and eventually Parker Weirdlove returned from a brief shopping expedition for some delicious pink embroidered underwear, to inform JLM that he was falling behind the curve and had better be getting a move on. Barney wrapped up the cut, which wasn't hard seeing as he hadn't done anything, and off they went.

✂

Barney got back to Edinburgh a little after three, having been dismissed before JLM's duties were over; JLM having pronounced that his hair was 'solid' for the day. Barney couldn't face his room, and had retreated to the World's End to hide behind a bottle of beer and some nuts. He'd discovered something else while in the Perth shopping mall, a fact that related to all these stories he'd been told about his puff, and he wanted to think about it over a large amount of alcohol.

Had spent a quiet hour or two contemplating his past and what to do about his future, when he was approached by two men seasonally attired in long coats and dour expressions, clutching large pints of lager in their cool fingers.

Solomon and Kent.

'Mind if we join you?' said Solomon, sitting down at Barney's table.

Barney smiled and waved the appropriate hand. Kent followed and both he and Solomon took long drinks from the watering hole.

'Nothing new for you today, I'm afraid,' said Barney. 'Although I did overhear the tail end of a conversation on the Nash Equilibrium which might interest you.'

'I doubt it,' said Solomon. 'I don't even know what that is.'

'Economics theory, apparently,' said Barney.

'Outstanding,' said Solomon. 'Who gives a shit? If you want to get into casual chit-chat, I'll be willing to discuss Tom & Jerry, but beyond that I'm not much of a conversationalist.'

'Ain't that the truth,' said Kent.

'Zip it, wise guy,' said Solomon.

'I never liked the Cat Concerto, for all the plaudits it got,' said Barney.

'I hear you, pal,' said Solomon.

'At least it got away from the sickening violence and depravity of some of the others,' interjected Kent.

'Listen to him,' said Solomon. 'Sergeant Kent's a bit of a girl sometimes. Anyway, we're not here to talk about T&J. We've got a little bit of a heads up, thought you might like to see if you can dig up a bit more.'

Barney nodded, tapped into some more beer nuts. Sat back, defensively folded his arms, offered himself up for negotiation.

'After I'd finished with you last night,' said Solomon, 'I had a few things to do, finally got around to your girlfriend's room at about two o'clock this morning. Thought I might as well be ballsy and rang the bell. Nobody home. So I decided to wait around.'

'Hid in a cupboard,' said Kent.

'Yeah, whatever,' mumbled Solomon.

'Like he was a broom or cleaning fluid,' said Kent.

'He gets the picture.'

'The DCI's found his place at last,' said Kent, smiling.

'Are you finished or am I going to have to put your face in a food blender?'

'I'm finished,' said Kent, easily. Fairly confident that Solomon would never actually do the food blender thing.

'Anyway, if I can continue the narrative. About ten minutes later, she shows up. The coroner reckons that both Benderhook and the other guy were stiffed by then, so she ain't off the hook. And here's the interesting thing. She was not alone. After your little night out with the girl, she was obviously feeling a bit lonely about the fact that she didn't get into your Homer Simpson boxers, you know what I'm saying?'

'Go on,' said Barney, a little warily, first signs of jealousy, to go with his regret at landing Blackadder with police surveillance.

'She was with another one of your crowd,' said Solomon, 'which is no surprise, as there's got to be no end of little shenanigans going on between the lot of you.'

'Weirdlove?' said Barney. Had had his suspicions.

'Even better,' said Kent.

'Like you were there, smart arse?' said Solomon. 'The priest guy.'

'Father Michael?' said Barney, surprised. So the guy did do more with his life than look at ridiculous depictions of JLM as Christ.

'That's the guy,' said Solomon.

'It was him who first doubted Dr Blackadder to me,' said Barney.

'Well,' said Solomon, 'who knows? Maybe he was giving her spiritual counselling because he's worried about her.'

'At two in the morning?' said Barney

'Exactamundo. More likely he was banging her senseless. You and I both know that that whole priest celibacy thing is on its last legs. Anyway, some time after three she kicks him out, kissed her on the doorstep, the usual routine. She closes the door on him, and I think, shit it's three in the morning, I'll let her go. See what the old priest is up to, because if there's one thing more suspicious than a psychiatrist creeping around at three in the morning, it's a fucking priest creeping around at three in the morning. Right?'

Not as suspicious as a grown man hiding in a cupboard, thought Barney.

'Exactamundo,' he said, instead.

'So, he doesn't go far, your priest buddy. Walks along the corridor, goes into his own room. I checked this morning where you all are. Right little hotel you've all got to yourselves there, eh? I just chance it, wait a while to see if he'll re-emerge. Police instinct you see. I knew not to wait around for the doc, I knew that the priest would come back out. So, ten minutes, fifteen, twenty, about to give up, when, here he comes, walking down the street. Hello! it's our friend the old shagger himself. Father whatsisname. And where should he go to this time, but to the room of the other fucking medico, or whatever these women are.'

'Louise Farrow?' said Barney.

Hadn't thought much about Louise Farrow, perhaps because his gut instinct told him that she was the one who was telling the truth about his past.

'Precisamundo,' said Kent.

'Listen to that fucking idiot,' said Solomon. '*Precisamundo*. Yeah, Louise Farrow, the GP. I starts snooping around outside, into various rooms using the old skeleton key. Brought the old guts into play to make sure I didn't walk in on anyone. Found a room directly opposite the doc's. The girl hadn't shut her bedroom curtains, I'm telling you, and what is that all about? She and the priest were going at it like fucking elephants. You know what it was like?'

'Can't begin to imagine,' said Barney.

'It was like watching tv with the volume turned down, you know. I could see her wee face screaming and yelling in pleasure. She loved it.'

'You stayed and watched, did you?' said Barney.

'Hell, yes,' said Solomon. 'And miss a show like that?'

Barney nodded.

'So,' said Barney, 'what are you saying here?'

'I'm saying nothing, Batman,' said Solomon. 'I'm just giving you a little information about your priest guy, that's all. I can't give you a clue about how to do it, but see what you can find out. There's clearly a lot of shit going on in that little fraternity of yours, this is just giving you a little more of a pointer in the direction you should maybe be headed.'

Barney nodded, drank some beer, stared at the floor. Had a mind to tell them about the note he'd received that morning. If this was a movie he'd be sitting there shouting at the character to tell the police about the frigging note, yet here he was, and he knew he wasn't going to mention it.

'But really,' said Barney, 'why should a priest and a doctor sleeping together have anything to do with the cabinet getting murdered?'

Solomon lifted his pint, which he'd hardly touched, and drained it in one smooth and quick gulp. Swallowed, belched massively into the back of his hand, placed the glass back on the table.

'Call it police intuition, Barn,' he said. Kent made a face beside him. 'When you've spent as long as I have doing this stuff, things begin to add up. Is there an automatic connection between the two? No. But all I can see is that the cabinet is getting murdered, which is a bit fucking odd, and on the other hand, there's a priest and a doctor having outrageous sex, not long after the priest has very likely knobbed a psychiatrist, and that's also a bit fucking odd. When you've got two seemingly unrelated fucking odd things going on, there's a fair shout that they're not as unrelated as you thought they were in the first place. You know what I'm saying?'

Made sense, in a roundabout kind of way.

'I'll see what I can do,' said Barney.

'Perfectamundo,' said Kent.

Solomon slung him a look.

'Are you taking the piss, or are you just an idiot?' he asked.

'I think it's sweet that you can't tell the difference,' said Kent.

Solomon looked at him with scorn, shrugged his eyebrows at Barney.

'Right, we're outta here,' he said.

'You want to tell me something first?' said Barney.

He trusted Solomon, felt sure he would get an honest answer from him to an honest question.

'Go on,' said Solomon. 'But be quick about it.'

'That story you told me about the brain thing,' said Barney. 'Bullshit?'

Solomon smiled.

'Total,' he said. 'How d'you work it out?'

‘Why d’you do it?’ said Barney.

‘Tell you the lie?’ said Solomon. ‘Just took a chance, you know. Yours is a pretty fucking weird situation, just thought we’d try to exploit it a bit to get you on our side.’

‘Thanks,’ said Barney.

‘You never actually believed it though?’ said Solomon.

‘Nah,’ said Barney, which was the truth.

Solomon stood up, lifted his glass to drain the last drops of it.

‘How’d you find out?’ he asked.

‘Doesn’t matter,’ said Barney.

‘Don’t suppose it does,’ said Solomon. ‘You’ll let us know in the usual manner,’ he added.

‘Sure,’ said Barney.

Solomon walked off, Kent quickly downed some more of his lager, nodded at Barney, and followed his superior from the bar. Barney watched them go, then leant back in his chair, bottle in hand.

So Louise Farrow was at it as well? He downed some more beer, stared at the table, wondered where it was all going to end. Fair enough, no reason for her not to be having relations, when the rest of them were at it.

And just because she was sleeping with a priest, did not mean that the story she had told Barney about his past had been a false one. Especially when Barney had found several copies of *Barney Thomson: Urban Legend* in a remainder bookshop in Perth. That he definitely did not look anything like the Barney of old had been verified; which had left only Solomon’s story out of the others which could’ve been true. And the final nail had just been firmly hammered into that one.

39

Barney takes confession

Barney stayed in the bar for the rest of the afternoon and into early evening. Sank a few beers, had *a medallion of sea bass, with Norwegian potatoes and an aperture of water melon*, which was tasty enough. Finally left at a little after seven, time to go home and get changed and have a shower. If he was going to get murdered at all during this clandestine meeting, he didn't want it to happen while he stank of cigarette smoke and alcohol.

He arrived back in his room, stripped, showered, got dressed in one of the Veron Veron inspired Chinese outfits and plonked himself down in a seat to listen to *In The Cool, Cool, Cool Of The Evening*, before venturing out into the cool, cool, cool of another early autumn's evening in Edinburgh. Visiting the Parliament Assembly building on a Thursday night, there would be a queue of security guards wondering what he was up to, and the same would go for whoever it was who had invited him there. So good chance he wasn't actually going to get garrotted or impaled on some spike or other.

✂

James Eaglehawk spent Thursday evening in an hotel room out near the airport. His wife was at home, minding the children, parked in front of Jurassic Park *V*, with a pint of cider and some Kettle chips. Herr Vogts had instructed Eaglehawk to excuse himself to her for the evening, the easiest thing on the planet for a politician to do, and to get around to this hotel. There would be a wee present there, he said, to cement their friendship, a confirmation of the brave new world that lay ahead for them both as part of this great alliance.

Eaglehawk had arrived to find several dossiers laid out on the bed. They were each marked accordingly, depending on which scandal against Jesse Longfellow-Moses they provided firm evidence of. *Hookergate* – sworn testimony that not only had JLM been aware of his secretary's business practice, but that he had also availed himself of those services, and had then conspired in her murder when she had threatened to sell her story; damning evidence, including photographs and DNA samples. (Even after checking in the first folder, Eaglehawk was laughing in amazement, wondering where Vogts had got hold of killer stuff like this.) *Disneygate* – a video tape of a speech JLM had given seven years previously, where he'd denounced Disney as prophets of evil. *World Cup 2014gate* – documented proof of discussions between JLM and the Faroes government to intentionally sink their own bid. *Entouragegate* – written evidence of JLM's team and their cost to the taxpayer. *Taxgate* – corroboration of the extensive tax avoidance measures which JLM had taken over the previous ten years or so, defrauding the Inland Revenue of over £300K. *Godgate* – tape of a conversation JLM had had with Father Michael, where they had jointly dismissed the Bible as 'the Disney of its times'. *Rwandagate* – evidence that JLM had applied pressure to the Herald to stop them running the story of the suspected war criminal living in Glasgow. *Shaggate* – substantiation of other affairs of JLM's, some where he'd paid for the pleasure, some where he hadn't.

It was never ending, file after file of doom, enough to sink a phalanx of First Ministers, not just the one. Eaglehawk couldn't even bring himself to read it all, it was all so glorious. He just fell onto the centre of the bed and lay there, crying with laughter. JLM was finished, absolutely dyed-in-the-bollocks finished. Eaglehawk could feel the glory of it in all the senses in his body. It was as if he'd snorted every known mind-blowing substance at once. He was floating, absolutely bloody floating. Flying high above JLM, and pishing on him from the loftiest height possible. He was in the stratosphere, JLM was in the mud, and he was going to dump on the bastard, and grind him into the slime and muck, so that he would become indistinguishable with it. JLM would become part of the suppurating ooze of the world, the repellent fetid gunk, as one with the rancid decaying pus. And he would leave him there to fester, and when the sun finally came out and once again shone on Jesse Longfellow-Moses, it would serve only to dry him up and turn him to dust. And in the end JLM would be blown away with the wind.

James Eaglehawk cackled hysterically.

'Fuck you, Jesse!' he shouted. 'Fuck you!'

There was a knock at the door. The laugh caught in Eaglehawk's throat.

He sat up, looked at the papers strewn around him on the bed, like rose petals strewn before a king. The knock came again. Relaxed, casual, inviting.

He got off the bed, heart beating even faster than before. What next? What other dreams could Herr Vogts have come up with? He opened the door.

There were two women, early twenties. One blonde, one Chinese. Wearing long overcoats and too much make-up.

'Hi,' said the blonde. 'My name's Willing.'

'And my name's Able,' said the Chinese girl.

Eaglehawk gasped, more or less.

'Where's Ready?' he asked with a smile, and Leslie Phillips couldn't have delivered the line better.

'We were hoping that'd be you,' said Able, wickedly.

'Ah,' he sort of croaked. 'Do come in,' he added, without the slightest hint of hesitation. A brief picture of Mrs Eaglehawk flashed through his head, but it was of a woman content with her lot, her cider and her video, and it had vanished as soon as it'd appeared.

The women smooched past him, brushing their hands against his genitals as they went. He shuddered at the touch, closed the door behind them, turned to face the room. He swallowed, couldn't believe the luck of what was about to happen. What a friend he had in Herr Vogts!

Willing and Able shrugged off their long overcoats, which fell at their feet, and Eaglehawk feasted his eyes on two fabulously horny women in incredibly tacky underwear. Then he walked slowly forward, into the lion's den, and buried his face deep in his own destruction.

✂

Barney opened the door to Conference Room 12 and walked in. Closed the door behind him, looked around the room. A large table in the centre, maybe twenty chairs around it. The usual whiteboards and projectors set up at one end, a table with a water cooler and coffee machine at the other. There was a beautiful hush, like walking into a chapel an hour before the service.

He walked to the window and looked out over the low central building, the leaf windows of the roof brightly illuminated. Two nights ago at this time, the evening had been muggy and warm. Now that the summer was over for another nine months, the evening seemed so much darker, the clouds heavy and threatening, the air cold.

He wasn't nervous, he didn't know if he was even interested. Had given it consideration while he'd sat in the bar, but the thoughts hadn't amounted to much. Presumably the message had referred to the murders. Presumably he'd been summoned because someone knew that he was involved with the police; it appeared to be, after all, a fairly open secret.

If he had to guess he would've gone for Veron Veron because the man had almost been invisible. They had all come to see him at some point, they'd all put in their tuppence ha'penny's worth. Who he was, where he had come from, who was behind the murders, why Napoleon invaded Russia when he did, why the Everley Brothers fell out over a bag of doughnuts live on stage in 1974. An endless series of pronouncements and opinions masquerading as facts.

All except Veron Veron, the joker in the pack.

The door opened. No Willing and Able here.

Barney turned, resigned. Here we go. Could hear himself being told he was in a Truman Show situation. His whole existence was a set-up for the television audience. Maybe the murders were all being committed for tv too. *Just a bit of fun.* Would it be all that far removed from what actually happened these days?

Father Michael closed the door and stepped into the room. Makes sense, thought Barney. The messenger returns with more news from the front.

'Mr Thomson,' said Father Michael. The same trepidation as before. As if he'd been called before God to account for his actions.

'Michael,' said Barney. 'What have you got for me today?'

Michael walked further into the room, round the conference table, came and stood beside Barney at the window. He looked out over the joyless grey skies of Edinburgh.

'The weather has changed,' said Michael.

Barney turned and followed the priest's gaze out over the city. To the west the clouds were darker still, worse yet to come.

'You've been standing outside all day to think of that one,' said Barney, caustically. 'Why am I here?' he added, voice cold.

It was a Thursday night and he had better things to do. Like sit in a bar getting drunk, or sit at home watching prodigiously awful survival shows on television hosted by former sports stars.

'The killing is over,' said Michael.

His eyes turned down, his fingers toyed with each other, tapping lightly against the glass.

'How can you be so sure?' asked Barney.

Michael hesitated in reply. He wasn't about to tell Barney the truth, and he was no politician. Lies and prevarication did not come so easily to him.

'It's over, that's all that's important,' he said. 'There will be no more death, tell that to your police contacts.'

'I'm sure they'll be delighted,' said Barney.

'I understand,' said Michael, then further hesitation as he considered his words, 'I know, I realise that they will want to bring someone to justice for these crimes, but tell them. Let them know that at the very least they will not happen again.'

'Whoop-de-doo and bad-a-bing,' said Barney. 'Only eight down, that's not important. There are a hundred and fifty deaths in Scotland every day, so what are eight more, eh?'

'That's not what I'm saying,' said Michael.

'Yes it is,' said Barney. 'And you're right, after all. Life, death, it's all one big bag. Particularly from your point of view when you don't actually think you're dying anyway. So, there were maybe 50,000 deaths in Scotland last year. What's another eight?'

'Well, yes,' said Father Michael, snapping just a little. Exasperated at Barney's tone. 'You could say that. Especially when some of them deserved to die.'

'Ah,' said Barney. 'Fine words for a priest.'

Father Michael closed his eyes, breathed deeply. This wasn't going well, but what had he expected? That Barney Thomson would be as spineless as he himself?

'Tell me why you're so sure,' said Barney, 'and I might speak to them.'

'I can't,' said Michael.

Barney nodded. Another unreliable witness.

'Fine,' he said, and he turned his back – that's how confident he was – and began to walk around the conference table. Waiting for Michael to say something else, because he would not have called him up here at this time in the evening for something as ineffectual as this. The man knew something, and he wanted to give the police some information, be it the truth or a false trail.

'Stop,' said Michael on cue, as Barney reached the door.

Barney turned.

'I don't want to hear any more crap,' he said.

'It's Blackadder,' said Michael. 'Dr Blackadder.'

'That'll be as opposed to Professor Blackadder, or Blackadder the Clown,' said Barney.

'It's not something to be facetious about,' snapped Michael. 'She's a killer. A cold-blooded killer. She's killed them all.'

'Blackadder the Killer,' said Barney, holding his arms up in a banner headline. 'Hannibal Blackadder. Buffalo Blackadder. Rebecca Bates. Rebecca Krueger.'

'My God!' shouted Michael, 'this is no joke! How can you say these things? It pains me to tell you this and you mock me. Mock me! Rebecca is a dear woman. I don't know her well, but she has confessed to me. Don't you understand? I have taken her confession. By telling you this I'm breaking my vows.'

'That must've been hard for you,' said Barney dryly.

Michael came forward, leant on the table, palms of his hands flat out.

'It is, Mr Thomson, it is!' he cried. 'This is the most awful position for me, can't you understand? But I know the killing is over. I thought maybe we could leave it at that. I accept the monstrous nature of her crimes, but I thought by letting the police know that there would be no more killing, perhaps it would be allowed to pass, that my betrayal of her trust would not be revealed.'

He looked imploringly across the table. The desperate words of a desperate man.

'What about God?' said Barney.

'What about him?' said Michael, standing straighter, bit of a wee worried look in his eyes.

'Aren't you concerned,' said Barney, 'about God? Even if Rebecca didn't know you had betrayed her, even if the police never knew you'd broken your vows, surely God would know?'

This, as they say in The Broons, put Michael's gas at a peep. Had he been a politician, had he been Jesse Longfellow-Moses or Tony Blair or Gerhard Schröder or George Bush, he would immediately have started spouting shite, smooth and easy like a blow hole on top of a sewerage. But he was a priest; not that he wasn't used to talking shite or anything, but it was all carefully prepared shite. Off the cuff stuff was a totally different matter.

'God?' said Michael, as if mentioning the name of someone he hadn't thought of before.

'Your boss,' said Barney.

'God will forgive me,' said Michael, quickly. 'He will understand.'

Barney smiled. Not like an agent of the Lord to come up with a cosy answer. All the bloody same.

'And what about the fact that you're shagging Rebecca?' said Barney. 'How's the big fella going to feel about that?'

Time stopped. The bell tolled. Father Michael's mouth opened slightly, his tongue edged out onto his bottom lip. The inside of his mouth went dry. Goose bumps broke out over his body, he shivered them away.

Barney watched with a kind of detached amusement. On the edge looking in, unlike some of his previous adventures, when he'd been stuck in the bloody middle of it all. He couldn't really have cared less. He didn't know for a fact that Michael was sleeping with Blackadder, a kiss at their door at two in the morning wasn't exactly proof. But the reaction he'd just given to the charge was confession enough. Decided to hold back the charge of sleeping with Louise Farrow until a further appropriate moment.

Michael said nothing. Barney shrugged. Turned his back again, opened the door.

'It was me,' said Michael, a little more convincingly this time, voice quiet.

'What?' said Barney.

'It was me,' he said. 'I murdered those politicians. I've got some things. I can prove it.'

Barney stayed halfway out the door. Wouldn't have believed anything that Michael told him now. But if he was telling the truth, then it was out of Barney's hands. He wasn't going to absolve the man of his crimes.

'You must've been interviewed by the police at some point in the last few days,' said Barney.

Michael nodded.

'Right then,' said Barney. 'They'll have left you a contact number. You know what to do.'

Michael stared silently. Beginning to sweat; hot under the dog collar. Dry tongue emerged again to lick drier lips. His nostrils flared. He swallowed.

'Did you really do it?' said Barney.

'Yes,' Michael responded quickly.

'Nice of you to try and stiff Rebecca then,' said Barney. 'Very Christian.'

Michael said nothing. Barney turned away, stepped from Conference Room 12, closed the door behind himself and walked away along the corridor.

Bloody religion, he mumbled as he went. He could remember everything about that.

40

Fortune favours the munificent

Jesse Longfellow-Moses burst dramatically into the sitting room, waving a blank piece of paper thrillingly in his hand. Classic kid in a sweetie shop expression on his face; that look of innocent excitement with the unbelievably trivial, the look that men never lose, and women never have in the first place. Boys' stuff.

Minnie was watching some trashy erotic thriller on Channel 5, with a name like *Lethal Fatality*, *Mortal Casualty* or *Fatal Death*, and pretended not to notice him.

'Champion!' bellowed JLM, 'absolute bloody champion!'

She looked away from the cheesy music playing over two naked, soft focus, wrestling bodies, by an open fire in LA in the height of summer.

'Won the lottery?' she said, half an eyebrow raised. Christ, she thought, there are so many better things I could be doing on a weekday night. So many more interesting people to be with.

'Better than that!' he said, standing between her and the television, forcing her to pay attention. 'Better than bloody that!' he repeated, and still the wonderful enthusiasm was in his voice.

She looked up at him; remembered with little regret the times when she had been amused by his boyish enthusiasms, had even found them attractive. But now? Now she had no time for them. And what man was any different? Shallow, pathetic and weak. That was what made women so much more interesting company.

'You have my undivided,' she said, as he more or less hadn't given her the choice.

'You know Larry Bellows?' he said.

She looked at him in much the way he deserved. Everybody knew Larry Bellows. In fact, the only person in the country who had his head stuck so far up his own backside that he might not know Larry Bellows, was JLM himself.

'Yes,' she said.

'Tomorrow night!' said JLM with triumph.

'How d'you mean that?' asked Minnie. 'Larry Bellows is always on on a Friday night.'

'No,' said JLM, waving the paper on which he was about to start making notes, as if it contained vital information, 'us. You, me, the cabinet, the team. They want to do us! Isn't it absolutely champion?'

'What are you talking about?' she said disdainfully. 'How are they going to do us? They set these things up months in advance. Do all sorts of planning.'

'Not today, Zurg!' he said. 'They've had a cancellation for tomorrow. They were supposed to be doing one of the scabby royals, apparently, but they've thrown their teddy in the corner and pulled the plug. They've been unable to pull forward anyone from the next few weeks, so they're looking for an interesting subject at short notice.'

The voice was still racing along at the speed of light, the wee kid trying to tell his mum and dad all about the goals he'd scored that afternoon for the Cub football team.

'National tv,' he said. 'National bollocking tv. The whole of Britain, isn't it bloody champion?'

'You're kidding me, right?' she said. But she knew he wasn't. JLM loved this stuff. Larry Bellows was an American talk show host contracted to the BBC for a few months to do behind-the-scenes docu-crap that went out live on a Friday evening. It was usually the Royal family or A-list celebs. Christ, thought Minnie, they must really have been struggling for business to stoop to Jesse Longfellow-Moses.

'This is wonderful,' said JLM. 'A national audience. Millions of people. That show got twenty-one million people when they did Posh & Becks. Twenty-one million! You imagine what it'll be like. We could have twenty-one million people listening to my vision for Scotland and for Europe. And the world, goddammit.' His face suddenly lit up even more. 'The world!' he said. 'BBC Prime, digital whatever, Christ, whatever it is they're doing these days. People all around the world are going to be listening to me. Me! Jesse Longfellow-Moses. One man! One dream! One vision!'

Minnie smiled. Did the man's conceit know no bounds? Well, of course it didn't, she knew that better than anyone else.

'It'll be a proud moment in your life,' she said dryly.

'Proud?' ejaculated JLM. 'It'll be a damn sight more than proud. Bloody magnificent. It'll be my Trafalgar, my Bannockburn, my Waterloo!'

'Would that be your Wellington's Waterloo or your Napoleon's Waterloo,' she asked.

'This is our chance for the name Jesse Longfellow-Moses to become synonymous with world statesmanship. Television is the new war, and this is my chance at glory!'

Minnie nodded. Very impressive. The viewers of the world would be geeked.

'If television is the new war, what's war then?' she sighed.

'There's not a person in any land on the planet will not know the name Longfellow-Moses,' he said, ignoring her.

'War is the new peace,' she said, staring at the floor.

'I'll be JFK, I'll be Martin Luther King, I'll be Frank Sinatra Chairman Mao.'

'War is the new ice cream.'

'We have to grasp this moment, seize the ruddy day! *Carpe diem*! Bloody Hell, I shall be magnificent tomorrow night. The world will be wowed by my munificence, my vision, my poetry. God, what an opportunity.'

'War is the new pink,' she said, then decided she should shut up. Might as well let the man get carried away by the weight of his own bum fluff.

'Right,' he said, suddenly considering practicalities. 'We have to mobilise the troops. We need to get Weirdlove, start working out who we need, what kind of set-up we're going to have.'

'Bloody champion,' he added, as he turned and marched from the room, still doing a Neville Chamberlain with the piece of paper.

Minnie watched him go, had a little flutter that she too was going to be on worldwide television, did not give in to it, at least, not yet, then turned back to the latest shenanigans on the Channel 5 movie. Two women this time, and she settled further down into her seat, for the best two minutes of the evening.

41

The usual roll call of late night visitors

Barney was safe in his room, channel surfing. Had briefly stopped on the same tripe as Minnie Longfellow-Moses, but on the whole was giving no show more than a minute and a half. On autopilot, zipping through the wonders of digital entertainment. Beach volleyball, stock car racing, Brazilian soap opera, documentary, docu-soap, docu-drama, docu-sport, docu-sex, docu-documentary, game shows, quiz shows, blooper shows, gardening and cooking and makeover and decorating. All utter, utter bollocks.

As ever, when Barney was sitting alone in his room, there was a knock at the door. He turned, looked at the time, a quarter to eleven, shook his head.

'Should just leave the bloody door open,' he mumbled, as he got up. 'Or put a sign up. *Enter All Ye Who Pass Within A Hundred Yards. Hang Around. Make Yourself At Home. Get On My Tits.*'

He opened the door. It was Tom & Jerry.

'Hi,' said Solomon, walking straight passed Barney. Kent followed, nodding his greeting with a slight facial movement.

'Come in,' said Barney. 'Nothing I like more on a Thursday evening than some Loony Tunes.'

Solomon stopped abruptly so that Kent walked into the back of him.

'Listen, cowboy,' he said, 'if you're thinking of the two of us as Tom & Jerry, that's as may be, I don't give a shit. But T&J were MGM, not fucking Loony Tunes. You got that?'

Barney held up his hands in a placatory gesture. He closed the door and leant back against it. Didn't want to walk back into the heart of the room, sit down, get comfortable. Didn't want this to last.

'Where were you between eight and nine tonight?' said Solomon abruptly. It was late, Solomon had been called away from a night of potential loving, and he was in no mood for messing around either. Something which Barney sensed, and so he did not even consider artifice of any sort. He wasn't about to start protecting Father Michael. What did he care about any of them?

'I was in the Assembly building,' he said.

'Too bloody right you were,' said Solomon. 'Caught by more fucking cameras than Kylie Minogue when she gets her arse out. You want to tell us what you were doing?'

'I received a note inviting me,' said Barney.

'Oh, very fucking clever,' said Solomon. 'You didn't want to tell us about it earlier?'

Barney shrugged. Wasn't going to allow them to put him on the defensive.

'Didn't know who it was from, what it was about. It could've been anything,' he said. 'I don't have to tell you every time I go for a shit.'

'Yeah, very nice, cowboy,' said Solomon. 'Can we take it you went to see the religious comedian, Father Michael?'

Barney nodded. It was inevitable that they'd know who else was there. More cameras than on Kylie Minogue's arse after all.

'Aye,' he said, but didn't volunteer any more information.

'Well,' said Solomon, 'you might like to consider that if you'd told us the fuck what was going on, Father Michael might still be alive.'

Barney's head dropped back against the door. Jesus, another one. And not a politician this time. It was spreading. Had he cared about Father Michael? Not in the least, but if he could've acted differently so that he might still be alive, then that was something to regret.

'You think I killed him?' asked Barney, raising his head, although the possibility did not bother him in the least.

'We know you didn't,' said Kent, sticking his wee nose into the conversation for the first time.

'He jumped from the roof. Enough people saw him before he took the final plummet for us to know it wasn't murder. Note in his own handwriting in his jacket pocket.'

'Oh,' said Barney. 'What did it say?'

'What did he tell you?' asked Solomon quickly.

Barney breathed in. Should he further implicate Blackadder? Why bother? The last thing Michael had said was to implicate himself, and just because Barney hadn't believed a word of it, didn't mean he couldn't share the knowledge as if it might've been true.

'Said that he'd committed these murders,' said Barney.

Solomon nodded.

'Right enough,' he said, 'that's what he wrote in his note. Confessed to it all. Did you believe him?'

Barney shrugged.

'No reason not to,' he said.

'Very well,' said Solomon. 'Told us where to find the bodies of the victims. We've already unearthed Malcolm and that Benderhook clown. Others'll take a bit longer. Bottom of the sea, most of them, apparently. Anyway, we've checked out his place, there's no end of incriminating evidence.'

'He say why he did it?' asked Barney, a little curious at last. Very surprised to hear that Father Michael actually had proof of his own guilt.

Solomon raised an eyebrow. Kent took advantage of the gap in conversation.

'God told him,' he said.

'Ah,' said Barney. 'What better reason could he give?'

'It's bullshit,' said Solomon.

'You think he's covering for someone?' asked Barney.

'As sure as a horse's knackers, he's covering for someone,' said Solomon.

‘Nah,’ said Kent, ‘you can read all sorts of things into it, but I reckon he did it. We’re clear.’

Solomon slung him a sideways glance, looked back at Barney.

‘Maybe,’ said Solomon, ‘maybe not. Who the fuck knows? We’ll have to do a bit more investigation, despite what Clark Kent here thinks.’

‘God, here we go with the Clark Kent jokes again,’ muttered Kent.

‘Did he say anything else?’ said Solomon. ‘Why did he call you up there in the first place?’

Barney held his gaze. Look ‘em straight in the eye and they’ll never know you’re lying.

‘Maybe he felt the need to confess before killing himself,’ he said.

‘Why not do it to a priest, then?’ retorted Solomon. ‘Barbers used to taking confessions, are they?’

‘All the time,’ said Barney quickly. Then he relaxed, took the edge from the conversation. ‘Look, I don’t know. Maybe he felt embarrassed about going to a priest. Maybe he wanted to confess but didn’t want to be judged.’

‘You’d think God would judge him,’ said Solomon flatly.

‘Not if God told him to commit the murders in the first place,’ Kent chipped in.

Solomon grumbled and moved towards the door. Barney stepped out of the way.

‘Expect you’ll have to answer a few questions to the investigating team tomorrow,’ said Solomon. ‘It could be all over, or it could be still out there, waiting to come back and grab us by the shorts. We’ll see. In the meantime, you shouldn’t have to employ too much guile to ask the others about him, see what they come up with. Blackadder and Farrow in particular, seeing as they were both shagging the bloke.’

They stood at the door, waiting to see if Barney would volunteer anything further. They could’ve waited all night. Solomon turned, walked out into the hall, Kent at his heals.

‘He didn’t mention Blackadder at all when you saw him, did he?’ said Solomon, stopping, casting one last significant look his way. 'You know, he implicated her a couple of days ago. Maybe he's covering for her.'

Barney shook his head, betrayed nothing. If there was more information to be discovered about Dr Blackadder, he would take care of it himself.

'Nothing,' he said.

Solomon nodded. Kent nodded. Solomon turned away and walked off down the corridor, Kent in his wake. Barney closed the door, stood inside looking at the confines of his prison, then began wandering around the room turning off the electrical appliances.

✂

He was garbed in rich blue Chinese style pyjamas, about to get into bed, teeth cleaned and face shinier than a pair of scissors, when there was another knock at the door.

He looked at the bed, warm and inviting, the sheets calling to him, much in the way that they do, then he turned and trudged through the apartment, mumbling, 'Pain in the arse,' as he went. Opened the door to find Parker Weirdlove.

'What?' said Barney.

'We need to talk,' said Weirdlove, and he pushed past Barney and stormed into the room.

Barney turned, left the door open, wondered about smacking Weirdlove on the mouth, but decided that electric blue pj's designed by Veron Veron were not a fitting outfit for getting into a fight.

'What?' he said again.

'Close the door,' barked Weirdlove, who was back in full blown arse-kicking mode.

'You were just leaving,' said Barney, not following his instruction.

Weirdlove thought about getting into a heated discussion, but decided that he couldn't have a serious argument with a man in electric blue pj's.

'You've heard of Larry Bellows,' said Weirdlove, as a matter of fact.

'No,' said Barney.

‘Talk show host,’ said Weirdlove. ‘Cutting edge. American. Great hair. He does behind-the-scenes stuff with A-list celebs and royals. Charles and Camilla, Posh and Becks, McCartney and Heather, the Blairs, you know, the usual suspects. They’re doing JLM tomorrow night.’

‘So,’ said Barney, ‘where does he fit into the A-list celebs and royals categories exactly?’

Weirdlove gave him an ‘I’m not answering that’ look.

‘We’re doing the show, that’s it. Not just Jesse and Minnie, but all his staff, X, me, the docs, you, the lot of us,’ he said.

‘But not Michael,’ said Barney, dryly.

Weirdlove hesitated.

‘You heard about that, eh? Well, the timing’s not great, the guy could’ve been instantly the best known priest in Scotland.’

‘You don’t think it’s at all questionable,’ said Barney, ‘to be doing a documentary like this when one of JLM’s team has just been revealed as the man who murdered most of the cabinet? Aren’t questions going to be asked about JLM?’

‘No they bloody are not!’ barked Weirdlove, taking a step towards him. ‘The man is above reproach, and don’t even bloody think about starting that kind of talk. You got that?’

‘Yes, kimosabe,’ said Barney with mock salute. ‘Now, tell me why you felt you had to inform me of this at eleven-thirty at night, then get the fuck out of my face.’

Weirdlove breathed deeply and noisily, nostrils flaring. Like a bull. Or a dolphin.

‘As I said, everyone close to the First Minister will be involved. He wants to present a united team. All of us, his family, the cabinet.’

‘The cabinet?’ said Barney, much in the tone that anyone would’ve used.

‘We will be working strenuously tomorrow to fill the vacant positions. This is our chance to show that, despite these setbacks, Scotland still has a fully functional, working government.’

‘Ah,’ said Barney. ‘You were fair farting around filling the vacancies before, but now that television has hoved into view, you’d better get on with it.’

'The First Minister wants to make sure that everyone is looking at their best. We're talking close to twenty people, so you've got a busy day ahead of you. You got that?'

Barney nodded. In his short space of time here, he had seen no signs of any panic or rushed action, not with any government difficulties and certainly not with the general slaughter and mayhem that was taking place. But, by Christ! here comes television, and it was all hands to the pump.

'Yes, boss,' said Barney. 'You intending to draft in outside help?'

'No, we bloody well are not,' said Weirdlove. 'You're it. JLM has kindly allowed you to work out of his private en suite. When we have a full list of participating names in the morning, we'll draw up an appointments list and you'll have to stick to it. No slippage or you're in trouble.'

Weirdlove walked to the door, stopped as he got to Barney, stood virtually nose to nose, so that Barney could smell the *stegosaurus of beef* which Weirdlove had eaten for dinner.

'Fuck up, and you're out of here,' said Weirdlove.

Another lingering look of suspicion bordering on animosity, then he walked quickly past Barney and along the corridor, the very way that Solomon and Kent had departed a short time previously.

Barney closed the door, turned off the light, stood in the quiet darkness of his sitting room for a short while, then walked wearily back towards the glorious welcoming arms of his bed.

✂

He lay there for an hour, head buzzing. Staring at the illusions the shadows cast on the ceiling. Thinking about Father Michael. Thinking about the cabinet ministers who had slowly been whittled away.

What value is a life? Because the press weren't interested, was the implication that the dead were not important? There were still mothers and fathers having to bury their children. There were children whose mothers and fathers would not be coming home for dinner. There would be husbands and wives left distraught. Because the press barely thought them worthy of mention, because most people in Scotland probably didn't even know that there was a Minister for Justice or a Minister for Parliamentary Business, did not mean that those lives were any less important than the lives of the rich and famous, who adorned the cover and inside twenty pages of every tabloid when they died.

This was no time to go charging into the full glare of trashazoid docu-soap. If they wanted to show Scotland was fully functional, they should have replaced the cabinet members as they fell, they should have shown a united front, Jesse Longfellow-Moses should actually turn up in parliament every now and again, they should act like a government, not a one-man collective, intent on following his own whim and ignoring the advice of everyone else.

But JLM was so far embedded into his own personal planet, so swept up in the glory of public appearances and media attention, that the timing was not important to him. Bugger disrespect, bugger the families of those who had died, bugger their friends: he was going to go on live television, and he was going to tell the world that it didn't matter that their mother or father or daughter or son or husband or wife or friend had been killed, and that it had made no difference to the smooth running of the country. In fact, if anything, it had improved it.

And after an hour Barney had finally reached the conclusion that the following day would be his last working for Jesse Longfellow-Moses. Maybe he owed his very existence to JLM; without him he might still be the guy who'd been found on Leith docks, with no past and no future, but he'd had enough of him, and enough of the rest of them. Except Rebecca Blackadder. But then, there was likely nothing he could do about that.

Tomorrow would be the end. He'd do the frantic day's worth of hairdressing that was required, might even enjoy it, and then he'd be on his way.

He turned over, closed his eyes, and eventually, through the uncertain thoughts that nuzzled away inside his head, sleep came to him.

42

Bing Velociraptor

They were each called to a ten o'clock the following morning. All the team, all the cabinet. Weirdlove had been up all night assembling the replacements for those who had been murdered. He'd had a brief discussion with JLM about it, but it wasn't as if the First Minister had actually heard of most of the MSPs who were left in the chamber, so Weirdlove had more or less been given the green light to formulate the next government. There was no need at this stage for him to have to stoop to the level of appointing deputy ministers, as they wouldn't be appearing in the tv special; he just needed to have the full cabinet in place.

So, a nip and a tuck here, the odd curious little placement there, a few late night or early morning phone calls, a bit of arm twisting, and Weirdlove had his team. JLM was obviously remaining as First Minister, although they would be the odd call for him to stand down from some of the newspapers once it emerged that it had been one of his crew who was responsible for the cabinet slaughter. However, none of the eight main Scottish dailies actually saw fit to change their front pages late on the Thursday when the story of Father Michael had emerged, none of the editors could be bothered writing a new editorial, so it wasn't as if there was too much condemnation. So, the papers all still went to press with the following headlines: Daily Record – *'I Shagged Survivor Babe' Claims Rangers Ace*; The Herald – *Bush 'Forgets' Hawaii Part of US, Nukes Honolulu*; The Sun *Blair To Be Next 'God'*; Aberdeen Press & Journal – *P&J Prevents Turnip Price Hitting Heights*; The Scotsman – *Israel 'Very Naughty' For Killing 1million Palestinians, Says Bush*; Daily Mail – *Massive Oil Deposits Discovered In Zimbabwe, US Sends Troops To Oust Mugabe*; The Express – *Blair Suspends*

Commons In 'Logical' Next Step; The Mirror – *Big Brother's Malky To Take It Up The Arse In Live TV First Shocker!*

After sifting through the possible candidates for cabinet positions, Weirdlove decided that there was not even the remotest possibility of finding the five people in the parliament that they needed who could so much as read and write, never mind actually string a coherent sentence together on Newsnight. So he took the decision to abolish three departments. Justice was an easy one, because most people didn't even know there was a Department of Justice, and if they had known it existed, they wouldn't actually have known what it did. Tourism, Culture & Sport was easily shelved, because tourism, culture and sport were things which pretty much took care of themselves in life and would almost benefit from a lack of government interference. Then there was Rural Affairs & the Environment; well, bugger it, the environment was going to pot anyway and there was nothing a wee country like Scotland could do about it, and while there might be a few people who were put out about the removal of rural affairs from the government's agenda, they wouldn't be Labour voters anyway, so they could whistle Dixie.

So, JLM remained as First Minister. In a display of his own quirky sense of humour, Weirdlove promoted Patsy Morningirl to be Deputy First Minister. (She had been reluctant until Weirdlove told her she'd get to go on BBC Breakfast and Top of the Pops and the like.) Alisdair MacPherson had already been promoted into Education, where Weirdlove was confident he would do bugger all for the next three years. Eaglehawk and Hamish Robertson were already in place in Finance and Parliamentary Business respectively, and he couldn't really touch Winnie without having his eyeballs clawed out. So the only other new appointment was the wunderkind of the party, Darius Grey, into the bloody mire of Health, where he was confident that the enthusiastic young socialist would be sucked dry of political zeal, to the point where he probably wouldn't even bother standing at the next election. Weirdlove often thought that there was nothing like taking the bright spark of political fervour, and then dousing it under the weight of red tape, bureaucracy, intransigence and unreasonable public expectation, to the point that the political zealot was sucked into the system and became everything he had set out to change.

So the line-up for the big special on BBC1 at 8pm was Jesse Longfellow-Moses, Minnie Longfellow-Moses, The Amazing Mr X, Parker Weirdlove, Barney Thomson, Dr Louise Farrow, the Rev Blake, Veron Veron, James Eaglehawk, Patsy Morningirl, Alisdair MacPherson, Winona Wanderlip, Darius Grey and Hamish Robertson. A magnificent band of cowboys to lead Scotland forward, to show its best face on live television, beamed around the world. Scotland the brave! Or, Scotland the fucking shambolic, whichever came out first.

Rebecca Blackadder had not turned up for the meeting. She'd had an angry confrontation with Parker Weirdlove at four o'clock in the morning, when she had told him how absurd and tasteless she thought the show was, given the news about Michael. The show must go on, Weirdlove had parroted, Blackadder had told him not to be so bloody stupid, Weirdlove had told her that she could leave JLM's employ any time she felt like it, and she'd said she'd be out by the Friday afternoon. Everyone was happy.

Weirdlove had had a similar conversation with Farrow, but in the end she had capitulated and agreed to the show. Dressed in black. Which was how she was attired, as she sat waiting for Jesse Longfellow-Moses to arrive at the meeting.

None of the others seemed to have any particular thoughts on Father Michael.

✂

'Right,' said Weirdlove, looking around the ranks of the assembled cabinet and JLM's team, 'The First Minister will be along shortly. He's going to say a few words, then we'll hand you over to Bing here,' and he indicated a man dressed in black, wearing preposterously stylish shades, from beneath which emerged thin and neatly carved sideboards. Bing Velure nodded and cocked a cool hand the way of the docu-saps. (Bing Velure wasn't his real name.)

'I don't think I need to emphasise to you all,' Weirdlove continued, 'the ball-breaking importance of tonight's show. The country is in grave need of reassurance. We present a united front, we stand behind Mr Longfellow-Moses as one. Some of you might be mourning the loss of Father Michael, but be that as it may, the guy is dead, his crimes are history. Today is a new day, today we start moving forward. A new cabinet in place, new ideas for the future, we stand behind the First Minister.'

The door opened and Jesse Longfellow-Moses walked assuredly into the room, wearing a Sunday grey suit, with a rather dashing purple handkerchief poking its nose above the jacket pocket. Veron Veron sizzled with quiet pride.

JLM stood before his collective audience, nodding and waiting for the tumult of genuflection to die down; which actually didn't take very long, what with it never even getting going 'n all.

'Thank you, thank you,' he said, thinking he was Sinatra playing Vegas, 'thank you for coming here today, and for giving your Friday over to this wonderful television broadcast.'

He looked around the crowd, smiling wholesomely. There were a couple of faces which he didn't recognise, which he rightly took to be the new cabinet members; although he couldn't actually be sure that they hadn't already been in cabinet and he'd never noticed them.

'I don't need to tell you the importance of tonight's event,' he continued. 'The world will be watching, this is our chance to achieve greatness. To become a player, a respected voice of reason in a world gone mad. The world as one; hundreds of millions around the globe will tune in tonight to see democracy at work. Tonight we speak to the oppressed and the downtrodden. We speak to the free world as well as to the enslaved, and we speak with one voice. Scotland is great, Scotland can lead the way, the world can follow, follow Scotland, and every country on the planet can be lead by our example, can do the things that we do, breathe the beautiful fresh air of freedom that we breathe, drink from the burbling waters of hope from which we drink! We shall show the world that we are kings, and the world will look up to us and fall at our feet in recognition of our majesty! The opportunity is there, if only we can reach out and grab it with both hands! We must take this chance, we must! Are you with me?'

They stared at him. One or two of the new kids on the block thought they should say or do something, so they kind of mumbled or nodded in agreement. Veron Veron looked upon his leader with wonder, thinking that the beauty of his speech befitted the beauty of the grey suit with protruding purple handkerchief. Winona Wanderlip wished that she had a gun she could pull out to, at the very least, kneecap the idiot. James Eaglehawk thought delicious thoughts of all the documented evidence he had against JLM, and of his moment of glory when he produced it live on television, of JLM's humiliation and embarrassment, and inevitable tears and resignation; and Eaglehawk also thought delicious thoughts of the two women who had remained in his company for more than four hours, and who had performed acts upon each other and upon him that had defied all the known fundamental laws of physical anatomy and mathematics. Barney Thomson had switched off, and was not listening anymore. He would do everybody's hair, make them look as ridiculous as possible, and then he would be gone, before the tv show broadcast had even begun.

'Champion,' said JLM in acknowledgement of the very lukewarm response to his world domination speech, 'Minnie and I are going off to have a working breakfast with Mr Bellows. We'll leave you in the capable hands of Mr Velure here, who should tell you everything you need to know. Any questions? No, lovely. Champion,' he added, clasping his hands together and walking swiftly from the room. Minnie eyed the crowd with a knowing look, and followed in his wake. JLM had done everything to try and get Bellows alone for the working breakfast, but Minnie had pulled the usual threats about exposing him for everything that he'd done, and he'd been forced to concede her a major part in the whole thing. If he was going to be King, she was going to be Empress Queen of the Universe.

✂

'Nice speech from your boss fella there,' said Bing Velure, addressing the crowd, 'but I wouldn't all go peeing in your pants if I were you lot. The show is only occasionally picked up outside the UK, and it's a dead cert this one won't be. Home viewing figures can be sensational, but for filler shows like this one, we'll be lucky if we crack a million at the start, and even luckier if anyone at all is watching by the end. No one gives a shit about your guy here, so let's use that as a starting point. Everyone cool with that?' he asked, pointing his loaded index fingers at the audience. There were a few nods of agreement from the crowd.

'Would it help if I got my tits out?' said Patsy Morningirl, raising her hand.

'Are you anyone?' asked Velure. He'd noticed Morningirl already, of course.

'I'm the new, em, what is it again?' she said, looking at Weirdlove.

'Deputy First Minister,' said Weirdlove to Velure, who smiled.

'That would be G-R-E-A-T great, darlin',' he said. 'I'll maybe need to check out your breasts beforehand just to make sure they're suitable, but yeah, breasts are going to be great for the show. Mandy,' he said, turning to his assistant, a straight-backed girl in this year's spectacles, 'get that out to the media as soon as we're done here.'

'Totally,' she said.

'Right,' said Velure, turning back to his public, 'maybe the audience figures won't be so bad after all. Anyone got anything else they think can boost the figures, let me know.' He looked speculatively around the crowd, no one volunteered anything in the 1.3 seconds he gave them, albeit one or two, including Eaglehawk, decided they'd have a word in private later. 'Right, we run a tight ship here, no one talks for more than the allotted time. In fact, some of you people just have to accept that you're window dressing, zip, that's it. You get your hair done, you put on your best clobber, and schtoom. You don't like it, you take your complaints to Mr Weirdlove here. The majority of the piece is going to be with Longfellow-Moses. On top of that, we'll have a few minutes with Wanderlip,' and he looked quizzically around the crowd, until Winnie raised a desultory hand. 'Excellent,' he said, ‘yeah, you’re like nothing to look at, but with a bit of lippy and some decent garb you’re gonna scrub up all right.’

Wanderlip bit one of her lips, the top one, and stared at the floor. The old familiar feelings of anger were beginning to rise inside her. Mandy leant towards Velure, whispered something in his ear, and dropped back down into her seat.

‘Hey,’ said Velure to Wanderlip, ‘Winnie. I hear you’ve got some great nipple action going on. We’re probably going to be able to use them.’

She looked up, employing one of Weirdlove’s destructo-ray looks. It more or less passed straight through him.

‘So, like,’ said Velure, ‘would you be willing to do a joint breast shot with the Deputy here, or are we talking the whole covered nipple thing, straining against tight fabric and all that?’

Wanderlip dug her nails into the palms of her hands, not entirely sure why she was restraining herself here. Who exactly was she protecting? But she knew, however, that if she gave this guy the slightest hint of ill-humour, he was the type to make some supercilious remark about her menstrual cycle. She could always fuck him one in the nuts, though.

‘I don't think either would be appropriate for Ms Wanderlip,’ said Weirdlove from the wings.

Velure glanced at him, gave him the benefit of two second’s thought, shrugged and looked back at his notes.

‘Right, we’ll talk to the Deputy, who’s gonna get her boobies out, and we’ll talk to Wanderlip, who’s keeping everything safely under lock and key. And hey, if I had bazookas like yours, girlfriend, I’d do the same, so no one’s blaming you. If the show crashes, really, it won’t be your fault, so don’t feel bad.’

He glanced sincerely up at her, sucked in at will the photon torpedoes she was firing, then looked quickly down the list.

‘The Reverend Blake, we got a Reverend Blake?’ he asked, looking up, and his eyes fell on her before she’d said anything, the dog collar being a bit of a giveaway ‘n all.

‘You’re Blake?’ he said, entirely superfluously. ‘That’s cool. We’re gonna have a word or two with you. You know, spiritual stuff in these dark times, your reaction to the Father being this weirdo psycho serial killer guy. You cool?'

Blake nodded.

'I shall happily speak the word of God,' she said, solemnly.

'Great,' said Velure. 'And where d'you stand on the breast issue?'

He engaged her eyes hopefully for a couple of seconds, realised he was getting nothing in response, nodded and turned back to the clipboard.

'That's about it. We might have a word with one or two others, it just depends on time. We're really going to be concentrating on the guy Longfellow-Moses, and Patsy here's breasts. We cool?' he asked, looking around the assembly.

Well, there were a few people who had a thing or two to say, but they all kept their mouths shut. Either with the thought of letting it all pass with as little fuss as possible or, like Eaglehawk, with the intention of drawing a few things to the attention of Velure, so that he would get his five minutes in the sun, live on air, when the time came. Patsy Morningirl's breasts were not going to get a look in.

'Terrific,' said Velure. 'Make-up and clothes are here between five and seven tonight. I believe you've got a guy doing hair and Weirdlove here's got the timings on that one. After seven, we'll then have an hour to chill, talk things over, maybe pop the odd relaxing pill, however you folks want to handle it. Then we're on at eight, it'll be forty-five solid, cake-your-pants minutes, then it'll all be over before you know and you'll wonder where the time went.'

Another look around the dull, expectant faces.

'It's a W-R-A-P wrap,' said Velure, then he placed the clipboard under his arm and, with Mandy falling in behind him, he was off.

They watched him go, they watched the door close, they turned back and looked at each other. None of them had anything to say, and eventually they all began to drift off in silent ones and twos.

43

More women than you can shake a stick at

Barney Thomson had walked down the steps of no.6 Bute House, the official residence of the First Minister, and started walking through the Georgian elegance of Charlotte Square, when he became aware of firm footsteps closing behind him. Someone old, someone new, someone borrowed, someone blue…

'Hey, Barn,' said the voice, to get him to stop. Barney recognised it, and walked on. He wasn't going to be picked up and dropped and picked up again by any old woman; any more than he had been already.

'Barn,' said the Rev Blake, coming up beside him. 'You got time to talk?'

Barney walked on without looking at her.

'Not really in the mood,' he said.

'Jesus,' said the Rev Blake, 'you're not pissed at me because I haven't spoken to you since we fucked, are you? That's schoolboy stuff.'

Barney put his hands in his jacket pockets, wrapped it more closely around himself against the cold wind.

'I've just had enough of you all,' he said. 'I don't belong in amongst all this absurd crap.'

He threw her a sideways glance.

'I wasn't bothered about your shag 'n dash,' he continued, 'but it was rude. It was schoolgirl stuff to do it, and then avoid me, like you were embarrassed or something. But look, I'm not getting into conversations about maturity or any shite like that. It's all bullshit. I just shouldn't be here, and once all this stupid bollocks is over tonight, I'm leaving.'

‘Why wait?’ she said quickly, a smile coming from nowhere.

He turned. She wasn’t wearing a coat – white collar, black shirt, long black skirt – and she looked very, very cold. Face pale, lips blue, eyes shining brightly in the chill autumn wind.

‘They asked me to sort everyone’s hair out, I said I would,’ said Barney.

‘Ah,’ she said, ‘the old Calvinistic work ethic. A beautiful thing,’ she added. Then she said, ‘You want to go and grab breakfast. I know a place they do a killer Bloody Mary at this time in the morning.’

Barney looked at his watch. He’d already had breakfast, brought to him by one of the angelic Chinese-garbed überchicks, but you can never have too much breakfast in life. You just need to leave a decent gap between your two breakfasts, and your second one will be fine.

‘Yeah,’ he said, ‘I could do that. Where are we going?’’

And they walked on in search of manna.

‘You think Michael committed those murders?’ said Barney, in between bacon that was only slightly overdone and scrambled eggs that were of near perfect consistency.

Blake quaffed a Bloody Mary, spread some more marmalade on toast, speared a sausage, licked her fingers; the last of which was extremely erotic, even for this time on a Friday morning.

‘Nope,’ she said. ‘Michael was a good man.’

‘Claimed God made him do it,’ said Barney.

‘Well,’ said Blake, ‘if he’d actually believed in God, that might’ve meant something. But he was stuck in the wrong job. His mother decided the damn second he was born that he was going to be a priest, and she had her way. Michael was just going through the motions until she died, and then he was out of there. I’m not saying he didn’t have his faults or anything, but he never killed anyone.’

‘So how come he knew where the bodies were?’ asked Barney, just before he took the time to savour a particularly succulent slice of black pudding.

Blake crunched deliciously into a piece of crispy toast, then licked the crumbs from her lips. She held Barney's gaze, smiled slyly, touched the corner of her mouth with her thumb.

'Well, Barn, you're the one working for the detectives. Can't you work it out?'

Barney did that thing where you take a little bit of everything on your plate – in this case bacon, scrambled egg, black pudding, sausage, potato scone, hash brown and mushrooms – crammed it onto his fork and popped it into his mouth. Never took his eye off her while he contemplated what she'd said.

Michael had evidence from the deaths, had maybe even handled the bodies, but he wasn't the killer.

'He was an unwilling assistant?' he said, after a good stiff mouthful of tea.

'Could be,' said Blake. 'I mean, it's not like I know. But I have my theory, and that's not it.'

Barney went around his plate, chasing some more food, munching away while he thought about it, irritated at himself for playing her game.

'What d'you know about Michael?' she said, leading him on, albeit unsure herself what Barney was going to know about him.

It seemed pointless to keep secrets, but he wasn't about to tell her about Michael and Blackadder and Farrow. Maybe she already knew, but if she didn't, it wasn't his place to fill her in. But perhaps that was what she was getting at. Michael had fingered Blackadder to him, first of all. He'd said that she'd confessed. Maybe it was more than that. Maybe he'd known she was committing the murders, and had followed her around, clearing up the mess.

So he was hopelessly in love, desperately covering the tracks of the killer. But was it Blackadder? He had also been Farrow's lover.

'You think he was covering for someone?' said Barney, with no intention of naming the names he had in mind.

Blake tapped her nails against her empty Bloody Mary glass.

'It would take a heck of a lot of devotion to do that,' said Barney. 'More than devotion,' he added.

'You can't deny,' said Blake, 'that whoever's involved with these murders, there are extremes going on. Extremes of passion, extremes of hate, extremes of love. Every base emotion, stretched to the limit. And when you pull the strings of emotion that tightly, they snap, and when they snap, Jesus,' she said, 'anything can happen.'

'So,' said Barney, 'who's he covering for?'

Blake stretched her hands out.

'Who knows?' she said. 'But it's going to be a woman, right? Shit, we all know what priests are like, but Michael wasn't taking it up the butt from anyone.'

'So he's protecting a woman,' said Barney, not knowing how much knowledge Blake was in possession of; whether she was leading him on, or working it out with him.

'Exactamundo,' said Blake, sounding, for all the world, like Detective Chief Inspector Solomon. Barney noticed. 'And let's face it, the guy never mixed with anyone outwith our little circle.'

Barney struggled with a tricky piece of bacon, that was just a little too crispy to be forked, scooped it up in the end, and crunched it.

'Blackadder,' he said when he was done, 'or Farrow. Or you,' he added, raising an eyebrow at her.

She smiled. She made a start on her coffee which had been delivered at the same time as the bloody Mary and was on its way to being too cold.

'Well,' she said, 'I can't argue that one. I fit the bill. Except, of course, that we all know that Michael was banging Blackadder and Lou, and he wouldn't touch me with a stick. Didn't think it was appropriate, bless him.'

'Only got your word for that,' said Barney, his eyebrow still doing that whole Spock thing. Scooped up the last of the scrambled egg with a piece of toast.

'That's true,' she said, and drank her coffee, looking at him over the rim of the large cup. 'And how can you trust the word of a vicar like me?'

'Exactly,' said Barney.

She drank her coffee and Barney drank his tea, and he wondered if the list of suspects was really as small as they had just reduced it to.

'There is someone else, of course,' she said, as if she could hear his thoughts.

'Go on,' said Barney.

Blake laid down her cup, rested her chin in the palm of her hand, elbow on the table.

'Have you met Minnie?' she asked.

Barney shook his head.

'This morning was the first time I'd seen her,' he said.

'Well,' said Blake, 'she's not been around much the past week. But all of us, in the past few months, have done for her whatever it is we do for JLM. Design clothes, minister, doctor, whatever, we've all done it. Michael will've seen plenty of her.'

'What's she like?' said Barney.

Blake smiled. She knew exactly what Minnie Longfellow-Moses was like; in all sorts of different ways, if you know what I'm saying.

'She's interesting,' said Blake. 'Wouldn't have her pegged as a killer, of course, but then whoever it turns out to be, we're going to be able to say that.'

Barney nodded. He surveyed the scene of devastation that was the breakfast table and decided he'd had enough. He'd reached the limit of breakfast number two, despite the seductive presence of a further three slices of toast.

'And maybe it'll turn out to have been just Michael after all,' said Barney. 'Some things are as plain as they seem.'

The Reverend Blake stared deep into Barney's eyes. He held her gaze, wondered at the blackness of its depth.

'That,' she said, 'would be the biggest surprise of all.'

And then again, that would depend on how you'd categorise surprise. Just because Michael had been able to leave a note detailing the whereabouts of all the victims of the Kabinet Killer, did not automatically mean that he had been the Undertaker, clearing up after the killer's crimes…

Barney got back to his room early in the afternoon. An hour to watch tv or get his head down or do whatever, then he would head over to JLM's office to start his round of appointments, with everyone penned in between two and five pm. (JLM had very kindly given his staff as much of the day off as possible, so that they would all look relaxed and stress-free for the cameras.)

Wondering what he was going to do with himself when he left here, because he had no idea. That, strangely, felt like a familiar, and almost comfortable emotion. Was it because Barney Thomson had been a wanderer before he'd fallen to his death; or because he wasn't Barney Thomson at all, as Farrow had told him, and the man he'd been in the past had been a wanderer.

It was enough to make his mind boil and spit, so he didn't think about it for long. After the stupid show that evening, a show he did not actually intend turning up for, he would spend one more night in his comfortable prison, and then he'd be away in the morning. A short walk down to Waverley train station and he could head north or south or west as the whim took him.

He opened the door to his apartment, and immediately smelled the light scent in the air even before he saw her standing at the window, looking out at the cold, grey day and the Victorian rooftops. He closed the door behind him, she didn't turn. He walked over and stood beside her looking out at the day.

They stood like that for a while, watching the formless grey clouds drifting at different speeds, minutely changing the shade of the sky with every passing minute. Eventually one of their hands found the other, and their fingers entwined. He felt the warmth of her touch, she squeezed his hand tightly, then relaxed.

'You go to the meeting this morning?' said Rebecca Blackadder eventually.

He nodded, she felt the movement.

'It's disgusting,' she continued. 'I know, I'm not at all surprised, but if ever there was a time for the man to show the least compassion.'

'He appears quite lost in his own little world,' said Barney.

'Michael was a good man,' she said, almost cutting Barney off. 'And they'll use this to neatly brush it all under the carpet.'

'You don't think he killed them?' asked Barney.

'Of course he bloody didn't,' she snapped. Her fingers tensed, but her hand stayed in his. 'Christ, you've seen what he's like, what Weirdlove is like. I wouldn't be surprised if they planted that note on Michael, planted the evidence on him. Jesus, I wouldn't be surprised if they'd pushed him off the top of the bloody building.'

Barney let the words go, let the anger fizzle out and die in the cold, grey afternoon. She sniffed, she wiped her nose and her eyes; but she never removed her hand from his.

'He confessed to me,' said Barney quietly. 'I saw him yesterday evening, before he died.'

She swallowed, bit her bottom lip. Breathed heavily.

'Did you believe him?'

'No,' said Barney quickly, and that was the truth. His words had most definitely had the ring of deceit. He was covering for someone, but he couldn't imagine for a second that it would've been Longfellow-Moses or Parker Weirdlove. 'He was trying to hide someone, but it wasn't JLM.'

She didn't reply. For the first time Barney turned and looked at her, and her face was cold and sad and drained. She was genuinely saddened by Michael's death; genuinely shocked that JLM should go ahead with his broadcast to the nation at a time like this. Nothing like Alison Blake's vague interest, bordering on amusement, that JLM should be so full of himself that nothing would stop his fifteen minutes of tv fame.

'You knew about Michael and Farrow?' she said slowly, her eyes diverting slightly to look at him.

Oh, yes, thought Barney. Him and Farrow, him and you, no end of malarkey. Doubt you're going to own up to your own little affair, though, are you? While all the time you implicate others. You're all the same, all jostling for position in the innocent corner, while pushing everyone else towards the guilty corner. *It wasn't me guv, but see that bastard over there, up to her eyeballs in motives!*

'Yeah,' said Barney. 'She seemed pretty quiet today. Didn't speak to her though, didn't see anyone speaking to her.'

'He loved her,' said Blackadder, her voice even smaller than before. 'He would've done anything for her. He hated the fact that they couldn't be out in the open about it. A relationship spent skulking about in the middle of the night.'

Barney turned and looked at her again. The one definite sighting he knew of Michael skulking about in the middle of the night, had been from Blackadder's room to Farrow's. She wasn't volunteering that little bit of information.

'Why are you here?' asked Barney suddenly, and she turned at his tone of voice.

Her eyes were pale blue and sad.

'I was lonely,' she said. 'I wanted to see you before I left.'

Barney swallowed. From one woman to another. But while Alison Blake had that raw sexuality about her, there was nothing behind the front. The passion was strangely passionless; the warmth was cold.

Blackadder was beautiful and vulnerable, greater depth, infinite warmth. And very possibly a liar, which made her all the more interesting, all the more inviting, all the more enticing, bewitching and impossible.

Barney moved slightly, drew her hand closer to his body, bent his head and kissed her softly on the lips. His other hand came up and touched her hair, brought her head in closer to his, and then their arms were around each other and they were enshrouded in an impassioned clinch.

Nice one for the big fella Barney, as Wally McLaven would've said, had he not had his throat slit.

44

All the world is queer save thee and me, and even thou art a little queer

Barney was flowing, zipping his way through three hours of haircuts, and the odd bit of styling for the womenfolk. In less time than it would take for a politician to mention himself in an interview, he had bestowed the following haircuts: to Veron Veron, a really rather wonderful 'Elton John, *Diana*'; a fuck me bob for Patsy Morningirl; a 'Bonfire of the Vanities' for Darius Grey; a short back & sides for Parker Weirdlove, in and out in a minute and a half; a James Bond for James Eaglehawk; and a 'Findus Feelin' Great ad', for the Reverend Blake.

He'd had a couple of minutes to himself, looking out at the low grey clouds sweeping across the hill, thinking about Rebecca Blackadder, when the door opened and in stepped The Amazing Mr X. Barney turned, dragged himself back from the oblivion of the romantic abyss, and slipped once more into his barber persona.

'X,' he said. 'Take a seat. What can I do for you?'

The Amazing Mr X eased himself into the barber's chair, imagined it was still warm from the heavenly Rev Blake, and looked at himself in the mirror.

He had been envisioning the best possible scenarios from the evening's events. If he played his cards right, if everything went well, it could be that he'd become a celebrity undercover bodyguard. Maybe he'd even get his own tv slot, talking about bodyguard issues. Or he could be the host of a game show such as *Big Bodyguard* or *Who Wants To Be A Bodyguard?* or *The Weakest Bodyguard*. Or maybe he'd get spotted by some

Hollywood babe, Sharon Stone or Halle Berry or one of that mob, and the command would go out for him to move to Beverly Hills. He had vowed to protect JLM with his life; but he did not suffer from the same delusions about the First Minister's place in the world. JLM was small fry, The Amazing Mr X was a big bodyguard, in more ways than one. He should be standing shoulder to shoulder, neck to neck, with the other behemoths at the Oscars and film world premiers. The Scottish Parliament, and the world of politics in general, was small potatoes. He should be out there with the big guns of the world of entertainment, where status, celebrity and power actually stood for something. That was where he belonged, that was his destiny, and this was his chance.

'What d'you think?' said X, willing to hand the reins over to the professional.

'You've got a good head of hair on you, X,' said Barney, giving his hair the once over; and deciding that when you're talking to a guy who, no matter how ridiculous he is, could rip your head off with his thumbs, it was best to butter them up than be perfectly honest. (The Amazing Mr X actually had a bit of an Elliot Gould, which is nothing if not a disaster. Look at, well, Elliot Gould.) 'I can pretty much give you what you want.'

'Legend,' said X, nodding, imagining no end of outrageous scenarios that were going to come from his fantastic hair. 'You know,' he continued, 'I want to look like a 70's porno star. That's a great look.'

Barney took a small step away from X and checked out his hair again.

'You're in the right zone, X,' he said. 'You might have to work on the 'tache and sideboards a bit though.'

The Amazing Mr X stroked his face and nodded.

'Yeah,' he said. 'I was thinking maybe one of those clean shaven 70's porno guys,' he said.

Barney looked at him, not entirely sure how to continue the conversation. *Shut up, you fucking loony* was obviously called for, but would have been just a little ill-judged. Probably best, in fact, to not continue the conversation at all, but to just get on with it and make him look like John Holmes *et al*.

And so, lifting a brush, a can of mousse, some sun-dried tomatoes and a bottle of balsamic vinegar, Barney got to work.

✂

The final entrant to the Barney Thomson hairfest was Minnie Longfellow-Moses. She arrived late, not that Barney was in the least bit concerned, marched in, somehow managed to invest the act of sitting in the chair with complete dominion, and engaged Barney's eyes in the mirror.

'I'll have a Roosevelt, please,' she said.

'Teddy, Franklin or Eleanor?' said Barney, with a certain acerbity, as he'd been instinctively annoyed by the brusqueness of her manner.

She raised an eyebrow at him, but didn't turn around.

'Watch it, Bud,' was all she said.

Barney smiled.

'Eleanor Roosevelt it is, then,' he said, and lifted up the chainsaw and comb to get on with the job.

Minnie watched him for a few moments, curious about getting to meet this man at last. She'd also read *Barney Thomson: Urban Legend*, but was not, however, entirely acquainted with the explanation of how someone who'd been dead for two and a half years came to be styling her hair.

She softened a little. (After initially thinking the tv thing an absurdity, MLM had seen the possibilities of it and had, as a consequence, gone into Lady Macbeth mode; becoming, in the process, as blinded as her husband to the fact that very few people would be watching; and those who were, would be doing so solely for the viewing experience of Patsy Morningirl's breasts and Winona Wanderlip's nipples.) Barney could feel the immediate alleviation of the atmosphere in the room and he caught her eye once more in the mirror.

'Who's doing *your* hair?' she said, a wee bit of a smile suddenly cropping up, to accompany the softer hue.

'No one,' he replied.

'It's perfect, is it?' she said. Feeling mischievous all of a sudden, as if Barney might be a good bloke with whom to flirt. She had heard tell, after all, that he'd given the Reverend Blake a good old seeing to.

'Two things,' said Barney, while he continued smoothly with the cut. 'Firstly, my hair's not great, but it's not so bad that it needs cutting for some ridiculous tv show. And second, I'm not going to be around for the tv show anyway, so it doesn't matter.'

'Oh, Barney,' she said, looking at him with mock disapproval. 'How could you miss it?'

Barney began to prep some nuclear fission fuelled curling tongs, which he'd had specially flown in from Kazakhstan. He gestured at her with a comb.

'You want to know how I can miss it?' he said. 'Because your husband is the most horribly ignorant, self-serving egotist I've ever met in my life.'

He felt like he was going out on a limb, unaware that Minnie had even more contempt for JLM than he himself.

'You haven't known many politicians then,' she said.

'And I don't want to,' said Barney. 'I'm leaving first thing in the morning, but before that I'm going to sit tonight and watch Jesse preen himself, and the rest of you suck up to his backside.'

Minnie Longfellow-Moses smiled again. Watched Barney at work for a short time, his hands flying backwards and forwards across the breadth of her hair, performing the work of a necromancer, for she had not the quality of hair necessary for an Eleanor Roosevelt.

'You don't like him, then?' she said, deciding to rejoin the flirtatious skirmish; not that Barney saw it remotely as flirtatious. He saw it more as 'trying hard not to slag off the boss too much to his wife, but wanting to stick a size twelve into him at the same time'.

'Look,' he said, 'I know he's your husband 'n all, but if you're going to ask, I'm going to tell you. I wouldn't fart on him if he needed his hair blow-dried.'

'I should certainly hope not,' she said.

'Maybe he's no better or worse than other politicians in the same circumstances, but he's the only one I've ever met, and I think he's shameful.'

'Well,' she said, 'I can see how you might think that. Why don't you come on the show and say that?'

'Go on live tv and denounce the First Minister?'

'Yeah,' she said. 'It might be fun.'

'No it wouldn't,' said Barney. 'All it'd mean would be that I was tonight's thing in the media, everyone having a bit of a laugh. In the papers tomorrow I'd be fitted in between Liz Hurley's latest Botox injection and Posh's current attempt to sell some crap piece of bollocks, masquerading as music. By Sunday, it'll have been forgotten about, because there'll be really crap football results from Saturday to be reported, and Pamela Anderson'll have had another breast implant. The media aren't interested in politics and the people aren't interested. I just don't want to be a part of it, full stop.'

She nodded sagely. She'd been making plans for her own political career, once her husband's had collapsed – an event which she envisioned occurring at some time just after eight-thirty that evening – but she was wise enough to know that Barney spoke the truth. However, she was also conceited enough to think that she would have the force of personality to change the media.

'You've suffered from them in the past,' she said.

'Maybe,' he replied, 'but it's not about that. I'm sick and tired of it, that's all. The people who run this country have been mown down, for God's sake, and the papers are still more interested in the fact that an English lassie refused to eat a live cockroach on Survivor last week. It's pathetic.'

Under the cape, which Barney had thrown on at the outset of the confrontation, she briefly applauded. He shook his head.

'Very moral of you, Mr Thomson,' she said. 'What are you going to do? Go and live on an uninhabited island in the south Pacific?'

'No,' he said, 'but I might go and live in Sweden or somewhere like that, where I won't be able to read any of the papers or understand any of the television.'

'Very brave,' she said. 'When you see something you don't like, run away. If it all appals you so much, then why not try and change it?'

Barney finally stopped his whirlwind dash round her Eleanor Roosevelt bonce, and stood still, brush in one hand, thermonuclear welding device in the other.

'How d'you mean that?' he said.

'Do the media give people all the junk because that's what they want, or do the people want all the junk because that's what the media give them?' she said, then continued talking like a true politician, without giving him the chance to answer. 'You can't blame the media, when all they're doing is meeting demand. If you want to change it, what you have to do is change the mindset of the people. And that's where a good politician comes in.'

Barney nodded. It seemed nicer to do just that rather than say the more honest, 'you've got to be fucking kidding me?' Even JLM had already come to the conclusion that he was in no position to do anything about society, and he was the leading politician in the country.

'And are you backing your husband to do all this?' asked Barney, 'or do you have ambitions of your own.'

Minnie Longfellow-Moses smiled again. Wasn't looking him in the eye. When she did finally make her royal proclamation of political intent, it was going to be to a much grander audience than Barney Thomson.

He watched her for a second, then started back on her 40's Ladies Auxiliary cut, with a touch of Sisters of Sappho for authenticity. Could tell what she was thinking. Another one carried away with the power of it all; and she didn't even have any power. Bloody idiot. That, and she was named after a mouse.

'Well,' she said, 'I'll say this, Barney. I suspect it might just be worth your time turning up at this show tonight. It might not be as dull as you think it's going to be. If you know what I'm saying.'

Barney paused, caught her eye again, recognised the mad glint of the megalomaniac, then powered up the Black & Decker three-in-one, and got on with the haircut in hand.

A woman with her own agenda, he thought. How scary is that? Still, if there was the chance that JLM was going to get his comeuppance, and to be served bloody right for having the nerve to participate in this show in the first place, perhaps it might be worth a visit after all. Didn't mean he couldn't get on the train the next day and head for the hills.

Maybe he would go, maybe he wouldn't. In the end, what would it matter?

45

Showtime

The show was due to start in five. The guests had gathered, nervous and ambitious, in the sitting room of the First Minister's official residence. JLM, MLM, Dr Farrow, Veron Veron, The Amazing Mr X, Parker Weirdlove, the Reverend Blake, Winona Wanderlip, Patsy Morningirl, James Eaglehawk, Darius Grey, and finally the two cabinet makeweights of Hamish Robertson and Alisdair MacPherson, men who were genuine politicians, and therefore of interest to neither the public nor television.

All-American talk show host, Larry Bellows, was still in his dressing room; show producer, Bing Velure, was about to give the participants a final run-through. It'd all been a bit hurried, but he thought he just about had enough to keep the audience interested. There would be Patsy's boobs, and then, well, he'd have to fill up the rest with people talking, but they'd wing it. There was also the thing that Eaglehawk had mentioned, although he wasn't sure that the total political and public humiliation of a politician that no one had heard of was going to make that great tv. Certainly wouldn't be a match for a fine pair of breasts. (And he had already taken the opportunity to verify their quality.)

He looked over the sorry bunch, because that was inevitably how he perceived anyone involved in politics. He was supposed to make forty-five minutes of interesting television out of this lot.

'Right, everyone,' snapped Velure, thinking already that this might be the nadir of his career to date – even worse than the documentary on the proliferation of cheap blue plastic bags in West Africa, narrated by Mel B, in which he'd allowed himself to get involved – 'we've only got a few minutes, so can I have your undivided.'

The gentle babble of conversation died away, to be replaced by the low murmur of nervous rectums.

'I'm looking at a quick run-through of events, so everyone please listen,' he began, and he looked sharply around his audience to make sure they were all paying attention. And they all were, except JLM, who was looking rather smugly out the window, thinking himself too important and too aware of everything that was going to happen, to have to listen to someone as lowly as a tv producer.

'As we open, the camera will pan around the room, starting with Mr Bellows, with Jesse and Minnie in the centre, taking everyone in, so the audience can get the picture of what they're dealing with here. And Patsy, we're looking for a quick flash of the boobs right from the off, just to get 'em hooked. You cool?'

'Totally,' she gushed.

'Sovereign,' said Velure. 'Don't linger on it, you know.' He snapped his fingers. 'That fast. It's almost as if the audience should've felt the presence of your breasts, rather than having actually seen them.'

An *'oh for God's sake'* escaped the mouth of Winona Wanderlip. Patsy Morningirl quickly sprang her blouse and closed it over again. All in a finger snap.

'Like that?' she spurted.

'Extreme!' exclaimed Velure. 'Nailed it! Right, then we're going to come back to Mr Bellows, who you're all going to meet in a minute. He'll do a bit of an intro, then he'll hang it round to Jesse, and we're off. Thereafter, he'll talk to both Jesse and Minnie, as like a couple or something, then we'll bring in some of the others, as either they or Mr Bellows see fit. Obviously, Patsy, we won't be bringing you in too early, because we don't want to smoke all our joints in the first five minutes. What we need is drama here, people. Drama. You know what I'm saying?'

He looked around the blank faces. *I'm not getting my kit off*, thought the other women. *I wonder if some of the other women are going to get their kit off*, thought the men.

'D-R-A-M-A drama,' said Velure, 'is the name of the game. We all need it, it's up to you lot to supply. Anyone have anything to say, ping it in there. We cool?'

A few nods.

'Doesn't matter what you want to get out there,' he continued, 'as long as it's not dull. Any of you comedians got any stuff about the welfare state or the Health Service or taxes, anything like that, we'll cut you off as soon as you open your mouth. Keep 'em coming, and keep 'em short. You'll know if we want you to keep talking, 'cause Mr Bellows will take you up on it.'

'We're on in one,' said Mandy, Velure's assistant, and Bing Velure pointed his forefingers at the crowd.

'This is it, people, let's think on our feet and do everything to bring in the punters. Every second needs to be B-I-G big, so that we catch the channel surfers.'

'Ah!' said JLM suddenly, drawing a sharp look from Velure. 'Rebecca, wonderful of you to come. I knew you'd have a change of heart.'

Velure turned round; a few in the room looked askance. Dr Rebecca Blackadder had arrived, looking pretty hot, because she always did, but frankly her hair hadn't been done that day. And she was expecting to do live television!

'Who are *you*?' barked Velure, casting a professional eye over her body.

'She's part of my team,' said JLM standing up. 'Come in, Rebecca, come in.'

'Thirty!' chirped Mandy.

'You going to get your clothes off?' cracked Velure.

'No!' Blackadder snapped back at him.

'Whatever,' he said, 'you're decent enough window dressing. Someone get her a seat.'

A seat was found, JLM sat back down still smiling and saying 'champion' to himself, a few others muttered, and Rebecca Blackadder joined the throng, looking daggers all the time at Bing Velure, and already questioning her decision to change her mind at the last minute.

The door burst open again and Barney Thomson entered the fray. This time, most of the room had a look of approval, as they were all still basking in the feel-good glow of great hair.

'Barn!' several of them cried, as if he were a long lost friend.

He stopped, regarded them with suspicion, then looked at Velure.

'Am I too late?'

'Fifteen!' cried Mandy.

'You're the hair guy,' said Velure as a statement of fact. 'Get him a seat,' he yelled, without enthusiasm.

Barney walked in, eyes on Blackadder, wondering why she was there. Cast a quick glance at one or two of the others, did not return the smiles.

'Ten!' chirped Mandy.

'Right!' bawled Velure, with unnecessary majesty, 'the lions have entered the Coliseum! Everybody grab hold of their bowels!'

'Five...'

Barney sat down next to Rebecca Blackadder, raising an eyebrow in question.

'Four...'

'Couldn't keep yourself away?' he said.

'Three...'

'I'm not bloody letting him away with it,' she said, her voice low.

'Two...'

And with a swish of magisterial authority, crisply shaven, smelling of unbelievably expensive aftershave and with his intestines recently having benefited from a $61 colon hydrotherapy treatment, Larry Bellows swanked into the room, not a second too soon.

'One....'

Bellows embraced his company with the aura of his magnanimity, silently greeted them with open arms, then he sat down and fixed the great and humble smile to his face, as Mandy chopped her hand to indicate they were on air.

46

Soap Opera 1

The cameras had trawled round the room, past the nervous, the excited, the resigned, the angry, and Patsy with her amazing flashing chest, finally settling on the legend that was Larry Bellows. He was a big man, with a large round head, a broad chest, and a stout belly, from the very depths of which was emitted the most bombastic of New England laughs. But he could also do quiet and sincere and sensitive as required, with the full range of emotions and sympathies in-between.

He was, in fact, the talk-show equivalent of Jesse Longfellow-Moses, in that he was really rather small-time back home, compared to Letterman and Leno and the rest. But just because he was a waiter at Big Al's One Cheese Pizzeria, did not mean that he couldn't act like he owned Pizza Hut. Especially when he was becoming a thing in the UK, and was being paid a decent wedge of the licence payers' money from the BBC.

'Hey, everyone!' he said, in his usual salutation. 'Welcome to Larry Bellows Tonight! Really, really fantastic display there from the little lady! And we'll be seeing more of that kind of thing later!'

And he smiled disarmingly, then switched on his serious face.

'Jeez, we have such a great show for you tonight. I am so excited personally, because this fella that I'm going to introduce you to has been such a hero of mine since I arrived in your country. It's been my pleasure, Hell, I've been honoured to be able to spend the day with him today, getting to know him and his lovely wife.'

(Translation: he'd never heard of JLM before that morning, then he'd spent ten minutes with him and Minnie, before spending the day allowing the BBC to honour that part of his contract which stated they'd supply him with women, alcohol and hard drugs in the run-up to each show.)

'So, ladies and gentlemen, I want to introduce you to the First Minister of Scotland, England, Jesse Longfellow-Jesus. Jesse, it's such a pleasure having you on the show.'

JLM smiled in a cheesy American way, which he thought might be appropriate.

'Hell, thanks Larry, it sure is great to be here,' he said. 'Champion.'

'It's Longfellow-Moses,' said Minnie, quietly, the words passing straight over Bellows' head.

'And your lovely wife, Minnie,' said Bellows, and he gave her a smile that suggested he seriously wanted into her underwear. Minnie smiled, but the smile was one of restraint, Bellows' look inducing in her a brutal desire to bury a hatchet in his head.

'It's really great to have a First Lady named after a mouse, ain't it?' he said, patting her on the knee.

Minnie simmered while playing along, thinking that it was, for the time, politically expedient.

'For just over five years now,' said Bellows, looking seriously at the camera, doing his earnest anchorman routine, 'the people here in Scotland have had what they call devolved government. Hell, now I'm an American, I don't even know what that means. Tonight we're gonna learn a little more about it, and about some of the....personalities...who...'

He became a bit distracted as the camera, which had been honing in on him, began to twitch, as if being attracted to something else. Bellows turned and looked behind, allowing the camera to follow his look.

Patsy, bless her, was already at it. Like a kid with a big bowl of ice cream placed in front of her and told to wait, she just couldn't contain her excitement. She was standing behind Bellows, very casual, leaning on the mantleshelf, blouse open, right breast obvious to the audience.

Bellows ejaculated his enormous laugh. A few of the others shook their heads; a couple were already contemplating abandoning ship. JLM smiled.

'Hey!' bellowed Bellows, the loudness of his tone demanding that the camera be switched back to him, as it duly was, 'isn't that great! Who is that little filly anyway?'

'She's the Deputy First Minister,' said JLM, smiling, and you know, even he felt a bit of a squirm as he said it.

'Fan-tastic!' said Bellows. 'Let's talk about your government's attitude towards sex!'

JLM smiled. Not quite off to the start he was expecting. Bellows was bigger and louder and filled the room with far too much of his own presence. And with so many enormous egos present, there was bound to be trouble. Add that to the fact that the Kabinet Killer was also in the room and was, by design, a little unstable; that The Undertaker was nearby, and had his own issues to resolve; that there were at least four people present who intended publicly humiliating Jesse Longfellow-Moses (even more than he was going to be publicly humiliated by the whole thing as a matter of course); and that there were six other internecine affairs to be revealed, and, well Bing Velure needn't have worried.

They were in, as Larry Bellows himself might've said, for one Hell of a show...

47

Soap Opera 2

Fifteen minutes in and everything was running smoothly, even if it was a little on the dull side. Everyone had calmed down from the drug and testosterone fuelled overdrive of the first couple of minutes, Larry had been fed a couple of pointers so that he actually knew what he was talking about, and normal service had been resumed.

Of course, most people who had started watching had already changed channel, and Velure was getting edgy. They needed something to happen, and Patsy had already blown the sex card.

To the dismay of several of those present, Darius Grey, the new Minister for Health, had stolen the early part of the show, and had gone off on a passionate discourse on the future of health care in Scotland. It was politics at its most raw and socially responsible. Only Winona Wanderlip was impressed, but with every second that Grey spoke, she'd begun to realise that here was a genuine political challenger in their midst. The lad was only twenty-five, but it didn't mean that the press wouldn't grab him by the nostril hair, and start turning him into a *thing*.

As Bellows nodded sagely to another one of Grey's points, Mandy passed him a note.

Larry. Time to ask Longfellow-Moses about Hookergate!

Bellows glanced at the note and looked up at Grey. The young lad was slightly thrown by the note thing – lack of experience, you see – which was enough to allow Bellows to break into his flow on radicalising health care for the elderly.

'Well, I think we all agree with your thoughts on that. One for the future, eh, Jesse?' he said, turning back to JLM.

'Absolutely, champion,' said JLM. 'My first priority in government has always been to promote the ideas of the young. You see, it's my…'

'Yeah, great,' said Bellows. 'Now, one of the things that a lot of people have been talking about is the little matter of Hookergate.'

The smile froze on JLM's face, but he did his best to keep his shoulders straight, and his mouth turned up at the corners.

'Hell, it sounds like something Bill Clinton would've got involved in, but it happened right here in little old Scotland. Tell us all about it, Jesse.'

JLM looked down at the carpet, nodding, sorting out his persona, so that when he looked up he would be in character. He'd had a meeting earlier with Velure, and they'd agreed on a variety of subjects that would not be touched upon. Hookergate had been one of them. If Bellows was going to pull that one out the bag, nothing would be inviolable. JLM cast Velure a quick and vicious glance, which television picked up in all its beautiful scorn, then smiled at Bellows.

'You know as well as I, Larry,' he said, 'what the media are like, especially in this country. While we strive to bring serious issues to the breakfast tables of the people of Scotland, the press are more interested in pointless tittle-tattle, in helping to create political legends such as myself, only so they can knock them down again. The first battle of any government is with the media. That is why it is the first instrument to be taken under state control in dictatorships. But in democracies such as ours, it is time that the media realised their responsibilities, it is time that they matured into the freedoms which have been granted to them.'

'A lovely polemic, Jesse,' said Bellows, 'but to get back to the question in hand. Is it true you porked your secretary, then had her stiffed when she threatened to talk?'

JLM laughed. Minnie pulled herself away from him a little, lovely body language, and waited to hear the bluster with which he would answer.

'Preposterous!' barked JLM.

'So, why is it you've been unable to recruit a new secretary since Mrs Walters was killed in a mysterious automobile accident? Some say it's because no one will touch the position for fear of the same thing happening to them. You're the First Minister for Chrissake, surely you can get someone to work for you?'

JLM hesitated. This was going way further than even the press had gone. They hadn't been aware that he was without a secretary. Someone from the inner circle must have talked. And if they'd talked about that...

'Look,' said JLM, and Minnie was now a couple of feet away from him, staring intently, 'Veronica was a very dear and lovely woman. Very sweet, very, very dear.'

'You mean, she charged a lot for sex?' said Bellows. 'Am I picking you up right?'

Minnie sniggered.

'She was lovely,' said JLM, with especial emphasis, 'a very lovely, lovely person. I never, never, never had relations with her. Ever.'

'Sexual relations?' said Bellows.

'I never had relations,' said JLM. 'And I can assure you that I was absolutely devastated when I learned that she had died so tragically. Devastated.'

Bellows did his sage nod, wished he was having this discussion with a politician who mattered, if there's such a thing, then gave Minnie a look of immense sympathy, as though she had cancer or something.

'Minnie,' he said, 'you've stood by Jesse through these difficult times. Was there ever a moment when you thought, I've had enough? I'm just gonna blow this guy off?'

The camera closed in on Minnie. Here we go, thought most of the people in the room, and almost everybody still watching on television. The usual stand-by-your-man crap.

'Hell yes!' said Minnie. 'And don't look at me as though I had cancer, Bud! I know I should stand by my husband, and the last thing I would want is for anyone to think me disloyal. But when you've caught your husband with his face buried deep between another woman's thighs, well you find that loyalty stretched.'

'That wasn't Veronica!' sputtered JLM, which probably wasn't the best rejoinder.

'Hey, Cowboy!' said Bellows.

'Who was it then?' said Minnie, looking outraged, but actually delighted that JLM had been so stupid as to be sucked in.

'Maybe it was this trollop!' said James Eaglehawk who had, up until now, been unable to get a word in, was feeling a bit left out and was desperate for an opportunity. And as he said the words, he stepped forward, thrusting several full colour photographs of JLM and an unknown woman into the hands of the other combatants and in front of the camera.

'Wow!' said Bellows, very impressed. 'Getta loada these!'

'Who's this?' said Minnie, indignantly, but not actually in the least bit bothered.

'Well, clearly that isn't me in the photographs,' said JLM with a politician's ease for the lie, even though it blatantly was him in the photographs. 'I've never seen this woman before in my life.' Not in a couple of months at any rate.

'Hell!' said Bellows, 'you shouldn't be embarrassed, Jesse. You take a great photo!'

'Oh,' said JLM, not sure what to do now. Never one to look a compliment in the mouth.

'Well,' said Bellows, 'Minnie, let's take a moment here. Remember we're on live television.'

Bellows reached out and took hold of Minnie's hand. He knew how to work the scene. A brief moment of hyperactivity, then slow things down; let everyone relax a little, then crank it way back up again. A rollercoaster. Suddenly he wasn't doing political insight, he was Geraldo or Jerry Springer. This would play great back home, if they ever got to see it.

'You've just been shown photographs of your husband having unbelievable sex with another woman. Millions of people have just watched as you were publicly humiliated. This man you call your husband has just degraded you in front of the entire world. You have been humbled, stripped of your dignity, your reputation lies like canine poop in the dirt. He has demeaned and cheapened you, to the point where there's not a single viewer out there who will consider you any better than some slimy, pustulant bug, ready to be squished on the windshield of history. How does it feel?'

JLM wanted to interject but somehow the moment wasn't right, even for him. Minnie stared at the floor, head racing. She hadn't intended that it should all fall out quite like this. She wasn't thinking about her humiliation, of course. Couldn't give a damn about that. She was, like all the best political animals, trying to decide what was going to play best with the voting public. What was going to get her the most sympathy? Anger, forgiveness, tears, outright venom? Difficult to make a decision without a team of highly paid advisors giving her feedback.

'You tell him to stick it up his ass, darling!' said a voice from the back.

They turned. Veron Veron had risen to his feet. It talks!

'Veron!' said JLM.

'Who's the poof?' said Velure, off-camera.

Veron bristled, and pointed a crooked finger.

'You are so much better than him, darling, so much better. You have so got to walk away.'

Minnie said nothing, eyed Veron Veron up for a short while, then turned back to JLM.

'This is, like, who?' said Bellows.

'He's supposed to be my dresser,' said JLM, attempting to give Veron a bit of a death stare.

Minnie remained silent. She too, turned and gave Veron a bit of a death stare. He was meant to be keeping his mouth shut.

'I'm her lover!' Veron exclaimed violently to the world, delighted with the release of the truth.

A few jaws dropped. Minnie felt speared by the revelation and said nothing.

'Cool,' said Bellows. 'And we all had you pegged as totally homosexual.'

'Minnie?' said JLM, looking at her like a lost dog, desperately hurt. That man-thing which allowed him to have no end of sexual partners, but as soon as he found out about his wife having one, he was devastated.

'Oh for God's sake, Jesse,' she said. This wasn't going to plan. No point in her husband's credibility being shot to pieces live on tv, when the same thing was happening to her. 'Don't look at me like that. You've slept with every tart you've ever met in your entire life.'

'I have not!' he protested.

'Ha!' said Eaglehawk from the back, and with that he threw some more pictures of JLM and an assorted bag of women into the mix.

Bellows grabbed at some of them and held them up for the camera. There were hundreds of them. Hundreds of photographs and hundreds of women. Big women, small women, short and tall women, Indians and Chinese, brunettes and blondes, wildly attractive to downright bogmonsters, the full panoply of the Scottish melting pot. JLM had had sex with more women than, well, Eleanor Roosevelt.

Bellows turned and smiled at the camera, then looked back to Veron Veron, fascinated that this man actually slept with women. Veron Veron remained standing, full of indignation, at the back of the room.

'Jesus,' muttered JLM.

'You're really porking this guy?' said Bellows to Minnie, while turning some of the photos of JLM to the camera.

'I love her!' exploded Veron from the back, 'and she loves me!'

Minnie dropped her head into her hands. Breathe, breathe, breathe.

'This is fantastic,' said Velure to anyone who was listening.

Things were getting a little out of hand, but Larry Bellows had decided that maybe it was time to stir things up and let this crowd of loons completely implode. He could step in and pick up the pieces later on; this was going far further than he'd anticipated.

'Startling revelations,' said Bellows, more fuel to the fire. 'Would you like to take this opportunity to resign from the post of Prime Minister, Jesse?'

'I bloody well would not!' answered JLM, ignoring the slip. In fact, enjoying the slip. Prime Minister sounded good.

There were a few looks thrown his way. And again, as he was primed to do for every set of circumstances from now on, James Eaglehawk stepped into the fray, this time waving printed documentary evidence.

'Here's the proof!' he exclaimed, 'the proof that you, Jesse Longfellow-Moses, had Veronica Walters murdered. It's all here. You're a killer, Jesse. You're going to prison. Prison! You're finished!'

JLM rose to his feet to meet the challenge of Eaglehawk head on.

'It's lies!' he shouted. 'All lies! I will not be cowed by these monstrous allegations!'

'Come with me!' shouted Veron Veron to Minnie. 'Let's leave this place together and go to Mykinos.'

Minnie's head sank a little lower.

'What about me?' said a quiet voice, in amongst the tumult.

Everyone turned and looked at Rebecca Blackadder who, like most of the others, had been silent up until now. Barney Thomson glanced to his side. This had been fun right enough. Wouldn't have missed it for the world, even though it must've been making fair viewing on live tv. But he was a little disconcerted by what Blackadder might be about to say, and he raised an eyebrow at her.

'Don't,' said Minnie, looking round and shaking her head. Suddenly, having been in control, she was now on the verge of tears. Just as much as it was going belly up for Jesse, it was going down the pan big for Minnie. They were *all* coming out of the closet.

The audience looked from Blackadder to Minnie to Blackadder. Blackadder quickly glanced at Barney, a guilty look, squeezed his knee, then leant forward towards Minnie.

'Minnie,' she said, softly, 'forget the men, forget politics. You don't need any of it. We have each other.'

'Heeeeeeey!' said Larry Bellows. 'Lesbians. Coooooool! Did you know about this?' he said to JLM.

JLM was beginning to look a bit lost.

'No,' he croaked.

'Minnie?' said Veron Veron, desperately.

Barney sat back, looking with some awe at Rebecca Blackadder. You think you know some people, and then, poof! Up in smoke. But then, Hell, he had never known her. God, he didn't even know himself.

'I thought you were sleeping with Michael,' said Barney, rather bluntly.

A little gasp went round the crowd at this information. Blackadder turned to look at Barney, her eyes boring into him, angry and upset.

'How could I be?' she said. She swallowed, becoming overcome with the emotion of the moment; the emotion, in fact, of Michael's death. 'He was my brother.'

A moment's silence, and then another, bigger gasp around the room.

'You slept with your brother?' ejaculated Larry Bellows.

'No, of course I didn't sleep with him!' said Blackadder, and this time Minnie rose from her seat and crouched down beside Blackadder, and the two women cuddled in next to one another.

Veron Veron, for his part, was outraged. He stood aghast, millions of hurtful insults galloping towards his mouth at once, all catching in his throat. Eventually the wee fella decided he just wasn't going to be able to get any words out, and stormed from the room, with a swish, a fizzle and a swoosh.

The camera followed him out, quickly shot back to Minnie and Blackadder, closed in on them hugging for a second or two, then moved back to the centre, Larry Bellows sitting next to JLM.

'This is getting a little weird,' said Bellows.

'You think?' said JLM, voice lost, eyes wide and unsure whether to stare at his wife with another woman, or at all the incriminating evidence that Eaglehawk had just thrown into the public domain. He glanced up at Eaglehawk and his Nemesis smiled cruelly back at him.

'How could you think that, Barney?' said Blackadder, regaining her composure, as she pulled away from Minnie. Thinking that she shouldn't have come, and that now would be a good time to leave.

'I'm sorry,' said Barney. 'I was misinformed,' he added, rather weakly.

Blackadder held his gaze, the hurt evident in her eyes. But then, who was she to talk? She'd led Barney along, and here she was with the person she really loved.

'It's her he was really sleeping with,' said Blackadder, bitterness in her voice, indicating Farrow with a nod of the head.

Farrow, who'd been one of the quiet ones, suddenly blurted out an exasperated cry at her name getting brought into proceedings. The happy sweet collective of JLM was spectacularly imploding.

'Well, why the Hell shouldn't I sleep with him?' she cried. 'I was his wife!'

Another gasp rippled around the room. There was a sharp clap as Bing Velure smacked his hands together with glee.

'Who are we talking about?' said Bellows.

'The priest,' said Barney, shrugging.

'The priest?' said Bellows. 'Isn't that a thing?'

'He never wanted to be a priest,' said Farrow, standing to fight her corner. 'It was a nonsense. We married in secret last year. He was waiting until his mother died, and then he was going to leave the church. He loved me.'

'Pah!' said the Reverend Blake, who up until now, etc etc.

Everyone turned to look at Blake. Farrow bit her bottom lip, close to tears.

(Generally here, the women were getting tearful and emotional, while the guys were open-mouthed or amused. Except Veron Veron of course, who was already on his way to Milan.)

'You're the new priest?' said Bellows, trying to keep up.

'I bloody well am not,' said the Rev Blake. 'I'm Church of Scotland, and if Michael loved this harlot so much, maybe she'd like to explain why he was banging me.'

A gasp went around the room. Again.

(As channel surfers flicked by, over 95% of them were stopping to watch, and the viewing figures were rising exponentially. The thing was getting completely out of hand, the problem being that it was a fight with no referee. It was in no one's interest to step in and bring it to a halt. It was magnificent, unabashed, outrageous television at its most puerile and far-fetched, and only JLM might have had the authority to bring proceedings to a close; but he had ceded that authority under the weight of Eaglehawk's testimony.)

'He was not!' exclaimed Farrow.

'Yeah, he was,' said Blackadder, softly, barely interested. Minnie lifted her head back to look up at her, a look that said she should be quiet and forget everyone else.

Farrow simmered just below the boil.

'Utter bullshit!' she exclaimed, despite trying to tell herself to be more erudite.

'He was,' said Blackadder, still quiet but with greater insistence. 'I only found out about it two days ago.'

Farrow strangled a roar, then slumped back down into her seat, her heart frozen. Couldn't look at Blake, who was watching Farrow, spit and venom in her eyes.

And suddenly the room was quiet, so abruptly that Larry Bellows was almost caught off guard. The revelations of the past few minutes had been gathering pace, achieving their own momentum so that one had led on to another, as the thing had spiralled and spiralled. But now, in an instant it had blown itself out, as everyone had said what needed to be said, and too many people had plunged into a sulk.

'Right, folks,' said Bellows quickly, 'I think it might be time for a commercial break. We'll be right back after these messages.'

And he sat back, let out a long sigh, and smiled hugely. This was fabulous. He was Adam Vinatieri and this was the Superbowl.

48

Soap Opera 3

Velure drew his hand across his throat. Bellows looked nonplussed. Someone on the set hurriedly scrawled 'BBC no adverts!!!' on a board and held it up. Bellows was about to start blurting out some stuff about the BBC being as commercial as any other organisation, but realised that it would be classical pissing in the wind so, ever the seasoned professional, he quickly schmoozed his way back into character.

'Welcome back to the second part of Larry Bellows Tonight! folks,' he said confidently, settling back into the old routine. 'Just in case anyone's missed anything so far,' and he started reading from another board which had been raised, written by Mandy, who'd been paying far more attention than had Bellows, 'tonight we've learned that the First Minister is an adulterer and a murderer, his wife's an adulteress and a lesbian, his dresser's not gay but is banging his wife, his psychiatrist is a lesbian and the brother of the priest who admitted multiple murder, but the priest was married to the First Minister's doctor and was also having an affair with the vicar.'

He'd read it all out in breathless fashion, then he turned and looked around his devastated audience, big cheesy grin on his chops.

'Wow, folks, what a ride! This is great. Anyone else got anything they'd like to contribute?'

Winona Wanderlip didn't have any amazing revelations, or at least none that she thought likely to be revealed that evening, but she thought it might be time to step forward and become the rudder that the Scottish Executive, the people of Scotland, and indeed this docu-drama were crying out for. This had been a humiliating farce for the whole country. At least some good would come out of it; Jesse Longfellow-Moses would be gone.

She was about to stand up and take the floor, when James Eaglehawk moved smoothly in to fill the void. Well, she thought, as she relaxed back into her seat, maybe it won't be too much of a bad thing. When one door closes…

'Yeah,' said Eaglehawk, 'I think it's about time that the full truth be told about the man who has led Scotland for the past nearly three years.'

And as he stepped forward, he was clutching folders and folders in his arms, the information with which Conrad Vogts had furnished him. He had already let loose an overture of damnation with the photographs of JLM's sexual abandon, now it was time to unleash the full nuclear strike force of accusation.

'What've you got there, Bud?' asked Larry Bellows, who could tell that this wasn't going to be as interesting as some of the other stuff that had gone before.

'You name it!' said Eaglehawk with triumph. 'Tax fraud, sex, pay-offs, strong arm tactics, manipulation, blackmail, collusion, murder! You're finished, Jesse. Finished!'

'Yeah, Bud,' said Bellows, reacting dismissively to Eaglehawk's claims, 'but you already cleaned him out about ten minutes ago.'

'No he didn't,' blurted out JLM, but even he knew he was clinging on by his armpit hair at this point.

'Tell us something new,' said Bellows. 'Bringing out more stuff on this guy is like putting a bullet in someone's face after you've cut their head off.'

'Right!' said Eaglehawk, 'I will tell you something new. I'll tell you that I, James T Eaglehawk, put myself forward as the new leader of Scotland, the man to take this magnificent country forward into a new relationship with Europe, where we can be a player, a broker, we can be the engine room *and* the bridge at the heart of the Starship Enterprise that is the European Union. This nation of ours…'

'Yeah, yeah, Bud,' said Bellows, stopping him in his tracks, which pleased more than a few people in attendance, 'we're looking for something a bit more interesting than that. You got anything about sex?'

'No!' said Eaglehawk. 'It's about time we started talking about serious politics.'

'What were you doing last night, then?' said a wee voice behind him.

Eaglehawk turned quickly. Bellows' ears perked up. Winona Wanderlip stood up from the midst of the small crowd and walked forward. She carried in her hand an A4 brown envelope. Slowly, deliberately, with immense cool, so she imagined, she began producing photographs of Eaglehawk in the buff, cavorting luxuriously with the girls Willing & Able, handing the pictures around the crowd, allowing the camera a view of each photo before passing it on.

'Vogts!' said Eaglehawk, spitting out the name.

'Hung by your own scrotum!' said Wanderlip.

'Ha!' said JLM, as some sort of last hurrah. 'I knew it. I've got a bigger knob than you, Eaglehawk.'

That's men for you. Size, size, size.

'So who are, like, *you*?' said Bellows, pointing at Wanderlip.

'I'm Wanderlip,' she said. 'Winona Wanderlip. And now that Longfellow-Moses has been uncovered as the scandalous crook we've all known him to be, I put myself forward as the only genuine and honest candidate here today, the candidate with the political nous and presence to be the leader of Scotland.'

Bellows nodded.

'Yeah, and you're the one with the great nipples, right?' he said. 'Are you going to show 'em to us this evening.'

'No, I'm not!' she said, remembering to keep calm, now that she was practically leader of the country. 'And I'll tell you something else. This charade is over. I'm leaving now, and anyone who wants to play a serious part in the future of Scottish government can come with me.'

She looked around the room, the question only really aimed at Grey, MacPherson and Robertson. The three of them nodded and began to rise from their seats.

'This has been farcical,' she continued. 'A disgrace, an absolute disgrace, and it's over. It's time for decency and honesty to become the bywords of the Scottish Executive.'

Larry Bellows sat back, studying Wanderlip's breasts for any sign of activity, and not sure exactly how to prevent the walkout, or whether to be pleased about it. It would still leave most of the main players in the emotional drama, and get rid of some of the political bores.

He needn't have worried, however.

'What do you know about honesty,' said a surprising voice from the sidelines. The one member of the crowd who had stood throughout, arms folded across his chest, jaw set in a particularly hard way, so as to impress watching Hollywood überbabes. A man for whom words were few, but well chosen.

Everyone turned.

'What d'you mean?' said Wanderlip, sharply. No idea what was coming. Genuinely no idea.

'Who's the 70's porno star?' said Bellows, looking around, and smiling at the camera, still demanding that the show was about him and not about all these fruitcakes.

'Don't!' said Parker Weirdlove suddenly, sitting across the room from The Amazing Mr X. X looked at Weirdlove; Wanderlip looked at Weirdlove; Weirdlove couldn't look her in the eye, and he stared belligerently at X telling him to keep his mouth shut.

Now Winona Wanderlip knew what was coming, and the fear crossed her face, her heart suddenly felt like it would burst through her chest.

'Go on, 70's porno guy,' said Larry Bellows. 'Tell it how it is!'

'X!' said Weirdlove. 'Leave it!'

The Amazing Mr X looked at Weirdlove one last time, then turned to face Larry Bellows. He'd had enough of the lies and the deceit. And of all the lies which had eaten away at him, of all the falsehoods and misrepresentations and economical truths that plagued government and of which he was part, the one lie that he could no longer face, was that he fancied women. All those thoughts, all that time spent fantasising about them, it had been to hide the undeniable truth. The Amazing Mr X had been taking it up the butt from Parker Weirdlove. And he hated Weirdlove for making him live in denial.

'She's no better than the rest of them,' he said. 'Ask her about university.'

Bellows stared at Wanderlip, who was looking a bit flushed around the chops.

'Well, Nipplebabe,' he said, 'what about university?'

Wanderlip didn't look at him; she was too busy boring terrified holes into Parker Weirdlove. Weirdlove swallowed, not at all happy with the revelations that were about to be released to the world. He just hoped nobody was watching.

'Murder!' barked The Amazing Mr X. 'Murder!' he repeated, in case anyone had missed it.

If Weirdlove had had a gun, he would've shot The Amazing Mr X where he stood. But then, murdering someone live on television to cover up a murder you committed several years previously lacks a certain purpose.

'Go on then, 70's porno guy,' said Bellows, 'you're the man in the know.'

'She and Parker were at university together in the early 80's. They murdered another student and buried his body in the moors above East Kilbride.'

'Cool!' said Bellows. 'And how come you're in on the secret?'

'X!' barked Weirdlove again.

'Pillow talk!' exclaimed The Amazing Mr X, as he looked at Parker Weirdlove, and by heck, but it felt wonderful to get it out at last. Suddenly he was running naked down a mountainside in summer, the wind whistling through his cheeks, the freedom to do or say as he felt.

Bellows looked from X to Weirdlove and back.

'Hell, a couple of queers!' he quipped. 'This is fan-tastic.'

Wanderlip gave Weirdlove another look of hopelessness and pain, then slumped back into the seat, from which she had risen just two minutes earlier to claim her rightful place at the head of the Scottish Executive.

‘Anybody else?’ said Bellows, enthusiastically, looking around the room.

Well, there was a fair bit of agitation going on, several people wanting to get things off their chest; albeit some of it being fairly minor, such as Alisdair MacPherson’s desire to admit to a fondness for Barry Manilow.

Just as the show seemed to be sagging a little, and Bellows was thinking that he might have to rejoin the fray and start working the crowd again, the door opened and in walked another two bit-part actors to join the crowd scene.

Bellows swivelled round, as the pair of comedians walked onto the set. The camera followed the look of the crowd, and so the viewing public got their first sight of Detective Chief Inspector Solomon and Detective Sergeant Kent.

‘Who the Hell are you guys?’ said Bellows, beginning to wonder if this might all be some mad set-up to which he wasn’t party.

‘DCI Solomon,’ said Solomon, holding forward his badge. ‘And yes, I’m wise as fuck. This is Sergeant Kent, we’re here to make an arrest.’

The crowd had pretty much given up gasping. They were all gasped out. (For the moment.) And most of them were too locked into their own private hell to be concerned about who was going to be arrested.

Barney Thomson raised another eyebrow. Well, actually, it was the same eyebrow as the one he’d raised previously, he just raised it again. Most of this stuff was just passing him by. So he thought.

‘Cool,’ said Bellows, as Mandy passed him another note. Bellows scanned it quickly, gave the camera a knowing look, then turned back to Tom & Jerry.

‘Hey, Federal Agent type guys,’ said Bellows, ‘I’ve been informed that you might like to check out the barber’s pockets. Don’t know what the Hell that’s all about, but it sounds outstanding.’

Barney stared at him, took a quick check around the room to see who was looking at him. As it turned out, everyone was now looking at him, glad suddenly to have someone else on whom to focus. He made a move to check his pockets, but was stopped by a bark from Solomon.

'Hold it, Buster!' he snapped. 'You might want to let us do that.'

Barney breathed out and held his hands above his head, thinking that there wasn't really likely to be anything of much interest in his pockets anyway. The odd coin, couple of bits of chewing gum, his I.D. card.

Solomon and Kent stepped forward. Kent stood in front of Barney, ensuring that he didn't suddenly dash off to Belgrade or somewhere. Solomon put his hands in Barney's jacket pockets and started rifling. Didn't take long.

A scowl crossed his face, then he came up with a small, clear freezer bag. He held the bag up to look at its contents, then let Kent have a look, then Barney, then anyone else who was interested, then, with a thespian flair for the dramatic, he turned and showed it to the camera, so that the watching audience of millions got a good swatch as well.

'A-mazing!' enthused Larry Bellows.

'C-double O-L cool,' said Bing Velure off-camera.

'It ain't mine,' said Barney, with undue extemporaneousness.

'Big surprise,' said Solomon. 'There ain't too many guys carry one of their toes around in their jacket pocket.'

Barney took another look at the toe, became even more aware of all the eyes that were resting on him. Bugger murder and infidelity and whatever else had just been revealed, suddenly all these politicians had something else to distract from their indiscretions, and they were all refocusing.

'You want to explain yourself, cowboy?' said Solomon.

Barney shrugged.

'Can't,' he said.

'I could be mistaken,' said Solomon, 'but I think this might be the toe of Nelly Stratton.'

The audience, right enough, weren't yet through gasping, and so they gasped again. Barney raised that eyebrow; if he wasn't careful he was going to be a victim of Repetitive Eyebrow Strain.

'You want to explain that?' said Barney.

'We found Mrs Stratton's body this morning, following evidence left by Father Michael,' said Solomon. Then he turned to the camera to wring maximum melodrama from the situation. 'She'd had one of her toes removed.'

Huge gasp from the crowd. Huge.

'Un-believable!' crowed Larry Bellows.

'What are you saying?' said Barney.

'Barney Thomson,' said Solomon, solemnly, with one eye on the camera, 'I am placing you under arrest for the murder of Nelly Stratton, and seven other members of the Scottish Executive cabinet. You have the right…'

'Whoa!' said Barney, although he wasn't entirely sure where that came from.

'What?' said Solomon.

'Well,' said Barney slowly, 'you know, I'm not really sure that I care all that much, but you don't think that this might be a plant? Why on earth would I come to a thing like this with a toe in my pocket?'

'Because you want to get caught,' one of the crowd barked, and a few others nodded and said 'yeah' in low voices.

'That's insane,' said Barney.

'Hey,' said Larry Bellows, and before he said anything else, everyone pretty much knew that it wasn't going to help, '*you're* insane!'

'Look,' said Solomon, 'do you even know what you've been doing the past few days? You're this weird thing, you don't even know where you've come from. Maybe you've been programmed to do this, and you don't realise.'

Barney was staring at Solomon. He tore his eyes away, turned to Rebecca Blackadder, who was still cuddled up to MLM and not looking like detaching any time soon. She did manage to give Barney a bit of an encouraging look, but accompanied it with a wee shrug of the shoulders to indicate she couldn't really help him out.

'I'm pretty sure I'll have alibis,' said Barney.

'We'll see about that,' said Solomon.

Barney lowered his eyes and stared at the floor. Madness. It was madness. But then, was the suggestion madness or was the madness his? Of course he hadn't killed anyone, hadn't ripped any toes off. But then, when somewhere in the region of fifty years had been lost to him, how could he say for sure that the odd hour here and there had not also been lost?

'Cuff him, Sergeant,' said Solomon, and Kent moved forward, showing his best side to the camera, and wondering if he could manage to get a word in. No need for Solomon to get all the glory.

The audience stared at Barney, trying to decide if it was cool or scary that a serial killer had cut their hair that afternoon.

'Full circle,' said Rebecca, looking at him and nodding. 'What goes around comes around.'

Barney shook his head, finally managed a wry smile. What the Hell. He'd felt like he'd been in prison for the past week anyway, what difference would it make? Whatever had gone before in his life, it seemed that by rights he shouldn't even be here. So, if someone wanted to frame him for murder, then maybe he should just let them.

Maybe that was it. Maybe that was why he'd been introduced into this absurd collective. To bring a former suspected serial killer into their midst, so that when people were murdered, he would be a convenient fall guy, set up with the most crudely planted evidence.

As a theory it had potential, but nothing in Scottish politics is ever thought out with that amount of forward planning, and the thought barely had time to gestate before it was proven wrong.

Kent was just about to clip the handcuffs shut on him, when Bing Velure excitedly yelped from the edge of the set.

'Hey fellas!' he said, 'check this out!'

The crowd turned and looked at a monitor sitting on a table just off set. Larry Bellows was thinking that this whole thing was getting ridiculously out of his hands, with even Velure having more of a say than was he, so he said, 'Yeah, good people, take a look at this!' in an overly-excited voice, even though he had no idea what was coming.

'We taped this earlier,' said Velure, in a bit of a gush. 'One of the technicians editing for highlights just picked it up.'

The camera closed in on the monitor, the audience leaned forward in their seats. It was video replay of Darius Grey declaring his good intentions for the elderly, and he himself smiled as he watched his own performance. There were a few glances around the room, as the crowd wondered why they were being forced to watch this again; but not for long.

'Look, look, look!' said Velure, aroused to almost carnal levels.

And there, behind the earnest figure of Darius Grey, was a woman's hand taking a small clear freezer bag containing Nelly Stratton's toe, out of her own pocket and slipping it into the pocket of Barney Thomson.

49

Soap Opera 4

The crowd turned, gasping. Again. There you are, but that's how it was. Finally, after all the revelations of the previous twenty minutes, the big Truth, the truth that had dwarfed them all, the one that had spread fear around the government and disinterest around the media, had also been revealed.

And so, the Reverend Alison Blake rose to her feet, backing off from the crowd as she did so, a look of madness springing to her face, her nostrils flaring in the wind.

'Hah!' she barked, 'I was wondering how long it would take you sad fuckers to catch up with me.'

Solomon and Kent said nothing. The crowd watched agog, those close to her backing off.

'You're the minister, right?' said Bellows, it being at least seven minutes since he'd engaged her in conversation, and needing his memory refreshed.

'Check the brains on that eejit!' she said. 'Stupid American bastard.'

'Hey!' said Bellows, but then he couldn't think of anything else to say to seriously object, because he was a stupid American bastard.

'Alison?' said JLM, looking a bit concerned.

'I had to do it, Jesse,' she said. 'I had to murder all those idiots in the cabinet.'

Larry Bellows turned to the camera, demanding that he be given some air time. Velure made the switch.

'So, what, like members of the cabinet have been getting murdered as well?' said Bellows.

Velure indicated the switch back to the Rev Blake, if that was the low level of insight that the host was going to bring to the occasion.

'Hey!' said Larry Bellows, off shot, but everyone was focused on Alison Blake.

'Alison,' said JLM, 'how could you? Why?'

Pleading with her, as if he'd actually cared about them.

'They needed culling,' said Blake. Her voice had settled down, and she was staring into the pit of madness as she looked at the audience.

'Can't argue with that,' said James T Eaglehawk, as a wee aside, settled firmly now in a complete humph as he was, and wondering if this latest item of news would somehow help him get into the seat of power.

'What harm had they done you?' said Rebecca Blackadder. Bitterness in her voice, because it was Blake's crimes that had indirectly led to Michael's death.

'Not me!' said Blake, eyes wide and loony. 'They were harming Jesse. Don't you see? That's why we're all here. We're here for Jesse. We wouldn't have jobs, we wouldn't exist if it wasn't for him. It's all about Jesse.'

'So you two are like banging?' said Bellows, directing his question at JLM, because frankly Blake was freaking him out a little too much.

JLM looked a little guilty but said nothing. This was all going so gloriously over the top that he was bizarrely beginning to think that maybe he could get out of it with his career still intact. Unaware of just how incontrovertible was the proof of his implication in the murder of Veronica Walters.

'Yes,' said Blake, 'but it's not just about that. It's about power. It's about respect. It's about love and decency and honesty and looking up to your superiors.' Frankly, she was beginning to sound like a Peugeot advert. 'Wally McLaven knew about Jesse and me and was going to blackmail him. He had to go. He had to be stopped.'

JLM nodded, without thinking. McLaven had been a sneaky little shit in politics, just as he'd been on the football field. The smiling assassin. Hadn't necessarily deserved to die, but the blackmail thing had been coming and would have needed to be dealt with.

'What about Honeyfoot?' said Eaglehawk, hoping that it would incriminate JLM even more.

'She was undermining him,' sneered Blake.

'I didn't ask you to do it,' said JLM weakly, aiming it more at the cameras and the policemen.

Suddenly, he and Eaglehawk were using Blake as a pawn, Eaglehawk trying to suck her into a close association with the First Minister, JLM trying to distance himself. Of course, Eaglehawk was playing her like Kasparov, while JLM was playing her like Mr Magoo.

'You didn't have to, Jesse,' said Blake.

'What about Filiben?' said Eaglehawk, egging her on.

'She was going to challenge Jesse's leadership. A turncoat and a traitor. Bloody Judas, masquerading as a serious politician.'

'And Stratton?' said Eaglehawk, intending to go through every one and make it as bad for JLM as possible.

'She was sabotaging him in the parliament,' said Blake. JLM groaned.

'Spiderman?' said Eaglehawk, loving every minute, and the fact that the longer it went on, the more that was revealed, the more chance there was of people totally ignoring what had been disclosed about him. JLM was miles in the shit, Wanderlip was a murderess and Darius Grey was still in nappies. There might be a way back yet.

'Looked at me funny once,' said Blake.

'Oh. McIntyre?' asked Eaglehawk, with a little more hesitation.

'Owed me a fiver,' said Blake.

'Right,' said Eaglehawk. 'Benderhook?'

'Never used to hold the doors open,' said Blake quickly.

Farrow, Wanderlip and Blackadder nodded in agreement, despite themselves.

'And Malcolm Malcolm III of the Clan Malcolm?' said Eaglehawk, realising that they were drifting well away from the agenda of incriminating JLM by this stage.

‘Used to wear Disney waistcoats to committee,’ said Blake, and looked contemptuously around the room.

‘Just got yourself a law suit there,’ said JLM resignedly, realising that this wasn’t going great for him.

‘What about me?’ said Wanderlip, a little indignant, rising from the ashes of her own shattered career. Of all of the cabinet, she thought she’d been the only one actually capable of mounting a serious challenge to Jesse. ‘How come I wasn’t killed?’

Blake spat out a laugh.

‘Winnie,’ she said, ‘you were beneath contempt. Pillow talk! I knew all about your pathetic little secret from university. Murdering you would’ve been too easy. I was just waiting for you to make your stupid little move, and then I was going to nail you up on the cross and watch you squirm.’

‘Soo-perb!’ said Larry Bellows very loudly, trying to attract attention to himself.

‘So,’ said Blackadder, ‘Michael was clearing up after you? God, he was such a fool to have loved you.’

‘He didn’t love her!’ exclaimed Farrow.

‘Yes he did,’ said Blake, ‘but it wasn't him who was clearing up after me.’

‘Who was it then?’ said Blackadder, getting the question in just before a few of the others.

The Rev Blake only sneered at her. The others looked around the room, waiting to see if anyone was going to own up to the strange deed. And, sure enough, it was that kind of evening…

‘It was me,’ said a surprising voice from behind. Everyone turned once more, gasps of astonishment now coming at a frightening rate. Patsy Morningirl, standing with her legs spread wide and her hands on her hips, stared defiantly at the crowd.

‘Patsy!’ exclaimed JLM.

‘What?’ said Blake, because she was suddenly a bit lost.

‘This is like having sex with eight women at the same time!’ ejaculated Bellows. ‘Coo-el!’ By this time, however, no one was even noticing when he spoke.

‘I know,’ said Morningirl, ‘you all think I’m this airhead bimbo. Well, you’re wrong.’

'You're a stupid airhead bimbo,' said Wanderlip, huffily.

'You're a moronic cretinous twat-brained breast-implanted fuckhead, who's so stupid you aspire to being an airhead bimbo!' said Blake with some joyous venom.

'Can she, like, say fuckhead on tv?' said Bellows off camera.

'I'm none of those things,' said Morningirl. 'I'm......'

She paused. The world waited. Then she put her hands up to her neck, and began to pick away at the skin. A line began to appear around her neck, the audience began to squirm. And then, with a sudden dramatic movement, she pulled the skin away from her neck and then up over her face and head, her hair coming away too, as she pulled off the latex mask under which she had been existing during daylight hours for the past year and a half. In an instant Patsy Morningirl was gone, and a fifty year old man, a touch of the James Woods about him, was staring back at the crowd. And the crowd was definitely staring at him.

Most of them had no idea who he was. Rebecca Blackadder knew, however. Her mouth dropped open, and tears immediately came to her eyes.

'Daddy?' she gasped.

'Yes, Rebecca dear,' said Dr Herman Blackadder, stepping forward, removing his outer shell of clothing, including the fantastic fake breasts, to reveal a small man with a slight hunchback, in a tuxedo. He looked with a mixture of hope, concern and humility at his daughter. 'It's me,' he said, 'I'm back.'

'God!' she said, as she rose to her feet. MLM still clutched her hand. 'But we thought you died in a train crash in the Andes in 1981, just after the Royal Wedding?'

Herman Blackadder tried to smile, but he was hurtin', hurtin' bad. He'd been watching his children for months now, but had spoken only to Michael. He'd taken at face value his son's assertion that Rebecca was deeply troubled and that meeting her father might tip her over the edge. However, like everyone else attached to the political world, Michael had had his own agenda. Fully cognisant of the details of Rebecca's affair with Minnie, he'd been trying to drive them apart; which explained his implication of her in the murders, an attempt to have her locked up and torn away from her lover. (Although, his thinking that prison was the best place to send a woman to get her away from lesbian sex, was probably a little out of focus.)

In time Herman Blackadder had realised that Michael was the troubled one of the pair, from his absurd marriage to Farrow, to his planetary infatuation with Blake.

'I'm deeply sorry, my sweet angel, I truly am,' said Blackadder. 'But it was all an MI6 plot. I spent twelve years in a Bolivian prison. Since then I've been working in a secret government research centre. There's not a day gone by when I haven't thought about you.'

'A secret government research centre!' she cried.

'Yes,' he said. 'We've been investigating reanimating dead life forms. In the last couple of years we've progressed onto human beings. We've kept bodies in stasis after they've been declared technically brain dead, and we've been able to bring them back, sometimes years later.'

'Oh my God!' exclaimed Rebecca, and automatically she looked at Barney.

Barney rolled his eyes.

'Yes, Mr Thomson,' said Herman Blackadder. 'You were one of our experiments, our most successful to date, in fact. I had you introduced into the First Minister's inner circle, to give me another excuse to get close to my family. I was so beginning to tire of this sordid Morningirl business.'

'Yeah, yeah,' said Barney.

'It's true! Everything that you've heard before has been a lie!'

'Don't care,' said Barney. And you know, he didn't.

'Daddy!' exclaimed Rebecca again, just because she was still in shock. Her old man looked at her with pity.

'I'm sorry, Rebecca, I should've spoken to you earlier, I know,' he said, 'but Michael counselled against it. When I realised the full horror of his infatuation with the Rev Blake, I started looking into her activities. I knew what she was up to, even before she started. I followed her around, clearing up after her, hoping that it would never come out, because I knew Michael would get sucked into the whole thing. And as it was, he found out in any case and could not handle it all.'

'He was a pathetic fool!' said Blake, a little put out that Morningirl had pulled off her mask and was massively stealing her limelight. For God's sake, she was the mass murderer here, the attention should be on HER!

'Excuse me,' said DCI Solomon to Blackadder, 'but you didn't think of informing the police at any stage?'

Herman Blackadder breathed deeply and shook his head.

'I truly am sorry, Detective Chief Inspector,' he said.

Solomon nodded. He liked it when people addressed him using his full title.

'That's fine, sir. Cuff her, Kent,' he said to DS Kent.

And then, live on television, in front of a viewing public that had reach the heights of 17million, DCI Solomon moved forward and placed the Rev Blake under arrest. The Kabinet Killer had been caught.

'And you know what?' said Solomon turning and looking at the crowd, who were all a little shell-shocked by now, 'we only came here to arrest Wanderlip for biting Longfellow-Moses on the knob.'

And so they arrested Winona Wanderlip as well, cuffing her with that extra set which DS Kent always carried about with him.

'We close in fifteen,' said Mandy suddenly, and the camera swung back round onto Bellows, who affixed the cheesy grin to his face and straightened his shoulders.

'Gee, folks,' he said, 'that was one helluva show. Totally unscripted, because you just couldn't write that stuff. Tree-mendous. See you next week on Larry Bellows Live! when we'll be meeting another couple who pass for celebrity in this country. Goodnight and God bless!'

The credits rolled, Velure exhorted the company to wave to the camera, which only the politicians did, and then the picture turned to black and it was all over.

There were a few in attendance who had it in mind to make a quick dash for it, but as soon as the show was finished, another couple of police officers – who'd ostensibly been there as security – charged onto the set and arrested JLM and Parker Weirdlove. And you couldn't say that they didn't have it coming.

In the end the police took everybody from the show, including Larry Bellows, into custody, just to save time, before releasing the appropriately innocent.

Champion, as Jesse Longfellow-Moses might have said, had he not been arrested with his political career in tatters at the end of the evening.

50

For the lips of a strange woman drop
as an honeycomb, and her mouth is smoother
than oil; But her end is bitter as wormwood,
sharp as a two-edged sword.
Her feet go down to death;
her steps take hold on hell

Barney Thomson sat in his room. Late Friday night, watching extended highlights of that evening's edition of the Larry Bellows show. It made good viewing, and he was pleased to see that he had been almost entirely excluded from the show. The toe thing got a mention, of course, but more as the device by which Blake had finally been trapped, rather than of any interest into whose pocket she'd secreted the digit.

For once the news headlines were actually paying attention to the drama surrounding the Scottish Executive, albeit the confession of the Kabinet Killer barely warranted a mention. Colour pictures of Jesse Longfellow-Moses and James T Eaglehawk in the buff were all the news, as well as the tales of lesbian and homosexual sex, and the variety of arrests that had taken place in the wake of the show.

Larry Bellows' agents were already in negotiation with the US networks, Bing Velure was already on a plane to New York.

Barney hit the off switch, lifted his beer and walked to the window of his apartment. He looked out at the courtyard, and the steady stream of drizzle that fell in front of the lights. He no longer had the desperate compunction to get away the next day, but he wasn't going to hang around much longer in any case. Someone, some time would be voted into the position of First Minister, he presumed, and it was unlikely that they would want the personal entourage with which JLM had encumbered himself. He would give it a day or two's thought, and then he would be on his way.

He put the bottle to his mouth, tipped the cold liquid down his throat. This seemed normal, somehow. Cast adrift from society. No friends, nowhere in particular to go. Just wandering alone, looking for something as much as he was looking for nothing.

There was a knock at the door and Barney dropped his eyes and stared down at the wet cobbles, three floors beneath him. One last visitor to cast a shadow before he turned out the lights.

'It's open,' he called.

The door opened and closed again, soft footsteps crossed the carpet, the woman came and stood beside him. She breathed softly, he knew who it was without turning. Had known, in fact, that she would come and join him at some stage.

They stood and watched the rain, falling from the Gods as if to wash away the stains that had blighted the Scottish capital that evening. Barney waited, she became lost in the restricted view, the cobbles shining under the street lights.

'I'm sorry,' she said, eventually. 'I should've told you about Minnie.'

'That's all right,' said Barney.

'No,' she said, 'it's not. It's just, people judged me. Michael judged me. He would've done anything to split Minnie and me up.'

'Yeah,' said Barney. 'Anyway, I don't think we were meant to happen. I don't think I'm meant to happen with anyone.'

'Don't say that,' she said, looking at him for the first time, although he never moved his eyes from the street below.

'Well,' he said, 'it's not self-pity or anything. I don't know, I just don't feel right. In this body. In this head.'

She said nothing, she looked back out at the cleansing of the night.

'Do you believe my father?' she said.

Barney smiled again, had another drink. It had just been another explanation thrown into the mix, right at the end of the show. Like a chef suddenly remembering to add bay leaves to the bolognaise ten seconds before dishing up. It seemed no more or no less relevant than any of the accounts which had preceded it. Brain transplant, coma, hypnosis, rapid cell development, reanimation, zombification, the undead, alien virus, cartoon character brought to life by ancient curse; they could go on forever. Did it matter? He was here now, and that was all that seemed important. He didn't care what had gone before, he just had the present to sort out, a future to decide what to do with. His life was like a field covered in snow; a fresh, clean canvas, waiting to be, well, fucked up probably.

'Sounds spot on, doesn't it?' he said, caustically

'God, I don't know. I'm sorry, I'd really like to be able to help you.'

'Maybe you're Dr Who,' she added, after a short silence.

Barney smiled. 'Christ, I hope not,' he said. 'Seven lives, I'll be around for bloody ages.'

'I should have told you about Minnie,' she said again, interrupting the mild outbreak of good humour.

'You said that already,' said Barney.

'Yes,' she said.

And they lurched once more into silence, and eventually their hands found each other and they stood together looking out into the wet of a cold autumn night in Edinburgh.

✂

The Prime Minister flicked off the television, stood up and looked out of the window onto Downing Street. He'd been in power for seven years now, and not once in all that time of rough-riding over others and no end of Machiavellian schemes, had any of his plans come off with such wonderful panache as this one.

He'd been in favour of Scottish devolution from the start, he'd backed it, he'd pushed it, he'd prodded it into place. And right from the off, it had been a complete disaster. The only possible way to get out of the whole thing without he himself looking like a turkey, was for it to completely self-implode. It had been going that way anyway, but a little helping hand had been all it had needed to push it over the edge. All right, they now owed the bloody BBC a thing or two, but that would be an easy enough favour to cancel out. What he had just watched, for the third time, had been more than worth it. And a particular delight seeing the Chancellor's little patsy, Wanderlip, get her comeuppance.

'It went well,' he said to the visitor, who was slouched on a sofa, bottle of beer in his hand. 'You did an excellent job.'

'Thank you, Prime Minister,' said the man.

'I owe you much,' said the Prime Minister.

'Nah,' said the man. 'I enjoyed it. Another German beer and a fine pair of women to snuggle down with for the night, and we'll be even.'

The Prime Minister turned and smiled. If only all the slime he dealt with in politics were as easy to satisfy.

'Certainly, Conrad,' he said. 'Did you have any specific women in mind?'

Where Are They Now

Despite allowing his hair to grow back into a piecey Tom Cruise (Time Magazine cover), **Jesse Longfellow-Moses** was sentenced to twenty years in prison for the murder of Veronica Walters. Two months later he was declared delusionally insane, and received a frontal lobotomy. The doctor also mistakenly removed his penis.

Minnie Longfellow-Moses married **Dr Rebecca Blackadder** in Reno, Nevada. They were both killed when the Southern Californian lesbian commune in which they were living was stormed by the FBI, looking for Moon Landing Conspiracy Theorists.

Dr Herman Blackadder is the Director of MI6.

Veron Veron is living in London, working for Stella McCartney. He is unmarried, and still bears a tattoo of Minnie Longfellow-Moses on his spleen.

The Amazing Mr X was picked up, as he hoped, by Hollywood. He was sacked from his position as personal bodyguard to Cameron Diaz for dressing in his employer's underwear. He is currently appearing in Oklahoma, off-Broadway.

James T Eaglehawk was proven to be a shallow, cheating, conniving, ruthless, duplicitous, underhand, lying bastard. He transferred to the Westminster Labour government and is now Foreign Secretary.

Dr Louise Farrow moved to St Andrews where she eventually married Prince William.

Parker Weirdlove was arrested for the twenty year-old murder of Alan Davis. He was repeatedly gang raped in prison, until his release, when he became principal secular advisor to the General Assembly of the Church of Scotland.

Winona Wanderlip was sentenced to ten years in jail for her part in the murder of Alan Davis. She escaped on her way to prison and fled to Beverly Hills, California. She was killed when the house in which she was living was stormed by the FBI, searching for New World Order Conspiracy Theorists.

Conrad Vogts is Chancellor of Germany.

The Reverend Alison Blake was tried for the murders of the eight cabinet ministers and found Not Proven. Unable to find employment with the Church of Scotland, she transferred to the Catholic Church and is now Archbishop of Argyll.

The Scottish Parliament was closed down and all executive powers transferred back to Westminster. The beautiful £400m building, which grew out of the land, was turned into a Museum of Modern Art. It was later inadvertently burned down by council workers after being mistaken for a landfill site.

Barney Thomson is walking the earth and getting in adventures. You can next read about him in the upcoming thriller, *Crouching Tiger, Hidden Barber*.